DISCARD

DETOURS

BETTE NORDBERG

GREENWOOD PUBLIC LIBRARY
P.O. BOX 839 MILL ST.
GREENWOOD, DE 19950

HARVEST HOUSE PUBLISHERS

EUGENE, OREGON

Cover by Koechel Peterson & Associates, Inc., Minneapolis, Minnesota

Published in association with the literary agency of Alive Communications, Inc., 7680 Goddard Street, Ste #200, Colorado Springs, CO 80920.

This is a work of fiction. Names, characters, places, and incidents are products of the author's imagination or are used fictitiously. Any resemblance to actual persons, living or dead, or to events or locales, is entirely coincidental.

DETOURS
Copyright © 2005 by Bette Nordberg
Published by Harvest House Publishers
Eugene, Oregon 97402
www.harvesthousepublishers.com
ISBN 0-7369-1342-4

Library of Congress Cataloging-in-Publication Data

Nordberg, Bette.
Detours / Bette Nordberg.
    p. cm.
ISBN 0-7369-1342-4 (pbk.)
1. Accident victims—Family relationships—Fiction. 2. Custody of children—Fiction. 3. Businesswomen—Fiction. 4. Orphans—Fiction. 5. Boys—Fiction. I. Title.
PS3564.O553D48 2005
813'.6—dc22   2004024318

All rights reserved. No part of this publication may be reproduced, stored in a retrieval system, or transmitted in any form or by any means—electronic, mechanical, digital, photocopy, recording, or any other—except for brief quotations in printed reviews, without the prior permission of the publisher.

Printed in the United States of America

05 06 07 08 09 10 11 12 13 / BC-MS / 10 9 8 7 6 5 4 3 2 1

For my husband,
Kim David Nordberg.

After thirty years, still the best part of my day.

Acknowledgments

Believable fiction grows from real life. Without the help of many experts, I could never begin to create a convincing story world. And so it is with sincere thanks that I acknowledge the sacrificial help of the following people:

Puyallup police officer Doug Kitts allowed me to tag along with Dora in his Canine Unit police car. He answered my endless questions with grace and kindness as I watched the action from his front passenger seat.

Harborview staff members Suzanne Robinson and Jennifer Magnani (Department of Social Work) helped me to understand the search for family members in the hospital setting. Jennifer, who provides service for Harborview's Trauma ICU, was especially helpful in clarifying procedural questions.

Puyallup attorneys Karl Zeiger and Gary Jacobson helped me to understand the nature of legal battles surrounding children. Gary even allowed me to join him in court and watch the proceedings firsthand. He endured my numerous phone calls with great humor. Thanks, Gary!

Steve Miller of the Washington State Patrol instructed me in the procedures of accident investigation and placement of dependant children.

Bob Bishop of the Pierce County Medical Examiner's office helped me to understand the procedures for unclaimed remains.

The Intake Group for Children and Family Services (Tacoma) helped me understand the procedures for unclaimed dependant children in Washington State.

The experts at Road Care helped me to understand children and grief.

Research librarians Greg and Jane, at South Hill's county library, regularly helped me with the pursuit of endless details.

No words could express my gratitude to friend Jeannie St. John Taylor, who reads all my work and suggests the perfect plotting solutions. If Jeannie didn't help, I think I'd quit writing. The expertise of editor Kim Moore, from Harvest House, made the editing process both enjoyable and enlightening. *Detours* is a better book because of Kim.

And finally, as always, I thank Chip MacGregor. His humor and professional savvy keep me going on the grayest of days. I couldn't do it without you, Chip!

And one last thanks to you, dear readers. Without your support, I wouldn't get to do what I love most of all. I owe you my career!

One

The bell, ringing over the door at Mountain High Coffee Company, caught Callie's attention. Though her hands did not stop moving, she glanced up to see a Washington State patrolman remove his gray Stetson and step inside. In the early morning light his tall, broad body threw a dark shadow over the dining room, his massive frame obscuring the light from the glass door behind him. He stomped his feet and slapped the hat against his thigh, dropping snow onto the dark green floor mat. Taking a step forward, he paused to brush the remaining snow from the shoulders of his jacket.

He stopped to look around, clearly inspecting the room.

Callie took a deep breath and savored the gust of cold air that blew across the coffee shop. After hours of steaming milk and dense humidity, she relished the cool relief across her cheeks. She nodded at the officer and smiled briefly.

He did not smile back. *One more*, she thought with weariness. On most mornings the rush would be over by this hour. Callie would have restocked the beans and filled the pastry counter. The tables in the dining area would be clean, and she would have mopped the mud from the tiles in front of the door. On most mornings she would have had a moment with the paper before heading home to the upholstery shop in her garage.

Not today, she thought, shaking her head as she shook wet grounds into the garbage pail. Today she would not get a single break between the two businesses that claimed most of her waking hours. At home in her shop, Callie had a newly recovered chair waiting to be delivered to its owners. She was already a week late with that project. And behind the chair a loveseat with a damaged frame waited for her to strip away its rotting fabric. The new fabric had finally arrived yesterday. She sighed.

Today she would barely finish her chores before her shift ended. Then she would jump in her car—but here, her planning suddenly ended in mid-thought. There would be no jumping in her car this morning. She didn't have her car at work.

Callie forced her attention back to the coffee counter, wishing for the fifth time that she had hired help for the early shift. Faint pink streaks tinted the tape that spiraled out of the cash register. The grinder sang the high-pitched sound of near emptiness; she could see all the way to the street through its cylindrical glass sides. The dining room floors needed mopping. The paper towel dispenser was empty. The pitcher in the dining room needed cream.

But what did she expect with six inches of new snow and temperatures dropping into the teens? This freak March storm had wreaked as much havoc in her coffee shop as it had on the roads outside. Callie didn't want to think about what the temerature was doing to the plants on the patio. With her luck, she'd have to replant the whole garden around the front walkway. She hoped both the storm and the chaos would soon subside.

With one hand Callie tucked a stray hunk of dark hair behind her ear and turned her attention to the stainless steel pitcher in her right hand. With an experienced touch, she took the temperature of the steaming milk inside. *Almost,* she thought, swirling the container around the steam spigot. Several seconds later, with the milk hovering at the perfect temperature, she poured it quickly into a paper cup, added espresso, ladled on foam, and stirred without disturbing the froth she had so perfectly swept over the drink's surface.

She added a double shot of amaretto flavoring and stirred again. Squeezing a lid onto the cup, she said, "There you are, Phil." She dropped the cup into a cardboard shield and held it out. "Just the way you like it."

"Thanks, Cal," he said, accepting the steaming coffee. "By the way, you're out of straws here." Phil pointed to a dispenser on the other side of the counter.

Of course, what should I expect? Callie sighed. "Just a minute."

Bearded, flannel-clad, with denim dungarees and steel-toed boots, Philip Kenterman pointed to a pastry in the display. "No problem. I'll have a pumpkin scone too," he said.

Discreetly, she glanced over Phil's shoulder to the patrolman, who now fingered the plastic cover of his huge gray hat.

To Phil, she teased, "I thought you were dieting." She bent down and opened the case. Removing a scone, she dropped it into a pastry bag and offered it to him.

He grinned. "I am," he said, taking the bag. "I skipped breakfast." Callie accepted the four one-dollar bills he'd tucked between his fingers. "Keep the change," he said, waving as he turned toward the door.

"Tomorrow, Phil," Callie said, adding, "and, hey, be careful." She smiled to herself as she rang up the sale and dropped the change into her tip cup.

Phil pulled the door closed behind him, waving through the front window as he turned toward his company truck. Callie shook her head. *Phil will have to skip more than breakfast to make any real progress on a diet.*

Before turning to her next customer, Callie glanced again at the officer standing quietly near the center of the store. "What can I get you this morning, Louise?" she asked the woman pacing in front of the counter. The policeman hadn't gotten in line for service. He didn't seem the least interested in the menu board on the wall behind her. Strange.

"I'm eating in the car today," Louise said. "According to the radio, the road between here and town is a skating rink." She shook her head.

"I might as well buy lunch too. It'll probably be noon before I get to work." In her black wool suit and high-heeled boots, Louise paused in front of the deli case, finally adding a muffin and juice to her tall Americano.

Callie pulled a bottle of Ruby Red from the cooler, and dropped a poppy seed muffin into a paper bag. "There you are," she said. "That's four twenty-nine."

Louise pawed through her handbag for exact change. "Thanks, Callie," she said.

"Stay warm, Louise" Callie countered, ringing up the sale. The pink on the cash register tape had turned bright red.

"Give me a break, Lord," Callie whispered toward the ceiling. As she dropped change into the till, she struggled to stay cheerfully professional, choosing to ignore the funny quivering she felt in her stomach. The worst of the rush had passed; only two customers remained. One sipped coffee as he read the morning newspaper from his seat near the front window.

The other, the mysterious police officer, approached the counter, still rolling the Stetson between his fingers. He seemed hesitant, uncomfortable somehow. Dark curls sprang out from below his close-pressed crown of hair. Hat hair, Callie called it. His dark eyes avoided hers.

"Are you Callie O'Brian?" he asked.

"Last time I checked," she said, swiping at the counter with a bar towel. Somehow her humor fell flat, and Callie reached up to tuck away another stray hair, feeling a sudden need to look presentable. What did he want? She searched his face for some sign, pausing as she looked into his brown eyes. Was it trouble she recognized there? She tried again. "Can I get you something?"

He ignored the question. "Are you the owner of a green '97 Ford Explorer?"

"Yes," she answered, feeling her stomach turn over as the flesh on her arms rose into bumps. She rubbed one elbow with the palm of her hand. "Why do you ask?"

"Can we sit down, ma'am?" The policeman brushed his mustache with stocky fingers. With his hat he gestured toward the tables in the dining area.

Callie shook her head. "There's no need to sit down. I have work to do, and you have something to tell me. What is it exactly?"

"I'm Patrol Officer Moriarty, ma'am. I've come to talk to you about an accident."

»»

"What do you mean delayed?" Marcus demanded.

"Relax," insisted the voice on the other end of the telephone. "It's normal. There's no need to worry. The DA assigned new counsel. There was a shift in staffing, that's all. It happens."

Marcus slumped against the back wall of the phone booth, fighting a losing battle with the discouragement that threatened to consume him. "Not on a big case. Why would they change counsel before an important trial?" Taking a deep breath, he ran one hand over his close-cropped hair, letting his palm drift down to his neck, where he wiped away a growing pool of sweat.

"I can't read minds, Marcus."

He glanced out at a group of teens draped across a bench as they waited for a city bus. One of them held an enormous boom box on his shoulder. From inside the phone booth, Marcus heard bass notes pulsing, beating against his thoughts. He closed his eyes against the sound, concentrating instead on the conversation.

"I'm not saying it's your fault." Marcus looked up again, glancing beyond the boys to the empty building behind them. Letting his gaze sweep the windows, Marcus made certain no one watched from the second floor. A black sedan cruised down the street toward him. He spun away from the door of the phone booth, holding his hand over the side of his face. "What about the trial?"

"Officially it hasn't started yet. They've had pretrial arguments. Fought over what evidence would be admissible. The usual stuff."

Marcus sensed there was more. Too much time had passed. Something had gone wrong. He pushed harder. "When exactly?"

"The judge granted a three-month delay."

In spite of his determination to avoid such a display of temper, Marcus swore under his breath. Three more months. Three months in a one-room apartment with a rickety, unreliable steam heater. Three months cooking on a hot plate. Three months alone in a city he hated.

Could Marcus survive three more months in this place?

Then a more frightening thought occurred to him. The crew had nearly finished this latest house. He had not yet heard about the next job. Would they find one?

Through the depth of an Illinois winter, his boss had trouble keeping the crew busy. What if more snow came now? Would he lay Marcus off? Though he'd worked with this crew for seven months, Marcus was still considered the newcomer.

"Are you there?" the voice questioned.

"I'm here," Marcus sighed. "Something's gone wrong. You aren't telling me everything. Spill it."

This time, the sigh came from the other end of the line.

"Tell me," Marcus hissed. "It's my life we're talking about. You can't hold back."

"There's a complication."

"A complication?"

"Presario disappeared."

"Disappeared?" Marcus felt a kick to the gut. "That's crazy. He's in custody!"

"They brought him to the courthouse for an appearance, and somehow he just walked away. They think he had help. The guard swears he had a gun. Turned out to be a soap carving. They found it in a first-floor bathroom."

Marcus gave a bitter laugh. "I'd expect that. The sheriff's department wouldn't admit they screwed up. It wouldn't go over very well with the constituency, would it?"

Another pause. The voice continued. "Presario was never the brains of the operation. He doesn't have the smarts to come after you."

"He didn't need brains. He had more than enough guts to make up for an empty skull."

"True," the voice agreed. "He's got guts all right. No one else would be gutsy enough to walk out of a county courthouse."

"No one else would succeed." Marcus pressed his fingers to his temples, trying to clear his thoughts. "So the prosecutor hopes the police will find Presario during the delay."

"It shouldn't be hard. There's no way he can disguise his face."

Marcus shivered at the memory of Presario's cockeyed smile. Someone in his past had given Presario a little gift to remember him by. The scar dividing Presario's cheek into perfect halves had severed a facial nerve, leaving his mouth partially paralyzed. When Presario smiled, only half of his face participated. Presario was as mean as his face was ugly, and that thought made Marcus shudder. He spoke urgently. "Listen. More than his mouth is twisted. Presario said he'd kill me, said it in front of a whole collection of witnesses. He's killed before. Why not come after me?"

"He's focused on staying out of jail. He can't afford to surface. Let's not worry about Presario until we have to."

"Let's?" Marcus gave a derisive laugh. "I'm the one he'll come after."

The voice took on an urgent tone. "He's going to be worried about staying out of jail, Marcus. Trust me. He doesn't have time to worry about you. Is there anything you need?"

Though the man on the other end of the phone had trouble with the truth, his kindness came through even across miles of phone lines. In spite of himself, Marcus smiled. "No. I'm fine for now." He shook his head. "Just find Presario, will you?"

"It's the top priority. You keep in touch, you hear me?"

"I'll call."

"Maybe you should give me a number where I can reach you."

"I'll call."

"When?"

"Next time," Marcus said, hanging up. He pulled up the collar of his denim jacket and opened the folding door. Ducking his head as he rounded the booth, he slipped on a pair of dark glasses. To this he added a navy stocking cap as he hurried away from the street via an alley behind a convenience store.

》》》

Callie eyed the police officer, still uncertain of his meaning. "An accident?"

"Did you loan your car to someone this morning?"

Her car? Callie remembered Celia as she had seen her that morning, scraping frost from the windows of her rusting Civic. The engine running, clouds of exhaust blowing white into the frigid morning air, Celia had leaned over the windshield, struggling to clear the crusted glass with nothing more than a credit card in her gloved hands.

Callie had walked to the guesthouse to check on her friend. She remembered the sound of the snow squeaking under her boots and the smell of exhaust as it curled and bounced against the siding of the carport. The morning was dark and cold. Celia looked tired.

"Yes," she said, nodding at the officer. "Yes, I did. I gave my car to my roommate because it has four-wheel drive." Though she meant to sound strong, Callie heard the little quiver that found its way into her voice. Celia hadn't wanted to take her car. She'd objected, more than once, worried that the unfamiliar vehicle might be more dangerous than her own.

Callie had insisted. She'd reassured Celia that the car was safe, insisted that Celia drop her off at the coffee shop and then drive to work in the Ford. In the end Celia agreed. Callie carried the car seat from the old Honda across the drive and fastened it into her car. Celia carried Keeshan, her sleepy four-year-old, and buckled him in.

"Ma'am?" the officer said, drawing her attention back to the present. "Who borrowed your car this morning?"

Without warning Callie's knees begin to tremble and she felt weak all over. She pressed her forearms onto the counter. Even though he had not explained the details, the implications of the officer's questions drove themselves home.

"Maybe we should sit down," he said, his voice as soft as his brown eyes.

"Maybe we should," Callie agreed. She picked up a bar towel and dried her trembling hands as she walked around the counter. Pulling out a wooden chair, she dropped down beside a round birch table. The officer sat directly across from her.

"Okay," she said. "We're sitting." This time, she made no effort to sound confident or controlled. She heard the high, frightened pitch of her voice and cleared her throat. "Tell me what's happened," she said, deliberately lowering her voice. "And I want the whole story."

Officer Moriarty leaned forward, once again smoothing his mustache before he began to speak. "I'm not completely sure. It looks as though your car hit a patch of ice while braking. The car slid into oncoming traffic and was hit by a station wagon traveling eastbound. The impact threw your car off the road and over an embankment, where it rolled several times."

"My car?" The quiver in her stomach had transformed itself into full-fledged trembling. Callie grew nauseous. "You're sure? I mean—there has to be a mistake."

"No, ma'am. I took the license and registration information myself."

"My car," her voice trailed off as she struggled to imagine an accident like the one he'd described. "But what about Celia? Where's Celia?"

The officer squinted. A glimmer of pain passed through his eyes.

Callie had her answer. "She's gone?"

He shook his head. "No, ma'am. She's in intensive care. We airlifted her to Harborview."

"Oh no." Callie dropped her forehead into her hands, pushing her hair away from her face. "It can't be. I gave her the car because she would be safe. I mean, with four-wheel drive…" She left the thought unfinished, struggling to control an unexpected rush of tears.

"Ma'am, four-wheel drive adds traction. It helps a car move forward, but it doesn't help a car stop—especially not with ice on the road. It was snowing hard when the accident happened. The highway was crowded, and there was almost no visibility. Witnesses tell us traffic just piled up before she had a chance to slow down." He shook his head. "No one can predict being hit by an oncoming car. These things just happen."

Callie fought rising panic. "I have to go," she said, standing.

"Actually, ma'am," he said without moving, "I came to ask for your help. We traced the car to you. And your address matches hers. I assume the two of you share a residence?" He took a small leather notebook from his chest pocket, opened it, and removed a pen from the elastic holder.

"She rents the guesthouse." Callie brushed at her hair again. "The guesthouse on the property where I live." She untied the strings of her apron and pulled it off over her head, pulling her baseball cap off with it. She crumpled the apron into a ball, pawing at it with her fingers.

He made notes on the small lined pad. Callie noticed that he was left-handed. He held his pen in the peculiar cramped position of those who struggle in a world made for the right-handed, his letters slanting tight and to the left. "How long have you known Ms. Hernandez?"

"I don't know exactly. A little over three years."

"What do you know about her family?"

Callie thought hard, trying to remember anything Celia might have said about family. Her mind drew a blank. *Did Celia say anything? Did I even ask her about her past?* She thought of the hours they'd spent together, watching movies, going for walks, riding bikes. Giggling. Working. For the life of her, Callie could not think of anything specific.

"I'm sorry. It seems so ridiculous. I just can't remember." Callie threw the apron onto the little table and collapsed back into the wooden seat across from the police officer. Putting her head in her hands, she let the tears flow. "I'm sorry. I just can't think right now. Give me a minute, will you?"

The officer nodded. "I understand," he said.

"You couldn't understand," Callie said, swiping her nose with the back of her hand. "Celia is my closest friend."

Two

Callie struggled to gain control. Her tears would not help Celia now. She wiped her face and glanced up. "I'm sorry. I—it's just so unexpected, you know?"

Officer Moriarty nodded. "Where does Ms. Hernandez work?"

Images flashed through Callie's memory. She saw Celia washing windows, her small frame standing on an overturned bucket. She remembered the last time Celia had delivered the check for the rent. "Celia is a classroom helper—an aide, or whatever you call them these days." Callie ran her hand through her hair and looked up at the ceiling. "I don't know what's wrong with me. It's a little elementary school on the way into town. I can't think of the name."

"In the Puyallup district?"

"No," Callie shook her head, frustrated. "I sound like an idiot."

"Can you think of where the school might be?"

"The district east of Puyallup, I think. Oh, shoot…Bethel. That's it. They started classes two hours late today."

"I can call the district office." He noted the information.

"Why do you care about where she works?"

"The hospital needs insurance information, and…"

"Insurance information?" Callie fumed. They'd sent the police about money?

"Please, Ms. O'Brian. Try to stay calm." His voice took on the tone of a parent with a recalcitrant child. "I also need to find Ms. Hernandez's next of kin. The hospital must contact her family in order to care for her. She may have told her coworkers something about her family. At any rate, I need to make certain her employers know about the accident."

"I'm sorry," Callie said again, dropping her head into her hands and brushing away another wash of tears.

"I understand," he said again, making another note. "News like this can be shocking. Unsettling. Is Ms. Hernandez married?"

"No," Callie answered, and then she reconsidered. "Actually, I don't know. She didn't live with a man." Celia had never worn a wedding ring, never mentioned a specific guy. "She never had anyone around the place—but that doesn't really mean anything these days…" At that moment a thought of staggering importance hit her, forcing her to sit up in the chair. "I can't believe I didn't think of this. Keeshan!"

"Keeshan?"

She leaned forward. "Was there a child in the car?"

Officer Moriarty frowned. "Now I'm confused."

"A child! Celia has a little boy. Was there a boy with her in the car?" Callie's heart raced. Why hadn't she thought of the curly-haired four-year-old before now? Why hadn't the officer mentioned the boy? "Well?"

"No, ma'am." The officer seemed to review the accident site in his mind's eye. "I was one of three patrol cars called to the scene. There was no child in the car." He tapped the end of the pen on the yellow pad. "I did see a car seat. Does the boy go to school? Day care, perhaps?"

"Day care," she answered. Perhaps Celia had already dropped Keeshan off at school.

"Do you know where?"

She shook her head, frustrated that she could not bring forth the name. Had Celia told her where she took Keeshan? It was somewhere on her way to work. Perhaps in calmer moments it would come to her. "I'm certain I've heard it, but I just can't pull it up."

"Okay. Maybe someone at her school knows." He looked over his pad. "Back to the other question. Is Ms. Hernandez married?"

"I honestly don't know," Callie answered, shaking her head. Though the officer had returned to his questions, Callie could not stop worrying about the child. She pictured her friend again, as she had seen her only that morning, the boy's head on Celia's shoulder. *The two of them were so close,* Callie thought. *Had Celia already gone to the day care? Where is Keeshan...*

"Ms. O'Brian?"

She forced herself to focus. "I asked Celia about it once, but she avoided the question. I just assumed that Keeshan was the result of some short-term relationship." Callie leaned back, frustrated. "I'm sorry. I'm no help at all."

Officer Moriarty made a few more notes. Callie noticed that his cramped left hand wore a plain gold wedding band. *Just like all the good men,* Callie thought. Then she chastised herself for allowing her thoughts to roam down this forbidden road. *Stick to the facts,* she told herself.

"What about family? A brother, sister? Parents?"

The weight of her ignorance struck Callie like falling bricks. "She did mention that she was the oldest of a large family, but she never told me where they lived."

The officer smiled sympathetically, his brown eyes brimming with compassion. From the inside pocket of his jacket, he pulled out a form, unfolded it, and slid it across the table. "We've had your car towed. You can call this number," he said, circling the telephone number at the head of the preprinted form. "They can answer any questions. Your insurance company can view the car in the lot. I'm no adjuster, but it's probably totaled."

Callie frowned. In her dismay she hadn't even thought of her car.

"I'd like to ask a favor," he said. "Would you consider going with me to the hospital? In cases like this, since the driver wasn't killed at the scene of the accident, the social worker at the hospital takes responsibility for finding the driver's family. They'll need you to answer some more questions."

Callie winced. "Celia isn't going to die."

He closed his notebook and slid it back into his jacket pocket, buttoning the flap over it. "I wouldn't know, ma'am. I'm no EMT. You'll have to check with the doctor on that. Since the roads are terrible out here, and I'm headed back to Seattle, I could take you along. You'd be able to visit your friend and speak with the social worker." He folded his hands on the table. "The hospital is really good at finding family. By the time we get there, you may have remembered something helpful."

Relief washed over Callie. Without this kindness, she'd have no way to get the hospital. And no matter what plans she'd had for today or tomorrow or next week, all she cared about was being with Celia. No one should be left all alone in the belly of a big-city hospital. And if it were up to Callie, Celia would have someone with her every minute. "I'd be happy to go along with you," she said.

>>>

A cold wind blew directly into Marcus's face as he walked, burning his skin and making his eyes water. The beard he'd grown since leaving Florida did not protect him from the biting cold. He tucked his chin into the collar of his coat. It didn't help that he'd lost almost twenty pounds. For a moment he envied the blubber his foreman carried around his middle. *At least Bill's fat keeps him warm,* Marcus thought.

He jogged across State Street and around the corner onto Pearl. Here, buildings protected him from the wind, and Marcus slowed as he considered the latest turn of events. His crew had just begun framing a new house. They should finish in another five days or so, leaving two days until payday. Then he would have enough for a bus ticket. It was time for a change, time for him to skip town. He'd already been here too long.

Though he'd made every effort to remain anonymous, dealing only in cash and using a false driver's license and social security number, every day he stayed in the same place left Marcus vulnerable. And now that Presario was free, the need to change locations grew even more pressing.

He shivered, wishing he'd invested in a down jacket like his coworkers wore. Down would protect him from the bone-chilling cold that saturated the bright Chicago morning. As long as he had to hide, he might as well hide where it was warmer, somewhere where the building industry was booming, where builders picked up nonunion framers without a single inquiry into their background. He could go south, heading for more temperate climates.

It might work, Marcus thought, feeling hope for the first time that day. Glancing at his watch, he realized that the morning break was over and he was late. At the next corner, he crossed the broken asphalt of a church parking lot and picked up his pace. Stuffing his hands into his jacket pockets, a peculiar shadow caught his attention.

He looked up at a brick planter, where a sign advertised the Sunday sermon. "He will protect us from the evil one," the sign announced in bold block letters.

"Yeah, right," Marcus muttered. "I wish." Pulling his arms from his pockets, he ran the last hundred yards to the job site.

>>>

Though she expected cold temperatures, nothing prepared Callie for the blast of wind she felt as she stepped onto the sidewalk outside. Blowing directly from the north, it carried the chill of a thousand glaciers as it cut through her mountain parka and seared her cheeks. Like so many others in the small town of Prospect, Callie didn't have much in the way of winter wear, only her rain-proof parka with its lightweight fleece lining. They didn't have this kind of weather often.

She pulled on a pair of fleece gloves, tucking the cuffs up under her sleeves. Grabbing the long end of her scarf, she wrapped it around her neck, pulling the knit fabric tight against the cold. As she led Moriarty through the patio, over the paving stones she had so laboriously set just the summer before, she glanced at her garden. The damage to her plants might not show for weeks. She'd worked so hard to turn the little house on Main Street into a comfortable, welcoming place. *Ah well,* she thought,

sighing. *Another setback.* On reaching the sidewalk, she turned toward
the white patrol car. Before she had taken two steps, she slipped on the
ice, her arms flying out as she tried to save herself from a nasty fall.

Officer Moriarty, walking just behind her, caught her by the elbow.
Without thinking, Callie jerked her arm from his hand, though she barely
managed to remain standing. "I'm fine, thanks," she said, brushing long
hair from her face. "It's a little slippery, that's all."

"Probably should have someone salt the sidewalk," he advised, turning
up his collar as he fell into step behind her.

At the car he opened the passenger door and she sat down, grateful
to escape the stabbing wind. Though Officer Moriarty had been in the
coffee shop less than thirty minutes, his car had already grown very cold,
and Callie shivered as the chilled vinyl penetrated the back of her jeans.
She tapped her feet against the floorboard, anxious for him to start the
engine. He opened the driver's door. "I'll have to clear the snow," he said,
pulling a long scraper from behind the seat.

Callie hugged herself as she watched him brush the front windows.
Apparently in no hurry, he slowly made his way around the car, whisking
snow from the side windows and roof as well. Callie prayed for Celia
as she watched the red numbers on his digital clock mark the passing
minutes. Her impatience grew, and shivering, her teeth began to keep
rhythm with her feet.

"There," he said, finally sliding into his seat and putting on his seat
belt. "Conditions are bad enough without being blind at the same time."
He started the car and turned up the fan. Then, touching switches and
dials, he brought two different radios to life. He opened the lid on a laptop
computer mounted from the dashboard. Punching in commands, he
worked until he was satisfied, adjusted the screen angle, and put the car
in gear.

Callie listened, trying to make sense of the conversations coming from
the two speakers. With so many voices speaking at once, she wished he'd
turn the whole thing off. "How can you stand that noise?"

Moriarty glanced at her, smiling. "I don't listen," he said. Adjusting
the temperature, he looked both ways for traffic, and eased his foot off
of the brake as he pulled into the street.

"How can you *not* hear it?" she insisted.

"I guess I've learned to tune out the stuff that doesn't apply. This one," he gestured to the speaker behind his head, "is the Washington state patrol channel. This one," he pointed to the speaker between the seats, "monitors the county and the city of Puyallup. If it doesn't pertain, I don't listen."

"You don't miss anything important?"

"Not often," he said, reaching forward to adjust the defroster.

As the patrol car crept along Main Street, Callie looked out over the snowy landscape. The road through town had been plowed and sanded, but accumulating snow blocked the entrances to nearly all of the side streets. There were no lights inside the Chevy dealership. Apparently, Don Boyer didn't expect to sell new cars in this weather. The parking lot in front of Harkness Furniture was a white expanse, untouched by tires. A closed sign hung in the front door of Sonja's Beauty Boutique, the shade pulled down behind it.

Callie glanced at her watch. Prospect had never been so severely affected by the weather. Normally things went on as usual, even in a snowstorm—though this storm could hardly be described as normal. "Mr. Moriarty, have there been a lot of accidents this morning?" she asked.

Moriarty laughed. "You can call me Mike. Everybody else does."

"Irish?"

"Pure blooded. My birth certificate says Michael Patrick."

Callie giggled. "You should see mine."

He glanced over at her, one eyebrow up. "Sometimes I wonder what parents are thinking," he said. "Especially these days. When I was a kid, I hoped no one would notice I was Irish."

"With a name like Michael Moriarty?"

He laughed. "You're right. It wasn't easy to hide." They approached a long downhill grade and Moriarty glanced in his rearview mirror, slowing the car to accommodate the slippery terrain. "You asked about accidents. We've had more than our share. We'll be getting accident reports for a while—fender benders, sliders, that sort of thing. Things have settled down, though, now that the sun is up. The temperature is warming too. Radio stations are advising folks to stay home. It should be raining by tomorrow."

"Other serious ones—accidents, I mean?"

"Not many. We tend to be a little overcautious around here." Moriarty switched his wipers on high. "I'm sorry about your friend, though. It must be hard."

She nodded and turned her face to the window. Though she and Celia had lived next door for more than three years, it pained Callie to realize how little she knew about her friend's past. How had that happened?

Celia had always focused her energy on the present. She was the kind of woman who exclaimed over every sunset, who enjoyed every rainstorm, and who dismissed offenses and daily struggles as inconsequential. As Callie thought back, she remembered that Celia had similarly dismissed her questions about the past. And, though Callie had tried to be a good friend, at the beginning she had been preoccupied, a woman recovering from her own troubles. Maybe she didn't know the truth because she never took the time to ask questions and wait for answers.

She glanced over at the officer, and caught him staring at her, one eyebrow up, apparently expecting her to speak. "Excuse me?" She pulled her hands from her coat pockets. "I think I just left the planet for a few minutes."

"Do that often?"

"My friend is in the hospital. My car is totaled. I'm worried about Keeshan. I think that's enough to distract anyone, don't you?"

"Sorry. I was just wondering how long you've lived in Prospect."

"A little over four years," she said. "I grew up in downtown Puyallup. My dad worked for WSU at the extension. A horticulturalist." Ten miles out of Prospect, they caught up with a long line of cars creeping west. Callie felt the patrol car slow and tried to control her impatience.

"Why move so far out in the country?"

Callie shrugged. This guy had no end of questions. She cleared her throat. "You know, this conversation is starting to sound like I should ask for an attorney."

He chuckled. "You're right. I ask questions all day, every day. Guess it just becomes a bad habit, you know. A way to kill time."

"I guess so," she said. No matter how nosy he was, she would not tell him everything. It was none of his business that she'd come home to care for her mother. That she'd returned single, humiliated, and determined to start a new life in a town whose very name implied possibility.

Officer Moriarty drove without speaking. Callie half-listened to the various radio transmissions blending together through the speakers. In the heater's warm air, she began to grow sleepy. She'd opened the coffee shop shortly after five; by the time Officer Moriarty arrived, she'd been working nonstop for nearly five hours. Her lower back ached, and the smell of coffee permeated the fabric of her clothes. Before she could stifle it, a cavernous yawn escaped her lips. "Sorry. I've been up a long time," she admitted.

"Me too. Worked the night shift. Now I'm going to pull a back-to-back."

For the first time Callie saw Officer Moriarty as a person—someone's husband, the father of kids, perhaps. A nice guy trying to serve the people in his community. "Must be hard on the family, having you gone at night."

"They get used to it."

"Kids?"

"Three. Two boys and a girl."

"Does your wife work?"

"That's funny, coming from a woman. Every mother works."

"You know what I mean."

"I do." He smiled. "She stays home with the kids. But on my days off, when I see how much she does, I'm amazed. I'd rather be a policeman. It's easier."

This time Callie smiled.

"You never told me why you moved to your parents' place."

"Convenience, I guess," Callie lied. "After my mom died, Dad didn't want to stay there alone. It was too much for him to take care of. My sister wanted him to sell it, but I couldn't stand to see it go. It would have been carved into a development—you know, the kind with the trees all cut down, a security gate out front, and some cheesy name like

Whispering Leaves." She shrugged. "I bought it. Dad built the house fifteen years ago, while I was in college."

He nodded, his eyes on the road. "Where's your dad now?"

"A retirement community." She felt the sting of tears and blinked hard. "Right after she died, he lost a foot to diabetes." Callie raised her chin, determined to speak without undo emotion. After all, it had been her father's decision. He wanted to be somewhere new, a place where he could meet people, stay active, and avoid the responsibility of so much land.

"Where'd you live before that?"

"San Francisco," she said, trying to stifle her growing resentment for this endless line of questions. *He's only trying to be polite. Be grateful. You're getting a ride into town.*

"That's a long way from home," he commented. "What'd you do there?"

"I worked for Hollingsworth Construction."

"Houses?"

She smiled. "No. They restore old buildings, turn dilapidated inner-city hotels into condos, that sort of thing."

"A woman in construction," he said. "That's unusual."

She bristled at his obviously sexist comment. "Not really. I have a degree in finance and a master's in project management."

"So what did you do?"

I played the fool, she thought. Without her permission, Scott Friel's face danced through her imagination. Callie closed her eyes against the memory and took a deep breath. "I was a project coordinator. Hollingsworth is an attorney—not a construction man. He loved buying unusual properties. Then he'd fight his way through the permitting and zoning processes. Once he decided what he wanted to accomplish with a property, he assigned the project to a coordinator. I specialized in the pre-construction phase, supervising the various engineers and architects."

"The design phase?"

"Yes, as well as the engineering and bidding process. Once the project broke ground, I passed it to a construction supervisor, who relocated to the project city."

"Sounds exciting."

She shrugged. "It was—for a while." She turned her attention to the side window, determined to mask her face against the emotions tumbling inside. The job had been exciting until she'd fallen for Scott. Then in only a few months it became a ball and chain, forcing her to see him, knowing he would never really be hers. Feeling the need to fill the silence, she said, "We restored some beautiful old properties to their former glory."

"Why'd you quit? Must have made a lot of dough."

She looked over at the officer, not quite believing her ears. Certainly he didn't think like that, did he? After all, he didn't choose police work for the money. "The old saying is true," she said softly. "Money isn't everything."

Three

Two hours after leaving the coffee shop, Moriarty and Callie pulled into Harborview's emergency department driveway. "Why don't you go directly to the admitting desk," he said. "I'll park the car and meet you inside. I need to check with my dispatcher."

Callie stepped out of the car and through steamy automatic doors to a bustling emergency room. Though Callie knew Harborview provided state-of-the-art trauma care for the Northwest, she'd expected a relative calm, considering the weather. Only the most desperate patients would be foolish enough to travel through unplowed streets to show up in the ER today.

It didn't seem to be the case in this hospital. Along the far wall, a group of people sat slumped in vinyl chairs. In the first, a pregnant woman hunched over a wire cart filled with clothes and small shoeboxes. Her dark hair hung in oily strands at her shoulders, and her jacket, easily two sizes too big, covered her fingertips. The woman's eyes, frightened and distracted, kept watch over the room.

Beside her a mother waited with a small child wrapped around her chest. Their position, mother and child facing each other, reminded Callie of a chimpanzee she'd seen at the zoo. Even now, with her mind focused on Celia, Callie sensed urgency in the slumped, unmoving shape of the child.

Near the center of the room, a mountainous African-American man lay draped across two seats, head back, snoring loudly. His possessions, wrapped in a worn wool blanket, lay beside him. On the other side, a hole had been dug through the vinyl chair cover, down into the foam padding below. As she considered the room, a smell assaulted her—something definitely human yet vile—something so strong as to make her step back, as if by moving she might avoid contact with the air itself. Without thinking, Callie brought her hand to her nose and looked for a safe place to sit down, a spot well away from the source of the odor.

A Seattle police officer moved toward her. "May I help you?"

Callie looked down at the diminutive woman in a freshly pressed navy uniform, her bullet-proof vest clearly visible beneath the polished fabric. Bewildered, Callie said, "I don't really know if I'm in the right place. A friend was brought in this morning after an accident."

"Your friend's name?"

"Celia. Celia Hernandez."

The woman nodded. "I'll let the ER clerk know you're here." She pointed to the waiting area. "Why don't you take a seat?"

By the time Officer Moriarty came through the automatic doors, Callie had given up on talking to someone about Celia. Instead, she'd chosen a two-year-old copy of *People* magazine and camped in the cleanest chair she could find. "Have you spoken to anyone yet?" he asked.

"I've talked to that policewoman," she said, pointing, "but no one else. Looks like they're pretty busy."

"I'll see what I can do," he said, glancing around the room and then checking his watch. "I have a few phone calls to make, so I may not see you right away. I'll be sure to check with you before I leave the hospital."

"I'd appreciate that."

As Moriarty turned to go, he nearly collided with a shapely woman in a dark brown suit. "Callie O'Brian?" the woman asked.

The officer pointed at Callie and turned to smile. "See? I'm fast," he said, touching his forehead in mock solute.

Callie smiled. "I'm Callie O'Brian."

"I'm glad to meet you," the woman offered her hand. "I'm Melinda Topping, the social worker assigned to the emergency room this morning." She took a seat beside Callie. "You can call me Melinda. This must be quite a day for you."

Callie ran her fingers through her hair, tossing it behind her shoulders. "You have no idea," she said, shuddering as she remembered the cold breeze she'd felt when she first spotted Officer Moriarty. Somehow, she'd sensed it; some strange foreboding had come over her as soon as he entered the coffee shop. "I need to know what's happened to Celia Hernandez."

"Why don't we go someplace more private?" Melinda said, her brown eyes intense. "We can talk in the counseling room."

Her words sent alarm bells ringing in Callie's imagination. Why did they need to go somewhere private? She followed Melinda through the waiting room to a single door opening off a play area. Under a spreading artificial tree, toys filled a large plastic box. There were no children playing; the space was as lonely as Callie's heart.

Melinda stepped inside. A small table lamp provided the only light. Several oak chairs lined burnt orange walls. Over them a cheap print hung slightly askew. Callie chose a chair near the corner table. Melinda Topping sat opposite her.

She appeared younger in this light than she had in the waiting area. She wore her blond hair in a trendy bob. She reached into her chest pocket and fished out a pair of reading glasses. Dispensing with chitchat, Melinda dove right in. "How long have you known Ms. Hernandez?" she began.

"A little more than three years."

"Is she married?"

"Not that I'm aware of." Callie took a deep breath and tried again. "I mean, she never mentioned a husband."

"What about family? Parents? Siblings?"

"She's the oldest of a large family. I know it sounds strange, but when I asked, she always tried to avoid the subject." Thinking back, it occurred to Callie that it was almost as if Celia Hernandez was born the day they'd met. "She didn't talk about her past."

"Did her family ever call? Did she ever call anyone from your house?"

"From my house?"

"Your address matches hers. I understood you were roommates."

"I'm sorry. I haven't made myself clear. Celia moved into the guesthouse on my property. It's a little place—only two bedrooms—about nine hundred square feet. She never used my phone; she had her own."

"So you don't have any record of the numbers she might have called."

"No. She paid her own phone bills."

"What about references? Did you ask for references when you agreed to rent to her?"

"Actually, I didn't. I needed financial help, and she came along when I advertised. She had a good job; she was clean and neat. I just—well, I let her move in three days after we met."

"Tell me about the child," she said.

Callie told Melinda everything she knew. It took no more than two sentences. "I don't really like children," Callie offered. "I only know Keeshan because he was always with Celia. We spent a lot of time together, but I don't think he liked me much, either."

Frowning, Melinda Topping made notes on her clipboard. Then, pushing the glasses up her nose, she stared off into space for a moment. "What about her work? Where did she work?"

"Look, I've already answered all of these questions with the police. But you haven't told me anything. How is Celia? When can I see her?"

"That's out of the question for the moment," Melinda said.

"I won't stay long. I just want to see her," Callie pleaded. "I've come all this way to be with her. I can't leave without seeing her."

Slowly, Melinda set her clipboard on the corner table. Folding her hands in her lap, she spoke carefully. "Normally, it's my job to guard the privacy of the patients in our hospital. But in this case, it looks like you hold the key to anything we might discover about Celia Hernandez. You're the only person we can talk to about her medical condition. At this moment, she is in very serious condition. The emergency room physician called in a neurosurgeon as soon as she arrived."

The words refused to settle. Callie could find no breathing space in the explanation Melinda Topping offered. "I don't understand. What's wrong?"

"Ms. O'Brian, your friend has sustained fractures to her left arm and leg as well as a very serious head injury…"

Though she continued speaking, Callie was unable to follow Melinda's explanation. Nothing made sense. Just this morning a healthy mother and child had driven out of her driveway on the way to a perfectly normal day. It shouldn't have happened. Not to Celia. And certainly not to Keeshan. What had gone wrong?

"Now, there is one more thing," Melinda said. Desperate to anchor herself, Callie focused on Melinda's face. She had wrinkles, tiny lines above her upper lip. "We must find Celia's family. They must be notified. And, as you know, her son needs someone to care for him."

"But I don't know anything."

"Do you have access to her house?"

Callie nodded.

"I'm going to ask you to look for documents, records, phone bills—anything that might help us locate her family. A marriage license. Birth certificates. Anything. Then bring these things back to the hospital. Celia will be moved to ICU after her surgery. You'll bring the information to this office," Melinda paused to write a name and office number on the back of her business card. "We need the information as soon as you can get it to us."

Callie took the card. "Not to you?"

"No. When a patient moves to another area of the hospital, so does the responsibility of finding the next of kin. ICU has its own social services team."

"Why don't we just ask Celia?"

"Unfortunately, in her condition, we don't know how long it will be before she can give us a coherent answer."

))))

In the surgery waiting area, Callie chose the chair closest to the reception desk. Here the chairs were comfortable, padded. Clean. Gold carpets and dark walls glowed in subdued lights, making the space more like a funeral parlor than a waiting room—with one exception. The chairs had been arranged in rows, like a theatre, all facing a single television suspended from the opposite wall.

Nearly a dozen people kept vigil with her, each suffused in his or her own anxiety. Whenever medical staff entered, every head looked up, every pair of eyes tried to guess to whom the next message would be delivered. Callie felt fear in the air.

Many of those waiting had brought books or paperwork. A woman on Callie's right balanced her checkbook. A man in the front row fiddled with an electronic Day-Timer. Callie had nothing. As the television delivered a contemporary soap opera, Callie wished they would turn off the sound.

The whole day has turned out like some soap opera, Callie thought. *A friend injured in a freak accident. A terrifying afternoon in a waiting room. Tune in tomorrow...* But this wasn't a soap opera, this was real life. And Callie found herself stuck waiting without a script. She found the waiting painful, like a balloon expanding in her chest, ready to explode.

She stepped into the hall and located a pay phone. With her insurance card in one hand, she waited through an entire Beethoven symphony before a live adjuster picked up the line. "I need to report an accident," Callie began. Though kind, the adjuster who answered the call had obviously had a busy morning. Harried, she ran through a list of routine questions. She had no empathy for Callie's predicament. Only when Callie explained about Celia's current condition did the woman display any evidence of interest.

"Did the driver carry insurance?" she asked, apparently alarmed.

"I'm sure she did. She had her own car."

The woman let out a long breath. "Well, I'm sorry about the accident, but your friend will have to file for personal injury coverage with her own company."

"I'm not trying to file for her. I'm just trying to replace my car. I'm stuck here at the hospital, ninety miles from home."

"Right. I understand," the businesslike voice returned. "I can give you a claim number. And, of course, we'll cover a rental until your car is evaluated and a settlement is reached. Would that be acceptable?"

"Can you have the car delivered? I'm at Harborview Hospital in downtown Seattle. I can't even get to a rental agency from here."

"Well, that is slightly unusual, but perhaps I can arrange that," the woman said, with more than a little reluctance. "I'll need to get some additional information."

Callie felt a gentle touch on her shoulder. She turned to discover Mike Moriarty standing beside her in the hall. "Can you hang on a minute?" she asked.

He pointed into the waiting area. "We need to talk," he said.

Callie covered the phone with her hand. "I'll be right with you." She hugged the telephone with one shoulder while she dug through her purse. "I'll take that claim number," she said.

In the waiting room, Officer Moriarty had chosen a seat in the last row of chairs. He signaled with one hand, directing Callie to the seat beside him. "Have you spoken to anyone yet?"

"Just the social worker in the emergency room."

"Any word on Celia's condition?"

"It's very serious, I think. They told me they're doing surgery to relieve pressure on her brain. They may have to remove some of the damaged tissue." Callie shrugged. "I don't understand medical stuff, but it sounds terrible."

"I've spoken to my supervisors and…" he hesitated, rubbing his mustache with one hand. "I know this is tough for you. I wish I didn't have to talk about this right now, but there is one detail that has to be taken care of. It can't wait."

"Go ahead," Callie said, turning slightly in her seat. What more could he possibly need from her at this point?

"I've checked the procedure in this case, and the truth is that someone has to decide where the Hernandez child is going to be placed."

"Keeshan? I don't understand," she said, confused. "I don't know who can take him."

Mike Moriarty smiled. "I don't expect you to place the child," he said. "That's my job. Washington State is woefully short on foster care. I've called the Department of Social Health Services and talked to the intake secretary. There just aren't enough good families to go around. I know you've been through a lot today, but I have just one more request."

Callie felt her stomach turn over as his meaning began to sink in. "I can't take him," she said, putting up one hand. "No way." Others in the room turned toward them, obviously startled by her tone. She lowered her voice to a whisper. "I've never been married. I don't have kids. I can't take him. I can't."

"I understand," he said. "I do. Really. But it won't be forever. I just need enough time to find the next of kin. It should only be a couple of days."

"I need to be here. Celia needs me. She doesn't have anyone else. Besides, I don't know what to do with a child. He doesn't even like me."

"You don't have to do anything," he said. "You just have to take care of him. Feed him. Keep him safe. I need more time to locate the family."

"But who will stay with Celia? Certainly you know someone more qualified."

"This isn't about qualifications. The boy knows you. He knows the house. If he stays with you, he won't have to change homes or day care. If I put him in foster care, he'd be placed with strangers. It's too much for a little kid who's just lost his mom."

"I can't do it. I'd make a mess of it. You've asked the wrong person," she said, trying to sound as forceful as possible. "I," she hesitated, taking a deep breath. "I just can't take him."

"I can't make you."

"That's right. It would be a mistake."

"I'm only thinking about the boy." Mike pulled the little notebook from his chest pocket, and removed the pen. Opening to a half-folded page, he began reading, "According to Child Protective Services, there aren't any foster homes on this side of the state. The closest is in Chelan County, a home with four other boys. He wouldn't know anyone. He wouldn't have any of his own clothes or toys. He'd be missing his mother and confused about everything happening to him."

Moriarty closed the notebook. "I understand though," he said, his eyes full of sympathy. "Kids can be pretty scary. It just seems that foster care is pretty tough for such a little guy. After all, it's not his fault his mom is in the hospital." Moriarty left the words hanging, feigning a sudden interest in the air freshener on the television screen.

"I know what you're doing," Callie said. "You're trying to make me cave. You want me to feel sorry for him." She took a deep breath and let it out slowly. "And, darn you, it worked."

Moriarty's face broke into a broad smile. "I thought it might," he said. "I can spot a softy a mile away."

"Why me? You don't know me from Adam."

"Actually, I ran a background check on you as soon as we reached the hospital," he said. "You're not only a softy, you're a clean softy."

"Great. Since I'm not a criminal, I've just inherited a kid."

"Looks that way to me," he said, grinning.

Four

Even with Moriarty's carefully written directions, Callie had trouble finding Keeshan's day care. Creeping along in the dark, she couldn't find the light switch for the dome light of her rental car. Holding her paper beside the dim reflection of the dashboard, she tried to read the words. Frustrated, she pulled off the road and held open the driver's side door, memorizing the directions before starting off again.

Out in the country, streetlights were nonexistent. Thick clouds covered what appeared to be a full moon. In the filtered light, Callie could barely read the road signs marking infrequent intersections. The driver of a Mustang, frustrated by her hesitation, blared his horn as he roared past.

Go ahead, she thought. *The hospital is waiting for you.*

Twice she made wrong turns, and when at last she neared the correct driveway, she drove past it before she recognized handmade numbers on a mailbox shingle. Carefully, she made a U-turn and headed back.

Thick snow covered the Mortensons' gravel drive as it wound through pastures, lined on each side by a chicken wire fence. Once as she came around a corner, Callie was startled by the glowing eyes of a small animal staring at her from beside the road. She braked hard, and the car began a slow skid toward the fence. Callie turned the wheel as she tried to control the slide. The raccoon scampered out of the way, ducking under the fence just as Callie's car came to a stop. She leaned her head against the headrest, breathing deeply as she let go of her fear.

At last she came to a square house with lights glowing from every window. The same wire fence marked the boundary of the front yard, where the bright beam of her headlights cut across tricycles and children's toys scattered across the lawn. Callie parked behind a pickup truck and turned off the engine.

For a moment she waited, trying to gather her confidence. Her logical side continued its relentless scolding. *What on earth do you think you're doing? You have no more business taking this child than you do performing brain surgery. Even the wicked witch of the west would provide better foster care than you can.*

Carrie shuddered and shook her head against the voice. "No," she said aloud. "Stop it. I gave my word. It's only temporary. The social worker promised to find Celia's family." She grabbed her purse and stepped out of the car, taking a deep breath. "I can get through this. He's only a little guy."

She rang the doorbell twice before an older woman answered. "You must be Mrs. O'Brian," the woman said, opening the screen door.

Callie didn't bother to explain her marital status. "Please call me Callie."

"All right then, Callie, I'm Peggy Mortenson. Come on in." Peggy wore knit pants and a green sweatshirt featuring a quilted bodice. "Forgive the mess. On Fridays everyone leaves at the same time. I haven't had a chance to pick up yet."

Callie entered the yellow living room, stepping carefully over a toy truck. "I'm sorry to be so late," she said. "I didn't get the car until after six." Her stomach growled in response to the rich scent of baking bread. "The roads in town are nearly clear, but it's still icy out here."

"Oh, no problem. The policeman came this afternoon," she said, closing the front door behind Callie. "He explained everything. Of course, I'd never have given Keeshan to you without that," she said, fanning the air with her hands as she spoke. "Celia was always so careful about not giving the boy to anyone else. What horrible news. It's such a terrible thing." She pointed to a couch. "Please sit down."

Callie hesitated. "Keeshan's been here too long already. I should be going."

Peggy waved the suggestion away. "He's no problem. Tell me, did you see Celia?"

Callie nodded.

"How does she look?"

Callie's mind flashed back to the hospital room, to Celia's blackened face and heavy bandages. Though Callie had only been allowed in the ICU for a moment, an instant really, the memory haunted her. How could she describe Celia's crushed body, the whooshing ventilator, the lines connecting every part of her friend to some inhuman medical device? Callie shuddered. Even if she could try, no words would convey the icy, trembling fear she'd felt speaking to Celia's unresponsive body. The utter terror of losing her. The inescapable sense that the Celia she loved was already gone.

"Well, she hasn't regained consciousness," Callie began. "She has a head injury. They performed surgery to relieve pressure on her brain." Callie took a deep breath. "They say the next twenty-four hours are critical."

Peggy made the sign of the cross. "I will pray," she said.

"That's all anyone can do, now," Callie agreed. She glanced around the living room. "Is Keeshan ready?"

The question brought Peggy back to life. "Yes. He's had dinner and he's watching television with Warren. Right this way." Callie followed her through the living room and past a hallway, where she noticed a rack of hooks; only one small coat remained. They walked to the door of a family room addition, apparently carved out of the garage. From the door, Callie noticed an elderly man fully reclined in a vinyl chair, his face hidden behind the front page of the *Tacoma News Tribune*.

"Keeshan," Peggy called. "Callie is here to take you home."

The boy sat cross-legged in the opposite corner of the room, his back to the television set, his face a mask of concentration. Wearing navy sweatpants and a Mariners sweatshirt, he held a large plastic building block in each hand. Before him stood a half-completed building.

"Keeshan," she repeated. He looked up from the toys, his brown eyes darting from Peggy to Callie and back again. A frown crept across his face. "Where's Mama?"

"Keeshan. Put the blocks in the tub and get your coat," Peggy instructed, pointing. "It's on the hook in the hallway."

Still confused, Keeshan dropped the blocks. His thumb went into his mouth as he leaned backward and his knees popped up in front of him. In this position he froze, his eyes large. "Where's Mama?" he asked, the words spilling out around his thumb.

Callie felt herself tense. No one had said anything to the boy.

"She isn't coming to pick you up today," Peggy said. "She sent Callie for you." She clapped her hands. "Come now, Keeshan," she encouraged. "It's getting late, and you need to head home." She reached for a clear storage tub and began tossing the blocks inside. Keeshan stood slowly, the thumb still firmly fixed to the roof of his mouth. He made no move to retrieve the blocks. "Help me with the toys," Peggy said.

Without removing the thumb, Keeshan picked up one block and tossed it inside. Again, Peggy pointed back toward the hallway. "Don't forget your papers," she reminded him. He started through the kitchen.

Callie watched his little tennis shoes recede, fascinated by the flashing red lights that marked every step. She hadn't noticed the shoes that morning. Why not? Would she ever get the hang of this children thing? "Cute shoes," she commented, shaking her head.

"Cute boy," Peggy agreed.

"You haven't told him anything?"

"Only that you were coming to get him."

"I'm not sure how much I should say. I don't know what he'd understand."

"In my experience, children always do best with the truth. Don't try to hide it or dress it up."

Callie shrugged and put her hands in her coat pockets. "I'm only a neighbor, really. Celia and I are friends, but I'm no child care expert. I don't know why they couldn't find someone more qualified to take him."

"You'll be fine, I'm sure. He's always been a good boy," Peggy said, crossing her arms. "Busy, but good. Well disciplined. I'd take him myself, but I'm just not able to take anyone at night. Actually, I may be in trouble as it is. I normally only provide care for the children from my church. Celia heard about us from someone at her school. I haven't obtained a license or anything. Until today, no one from the state even knew I had children here."

"Well, that's over," the man in the recliner said.

Peggy frowned toward the voice. "This is my husband, Warren," she said, pointing as she spoke. "Warren, this is the woman Celia rents from. Callie O'Brian."

Warren managed to nod before disappearing again behind the newspaper.

"How long will Celia be in the hospital?" Peggy asked.

Clearly, this woman did not understand the seriousness of the situation. "I don't think anyone knows for sure," Callie hedged.

Peggy nodded. " I'm sure you'll do fine. Keeshan almost takes care of himself. Do you have everything you need?"

"Since I've never done this before, I don't know what I need."

"Well, a car seat, for instance. Even preschoolers need them."

Callie sighed. "I didn't think of that. Celia's seat was in my car. Unfortunately, the car is in an impound lot."

"I can loan you one. It was donated by one of my students."

Keeshan returned, his arms hugging his coat, his fingers clutching two pieces of paper. "Good job, Keeshan," Peggy said. "Here, let me help you with your jacket."

"I can zip it," he said, slipping one arm inside. Then, transferring the papers to his other hand, he made a fist and shoved the other arm down the sleeve. "I can do it myself."

They waited while Keeshan put his papers on the couch and struggled with the two sides of the zipper. Though he managed to connect the ends, he could not pull up the zipper. His face scowled with concentration.

"Do you want me to help?" Peggy asked.

"I can do it."

The minutes passed. Eventually Keeshan heaved an enormous sigh. "It won't go," he said, shrugging. "I can't do it."

"Sometimes you just need a little help, Keeshan," Peggy said, bending over as she zipped his parka for him.

Don't we all, Callie thought.

>>>

The temperature had dropped and the fog had cleared by the time Callie pulled into her carport. A full moon glistened white against the dark sky, the stars marking the constellations. It was a night for fairy tales and romance, not accidents and hospitals. Exhausted and emotionally drained, Callie wondered why such a glorious night should be wasted.

The boy had not spoken during the twelve-mile trip from Peggy's house. Did his silence mark fatigue or confusion? He acted cautious and undecided rather than fearful. Wide-eyed, he seemed to observe Callie's every move, as if gathering evidence for judgment.

Even as she walked around the front of the car, she felt his dark eyes following her. She plastered an enthusiastic smile on her face as she opened the passenger door. "Well, Keeshan. Tonight you'll be sleeping at my house," she said, waiting for him to get out of the car. When he made no move, she remembered he was buckled in. She opened the latch and reached for his left hand. "Won't that be fun? Just like a sleepover," she said. Turning him in the seat, she helped him off the bench.

"I need my jammies," he said. "And my toothbrush."

"Right. Toothbrush and jammies," Callie agreed, with too much enthusiasm. "Not a problem." Still holding one hand, she let him jump, two-footed onto the floor of the carport. "We can go over to your house later and pick up everything you need. Do you have a favorite animal? Something you sleep with?"

He nodded, his face serious. Callie wondered if the boy ever blinked. His dark lashes curled upward, framing his eyes with the detail of an ink pen. The effect gave him an attentive, curious appearance. His lashes complemented the curly ringlets that covered the rest of his head, reminding her of a beautiful child in a clothing catalogue.

In spite of his dark complexion, bright spots of red bloomed on the apples of his cheeks. Callie decided he was cold. "How about we get inside and warm up first?" she asked. "We can start a fire in the fireplace, and drink something hot. Sound good?"

Again he nodded. Callie wondered if comedians felt this way before a hostile audience. Letting go of his hand, she pulled his backpack from the floor of the car. Keeshan had not yet smiled. She had not heard him laugh. "Let's use the back door," she said, leading him through the carport.

Inside she moved through the house, turning on lights first in the laundry room and then the kitchen, adjusting the thermostat in the hallway. She shivered, aware of the brutal cold front that had penetrated the walls of her parents' home. Her home. In the entry hall, she flipped on lights and swung around to retrace her steps through the kitchen. In the process, she collided with the little boy, who had followed silently at her heels.

"I'm sorry, Keeshan" she said. "I didn't see you." His thumb returned to his mouth. "All right. How about we take off your coat?" Sighing, Callie bent down on one knee to face him, reaching out for the jacket. "Want me to unzip?"

He stepped back.

This is going to be a long night, she thought. "No problem," she said, standing. "Would you like to do it?" No movement. No response.

"Okay. Well, then." Unnerved, she brushed her palms together. "I'll start some hot chocolate. When you feel warm enough, you can take off your jacket." In the kitchen she poured milk into a saucepan and turned on the stove. She brought out hot chocolate mix, shaking it as she set it on the counter. Thankfully, loose powder rattled against the sides of the tin. In the four years she'd lived here, she couldn't remember making hot chocolate from this mix. It had been her mother's cocoa, something she enjoyed on late winter afternoons. Something she made for the grandchildren.

As she prepared the cups and milk, Keeshan stood sentry in the farthest corner of the kitchen. Callie kept up a one-way conversation. "This was my mother's hot chocolate. She liked to drink it in the winter when the sun went behind the trees and the house got cold." Callie stirred chocolate into the milk. "Of course, she always started a fire in the fireplace. That helped," Callie continued. "Even when she was very old, my mother would lay a fire for the afternoon and sit in the rocking chair with her chocolate."

Callie pictured her mother in her last days, lying in bed, her body consumed by cancer. Even then she had insisted upon the ritual. Though she needed help to sit up, she insisted on holding the fragile teacup in her bony hands as she sipped chocolate.

Callie shook her head. "When we make a fire, I'll let you help, okay?" She glanced over at the boy, who had not moved, had not spoken. *What do real mothers do at a time like this?* she wondered. *How does a real mother engage a child? How does she share bad news?* Callie had no idea. She had never been a mother.

Finished with the hot chocolate, Callie carried two mugs to the table. Pushing aside her collection of spring gardening catalogues, Callie set a cup down on the same placemat she had used for breakfast. "There you are," she said. "Climb up here, and you can have some." Cautiously he came near. His thumb exited his mouth only when he needed two hands to climb onto the chair and kneel before the table. "Go ahead," she encouraged.

He bent his head to the steaming cup, closed his eyes, and smelled it. With two hands he brought it up to his lips and sipped. With a jarring scream, Keeshan dropped the cup, spitting chocolate across the table. Fluid ran from the overturned cup onto the placemat and over her catalogues. The single scream turned to tears, ragged and frightened as his features crumpled in pain. His little hands came to his lips, both palms touching his tear-streaked face.

At the spilling of the chocolate, Callie jumped to save her beloved catalogue collection. But Keeshan's face, disconsolate, changed her mind. With one motion, she scooped the boy from the chair and brought him to her chest, holding him as he sobbed.

Five

"About time you got your black hide back to work."

Drawing a deep breath, Marcus leaned forward to close the buckle of his leather tool belt. In spite of himself, he felt his heartbeat accelerate. No matter how many times he heard these kinds of expressions, they still ate at him. Cut away at his pride. Carefully, he slid his hands into his work gloves. Determined not to respond, he leaned one arm against the foreman's truck and looked toward the house.

Bill Rice, short and broad, stood on the front porch glaring at him, both hands on his hips, as if to challenge Marcus to a school yard brawl. Marcus refused to take the bait. "Sorry. Had to make a phone call."

"Sorry, my eye. I pay you by the hour. I expect the whole hour."

"You'll get it, Bill," Marcus answered. "You always do."

Bill pointed at his brand-new pickup truck. "Bring the Sawzall from my toolbox, will ya?" He started to turn away but turned back to fling one more barb. "And try and get it up here before lunch, if you can."

Marcus nodded. *Just once I'd like to tell that guy what a jerk he is.* He expected to earn his place; after all, he was the newest hire. He expected to be the designated errand boy for a while, the man who cleaned up after everyone at the end of the day. The grunt. But as of this minute, the tradition had lasted too darn long, and Marcus resented it. *If I didn't need the money so badly,* he thought, *I'd have left this job months ago.*

Of the two toolboxes built into the truck, one lid stood open. Marcus peeked inside. Layers of plastic shelves held his boss's carefully organized tools. No room for the Sawzall here. He walked around the front of the truck and released the latch on the other box.

The cutting tool sat on top of several smaller cardboard boxes. Marcus leaned over the truck to lift the heavy saw. As he did, bright yellow labels caught his attention. "Heavy Duty 'Star Drive' Construction Screws" the label read. Surprised, Marcus lifted a cardboard box from below the saw. The whole crew had spent most of yesterday morning looking for those screws. Eventually, they'd given up and ordered more.

In an instant, Marcus understood.

Carrying the saw in one hand, the box in the other, Marcus walked into the house. With every step, his anger grew. *The nerve,* he thought. *It's one thing to steal, but to be so blatant about it?* Part of him wanted to deck his foreman.

Easing himself between a long row of two-by-fours, Marcus stopped in front of Bill. His anger rose, a hot burning flame. He took a deep breath, trying to swallow it, determined not to let his temper get the best of him this time.

Bill didn't even look up. Unhurried, he held down one end of a chalk line as he snapped it against the floor. "Okay," he said, turning the handle of his marker. "That's the east kitchen wall. Now let's measure across to the hallway."

Marcus cleared his throat and Bill looked up. Marcus watched Bill's gaze travel from his steel-toed boots all the way to his hard hat, finally settling on his face. Bill nodded. "Thanks," he said. "Put it over there," he jerked his head toward the rear of the room.

Barry, who had been helping Bill mark wall positions, froze. Marcus ignored him. He tuned out the sound of the compressor as it switched on to power the nail guns. "I found the Sawzall in your toolbox," Marcus began.

"Great," Bill said. "Now get back to work."

"I found these too," Marcus continued, holding up the cardboard box and shaking the screws inside. "The Star Drives we were looking for yesterday."

"Oh?" Bill stood up, glancing from Marcus's face to the box and back again. "Where did you find those?"

"In your toolbox."

Bill spread his feet and pulled his tool belt up. "Well, I sure could have used those yesterday," he said. "Glad you found them."

"You already ordered more," Marcus said. "I heard you on the cell phone."

"I did. City Lumber dropped them by this morning."

"You accused them of leaving them off the order."

"Well, I must have made a mistake."

"Yeah, right." Marcus shook his head. He could hardly control his disgust over Bill's obvious theft. It had gone on so long. Lumber. Wire. Tools. When would it end? "I guess that means you'll be returning these."

"Sure. I'll do that later."

"I'd like to hear you call them now."

Bill frowned and stepped forward, his fat belly hanging over his tool belt. "Marcus, I'll remind you that you work for me." He poked his index finger on Marcus's chest. "Don't you go getting your black hide all uppity about this. It was a mistake. Plain and simple."

All sound ceased. Barry crossed his arms, waiting quietly for the storm to break. The thumping compressor gasped and stood silent. The table saw sat motionless. Though they tried to be subtle, Marcus felt the rest of the crew move forward as they listened in.

"Doesn't look that way to me," Marcus said.

"What are you saying, Marcus? How does it look to you?"

"It looks like you're trying to rip off the company, Bill. A little lumber here, a few screws there. It looks to me like you put those screws in your truck yesterday, and then you accused the supply company of forgetting to send them so that you could take some home for yourself."

"I don't think you'd better say another word, Marcus Jefferson," Bill said, his words slow and deliberate. He stepped closer, his belly rubbing against Marcus. "'Cuz if you do, you're outta here. I don't tolerate dis-respect from my crew."

For just a moment, Marcus hesitated. He didn't have another job and still owed a week's rent on his room. Martha Putnam needed that money, and he wasn't about to skip town without paying. He had some cash but nothing extra. No plans. No hope. And as of this morning, a trial delay. A madman on the loose.

Then, in spite of his determination, anger flashed and exploded in his chest. "You don't have to warn me, Bill," Marcus agreed, his words powered by hot rage. "You're right. Your crew should respect you. But since I can't, I quit." He set the saw down and dropped the box of screws beside it. "I'll be by for the rest of my pay on Friday," he said, tucking his gloves in the back pockets of his jeans. "Have it ready, or I'll make the call to City Lumber myself."

And with that, Marcus turned and walked off the job.

>>>>

When at last Keeshan stopped crying, Callie offered the chocolate again. "I can add milk. It won't be too hot, I promise."

"I want my mama," he said, tears clinging to his eyelashes. "I want my mama," he repeated, desperate and growing hoarse.

Callie looked around the kitchen for inspiration. She had no clue about these kinds of situations. After all, a real mother would never have served chocolate so hot that it burned the boy's tender mouth. A real mother would have known better. A real mother would know what to say to console him. But Callie was not a real mother. No one had trained her for moments like these. He wanted Celia.

Now would be the time to explain what had happened to his mother.

But Callie panicked. *What if I make a mistake? What should I tell him?* She knew so little about children. *How much of the truth can he handle?* In this case, the fact that his mother fought for her life in a Seattle hos-pital bed was too much information—even for Callie. But what if the worst should happen? Should she try to prepare the boy?

She didn't want to frighten him. "Keeshan," she began, "your mom was in a car accident today. I know she'd really like to be here with you tonight, but she can't. She's very sick."

Without warning the crying stopped. Keeshan put his thumb in his mouth and turned to her, his brown eyes searching her face. "Nathan has a cold," he said around the thumb.

"Is Nathan one of the boys at your day care?"

Keeshan nodded, his eyes serious.

"Well, your mom is very sick, much worse than a cold. And until she comes home, you'll have to stay with me. Do you understand?"

His face crumpled, and the tears began again. "I want my mama."

Callie tried to distract him, making her voice light. "I'm so sorry about the chocolate. I've never had children. So I'm probably going to make a lot of mistakes. I think I'm going to need a lot of help taking care of you." She put one palm to her cheek, shaking her head in mock desperation. "Do you think you could help me?"

With the thumb still in place, he rewarded her with the tiniest of smiles.

"Good. Then why don't you start by helping me build a fire in the fireplace?"

Keeshan sat on the hearth while Callie removed the ashes of her last fire. "Now, Keeshan," she said, pointing at the wooden bucket behind him. "I'm ready for the kindling. Would you hand me those little pieces of wood—one at a time?"

He turned to the bucket and pulled out one piece.

"Good job," she said. *At this rate, we should have a fire around midnight.* She brushed aside an inclination to do the job herself. Keeshan needed to feel included. Tonight of all nights, he needed to feel at home.

With a long fireplace match, she lit crumpled newspaper in several places. Bringing the match to her face, she intended to blow it out when she happened to glance down at the boy. His dark eyes followed the light. "Would you like to blow it out?"

He looked at her, his face confused. "Like birthday candles," she said. "Take a deep breath." She did so herself. "And blow it out."

He filled his little lungs with air and began to blow through his lips. Just as he ran out of breath, Callie placed the match in front of him. The light went out, and his face lit up with a smile that warmed her heart more than any fire ever could.

>>>

At the bus stop, Marcus leaned against a signpost, his tool belt slung over one shoulder, arms across his chest, watching traffic whiz by. He lifted his face and let the warmth of the morning sun warm his skin. These days, he enjoyed whatever small pleasures came his way. After checking the time, he glanced up the street, watching for the blue number twenty-seven headed toward Welsh Hill.

The early commute was long over and fewer busses moved about town this late in the morning. He sighed, resigned to a long wait.

It didn't matter anyway. He had nowhere to go.

Marcus forced his mind to relax. He couldn't afford to think about the future. He had no future. At least, not until the trial was over. And now, with the trial delay and Presario's disappearance, Marcus would have to postpone any hope of resuming a real life.

Eventually, this job, this city, this experience would meld itself into a period of time he would file away into a parenthesis in the long essay that would become his life. Someday he'd refer to it as the time before the conviction. Then, after many years, he would come to see it as nothing more than an interruption, a break, a blip.

But for today, as he waited for a bus in a strange city, with no job and no future, it seemed as though the interruption would never end.

He tried not to think about his landlady, tried not to imagine her reaction when he told her the news. After all, he hadn't promised to stay forever. He'd told her the truth, or most of it. Just drifting through, he'd explained, looking for temporary work.

In spite of this, the image of Martha's face as he'd accepted the room—happy, hopeful—popped up in his memory. She'd even brushed away a tear. Marcus shook his head. She wasn't his problem, after all.

She'd just have to find another renter; he'd pay his bill and be on his way. Martha would have to fend for herself.

"Wait, Marcus!" Barry Sattler jogged up the street, waving one hand. Marcus looked the other way. "Wait. Just talk to me, man." Barry panted heavily, moving more at a trot than a run. He stopped in front of Marcus, hands on his hips, beads of sweat dripping down the creases in his lined face.

"You should get in shape, Barry."

"Back off, man," he shot back, holding his palms up. "Whew," he said, bending over to catch his breath. "I ran all the way."

"A waste of energy."

"Mine to waste," Barry said. He pointed one thumb over his shoulder. "You can't just take off like that, man. We need you. We got to finish in a couple of days."

"Look, Barry, I've had it with Bill. I'm done."

"He treats us all that way."

"I can handle his attitude," Marcus said. "I've had people ride me all my life. Bein' black, I expect it. But I can't stand the cheating. The thieving."

"Look, man. Everybody does it."

"I don't."

"Okay, the rest of the world, then. If you quit every time this happens, you won't ever work more than a week at the same job."

"If it were just the screws, I might agree with you. Maybe it was a mistake. But what about the subflooring?" Marcus shot back, his anger growing hot again. "Bill deliberately sent me out on an errand so he could get that plywood down before I got back. He knew the specs called for tongue and groove. He put that cheap stuff down hoping nobody would notice. He didn't even use glue." Marcus recrossed his arms. "You know as well as I do that he was hoping to pocket the difference in cash."

Barry spread his arms wide. "It ain't our problem. That's what inspectors are for. We just do what he tells us. If he's dishonest, it's him. It ain't us."

"I can't be a part of it, Barry." Marcus said. "Not anymore."

"You're just gonna leave?" Barry cocked his head to one side and drew up a single eyebrow. "You're gonna let us kill ourselves trying to finish on time?"

"What you do is your business," Marcus said. "I have to live with my conscience. I can't go along with it any longer."

Barry nodded, letting the silence swell. "So, where you goin'?"

Marcus shrugged. "Don't know for sure."

"Won't see you again." It was a statement.

"Probably not." Marcus avoided his eyes.

"Well, then." Barry held out his hand. "Good luck," he said. "Good luck with everything."

Six

By 9:30, as the fire crackled in the stone fireplace, Callie and Keeshan warmed themselves in the old oak rocking chair her grandmother had brought from Oklahoma. Though she'd tried to hold the boy, Keeshan managed to squirm off her lap twice, pushing her away with both hands as he landed on the wooden seat beside her. Unwilling to squabble, Callie made room by twisting sideways, holding one hip up against the hard edge of the chair arm.

With the toe of one foot she kept the old rocker moving, an old familiar creak marking the end of every arc. As her fatigue grew, she wondered how long she could stay in this position before the pain of the chair grinding into her thigh would overcome her willingness to share.

Keeshan yawned. Callie responded with a yawn of her own. The day's bewildering rush of emotions and fears had completely drained her. Even the promised trip to the guesthouse seemed too much for now. *Forget the toothbrush,* Callie thought. *We'll go in the morning.*

She'd have to put the boy to bed soon. Finding a place to sleep would pose no problem. Callie had plenty of space in the ranch-style home her father had built. When she moved in, she had claimed the back bedroom for herself, saving her parents' room for guests. Keeshan would be comfortable in her mother's sleigh bed, with its new mattress and down comforter.

As for pajamas, she certainly didn't have anything small enough for him. And, of course, she had no toothbrush for his tiny mouth. *What else does a child need to go to bed? And what about bedtime routines?* Had Celia devised some unalterable pattern for sending him to the Land of Nod? Knowing her as she did, Celia had gone about the process in a methodical yet magical way—full of bonding, bedtime stories, Bible instruction, meaningful prayer, and who knew what else.

For the first time, Callie began to regret not having spent more time with her own niece and nephew. She thought about her sister's two children—how old were they now? Eight and eleven? No, she shook her head, Brian had turned twelve in November. Callie had forgotten to send a gift.

Over the years, twice that Callie could remember, Erica had brought the children to visit. Though she was not inhospitable, Callie had always lived in downtown apartments, high rises without playgrounds or parks. Certainly not the ideal place for visiting children. Over the years Callie and Erica had shared most of their time together right here in this house, when both had come to Prospect to visit their parents.

On those visits Callie had been content to let Erica do all the child care—at least, whatever chores their mother had not taken over. Callie's mother doted on the grandchildren, making blueberry pancakes every morning and fresh cookies every afternoon. She took them on walks through the forest surrounding the house, once hiking all the way to the valley floor in the cool warmth of an August morning.

Callie thought she'd never hear the end of the glowing reports the kids gave when they ended up in the kitchen, dipping cookies in Kool-Aid floats, of all things, and topping the snack with jellybeans. Though Erica had protested the feast, Callie's mother defended herself.

"Athletes need carbs," her mother said with authority. "Hiking takes energy."

Though Callie had never ignored her niece and nephew, tonight, as she sat in the narrow corner of the rocker, she realized she hadn't stayed close to them, either. A twinge of regret twisted her heart and settled in her throat. For a moment she thought of calling Erica for advice. Erica would know how to put a four-year-old to bed.

Glancing down at Keeshan, Callie noticed that his eyelids had grown heavy. With every blink, the lashes took longer to lift. She didn't have time for a consult with Erica; she needed to make a move, and soon. "Keeshan, what do you say we head for bed?"

The boy looked up. To her surprise, he nodded. She smiled. "How'd you like to sleep in one of my T-shirts?" she asked.

Without moving his thumb, he shook his head. "Too big," he said.

She pulled his thumb from between his lips. "Say that again? I can't understand you."

Unimpressed, he slipped it back inside. Muffled words escaped around his soggy thumb. "I can't wear yours. You're too big."

"Hmm," she said, rolling further onto her left thigh and pushing up from the chair. "Why don't you come to my room and see if you're right?" She faced the rocker, offering her hand. "I think I have a T-shirt you'd love."

Taking her hand, he followed her toward the hallway. At the exact place where the dark hall swallowed the entry light, he stopped, leaning back, pulling his hand from hers.

"Come on, Keeshan. You said you want to go to bed."

"Dark," he said, though the consonants were lost as they collided with his thumb.

"Ah, yes." Callie smiled. She flipped the switch and light filled the hall. "I don't like the dark, either," she agreed, offering her hand again. "Now, would you like to see my Mickey Mouse T-shirt?"

He nodded and slipped his hand inside hers, his small wet fingers closing around her palm. His skin was soft, and she relished the feel of his little hand in hers. It seemed so right to have him here, so natural that he should visit. And she had no more than enjoyed him like this, his hand in hers, when she remembered his mother, fighting for her life in a Seattle hospital bed. The sharp twist in her gut returned, and Callie blinked away fresh tears.

At the end of the hall she switched on her bedroom light and picked Keeshan up, placing him on the edge of the bed. "I'm pretty sure that shirt is just your size," she said. Callie searched through two dresser drawers before she found the shirt. Over the years the poor thing had faded and shrunk almost beyond recognition. In spite of this, the mouse on the front continued to wave his arm in a cheery greeting. She held it toward Keeshan. "Would you like to wear this tonight?"

He nodded, smiling, his thumb still entombed by his lips. She held the shirt out to him. He stared back at her, questioning. "You can dress yourself, can't you?" Keeshan rolled and slid off the bed, standing with one hand over his head, the other in his mouth.

Clearly, he expected Callie to do the dressing. Obligingly, she pulled his Mariners sweatshirt over his head. He shivered and hugged himself. Callie hurried to replace his shirt with her own. "I could use a little help here," she said. "Put your arm through this hole." She held the sleeve open.

The boy was as cooperative as a garden scarecrow.

She managed to pull down his sweat pants, only to remember the tennis shoes still on his feet. She had to lift him onto the bed, take off the shoes, and drag off his pants. By the time he was ready, she felt as though she'd wrestled a sixteen-foot alligator.

"All right," she said. "Let's go check out your bed."

Callie rarely entered her mother's bedroom, and she couldn't help the feeling of sadness that passed over her as she switched on the light next to the old bed. She had not wanted to change a single detail. Patterned wallpaper in jewel tones of burgundy and blue swirled behind the dark headboard. A mountain of pillows, all covered in matching shams, stood guard at the head of the bed. Callie turned back the covers. "Here you go, Keeshan," she said.

"Potty," he said, as through mashed potatoes.

This time, Callie didn't bother to pull out the thumb. Instead, she squatted down, her face near his. "Can you do that yourself?" she asked. He nodded.

"Okay," she said, switching on the bathroom light. "You get your very own bathroom for as long as you stay here with me. Pretty cool, huh?"

He followed her across the carpet, his feet peeking out from under the hem of the faded T-shirt. Holding on to the door jam with one hand, he peered around the wall. Apparently satisfied, he pulled out his thumb and used both hands to push Callie out of the doorway. "By myself," he said, and pushed the door shut.

>>>

By the time the old bus landed in Casa Grande, Marcus found himself fighting to contain both a pounding headache and a very full bladder. No matter what destination he'd paid for, he could not face another minute of shuddering brakes, diesel fumes, and swaying seats.

Before the driver opened the power door, Marcus grabbed his duffel bag and bounded down the aisle. In the parking area he swayed for a moment, dizzy from two days in a rocking bus, as he tried to get his bearings.

"Bus stops here for ten minutes," the driver behind him announced. "I'll open the baggage compartment. Passengers continuing to all points south should reboard at 2:40."

Hearing the scuffle of other passengers, Marcus checked his watch and hurried across the sweltering pavement into the station. With any luck, he'd be the first to find the restroom.

From Chicago, Marcus had traveled by bus through Bloomington, Springfield, and St. Louis. From there, he'd gone north to Kansas City, where a highway glimpse of a burned-out apartment complex led him to a two-week framing job. Though he'd slept on the floor of a neighboring apartment, he'd made enough money to replace what he'd given his landlady when he left Chicago. He smiled, remembering the shuddering of Martha's chest as she'd enfolded him in a tearful goodbye. He'd nearly suffocated.

With additional cash padding his wallet, Marcus bought a bus ticket west. He'd stayed briefly at the YMCA in Denver before following a job lead to Fort Collins. Hitchhiking north, he spent seven hours in heavy winds and cold temperatures, arriving at the promised job site exhausted. There, with his stomach growling and his feet aching, he discovered that the foreman hired union carpenters only.

Marcus had no union credentials. In fact, he had no genuine social security number or employment record of any kind. He had no referrals, no recommendations. No resume. For that matter, he no longer used his real name.

Marcus Jefferson had left his real life far behind.

These days, he looked only for jobs where none of these technical complications were required. Marcus needed cash. Tired of the Colorado cold, he bought a bus ticket and headed south. If he were going to starve to death, at least he would be warm when it happened. The trip to Albuquerque took fourteen hours, and from there to Flagstaff, Arizona, another six.

From the moment his bus left Chicago, his frustration with the bus company and its unreliable schedule nearly drove him mad. He'd suffered through breakdowns, driver illnesses, and schedule changes. It galled him that the company could be so negligent.

Before long, Marcus realized that he no longer cared. He paid no attention to the names of the cities he passed through. He slept whenever he could, eating day-old sandwiches from bus terminals all across the Midwest, washing them down with Diet Coke or bottled water. His only real concern these days lay in the dwindling pile of bills in his wallet.

Though he had learned to live without home or possessions, to become an anonymous passerby on the streets of any city, he still needed money to survive. Even as he traveled south, he struggled with the certain knowledge that he had to find work soon. He needed to hunker down and stay in one place long enough to save some real money.

Only then, when he'd joined a long-term construction crew, would he be able to refinance his life. He looked forward to living in a rented room again, sleeping in a real bed. Using a shower. Buying food with taste and nutrition.

Inside the Casa Grande restroom, Marcus crossed broken floor tiles to the urinals, dimly aware of the graffiti-covered walls and the shattered mirror hanging over two sinks. As he washed his hands, he discovered that management had turned off the hot water and the towel dispenser was empty. Shaking his fingers dry, he slung his duffel over one shoulder and walked out of the restroom.

The waiting area was clean, though depressing. A working upholstery shop filled one side of the room, individual chairs and vending machines the other. For a moment he watched his fellow passengers as they bought food from machines in the far corner of the room. Marcus did not feel hungry. Instead, he longed to stretch his cramped legs.

He glanced at the clock over the exit doors and wondered if he had enough time to stroll around the block before reboarding the southbound bus. In the middle of the Arizona desert, with temperatures soaring, he wondered about the wisdom of going for a walk. *At least the air-conditioned bus will be welcome,* he thought, turning toward the street.

Pulling his bag higher on his shoulder, Marcus stepped out onto the sidewalk, where a slight wind blew from his right.

It was cooler here. Refreshed, he turned to his left and started out at a brisk pace. As he continued past the first intersection, his shoulders relaxed and the cramp in the small of his back began to ease. Covering the next block quickly, he turned left at the second stoplight. At this pace, he would return to the bus station with time to spare. In spite of the afternoon heat, Marcus already felt better. Alive again.

As he passed the second entry on the left, he looked up just as a small man stepped out from the space between two buildings, his face partially covered by a mass of long disheveled hair. Without thinking, Marcus stepped sideways, allowing ample room for the stranger to pass. As he approached, Marcus noticed a change in the stranger's face. A malevolent smile began to spread across his dark features. Marcus felt his stomach squeeze.

The stranger nodded. With his attention fully focused on the small man before him, Marcus did not hear someone approach from behind. Then, startled by a painful blow across the back of his calves, Marcus collapsed onto his knees, sprawling forward, face-first onto the pavement, scraping skin from his palms. His chin took a slide as well, and Marcus tasted blood.

Stunned and suddenly angry, he pushed himself up. He'd hardly straightened his elbows before a foot came down hard in the center of his back. Again, his face met the concrete. As he struggled to free himself, the smaller man grabbed the strap of his duffle bag. Yanking it off Marcus's shoulder, the thief turned and ran down the street.

Confused, Marcus struggled again to rise to his hands and knees. He could not let his bag go. It held all his earthly possessions. His tools. His tool belt. His clothes.

But the foot on his back kept him down. Instinctively, he went limp. As he felt the pressure on his back ease, he rolled, grabbing the stranger's ankle. The maneuver worked, and the attacker lost his balance, falling onto the sidewalk beside Marcus. With both arms, Marcus pushed the body away and scrambled to stand. "Stop," he yelled at the figure receding up the street. "My stuff. I need my…"

Stumbling, Marcus began to run. He took no more than two steps before the baseball bat struck him again, this time on the side of his chest. Air rushed from his lungs as he fell again to the sidewalk. He gasped, mouth open, his muscles fighting to pull in the stubborn afternoon air.

Fear grabbed hold of him, and his Indianapolis street smarts returned. Ignoring his pain, Marcus curled into a fetal position, protecting his ribs with his knees, his head with his hands. As the bat rained blows on his shoulder and back, he coaxed his mind into action. *Think*, he told himself. *Get out of here.*

Sneaking a look between his elbows, Marcus focused enough to spy a pair of Puma tennis shoes spread wide before him. He took a deep breath and waited for the pause between blows. Then with a roar, Marcus sprang out, both arms low, hitting the attacker hard around the hips. Both men dropped to the ground. It was a tackle that would have made his high school football coach proud.

Without looking back, Marcus sprang to his feet. He wanted to sprint down the sidewalk after the thief. But his head swam, and he could not catch his breath. He staggered for a moment, breathing hard. When he looked up again, the small man had disappeared.

He couldn't have gotten far away—not in the middle of the afternoon. Certainly someone had noticed such a bold thief in the bright light of day. Marcus could follow him, hear something, footsteps, heavy breathing, maybe even a barking dog. Marcus couldn't afford to give up.

Taking a shallow rasping breath, Marcus started at a jog down the sidewalk. At the first intersection, he paused to look for the smaller man. Seeing none, he turned left, away from the main street, passing two small houses before he came to the opening of an alley on his left. Somehow, knowing with certainty that the thief had turned here, Marcus started down the narrow alley.

Marcus tried to pick up speed, but his body would not obey. This was the direction his brother would have gone. Somewhere in this alley, he would find his duffle bag. His possessions.

He moved along the back of one building, behind a detached single car garage, and toward a full-sized van parked on his left, listening carefully for the sound of footsteps on the gravel nearby. He heard nothing.

Marcus slowed, his body demanding rest, his chest screaming at him. Just as he passed the end of the van, a long two-by-four came swinging at him from in front of the van, slamming into him directly above his left eye. Marcus never even raised his arms to protect himself. The last thing he felt was gravel slamming into his cheek as he hit the ground.

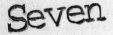Seven

Callie had barely closed the door to her mother's old bedroom before she decided to head for the shop. In her own room she changed from jeans into a pair of fleece tights and a winter jersey. Over this she threw a hooded sweatshirt. From the closet she picked up her bike shoes and a pair of wool socks. She recognized this urge; she'd felt it before. Somehow, she had to burn off the anxiety she felt. As always, she needed to move.

Sweating always helped Callie to think clearly.

As she slipped on a pair of bike gloves, her worries assaulted her. What on earth had come over her? What made her think that she could take care of this boy? Even for a moment—an hour—an afternoon. She couldn't do it!

Of course, someone had to; she recognized that. And yes, she felt sorry for him. Anyone would. After all, the last twenty-four hours had turned his life upside down. His mother had left him at day care, and somehow—at least as far as he understood—dropped off the face of the planet. How could any four-year-old understand that?

Callie wished she could make things better. Something nearly maternal had risen inside of her, something that wanted to comfort him, to support him to…and suddenly her thoughts collided with an idea so strange that she caught her breath.

You want to keep the boy.

It couldn't be. It wasn't her job. Celia should have said something about her family's whereabouts. If she couldn't tell Callie about her past, she might at least have told someone at day care or her work.

Callie thought about that. When she worked in the city, none of her coworkers knew anything about *her* family. It wasn't that she had anything to hide. It simply never came up. Callie shook her head. Maybe it hadn't come up for Celia either.

After all, no one expects to land in ICU.

Callie went through the house to the back door, where she reached up and grabbed the shop keys as she backed through the screen door. Then running across the yard, she headed through the moonlight to her detached shop.

Shivering, she unlocked the door and turned on the fluorescent lights. Ignoring the chair she hadn't delivered and the loveseat she hadn't stripped, Callie lifted her road bike from the wall and placed it on the training rollers. Leaning the bike against her hip, Callie twisted her long hair into a knot and caught it in a soft band. With a deep breath, her emotions roiling, she threw one leg over the top tube and mounted the bike. As she began pedaling, Callie shifted quickly, increasing the resistance until her heart began to pound and her breath came in deep gasps.

As her legs warmed up, Callie prayed. *Lord, I didn't ask for this, you know. I was only trying to help Celia. That's all. I lent her my car and look what's happened. It's totaled. Celia is in the hospital, and now I'm a babysitter. You know I love Celia, but I never meant to take care of her child. I want to be at the hospital, taking care of her.*

She changed gears again and let her breathing settle into a rhythm as she pushed herself to a faster pace. In spite of the cold temperature, she felt her body respond. White puffs of condensation escaped from her mouth. Sweat began to trickle between her shoulder blades and collect at the small of her back. Her legs, which at first objected to the effort, fell into a cycle of ups and downs so perfectly timed that she no longer bounced on the seat. She changed gears again, hoping exertion would quiet her inner turmoil. Again, she prayed.

Now what am I supposed to do? I didn't plan this. I don't want it, Lord. I know I'm supposed to be your servant. But a child? How can I care for a child? I'm single. I'm broke. I can hardly care for myself. Would you just heal Celia and bring her home quickly? I can't do this for long, Lord. It wouldn't be fair to the boy.

She leaned over, gripping the handlebars in the drops. *I'm telling you, Lord. I don't have any idea how to take care of a child. I'll mess it up. I know it. They tell me you never make mistakes. But this, I guarantee, is a huge mistake.*

Callie continued to push herself, gradually increasing her speed and effort until the trainer whined as it kept pace. Her breathing labored and she felt her thigh muscles swell and fill with blood as they strained to keep up.

Even as she panted, a tiny thought hovered in the back of her mind—a thought so alarming, so frightening that she refused to vent it in prayer. If she did not acknowledge the thought, perhaps it would go away. She pedaled even faster, but the thought caught up with her. Pestering. Irritating. Frightening. The alarmingly tempting thought whispered over the whine of the trainer.

If something happened to Celia, you could keep the boy.

She shook her head and pedaled even faster, her heart pounding in her ears. No. She would never keep the boy. She was happy as she was. Contentment had come at a high price. She had worked hard, sacrificing much to come to a place of peace in her life. She could not, would not allow a four-year-old to shift the balance she had fought so hard to win. No. Keeping Keeshan was out of the question.

Over the soft whir of the wheels and the high pitch of the rollers, Callie did not hear the door open behind her. Did not hear little feet pad across the bare concrete floor.

Callie had no way of knowing that Keeshan was in the room—that is, until he touched her right hip.

The touch, so sudden, so completely unexpected, startled her and she screamed, losing both her rhythm and her balance at the same time.

The bike tipped, and Callie barely managed to get her shoe out of the pedal before dropping it on to the concrete. She stood on one foot, still panting, her heart pounding. "Keeshan, you scared me!"

Eyes wide, his thumb slipped back into his mouth. He backed away.

Seeing his expression, she softened her tone. "Why are you out here?" she asked. "You'll freeze walking outside on a night like this."

"I want Eddy," he explained. As Callie looked more carefully, she noticed that his cheeks were wet with tears.

"Eddy?" Callie struggled to understand. "A stuffed animal? You want a stuffed animal to sleep with?"

"My kitty," he said, nodding. He pulled his hand away from his mouth and caught a river of drool as it slid down his chin. "I want Eddy."

Callie laid the bike on the floor, and moved toward Keeshan, squatting in front of him. "Where will we find Eddy?"

He shrugged. "At my house."

"You want to go over to your house to find Eddy? Now?"

He nodded.

Callie glanced at her watch. Seven minutes after eleven. Though she had a key to the guesthouse, she had never, in all the time Celia had lived there, gone in without permission. Callie believed in giving the little family as much privacy as she would want in their place. It bothered her, going in when Celia wasn't home. Even now, under these strange circumstances, she hated the idea.

She put her hands on his shoulders. "You can't possibly sleep without Eddy?"

He shook his head as his eyes filled with tears.

The sad, lost expression made Callie's heart weak. Of course they could go over and look for the stuffed animal. It would only take a moment. After all, if he needed the animal to sleep, it would probably be on his bed, or in his room, exactly as he'd left it when he'd gone to school this morning.

Callie took his hand. "All right," she agreed, turning for the door. "I'll help you get your kitty. You promise you'll go right to sleep as soon as we get back?" He nodded and smiled. For the first time, the smile reached his eyes.

She steered him toward the back door. Giving his hand a squeeze, she said, "Sounds like a deal to me."

>>>>

The feeling of a sharp rock digging into his cheek dragged Marcus from unconsciousness. Even before he opened his eyes, he recognized the headache raging in his temples. As he lifted his head to relieve the pressure on his cheek, a jolt of electricity shuddered through his neck. He groaned and pushed up onto his hands. The effort revealed yet another source of injury; a new pain stabbed through his rib cage.

He cried out and flopped onto his back, covering his eyes with his forearm. "Lord," he complained aloud, "I could use some help."

From this position he wiggled his toes, bent his knees, and flexed his hips one after the other. Things below the waist seems to be working fine, he realized, though all motion made him wince. He poked along his ribs with his left hand, searching for the source of the throbbing pain. It didn't take long to find a long, wide section of rib bone, situated just below his right armpit, so tender that his eyes watered when he touched it.

Broken, he thought, gritting his teeth.

Marcus knew he could do nothing for a broken rib. No casting, no taping, nothing to ease the unending pain. He'd simply have to wait it out. After all, no one ever died of a broken rib. At least, not anyone he knew.

Removing his arm from his eyes, he looked up into the slanting light of sunset. His entire face seemed to be on fire—a condition he attributed to falling face down in the gravel. Still, something about the view wasn't quite right. He covered the left eye, and peered up with his right. The branches of a tree fluttered in the evening breeze. He repeated the motion, this time covering his right eye. The tree disappeared.

His left eyelid seemed stuck at half-mast.

Running his fingertips carefully along the skin over and around his left eye, he found a new tenderness. Holding his hand to the light, he examined his fingers. Blood. Marcus found dried blood on his left eyebrow and cheekbone as well. *Well, that explains the view.*

He tried to sit up, but the knifing pain from his ribs stopped him before his head ever left the ground. He cried out, grabbing his chest with both hands. He waited for the pain to pass. Then, rolling like a log, he moved onto his left side.

Bringing up one knee, he got onto his hands and knees, though the horizon swirled around him. This time as he moved, his neck did not complain, and Marcus noted this slight improvement with gratitude. Still, his chest ached as though he'd been run over by a tractor.

He inched his left knee forward, gradually bringing it off the ground. Closer, closer, he brought his foot toward his hand. Then, holding his breath, he managed to get his feet underneath him and stand. Swaying a bit, he remained bent, his hands on his knees, focusing on a small cactus garden beside the road. Gradually, the dizziness settled.

He straightened, stood, and for a moment, took in his surroundings. In the dim light he spied the van that had sheltered the thief. Marcus took a couple of steps toward the vehicle and reached out to lean against it, resting. With one hand on his ribs, he looked around, hoping the thief had found the contents of his gym bag uninteresting, or worthless, and left it behind. Though he knew better, he scanned the alley and a nearby driveway.

It was gone. Everything. His tools, his clothes. Everything was gone. Only then, as he mourned the loss of his father's hammer, did Marcus remember his wallet. Feeling certain dread, he reached down and patted the back pocket of his jeans.

The thief had not forgotten.

Turning his back to the van, Marcus slid down the warm metal, coming to rest against the side door, his legs bent, his chest aching. Resting his elbows on his knees, he dropped his forehead onto his arms and allowed himself to feel the first stirrings of self-pity.

He couldn't go to the authorities. He knew enough about the police to understand that such petty thievery hardly found its way onto the priority list—no matter where the crime occurred. *And in this tiny southwestern town, no one will care.*

Marcus rested against the van for some time before he felt strong enough to move. By then the sun had gone down and the temperature had begun to drop. As the last vestiges of sunlight glimmered along the horizon, he made his way back to the main street. Slowly, one hand holding his aching chest, he inched along.

As he exited the alley, a small car approached the intersection. Inside, a woman glanced at him with disgust. Turning her face from him, she pressed her foot against the accelerator and the car shot away. She did not stop at the intersection.

Marcus would forever remember the look that crossed her face as her eyes fixed on him. He swallowed a strong feeling of humiliation as he considered how he must have looked, a stooped black man, his face battered, staggering down the street. No wonder she was disgusted. Anyone would feel the same way.

>>>

Callie snatched the keys from a cabinet above the dishwasher in her kitchen. "Okay," she said. "Follow me." In the mudroom she picked up the boy and wrapped him in an old wool coat as she struck out through the moonlight for the guesthouse. Even as they hurried across the lawn, Callie felt his little frame shiver.

She wrapped the coat tighter and pulled him against her chest.

At the guesthouse Callie deposited Keeshan on the porch and moved to the door. She held the keys up to the lamplight and struggled with the lock as the little boy waited. Her key was old, and the lock was resistant. In the cold her fingers grew clumsy and stiff. As she struggled, she heard Keeshan's teeth begin to chatter.

At last the lock gave way, and she pushed open the door. With the old barn coat flying loose, Keeshan darted around her legs and ran inside. "Eddy," he cried. "We're here!"

Callie walked in and pulled the door shut behind her. Light, passing through the ruffled shade of a small lamp, cast a soothing glow over the room. Though Callie had spent many hours here, tonight, without

Celia, it seemed different—changed somehow—as if the entire house stood waiting, incomplete without her presence.

Callie saw Celia's couch in a new light. Though she'd often enjoyed late night videos, popcorn, and girl talk on that couch, she had never felt such loneliness from the threadbare fabric or the cushions sagging like a hammock strung between trees.

Moving to the table, Callie picked up a frame holding the grainy image of a young Hispanic woman and a baby. A picture of Celia and Keeshan, she guessed, though the woman in the picture had her face partially turned from the camera. The mother glowed with pride, her gaze fastened on the bundle she held. Wrapped in a white blanket, the dark baby seemed to be all eyes—beautiful dark eyes. His hair, even as a baby, formed perfect ringlets.

As always, the house was immaculate. There were no toys on the floor, no laundry waiting to be folded. There were no magazines or books strewn around the room. No mail on the table. Callie turned to look at the kitchen. Here too, the sink was empty, the counters wiped, dishes put away. The floor sparkled. There were no fingerprints on the refrigerator door. No water spots on the window above the sink. The table had been set for dinner, with two place mats, fabric napkins, and dishes.

There was no Eddy in the living room. In a few quick steps, Callie entered the hallway, where she poked her head into the bathroom. Bath towels hung neatly on racks. The sink was clean and the mirror spotless. No clothes on the floor, no towel draped over the toilet. No Eddy.

"Come here," Keeshan yelled from the back of the house.

"Did you find Eddy?" she asked, expecting to find Keeshan in his bedroom. But he was not there. Instead, he stood in Celia's room, his thumb in his mouth, staring up at the closed door of Celia's closet. "Where is he?" she asked.

"In there," he said, pointing at the doors.

Callie put both hands on her hips. "Why is Eddy in your mother's bedroom?"

Relentlessly, Keeshan pointed up at the closet.

It seemed a little excessive, putting a favorite animal in the closet every morning. But considering the neatness of the rest of the house, this did not seem completely out of character. Callie slid open the closet door.

As the light from the room spilled into the closet, Callie heard the angry meow of a very unhappy cat. "Eddy," Keeshan cried, falling onto his knees in front of a line of matched shoes. The cat meowed again, though more gently this time, and Callie watched in amazement as Keeshan opened the door of an animal cage hidden under long coats at one end of the closet.

With tiny fingers he pulled out the largest gray cat Callie had ever seen. Staggering beneath the weight, Keeshan stood, the cat draped over his forearms. "I'm sorry we're late, Eddy," he said, laying his cheek along the feline backbone. As he closed his eyes, long lashes showed clearly against the skin of his cheeks. "It's been a very bad day."

Amen, thought Callie. *Amen.*

Eight

As Marcus made his way back to the bus station, he noticed the darkened sidewalks, the closed businesses, the quiet of the street, and for the first time he wondered how many hours he had lost to the effects of the attack. He hadn't eaten a genuine meal in days, and hunger knotted his stomach. He glanced at his wrist, relieved that the thief had left him his twenty-dollar watch. It was nearing 4:30.

At the station he realized with a sinking disappointment that the windows were dark. Too dark. He pushed against the front door, hoping that the lobby remained open. The door held fast. Marcus leaned forward, cupping his palms around his eyes, and looked inside. Not even a cleaning lady.

Only then did he notice the small sign. Tiny white letters on black felt announced that the station had four daily departures. The next southbound bus would leave at 10:00 A.M.

Forgetting the injury to his ribs, Marcus took a deep breath. The instant stabbing reminded him immediately of his mistake, and he turned to lean against the door, his arm across his chest as if to hold off the pain. Focused on his agony, he shut his eyes, squeezing off the tears that threatened. Fighting to regain his composure, he blew air through tightened lips.

He stood up again, though in slow motion. Fatigue, along with the ever-present ache of the beating he'd taken, dogged him, weighing down his arms and legs. He needed rest and food. He needed to find some place to spend the night—some safe, quiet place. He could deal with his failed travel plans later.

Only then did he spot the police cruiser coming to a stop along the curb. In spite of his injuries, he brought himself up to his full height and forced a smile. A uniformed officer exited the driver's side door.

"Good evening, sir," Marcus said, softly, evenly.

"Hello," the man said, pausing to put his hands on his hips. "You from around here?"

"No, sir. I came in on a bus," Marcus said, pointing over his shoulder with his thumb. "Arrived this afternoon."

"You don't look too good. Something happen to you?"

"No, sir." Marcus took a moment to read the name on the officer's name tag. Quiñones. Marcus had no idea how to pronounce it. "I went for a walk after my bus came into town. Fell asleep down the street there. I was a little woozy when I woke up." He put his hand to his face, touching his eyebrow gently. "Coming back here, I walked straight into a light pole."

"Just like that." Suspicion radiated from the officer's hazel eyes.

"Yes, sir. Just like that."

"You been drinking?"

"No, sir."

"You planning to catch a bus out of town?"

"Yes, sir."

The officer paused, tipped his head, and eyed Marcus from head to toe, evaluating him, judging the strength of the story. Marcus closed his mouth, crossed his arms over his chest and waited, praying the officer would decide he was just a vagrant. A man passing through. Not worth harassing.

Evidently satisfied, the officer dropped his hands. "Casa Grande is a peaceful place," he said, using one finger to emphasize his next point.

"We don't tolerate violence or law breaking around here. When that bus leaves here in the morning, you be sure you're on it." He paused and gestured toward the corner where Marcus had been mugged. "In the meantime, we have a Lucky Six down the street. I'd suggest you sleep off your troubles. It'll be safer for everyone." He turned back to his patrol car.

"Thank you, Officer," Marcus said, with respect he did not feel. *Thanks for nothing.*

>>>

Callie lugged the animal carrier and a half-opened bag of cat litter back to the house. Keeshan insisted on carrying Eddy, though he could hardly manage to see where he was going with the animal draped over his little forearms. Stumbling through the snow in oversized cowboy boots, Keeshan offered the tranquil cat an unending litany of apology.

When Celia moved in, Callie had insisted there be no pets. But, since she and Celia had become frinds, Callie couldn't understand why Celia kept the cat a secret. Was Celia afraid to put their friendship to the test?

Inside the house, Callie put the carrier in front of the dryer, depositing the bag of litter on the floor beside it. Then she hung up the barn coat. "Keeshan," she called, stopping him as he stepped into the kitchen, "how long has Eddy lived at your house?"

He shrugged. "A while."

"A month?"

The boy shrugged. "I don't know." Then, folding himself in half, Keeshan set the cat on the floor. Eddy began to sniff around the walls of the room, pausing to inspect a basket of folded towels. He jumped onto the towels and began kneading. Circling twice, the cat curled into a ball.

Callie hung up her keys. "I think Eddy should stay in the laundry room tonight. He'll be more comfortable here."

"No," Keeshan said. "Eddy sleeps with me."

"I don't think Eddy should sleep in your room."

Keeshan shook his head. "Eddy sleeps on my bed."

"At my house, we don't keep animals on our beds."

Keeshan's lips tightened and he picked up the cat. Callie heard the cat squeak as the air was squeezed out of his chest. "I can't sleep without Eddy," Keeshan complained. "You said we could go get him. You said I could sleep with him."

"But I didn't know that Eddy was a real cat."

Keeshan's frustration turned to a whine. "Eddy is real!"

Callie took a deep breath, resisting the urge to run screaming to her bedroom. "I can see that now, Keeshan. But I didn't know he was real when I promised. I thought he was a stuffed animal. Like Garfield." She bent down beside him, trying another tact. "Aren't you tired? You should be in bed. I'm sure the kitty would prefer to sleep out here where it's warm. I'll put his bed here, and he'll have his food dish and his litter box…"

"No," the whine turned to a wail. "He sleeps with me." Tears overflowed his dark eyes, spilling down over his cheeks.

Actually, Callie was the one who was tired. To a long, tense day she had already added four exhausting hours of parenting. She gave in.

After all, Keeshan wasn't her child. She could spoil him if she wanted, and then, when his mother got out of the hospital, or the authorities managed to locate his family, she would simply hand him over. She just needed to survive until then.

Someone else could have the pleasure of developing character in this child. For now, Callie wanted only to crawl into her own bed and turn out the light. Though she had grown up in a home where animals did not sleep on human beds, she was about to make a distinct policy shift. "All right," she said, with some irritation. "Eddy can sleep with you. Don't blame me if you wake up with fleas."

With that, she picked up the cat things and led the boy back through the house to her mother's bedroom.

>>>

Marcus watched the patrol car pull away from the curb and turn at the next corner. His hunger had grown, demanding more than attention; it drove him to action. Marcus crossed the boulevard to the large grocery store facing the depot.

He'd shopped at similar chain stores in other locations, back in the days when he had a family and a real life. Marcus pictured the inside of the store, and for a moment, he remembered stopping on the way home from work for a gallon of milk, a package of cheese, a carton of whole wheat crackers.

He shook the image away as his stomach squeezed in anticipation. Stepping into the parking lot, he paused. Shopping carts were scattered across the asphalt, indicating a thriving business. But at that hour, only a few cars remained.

The air had cooled slightly, the last of the sun having sunk behind the hills. Still, the pavement radiated heat. A slight breeze ruffled the American flag over the entrance. Keeping his head down, Marcus tucked his hands in his jean pockets and made his way across the lot and around the side of the building.

Not certain of his destination, he hoped to find something, anything the store might have discarded. Perhaps damaged fruit or leftovers from the deli. Perhaps the bakery might have thrown something out—something burned or out of date. As he walked, he prayed. *I'm hungry, Lord. I don't know how you can help, but I've got to have food.*

It was then that something inside Marcus changed. Though he'd grown up among thieves, he'd never stolen anything in his life. He'd been with friends who shoplifted. He knew boys who'd been sent to jail for breaking and entering. Intellectually, he'd always understood their willingness to steal. In the inner city, with absent parents and constant poverty, some of his peers stole to live. Some stole for reputation. Others stole for the thrill of it.

But with every step, as hunger twisted his stomach, and he felt the beginning of lightheadedness—Marcus knew what it was to be driven by hunger. Though he planned only to raid the dumpster, Marcus understood how others became desperate enough to steal food.

For the first time, Marcus Jefferson identified with those driven by poverty.

The parking lot lights had already come on, and in their orange glow he scanned the narrow lot for a dumpster. Near the loading dock, Marcus found a cardboard recycling machine, the holding cart full of flattened and bound cardboard. Walking around the loading dock, he had just turned back toward the building when a scraping noise, coming from a partially open side door, caught his attention. He froze.

An older voice spoke. "Don, did you set out those overripes?"

"Not yet."

"Are they off the floor?"

"Not yet."

Marcus crouched low, hiding himself in the dock's squatty shadow. From here, light spilled from a door blocked open by a plastic five-gallon bucket. The older voice swore. "I told you to get those bananas when you first came on. Can't you do anything I ask?"

"Sorry. I'll get it before I go on break."

"Get it now. And clean up this mess."

"Yes, sir."

Marcus crept through the shadows toward the door. He heard the sound of cooler doors being slammed. If things went as he expected, overaged fruit would soon be removed from the sales floor and discarded. If he were lucky, Marcus could make a meal of the castoffs. Though it wouldn't satisfy for long, it would keep him through the night. It might even hold him until he figured out how to earn his next meal.

If he could just get to the fruit before the store disposed of it.

He waited, perfectly still in the darkness as the minutes crept by. His left knee began to ache and before long he felt a cramp in his calf. He dropped onto his hands, pushing the foot out behind him, stretching to ease the spasm. Just then, the door opened wider and Marcus froze. Glancing at the door, he stopped breathing.

A boy, no more than eighteen, stepped outside carrying a roll of garden hose. The sound of his footsteps grew louder, and Marcus sensed him moving near—very near. The boy attached one end of the hose to a spigot not ten feet from where Marcus lay in a partial push up. He heard the faucet open and water rush into the hose. The steps retreated and the door opened again, squeaking as it fell closed.

With a rush of air, Marcus lowered himself gently onto the pavement. His ribs screamed from the position he'd been forced to hold. *Too close. Far too close.*

Marcus heard the sound of pressurized water spraying concrete as water streamed out from under the door. The boy was washing the floor. Would he ever put out the fruit?

For a moment Marcus considered begging. Perhaps the produce men would have mercy on him. As his cheeks grew warm, Marcus knew he couldn't ask for help. People would take one look at him, at his broken face and his torn and dirty clothes, at the color of his skin, and they would know he wasn't worth helping.

Marcus understood that much about people. He wouldn't give them the satisfaction of turning him down. No. Tonight he would take care of himself.

He crawled closer to the building, and in the dark corner where the loading dock touched the rear wall of the grocery store, Marcus turned around and sat down, tucking his arms across his chest. With what was left of his patience, he waited for the boy to finish his assignment.

>>>>

Dimly aware of noise and daylight, Callie rolled over and pulled the covers up around her chin. Her eyes felt heavy and her mind thick. *Too early,* she thought, burying her face in the pillow. *It's too early to get up.*

When tiny fingers pulled her right eyelid open, Callie jumped.

"You up?"

Flying onto her knees, heart pounding, Callie put one hand over her eye. "Did you have to do that?"

"I thought you were awake."

She collapsed onto her stomach and rolled over, rubbing her eyes with both hands. She couldn't quite rid herself of the feeling of her eyelid being peeled back. "I wasn't awake," she said, still irritated. Opening her eyes, she found his face bent over hers, apparently worried that she might have fallen asleep. "And you shouldn't be awake, either."

"But I am."

"I can see that."

"I'm hungry."

"Okay." Callie threw one arm over her eyes to block the glaring light. He dragged her arm down.

"I want some breakfast," he said, his impatience growing.

"I want some sleep," she answered, closing her eyes. In the long silence that followed, Callie realized she could never go back to sleep. Giving up, she opened her eyes and found his nose no more than four inches from hers. It took fortitude not to jump. "What would you like for breakfast?"

"Dynobuddies."

"Dynobuddies?" Callie could not imagine any food by that name. "Is that a cereal?"

"With candy crunchies."

"Sounds good for you."

"I'm hungry," his request was now a whine. He pulled at her arm. "Get up."

"I'm coming," she said, throwing back the covers.

Keeshan wrapped one fist around the elastic in her pajama bottoms. "Come on," he said, dragging her out of bed.

Obediently, but with growing resentment, Callie followed the boy, slowing only to reach for the terry cloth robe draped over the end of her bed. Saturday was her only day to sleep in. Didn't this little guy realize that? Couldn't he give her just one morning of real rest? "Wait a minute. I need to stop here," she said, turning toward the bathroom.

"No!" With both hands, Keeshan threw his whole weight against her hips, blocking her path to the door. "I want breakfast now!"

Callie stepped around his outstretched arms. "You'll get breakfast when I'm good and ready," she said. With that, she stepped into the bathroom and locked the door behind her.

She tried to ignore the sound of his crying. Closing her ears to his escalating wail, she washed her face. And to spite his temper tantrum, the accident, and the luck that brought him to stay with her, Callie took an extra few minutes to brush her teeth before she emerged to make breakfast.

Nine

Gradually, the sound inside the grocery store diminished, and Marcus found himself fighting sleep. Drifting off, his head bobbed onto his chest. He dreamed of cookies and of steaks sizzling on an outdoor grill.

Hunger, now his master, taunted him even in his sleep.

A bang, coming from the produce department, jolted Marcus from his dreams. Fully alert, with aching chest and throbbing head, he remembered his surroundings. Once again his stomach screamed for food. He had drooled in his sleep, and feeling shame, he wiped his chin with the back of his hand.

Marcus rocked gently on his buttocks, stretching his legs as he tried to regain the sensation in his feet. Then he peered through the darkness to the back door. Someone had left it propped open. In the light coming from inside, Marcus saw what he'd been waiting for.

Just inside the open door, he spotted several large milk crates filled with discarded produce. His mouth watered as he rolled over and began crawling through the darkness toward it. The sudden, intense prickling of his legs as they came back to life stopped him, and he dropped his head, waiting for the sensation to pass.

More slowly, he crept forward, his eyes on the open door, his ears tuned to the sounds inside. His breathing came in shallow gasps and all of his muscles tensed. Staying low, he brought himself to his feet, hiding behind the door.

Certain there was no one nearby, he crept around the door and entered the back of the store. The bright light stung his eyes as he moved quickly and silently to the stack of milk crates. Bananas, bruised and dark, filled the upper crate. Hurriedly, without examination, Marcus stuffed the fruit into his jacket pockets. He dropped several down the neck of his T-shirt, where they bounced against his bare stomach.

Emboldened, he picked up the top crate and moved it. The next crate held the bruised cuttings from lettuce heads. Below that, Marcus found bruised apples. Though soft and brown, he could not resist the sweet smell rising from the crate. Hungry, and uncertain of his future, Marcus took four of these, two in each hand.

Realizing that he could not carry any more food, he stopped and looked around. If he could hoard enough, find something to carry more food, he might be able to make it to Tucson and a job. As he considered his surroundings, the door separating the storage room from the rest of the store swung open, banging on the wall behind it. Marcus looked up into the surprised face of the produce boy.

Marcus turned to run.

"Wait!" the boy yelled. "Stop! You can't steal food from here!"

Still clutching the apples, Marcus darted out the open back door. The boy followed him outside, where, apparently blinded by darkness, he stopped the chase. "I'm going to call the cops!"

Marcus dropped behind the loading dock and froze. From here, he watched the boy peer into the night, heard his threats.

Police. Marcus felt his forehead bead with sweat. As the boy turned back inside, Marcus made his decision. Desperate, he dashed along the store's back wall. Panting, sweating, he planned to run to an empty field he'd spotted earlier in the afternoon. If he could run fast enough, freedom lay just down the block under the cover of wild scrub.

He ran full speed toward the corner. As he came around the building and started up the narrow sloping driveway, a white pickup came toward him, the vehicle's headlights blinding him. Marcus threw up his arms, using the fruit to shield his eyes as he searched for an escape route. He had to get out of there. He had to.

The pickup did not stop. Still moving forward, Marcus noted that the truck hugged the left side of the drive, leaving him no room to escape in that direction. Marcus glanced to the right, where a ten-foot block wall stood sentry. He could never scale the wall, not without dropping the fruit.

Still clutching the apples, he made another choice. He stepped sideways and turned his back to the truck, as if to head back to the loading area. Then suddenly, with speed he had not used since his days in football, Marcus pivoted and ran straight for the driver's side of the pickup.

As he did, he heard steps behind him, and the voice of the boy calling "Stop! Thief!"

This is my only chance, Marcus thought, knowing with certainty that the boy had already called the police. Putting his head down, Marcus rushed the space beside the truck. As he reached the pickup's hood, the headlights went out, and the driver's side door opened. The edge of the door touched the block wall on his right. Instantly, Marcus knew he'd been trapped.

Dropping his torso, Marcus advanced his right shoulder as he ran directly into the door. With a classic football block, he hoped to surprise the driver, forcing the door back. He would escape between the door and the wall.

As Marcus slammed into the door, he felt it give way, nearly closing against his impact. His ribs screamed in objection, but he did not stop. He could not.

As Marcus stepped sideways, the door opened again, only this time with a mighty shove. For this, Marcus was unprepared. And whether by surprise or by the force of the moving door, he was thrown back, hitting the ground with a thud.

The air rushed from his lungs and he rolled away, but before he could get up, Marcus found one knee planted firmly against his gut. Big hands held him by the lapels. "Seems to me," a voice said, panting, "that this boy wants you for somethin'. I think you'd better slow down and talk this out."

Marcus held up his hands, still clutching the fruit. "Okay," he said, surrendering. "Okay. I give up."

>>>>

In the kitchen Callie glanced out the window. Yesterday's snowstorm had already changed to rain. Water dripped off the roof and pelted tiny holes in the snow. She could see asphalt showing through parts of the driveway.

She felt a tug on her pajama bottoms. "I want breakfast."

"I'm working on it," she hedged. Callie wondered what she had in the house that might feed this little hunger-driven monster. She never ate cold cereal, at least not any of the sugar-frosted types. Callie preferred natural, unprepared foods. Having watched her dad struggle with diabetes, she focused on eating well. The idea of Dynobuddies made her shudder.

As she looked through her cupboards, the boy stayed at her feet, dodging her steps and filling the air with complaints. "I said I'm working on it," she repeated.

He dropped onto the floor and began to cry. "I want Mama," he wailed.

Callie wondered how a child could make so much noise with his thumb still in his mouth. *I can't keep this up.* She put her hands on her hips and turned back to the cupboards. Spying a carton of oatmeal, she remembered her mother serving it to Erica's children under a thick coat of brown sugar. *That ought to satisfy anyone who eats Dynobuddies for breakfast.*

She pulled a pot from under the counter and filled it with water as a sudden calm came over the kitchen. She glanced down at Keeshan. He was lying on the floor, thumb in place, eying her every move. Though she felt like a zoo animal, she refused to worry about it. *Peace is peace,* she thought appreciatively. *I'll take it.*

Movement against her leg made her jump, and she looked down to find the cat rubbing against her. "Keeshan, why don't you hold the cat while I cook," she suggested. "I don't want to step on him."

"His name is Eddy." Keeshan made no move to hold the cat.

She bit her tongue. "Right, Eddy," she said. "Sorry." She gave the cat a shove with the toe of her slipper. *Patience,* she told herself.

As she brought the oatmeal to a boil, she wondered about the assignment the social worker had given her. Where would she find the kinds of papers the hospital needed? Where did Celia keep such documents?

Callie had no idea where to look. She thought of her own papers, the house papers, her copy of her parents' will. She kept those things in a tiny fire safe her father had built into the wall of the master bedroom. But what had Celia done?

The sound of boiling oatmeal brought her back to the task at hand. She poured the cereal onto a wide flat bowl and spread it out to cool. She might not be a real mother, but even Callie learned from her mistakes. "Breakfast is almost ready," she said. "Maybe you should go to your bathroom and wash your hands first."

Sitting on the kitchen floor, Keeshan pet the cat. "I did."

"Do it again."

He did not answer.

"Keeshan, I asked you to go wash your hands."

He pulled the cat into his lap. "I want to eat first."

Callie considered her options. Tired and hungry herself, she grabbed a clean rag from a drawer and rinsed it in the sink. "We wash before we eat here, buddy," she said, pulling his hands from the cat as she gave Eddy another shove. "And you'll do as I ask."

"I want my mommy," he said.

"I do too."

Callie ate homemade granola with soy milk and sipped organic coffee while Keeshan scraped liquid sugar from his cereal. She remembered a connection between sugar and bad behavior, and as she watched him eat, she hoped it was only a rumor. "Keeshan, we have to go over to your house this morning," she said.

He looked up, licking the spoon.

"The hospital wants me to find some of your mother's papers." She watched for signs of understanding. "You know, important papers."

"Like mail?" He asked, curling his tongue around the handle.

She nodded. "Maybe. But more like mail that you keep. Stuff that you keep forever." She waited while he licked off another spoonful of brown sugar. She could almost watch his pancreas fail. Surely Celia would be back on her feet before this boy died of malnutrition. "Have you ever seen your mom put away photos? Or bank statements? Maybe she does something with her paycheck?"

He shrugged. "Can I go outside and play in the snow?"

Callie didn't have the heart to tell him that the snow was nearly gone. "Maybe. First we'll go over to your house and get some clean clothes. And then we'll look for your mother's papers. After that, if there's time, you can play outside."

>>>

The man who faced Marcus had coarse red hair and ruddy skin. His body was thick and muscular, like a man who regularly lifted weights. Wearing a tropical print shirt over jean shorts, the blond hair over his well-shaped legs was as thick as fur. His white court shoes were badly scuffed, the stitching coming apart in places. His blue eyes seemed troubled rather than angry. "This is the man who stole the food?" he asked.

"That's him," the boy replied.

Marcus sat on a crate in the produce office. He had never stolen anything before in his life. In fact, he'd always despised thieves, starting with his own brother. And now, to his everlasting shame, he had become one. Heat burned his face, and he avoided looking into the pale eyes of the red-haired man.

The teenager, himself as lanky as the older man was thick, spoke again. "I came back here to move the crates outside where you could pick them up." The strain in his high-pitched voice betrayed anxiety. "When I came in, I saw him stuffing his pockets with food."

The man moved closer to Marcus, still half-squatting. "You hungry?"

Marcus could only nod, turning his face away from the stranger's concern. He couldn't hold it in much longer. All the bad times, the running, the misery, threatened to spill over like a cascade of water over a mighty cliff. Marcus shivered and tightened his lips.

"How long has it been since you've had a decent meal?"

Marcus cleared his throat. "Most of three days."

"Call the police," the man said without turning to the boy. "Tell them there's been a mistake."

"But he stole the food," the boy said. "It's still in his pockets."

"Look," the red-haired man said, this time with emphasis. "Your store donates food to our mission. We feed the hungry." He pointed at Marcus with one index finger. "This man is hungry. I think it's a misunderstanding." Looking into Marcus's eyes he spoke again, this time more kindly. "Call the police and tell them we don't need their services."

The boy held up both hands, as if to object even as he moved to a wall phone.

"Why don't you call from the store manager's office, James? Give us a minute or two. All right?"

Shrugging, the boy turned and slammed through the swinging door. The red-haired man turned again to Marcus, this time holding out his right hand. "My name is Sean," he said. "Sean Boyer."

"Marcus Jefferson," Marcus said, taking the hand.

Sean bent over one of the crates and selected an overripe, unbruised banana. "This might hold you for a minute or two," he said, offering Marcus the fruit. As Marcus peeled the banana, Sean pulled up a small stool and sat down, his face level with Marcus. "I work with the Oasis Mission Foundation in Tucson," he said. "This store is part of my regular run. Most grocers throw away produce that has become too old or too damaged to sell. We've convinced a few in this area to let us have the unused food. I pick up grocery items that are past the pull date—you know, bread, bakery goods, dairy products. I come by with my truck—the one you tried to run down—and take the food back to the mission."

He paused, smiling as Marcus finished the last of the banana. "Right at this minute, I don't think I've ever seen anyone hungrier than you. Would you like another?"

Marcus nodded, accepting the banana. Trying to hide his trembling hands, Marcus took particular care in peeling away the skin. "Why are you telling me all this? You could have called the police."

Sean answered with a question of his own. "You're not from around here, are you?"

Marcus shook his head.

"You seem a little out of your comfort zone. I'll bet you've never stolen anything in your life."

Marcus looked up, surprised. "I've never had to."

"You didn't have to tonight. You just didn't know where to go for help." Sean leaned forward. "Tell me, you have any skills?"

A bitter laugh escaped before Marcus could stop it. Sean wouldn't believe him if he told the truth. He'd certainly never guess that Marcus held a degree—an engineering degree from a prestigious private college. Marcus hardly believed it himself anymore.

Deliberately, he chose his words. "I'm a carpenter between jobs. I came in on the bus this morning." He threw the peel at the garbage can. It hit the rim and fell in, a perfect landing. "Missed the bus out of town, though. And I don't have money for food."

"A carpenter, eh?" Sean leaned forward, his elbows on his knees. "What kind of work do you do?"

"I've done a lot of framing," Marcus said. "But I can do finish work. I've drawn up remodels and framed them—that sort of thing."

"You interested in work?"

"Maybe. What kind?"

"The kind that comes with a roof and all the food you can eat."

Marcus could hardly believe Sean's words. Still, he held himself back. "Yeah, sure. I'm interested." He worked to swallow the laugh that threatened to bubble up from inside him. "I'm interested," he repeated. "But I wonder, do you think we could start with the food part?"

Ten

In a sports restaurant not far from the grocery store, Sean and Marcus faced one another across the glossy surface of a table for two. Ignoring the sound of basketball blaring from the television over the bar, Marcus tried to imagine what kind of man would offer dinner to a would-be thief.

Marcus had to force himself not to lean toward the waiter carrying entrees to the booth behind them. The scent of roast beef turned his head, and the pungent smell of onions and sage dressing on another plate made his mouth water and his stomach squeeze painfully. He forced himself to look at Sean, who sat with his fingers laced, his hands resting on the table in front of him. He seemed relaxed, interested—as though he had all the time in the world. "So, Marcus," he began, "tell me about yourself."

Ignoring the smells around him, Marcus felt anxious. The tips of his fingers began to sweat, and the muscles of his shoulders tightened. He didn't want to lie to this man, who had already been so kind, but he couldn't tell him the whole truth, either. There was too much at stake, too many lives riding on his silence.

So, though Sean deserved more, Marcus gave him only bits and pieces. "Like I said, I came into town on the bus," he said. "I didn't have much, just my tools, my clothes, and a little money. We had a layover, and I went outside to stretch my legs. Some kids jumped me." He glanced away, shaking his head. "They took everything I had, the little demons."

"You didn't report it?"

"I blacked out. By the time I came to, they were gone. The police don't care about some stranger claiming he'd been jumped by a gang. I couldn't prove anything."

A middle-aged waitress came to the table, her white-blond hair pulled into a thick ponytail. "You boys ready to order?"

Sean nodded. "I am. How 'bout you, Marcus?"

Shame flooded Marcus. He couldn't shake the feeling of undeserved charity. He glanced up at the waitress and nodded.

Sean ordered the three-egg omelet, including hash browns and pancakes. He added juice and coffee and then pointed to Marcus, indicating it was his turn. "I'll have the skillet special," Marcus said, handing her the menu.

"Aw, that won't do." Sean said. "Not in your condition. You won't get two hours out of that little meal. Order something substantial."

Marcus tried again, this time ordering a Denver omelet with all the trimmings.

"This boy's been a long time without a decent meal," he told the waitress. "Got to fill him up."

She tucked the menus under one elbow and winked at Marcus.

Sean cleared his throat and leaned forward. "Okay. So you had some bad luck this morning," he said. "It always seems that when you need help the most, you run into trouble. Do you need to see a doctor? Your face looks like you could use some stitching up."

Marcus fingered his eyebrow tenderly. "I'm fine, I think. Just a little sore."

"Anything else injured?"

Marcus shook his head. He couldn't let the injury to his ribs risk the opportunity for work. "I meant to find work in Tucson. I've been on the road a while, and I'm out of cash."

"What about a place to stay?"

"Usually, once I get a job that isn't too hard," Marcus said. "I don't have trouble finding work; it just never lasts long. So I have to keep moving."

"No family?"

Marcus closed his eyes and shook his head. "Not anymore," he admitted. The crowd around them erupted into cheers. A slam dunk put the home team ahead. "My father died years ago and my mom passed away last winter."

"I'm sorry."

"Me too," Marcus said. "My dad was a good man. He did his best to teach us right from wrong. I miss him. I miss both of them."

Sean reached for his glass of water. "He teach you to carpenter?"

"He taught me to work with wood from the time I was a little boy— loved anything that had to do with a hammer and nails."

"No school, eh?"

"Not for construction, exactly" Marcus hedged. "I learned everything I know from my daddy's hands or on the job. I've built just about everything—commercial, residential—you name it, I've done it."

A small smile crept across Sean's lips as he brought his fingers up to his chin and rubbed it gently. "You can do anything, eh?"

"Most anything."

Sean shook his head. "Well, I'll be," he said. "You know? This meeting may just be a divine encounter."

"Divine?" That might be a slight exaggeration. The encounter he'd endured earlier in the day seemed to be of the opposite kind.

"Don't you believe in divine encounters?"

"Well, sure," Marcus said. "I'm just not sure I've ever been part of one."

"You're a believer, then? A Christian?"

"Since I was a boy in Indianapolis."

"And you've never had a single divine encounter?"

"Not that I know of." Marcus shrugged. "Most of my life feels like what happened this afternoon. I tend to end up on the broken end of things."

"Well, starting today, I think your luck is gonna change."

>>>

With the breakfast dishes in the sink, Callie propped Keeshan in front of the television while she headed down the hall to shower and dress. The program looked safe enough, a cartoon for young children. If she hurried, Callie would finish before the next show began.

After her shower she wrapped herself in a bath towel and snuck down the hall to her room. Just as she opened the closet door, a noise behind her made her jump. She barely managed to keep her towel around her body. "Keeshan, I though you were watching TV."

"It's a dumb show," he said. "For babies." Keeshan had followed her into her room with Eddy draped over his forearms.

With one hand holding the towel, Callie plucked a pair of pants from the closet. "Well, maybe you could change the channel. Surely there's something else you'd like to watch."

He walked over to the bed and dropped Eddy on her comforter. "I wanna be with you."

"Keeshan, I'm getting dressed. Can't you wait in the hall until I finish?"

He climbed up on the bed, grabbed the cat around the middle, and dragged it into his lap. "I'll wait here."

Clenching her teeth, Callie moved to the dresser, where she chose socks, underwear, and a wool turtleneck in dark charcoal. "All right," she said, still clutching the towel. "I'll change in the bathroom." This time she locked the door behind her.

He was sitting on the floor in the hall as she came out, the cat purring in his lap. "Well, at least I always know where you are," she said. "Now it's your turn."

Callie helped Keeshan to bathe, drying his hair with a hand towel. His dark curls fell into perfect ringlets. "I can dry myself," he said, pulling the towel from her hands.

She gave in without a fight, choosing instead to blot the puddle underneath his feet. "We'll have to get some clean clothes today," she said. "We can do that this morning at your house." She held up his Spider-Man underwear.

"I can dress myself," he objected, clearly offended. He snatched the pants with such energy that he nearly fell over, his tiny square feet backing away.

"Okay," she agreed. "Then put those on. We need to hurry."

He sat down. "What for?" he asked, his dark eyes wide.

"We're going to the hospital to see your mom."

"Right now?"

"As soon as we can," she said. "But we need to find those papers first."

Ignoring her, he concentrated instead on stepping into the waistband. He lifted one leg, balancing carefully on his behind as he held the foot high in the air. With his mouth tight, he stuffed his raised foot through the pantleg, slapping the floor with the sole of his foot.

Patience, Callie told herself, as he repeated the process with the other foot. *It's only for a few days.* Keeshan rolled over onto his hands and knees and stood up, his head hanging down between his knees. From this position, he pulled the pants up with both fists. In spite of his supreme effort, he'd managed to put his underwear on backward, though he didn't seem to notice until they were all the way up to his waist.

Stomping his foot in frustration, he yanked them down again, stepping out of them as he began to cry. "Backward," he said, plopping his thumb between his lips.

"I'll help."

"No!" A single tear began to roll down his round cheek. His face crumpled in defeat.

"Okay then," Callie said with a calm she didn't feel. "Let's just try again. I'll hold them while you step in."

Though she hadn't had enough sleep or nearly enough coffee, she determined to present a cheerful face. Every new difficulty brought another round of fresh tears. By the time she pulled his sweatshirt over his head, Callie felt herself fighting tears too. Surely he was tired, distressed, a little lost, but couldn't he try to make it easier for both of them?

After all, she was hurting too.

They hurried through heavy rain to the guesthouse. Inside Callie turned on the television, hoping to distract Keeshan. Instead, he followed her, step for step, as she began her search for Celia's records.

She started in the kitchen, looking through drawers and cupboards for some sign of the necessary papers. Surely Celia had a birth certificate for Keeshan. Perhaps a record of his immunizations. Maybe she had a marriage license or divorce papers. The social worker had asked for Celia's telephone records. Certainly Celia kept her bills where Callie could find them.

Callie found nothing in the kitchen. Within moments she'd searched the living room, checking the drawer in the end table, even looking behind the couch. In the hall linen closet, Callie found nothing but sheets and towels and toilet paper.

Moving to the smaller bedroom, Callie found Keeshan's clothes in the closet along with a laundry basket filled with trucks and cars. Again, no sign of important documents.

"Keeshan," she called, "come in here and help me choose some clothes." A hand on her thigh made her jump. He'd done it again. The boy followed her around like a ghost. It unnerved her, his sudden appearing in every room. She took a deep breath. "My goodness, you do know how to startle a person, don't you?" She emptied the toys on his bed, and placed the empty basket on the floor. "Why don't you tell me which things you'll want at my house?"

Without interference, she let Keeshan choose his favorite clothes. He showed a particular fondness for character apparel, including items from Shrek, Spider-Man, and VeggieTales. The boy was a walking advertisement.

He preferred jeans without an elastic waist, socks with shaped ankles, and sweatshirts without hoods. He certainly knew what he liked. "Now can we go see Mama?" he asked.

"Soon," she said, affectionately ruffling his hair. "Let's go look in your mom's room. Maybe she kept her papers in there."

Keeshan climbed up on Celia's bed while Callie opened the closet. The distinct smell of scented cat litter wafted out from the open doors. Callie scanned the closet. On the hooks at one end hung Celia's nightgown and robe. At the other end, sweaters and T-shirts had been rolled into perfectly shaped logs and nestled in the individual cubbies of a wire storage unit. Two rows of shelves lay above Celia's hanging clothes. From the ground, the contents of the shelves seemed organized, though Callie could not see clearly enough to identify anything.

She returned to the kitchen to grab a chair. Dragging it back to the bedroom, she stumbled into the boy. "Keeshan, you don't have to follow me like this. I was just bringing a chair so I could see up in the top of the closet."

The thumb slipped back between his full lips; his dark eyes looked hurt.

Callie relented. "It's all right. I'm just not used to having a little boy around." She patted his black curls. "I'll calm down before your mom gets home, I promise. Things will be back to normal in just a few days. Would you help me carry this chair back to the bedroom?"

His face brightened as he put his little palms under the seat of the chair. Callie took the back of the chair, lifting most of the weight. Backing up slowly, with short erratic steps, he moved as if he carried his half of a grand piano. Together they manipulated the chair down the hall into Celia's room and put it before the closet.

Callie climbed up on the chair, tucked her head sideways, and stuck it through the small space between the wall and the shelf. Here she found the residue of Celia's previous life. There was a stack of photo albums, several shoe boxes labeled with Keeshan's name, and two cardboard boxes large enough to make Callie wonder how Celia had managed to get them up on the shelf in the first place. There was enough dust to make Callie sneeze. She wiped her nose with the cuff of her sweater.

Keeshan crawled onto the chair beside her, pushing her to make room. "Keeshan, get down. I don't want you to fall and hurt yourself."

"I won't," he said, wrapping one arm around her thigh. "I'll help you look."

As Callie turned her head to look at him, the door's track system attacked the back of her skull. "Oh, crud," she said, tilting her head forward again and rubbing the sore spot. "All right. You can help me." Her voice sounded tired and grumpy—in spite of her conscious effort to keep positive. "I'm going to hand you things from this shelf. You carry them over to the bed."

From the top of a pile of photo albums, she pulled down a short stack of envelopes. "Here, start with these." Though she could not see him, she felt his little hands take the envelopes from her. She heard a thud as he threw them to the floor.

"I could drop them myself," she said.

He did not answer. Instead, she felt his arm wrap around her legs. She considered how difficult it had been to fit her head inside this confined space in the first place and dismissed the idea of climbing down with every item she brought out. "Okay," she said, resigned, "here is a really big book. Hold on tight."

He grabbed the book and dropped it to the floor. Callie took a deep breath and reached up to the highest shelf, this time struggling to scoot the largest box toward the edge. She wrestled it through the narrow opening, turning it as she did until it cleared the door.

Eventually, between the two of them, they emptied both shelves. Callie settled herself on the bed and began looking through the envelopes. The first contained a stack of letters written in Spanish and postmarked from Mexico. None included a return address. Ignoring the body of these letters, she scanned the signatures. They had been written by only a few persons. *Family,* she surmised, tucking one of the envelopes into the back pocket of her jeans.

In a large manila envelope she found a record of Celia's school years, including photographs, transcripts, and a diploma from a Miami high school. Under these she found individual report cards and a membership in the honor society. To her surprise, she found a letter of acceptance from Florida State University. Celia had never mentioned going to Florida State.

In all of these things, Celia was listed as Celia Hernandez—the only name Callie had ever heard her use. It was the name she used to sign her rental checks. According to the state patrol, it was the name on her driver's license, the name on her employment information. Had Celia never married? Without Keeshan's birth certificate or an actual marriage license, Callie couldn't be sure. Still, she'd found at least part of the puzzle the social worker had requested. She knew that as a young person, Celia had lived in the Miami area. And her maiden name was Hernandez.

Perhaps this information would help them find Celia's family.

Callie could only turn this information over to the hospital and hope for the best. She lay aside the diploma and the acceptance to Florida State, and reached for the next envelope. Here she found a stack of photographs—most of these included faces Callie had never seen. Only a few included Celia. Callie had not yet found any sign of Celia's bills or financial records. Where did Celia keep them?

She looked in the bedside table. Nothing. She threw back the bedspread and inspected the floor under the bed. Here, Callie found several cardboard gift boxes.

Lifting the top of an especially promising one, she found several manilla files, each bearing a neatly printed label. Callie found one for utilities, insurance, tax records, banking, savings, and car maintenance. The last file was labeled TELEPHONE and Callie barely contained her delight.

This would include the telephone numbers of Celia's family!

Without looking at them, Callie set the telephone records aside and opened the next box. Here she found a stack of photographs and papers. Below these, she found an address book, a list of baby gifts and thank-you notes, and on the very bottom, an envelope containing Keeshan's birth certificate.

Emptying the envelope, she slid the telephone records, the address book, and the birth certificate back inside. As she closed the envelope, a rhythmic banging caught her attention, and she realized that she had lost track of the boy.

Callie walked around the bed, where she found Keeshan lying on his back on the floor. As she watched, he rocked himself, dropping a leg again and again, each time allowing the foot to bang against the floor. In one fist he held his mother's satin nightgown balled up around his tiny fingers. Rubbing the satin against his cheek, Keeshan rocked himself as he sucked his thumb.

Comforting himself this way, Keeshan had put himself to sleep.

Eleven

"That's the original church," Sean said, pointing to his left as he drove past a large two-story stucco building. Considering the day he'd just survived, Marcus was doing well to glance over at the building. His body ached from his eyebrows to his knees. His neck seemed to scream at him, begging for rest. All he could think about was the bed Sean had promised. "Not bad, hey?"

To Marcus, it looked like any ordinary church, complete with a steeple and stained glass. As they approached the next light, Sean switched on his turn signal and pulled into a turn lane. "The mission started out providing health care for Hispanic children."

"And now?"

He laughed. "Well, that's a different story. These days, it would be easier to tell you what we don't provide. We have volunteers doing just about everything you can think of, teaching English to adults, tutoring children. We provide work training, health care, parenting classes, drug prevention, and addiction programs." Sean chuckled, driving the truck around the corner. "And, of course, we have traditional Christian education programs."

"That's quite a project you've taken on."

"It's not like we meant to choose an impossible task."

"It chose you?"

"Sort of like that." Sean smiled as he pulled the pickup into the gravel lot behind a small square house, shut off the engine, and turned to face Marcus. "If I were to tell you the whole story, we'd be here all night. But I'll give you the fifty-cent version."

As Sean spoke, Marcus let his gaze drift from darkened building to darkened building. In the course of a city block, it seemed that every single house had been commandeered to serve as part of this ministry, whatever it was. Hand-lettered signs, in both English and Spanish, marked building entrances, parking areas, and walkways. From the outside, anyway, it looked like a ragtag operation. Nothing matched. None of the buildings had been built for their current purpose.

"Thirty years ago, this church was dying," Sean began. "Most of the younger families had moved to more affluent neighborhoods. The homes around here became rentals; the rentals were torn down and replaced by apartments. The apartments became gang territories.

"At first the church tried to hang on to the old congregation. But as the older generation passed away, even that became impossible. In 1971 Pastor Enrique Gutierrez took the pastorate. He was barely twenty-five. Instead of fighting to keep things like they were, he decided to meet the needs as he found them. Somehow, he convinced a retired doctor to come into the church basement and give free children's exams. Things just grew from there."

Sean pulled his keys from the ignition. "The short version is that those first families came to know Jesus. As their lives changed, they took over ministries and started new ones. Now we have this." He swept his hand across the buildings beyond the lot. "We've finally obtained permits to redesign the facilities. That's where you fit in."

He opened the door of the truck and slipped out. Ducking his head back inside he said, "If you want a good night's sleep, we'd better get moving."

〉〉〉

Armed with the papers she'd been asked to bring along, Callie loaded Keeshan back into his car seat and drove through the rain to the county hospital. Though slush marked the edge of the highway, there was little evidence of yesterday's deadly snowfall. Saturday morning traffic crawled into the city.

With the defroster on high, and windshield wipers slapping a quick rhythm across the window, they listened to the radio on the way into town—a drama program designed for kids. Keeshan, buckled into his car seat, sucked his thumb and gazed out of the car window.

From behind the wheel, Callie couldn't get her mind off the papers she'd found at the bottom of the stack of envelopes in Celia's closet.

Keeshan's birth certificate listed his mother as Celia Hernandez Williams. The baby had been named Keeshan Marcus Williams. At the time of Keeshan's birth, Celia lived in Saga Bay, Dade County, Florida— a tiny rural community Callie had looked up on the Internet only this morning. The certificate listed Andre Williams as the baby's father.

Callie turned her windshield wipers down as the rain eased. Who was Andre Williams? Where was he now? Would the social worker at the hospital be able to locate him? Maybe Andre didn't even know about the child.

Questions swirled through her mind until she felt the beginning of a headache creep across her forehead. She glanced into the rearview mirror. Keeshan, his thumb in his mouth, had grown drowsy, his eyes hanging at half-mast. Poor boy hadn't gotten enough sleep.

Neither had she.

Under the birth certificate Callie had discovered pictures of Celia, apparently leaving the hospital with her newborn. In a wheelchair holding the baby, her full attention on Keeshan, Celia wore the same adoring expression Callie noticed in the photograph in the living room.

In the picture hidden in the closet, a young African-American man stood behind Celia, his hair in cornrows, his face partially turned from the camera. Was he the baby's father? A relative? A friend?

Though she could not be certain, Callie sensed a vague anger emanating from the man's blurry image—as if this photograph were an imposition of some kind. She saw it in his posture, in the tension of his features, the grip of his hands on the wheelchair.

Callie felt stung somehow, looking at the picture, and she could understand why Celia had chosen to leave the picture in the envelope with the birth certificate. It was not an image she would display.

As she drove down the highway, Callie could only hope that her instincts about the man were wrong. Keeshan had curly hair; his mother had straight course hair. While his father might have been African-American, he might just as easily have any number of other backgrounds. Something in Callie hoped that the man in the picture was not Keeshan's father. In searching Celia's house, Callie found more questions than answers.

Right now Keeshan needed someone who loved him, and Celia needed family. Praying along with the rhythm of the wipers, Callie asked for divine help. Finding Celia's family seemed a daunting task.

At the hospital's west entrance she helped Keeshan from the car, left her rental with the valet, and dashed through the rain into the luxurious lobby. There she and Keeshan took off their coats, their dripping clothes making a puddle on the marble floor. A policeman directed them to the information desk, where they asked for directions to the social worker's office. Then, taking Keeshan by the hand she started down through the bowels of the enormous building.

As they walked, she tried not to notice the worn linoleum and peeling paint. After all, this hospital was very old—as old as her first childhood memories of the city. Clearly, the reconditioning of the west entrance had not yet reached the tunnels that connected the four hospital towers.

In the cool hallway, Callie shivered. "Almost there, Keeshan," she said, punching the up button on what she hoped would be their last elevator ride. "After we drop these off," she said, indicating the envelope in her hand, "we can go see mommy."

Inside the elevator, Keeshan did not speak, and Callie suspected that the sights and sounds of the hospital had frightened him. When the doors opened, he did not move. She urged him out, pushing him forward. They stepped into a brightly painted waiting area—a stark contrast to the halls they'd just passed through. Callie consulted the directions she'd received from the receptionist and turned left. Halfway down the hall, she found the social worker's office. She knocked and waited.

Nothing.

Frustrated, Callie wondered what to do with the papers she'd worked so hard to find. If the woman didn't work on the weekends, she would not begin to look for Keeshan's family before Monday. Callie felt a knot of resentment twist her stomach. As far as the social worker was concerned, there was no hurry; the boy was well cared for. "Enjoy your weekend at home," she muttered. Keeshan looked up, confused. "Never mind," she said. "She's not here today."

Though there was a plastic records holder beside the door, Callie chose not to leave Celia's documents there. After all, these were private papers. Instead, she took Keeshan's hand and went to the check-in desk at the ICU.

When the clerk finished making copies of the documents, Callie stapled them together and dropped them into the manila envelope she'd brought along. Tucking the originals into her purse, she returned to the social worker's office and slid the envelope under the door.

They waited outside the intensive care unit while nurses finished Celia's morning routine. Keeshan watched a small television, fascinated by the story of a green ogre and a beautiful princess. Callie tried to focus on the movie, but she found herself distracted by nervous anxiety.

Instinctively, she knew she should prepare the boy. But practically, she had no idea how to begin. Bewildered, she said nothing.

When at last the clerk called their names, Callie dragged Keeshan from the television and through the electronic doors to Celia's room. On one side of Celia's hospital bed, a woman in print surgical scrubs replaced an IV bag. She nodded as Callie and Keeshan entered. "Good morning," she said. "I'm just finishing up here. Then she's all yours."

From the foot of the bed, Callie inspected Celia. There seemed to be no improvement. Celia's eyes remained closed, her body relaxed. To Callie, Celia looked no worse than she had the evening before, though the bruises on her face had deepened. Various monitors continued to beep and chirp behind her. A ventilator continued to force air into Celia's lungs; the loud hiss of pressurized air passing through a narrow hose cast a mechanical chill over the room.

If Celia was aware of their presence, she did not respond.

Today, her left leg seemed less swollen, though Callie could hardly stand to look at the place where a rod punctured the skin through both sides of Celia's thigh. The sling holding her leg had been lowered slightly, and Callie thought it looked less uncomfortable than before. Blue bruises covered the entire sole of her left foot.

Celia's left arm, casted from above the elbow to the base of her fingers, had been propped up on pillows. An ice pack covered the wrist. Celia's fingers looked swollen and black. Callie could hardly recognize the knuckles on what had once been a delicate hand.

Callie's attention was drawn back to the nurse, who, without missing a beat, added bags, changed lines, and flushed tubes. In moments, the nurse turned again to Celia, smoothing the light covers on her bed and patting her patient's shoulder. "There now, Celia," she said, "that should take care of you for an hour or so. You have visitors, so enjoy them. Don't get too rowdy, though." She winked at Callie and turned to Keeshan. "Hey there, big guy," she said. "Is this your mama?"

He nodded.

"Would you like a chair so you can talk to her?"

Keeshan slipped his thumb back into his mouth. "Yes," he said. As she turned to leave he added, "Thank you."

After Callie helped Keeshan onto the chair, he leaned over the bedside. Callie slipped one finger through his belt loop and watched as he looked up and down the bed. "Mama," he said quietly. Her eyes remained closed; she did not move.

With both hands, he shook her good arm and repeated his request. "Mama, wake up."

"Gently, Keeshan," Callie whispered. "She's been in an accident. Don't hurt her."

He looked up and nodded. The thumb slipped back in his mouth. Using his free hand, he touched her arm, pointing at the skin with a single index finger. He ran his hand up to her shoulder, and leaning over the rail, caressed her hair.

Before she could stop him, he reached for Celia's face. Prying her right eyelid open, Keeshan looked inside. "Mama," he whispered, "are you in there?"

>>>

Before Marcus could manage to unbuckle his seat belt, Sean bounded up the steps and unlocked the back door of the little house. Stepping inside, he flipped on lights. Marcus caught him just inside the door as he punched numbers into a security pad.

"These days, we use this house for administrative staff."

They stepped into a small 1950s-style kitchen, where Marcus let his eyes adjust to the wild flickering of overhead fluorescents. "But we keep a room in the basement for visitors. I'm going to put you there. The sheets are clean and there's a small bathroom on the main floor. I think you'll be comfortable."

Sean opened the refrigerator and pulled out a pitcher of purified water. "Here," he said, pouring a glass for both of them. "In Tucson, we take water very seriously." He handed Marcus a glass, picked up his own, and raised it in a mock salute.

As they leaned against the counter, sipping water in silence, Marcus took in his surroundings. Cabinets and walls had been painted the same soft turquoise. The floor was covered with printed vinyl squares. The sink was empty and the counters bare. Still, he saw age everywhere, in an obvious depression in the center of the floor, in the failing windows, in the dented woodwork.

In an alcove off the kitchen, Marcus spotted a table covered with stacks of papers, a stapler, and several boxes. Sean spoke again. "I'll give you a little tour before I take you down to your room," he said, setting his glass in the sink.

The two men walked through the little three-bedroom house as Sean explained the functions of the various spaces. In the dining room, two desks marked a reception area. "Gina and Marianna work here. Gina handles all our requests for assistance. Marianna does staff support."

He opened the door to the first and smallest bedroom. "Our director of education uses this office," Sean said. At the next door he announced "And here, we have our Ernesto Ministries leader. Ernesto takes care of all the physical needs—food, housing, that kind of thing."

Sean barely opened the door to the corner bedroom, clearly the largest office thus far. "This is my office," he explained. "It's a mess right now, though. With the building permits and planning, everything is in flux. All of the blueprints and paperwork end up in there. They have to go somewhere, I guess." He turned abruptly and showed Marcus built-in shelves covered with neat stacks of office supplies.

Sean stopped to point out the main floor bathroom. "There's a basket of new toothbrushes under the sink. We often have visitors, so we keep soaps, shampoo, and towels in the cupboard over the toilet. I think you'll find anything you need," he said.

From the kitchen they started down a narrow wooden staircase. At the bottom of the stairs, Sean pulled a hanging cord. A single bare bulb cast a dim light over the basement.

"We kept the washer and dryer, but we don't use them. The church has its own laundry facility. There's detergent on the shelf over the washer. Help yourself." He caught himself and chuckled. "When you have clothes, that is." He turned left and opened another door. "This is your room. It isn't a four-star hotel, but it's comfortable," he said, turning on a switch.

A glass fixture hung over the center of the room, which, to Marcus, resembled a monastery cell. Against the far wall was a double bed covered by a yellowed chenille spread. A bare wooden desk stood to the left of the bed, the kind a teenager might have used years ago. Light from the parking lot streamed through a small square window over the desk. On the other side of the bed was a small four-drawer chest.

"When you get some clothes, you can put your things in the chest," Sean observed. "There's no closet down here, so you'll have to hang things up in the laundry room."

Marcus nodded. "It's fine. More than I expected, really."

"Tomorrow morning we'll see if we can find some clothes in the company store."

"I don't have money. The kids took everything."

Sean laughed. "The company store is our term for the clothing out-reach. You can have anything that fits," he said. "It won't be easy, though. Most of our stuff is for folks much smaller than you." He put his hands on his hips and tipped his bushy head. "I guess that's it. Wish we had more creature comforts down here. Seems a little bland. I never really looked at it like this."

Marcus blinked back the moisture that threatened to fill his eyes. "I'll never be able to thank…" He choked up a bit and stuck out his hand.

Sean took the hand and pulled Marcus into an embrace. "I'll be thanking you if things go as well as I think they will. Don't you worry about it now." He let go of Marcus and stepped to the door. "Anything else you can think of?"

Marcus shook his head. "Not really." He sank down on the bed. Sean stepped out of the room, pulling the door closed. "Wait!" Marcus said. "You never told me what part you play in all of this. Where do you fit in?"

The door stopped moving. "Me?" Sean stuck his head back in the room, a broad grin covering his face. "Well," he hesitated, shaking his head as he searched for words. "Actually, I run the place. See you in the morning."

Twelve

Unable to sleep soundly, Callie began her Sunday morning early, far earlier than usual, climbing onto her bicycle before daylight. Listening to the radio as she pedaled, she caught both the morning news and a full half hour of oldies. She rode hard, working up a heavy sweat as she alternated between standing and sitting, shifting to harder and harder gears. By the time dawn spilled through the windows, she had kept her heart rate at her target zone for forty minutes.

When she finished riding, Callie wrapped a towel around her neck and slipped on a hooded sweatshirt. She went back into the house and poured herself some coffee. Then, settling down in a kitchen chair, she called the hospital. The ICU nurse assured her there had been no change in Celia's condition. "Continues unconscious," the nurse said, without emotion. "But her vitals are strong. No change in status. She seems comfortable."

Nothing about her friend looked comfortable to Callie. She thanked the nurse and hung up, disappointed. She had convinced herself that Celia would be awake this morning, moving about in bed and asking for her son. Callie tried and failed to wipe the picture of Celia's damaged body from her memory. Praying for her recovery, Callie reached into a cupboard and pulled down a brand-new box of Dynobuddies. She opened it smiling. Keeshan had been so excited over one silly box of cereal. He'd nearly bounced out of the shopping cart, hugging the cereal and singing his thanks.

You have other motives. You want him to love you.

No, she argued with herself. *I only bought the cereal to make things easier for both of us.* After all, she would only have Keeshan for a couple more days. Why try to change his eating habits? Why make it any harder than necessary?

Callie poured the cereal into a small bowl, keenly aware of the sugar-coated empty calories falling from the box. If she were a mother, she would never let a child eat this kind of food. How had Celia let such a terrible habit get started?

Once the authorities found Celia's family, Callie's very first action would be to empty the remaining Dynobuddies into the trash can under the sink. *It won't be long.*

As she carried the cereal dish to the table and placed it where Keeshan usually sat, Callie wondered about the glimmer of sadness that flitted over her. Like a shadow passing over a sun-filled lawn, it disappeared in an instant. She would be glad to send the boy back to Celia, wouldn't she?

She sat down at the table, confused by her own thoughts. These feelings were ridiculous; her only obligation was to keep Keeshan until Celia returned from the hospital. Nothing more.

Remembering how low he sat in her dining room chairs, she turned to the drawer below the telephone and retrieved the county phone book and placed it on the seat of the chair.

Picking up her cordless phone, Callie called her only employee. "Jan," she said, "I hope I didn't wake you?"

"Who me? Sleep in? What makes you think that?"

Callie heard sarcasm dripping from her voice. "I wouldn't call if it weren't important. I have a problem."

"I've heard."

"What have you heard?"

"Jim came in yesterday. He told me that you rushed him out of the shop after a patrolman showed up. Of course, the accident was on the news Friday night."

"Sometimes I forget how small this town is."

"How's Celia?"

"The nurse said she's holding her own."

"You have the boy?"

"Who told you?"

"Marina. She saw you at the grocery store with him."

The Prospect gossip factor took some getting used to. In the city Callie could hide in her apartment for months without ever seeing her next-door neighbor. Not so in Prospect. She turned to the window, took in the view of the forest beyond, and drew a calming breath. Marina, their most predictable customer, bought a triple caramel latte every afternoon at three.

"You can set your clock by Marina," Callie said.

"So what did you need?"

"Well, I do have Keeshan—at least until they find his father, or Celia's family. And until then, I need to change my work schedule."

"What's the plan?"

"I need to take the late-morning shift. I'll take him to day care first and then come to work. Otherwise, I'd have to drag him to day care at four-thirty in the morning. Too early for such a little guy, don't you think?"

"Can you still take care of ordering and stocking? I don't know how."

"Sure." In the long pause that followed, Callie recognized Jan's hesitation. "I know you hate the early shift." She added a promise to sweeten the deal. "After this is over, I'll do some of your weekend shifts so you can have more time with your family. Sound okay?"

"Rod'll have to get the kids on the school bus."

"He can do that. He's a 'Mr. Mom' kinda guy."

More hesitation. "All right. But only for a while."

Callie spotted Keeshan coming down the hall. "Great. Shouldn't last long." she said. "You open tomorrow morning then. I'll see you at church. Gotta run."

"Happy mothering!"

"Happy opening," Callie said, and hung up.

〉〉〉

Marcus woke to the sound of a ringing telephone. Without opening his eyes, he tried to shake the clouds from his memory. There had been so many cities. So many beds. Where had he landed this morning?

He rolled over, groaning from the pain in his rib cage. Ah yes, the mugging. He tried to open his eyes and found that only one operated normally. The other refused to cooperate. He reached up to touch his eyebrow. Thick swelling blanketed his eyelid.

With his one good eye he spotted a thick column of sunlight pouring through the window. Already the temperature in the room had begun to climb. Tucson. The mission.

He remembered now. The beating. The grocery store. Dinner with the mission director.

Sean's face floated through Marcus's memory and silently he thanked God for the kindness the man had shown him. If it hadn't been for Sean, Marcus might have spent the night in jail. Instead, he'd enjoyed clean sheets and the promise of a job.

Hugging his rib cage, Marcus climbed out of bed. Gingerly, he slipped into his clothes, holding himself upright with one hand as he eased his feet into his pants. Holding his breath, he slipped his right arm into his shirtsleeve. Every bone in his body resisted his decision to rise and dress. His head throbbed and his mouth felt dry.

He wanted to crawl back in bed, but he'd promised work in exchange for his keep. Obligation drove him forward, and he sat down on the edge of the mattress to put on his dirty socks and steel-toed boots. Bringing one foot up over the other knee, he cried out with a fresh wave of sharp pain. How could he work with this kind of discomfort?

Marcus leaned back, resting on one hand. "God help me," he whispered. Then, taking a shallow breath, he held it as he tied the boot. He longed for a shower and clean clothes, but those luxuries would have to wait. What little he'd had in the way of clothes now belonged to a gang of teenagers in Casa Grande. Cautiously, Marcus pulled the covers back over his bed.

Pulling himself up by the handrail, he climbed the stairs to the main floor. At the top step, he opened the door slowly, peering out before stepping into the kitchen.

"Marcus! Good morning," Sean Boyer's voice boomed from beside the sink. He had on long baggy shorts and a bright yellow T-shirt. His furry legs ended in Birkenstocks. With a half-wave, he offered coffee from a drip pot. "I thought I'd have to go roust you out of bed myself pretty soon." Still holding the pot, he turned toward the kitchen table and pulled out a chair. "But, considering what you've been through, I decided to let you sleep it off. Have a seat and I'll pour you some coffee," he offered. "Do you take anything in it?"

"Black, thanks," Marcus said, using both hands to lower himself to the chair.

Sean opened an overhead cupboard and selected a mug from a collection of mismatched cups. He handed it to Marcus before taking the other chair. Coffee steamed through the spout of his bright red commuter mug. "I've already called the medical clinic and asked them to take a look at that cut on your face." He gestured to his own eyebrow. "I hope you don't mind. I can't afford to have you get an infection," he said.

Marcus nodded. "I can't afford it either."

Sean smiled. "Dr. Torres will have you fixed up in no time. They told me it's probably too late for stitches though." He shoved a white cardboard box across the table. "I brought some donuts in. And I took the liberty of raiding the thrift shop for clean clothes on my way across the parking lot. I had to guess your size. Hope it's okay. It's all in the bathroom for you."

Marcus felt his face heat up. "I won't ever be able to repay you. It's sort of overwhelming."

Sean laughed. "Before we're done, I'll be the one doing all the thanking. I told you last night that I need your help. I'm pretty sure our meeting was an answer to a lot of prayers around here." He chuckled and shook his head. "Who'd have guessed?"

Standing, he pushed in the chair. "I've got some work to do in my office this morning. I forgot to mention there's a new disposable razor in the bathroom. You go ahead and eat. After you've showered and dressed, I'll take you over to the health clinic."

Two hours later, Marcus stepped into the hot morning sun. The clothes he wore were clean, though not new. Sean had chosen jeans that fit well around the waist, though they lacked a good two inches of covering the tops of his boots. His newly acquired black T-shirt absorbed the blazing sunshine, amplifying Marcus's discomfort in the unfamiliar heat of southeastern Arizona.

Wiping sweat from his forehead, he followed Sean to the back side of an old house that had been transformed into a small medical clinic. They entered behind the front desk. After introducing Marcus to the office staff, Sean led him down the hall to an empty exam room, where a nurse took his blood pressure. "I'll get Dr. Torres," Sean said.

Twenty minutes later, his chest heavily taped and butterfly bandages holding what was left of his eyebrow together, Marcus left with samples of pain medications and instructions to take it easy for a few days.

Though it hadn't surprised Marcus to find that he'd cracked two ribs, taking it easy was out of the question. He'd promised to work for Sean. And work he would, no matter how badly his chest hurt. He followed Sean outside.

"This project is our first priority," Sean began, stepping over a mound of dirt. "Of course, we won't start until you're feeling better. You saw the people lined up in the waiting area. We need more medical help to care for all those patients, but we can't bring anyone in until we have more space." He pointed to flags outlining an addition at the end of the house. "We have the funds to build this extension. We even have the permits and the plans. But last month our lead carpenter left us. We've been stalled ever since."

"Lead carpenter?"

Sean shrugged. "I guess that's a bit of a misnomer." He spread his hands. "We have a group of handymen, but they aren't really trained. He was the best we had."

"And you think I can do this?" Marcus indicated the addition. "By myself?"

"Oh, not by yourself. I have a crew." Sean turned toward him, squinting against the sunshine. "You said you could do anything."

Marcus looked down at the hard dry ground. "Almost anything. I haven't done anything this extensive by myself before."

"We'll pay the best we can. Fifteen dollars an hour with room and board."

"I need the work," Marcus began. "Real bad." He glanced off toward the blue hills surrounding the town, considering. Could he afford to stay here that long? And if he did, should he tell Sean? Didn't he owe him that much? "I do need one thing."

"Name it," Sean said.

"I need to lay low for a while. I can't explain. I haven't broken the law. I just can't let anyone know where I am. Can you go along with that?"

Sean frowned, clearly uneasy with the news. "The law isn't involved?"

Marcus shook his head. "I'm clean."

"And there won't be any drugs or alcohol here—or at the house?"

"None."

"What about taxes?"

"I can't be on your official labor role. You can't report my income or my presence to labor and industry. I have to fly under the radar for a while."

"Not report you? No social security payment? Nothing? That's illegal. I'd go to jail."

"I know. If you can't do that, I understand. But if you report me, I'll be in a worse place than jail. I'll be dead."

"Look, Marcus, you're in trouble. I've known that from the first moment I saw you. I know the look, the way you keep glancing over your shoulder. But you can't live like that. You can't keep running."

"I don't intend to. If I can just hang on a little longer, I may beat this thing. But if you report me, I'm dead. That's all there is to it. I promise to make it right with the government as soon as I can."

Sean looked at Marcus for a long time. "I wish you'd trust me enough to tell me the whole story." He shook his head and ran his fingers through his sandy hair. "You've backed me into a hard place."

Marcus smiled. "I know, and I'm sorry."

"This isn't really about taxes. I hate to put the ministry in jeopardy."

"Sean, the tax people are the least of my worries."

"But they could be the worst of mine. Can I think about it?" Without speaking, Sean stared into Marcus's eyes for a long time—until Marcus began to wish he hadn't asked. Those blue eyes, it seemed, saw all the way into Marcus's soul. They recognized his troubled past, measured the pain Marcus had survived, the pain he carried still. Sean's eyes saw too much.

Yet, part of Marcus wished that Sean could see it all. Part of him believed that it might be wonderful to let someone know everything. Marcus had been too long without a friend.

"I don't know why, but I trust you, Marcus," Sean said at last. "I want you to work for us. You'll be safe here for as long as you need to be." He reached out and offered his hand. "And if you ever need someone to talk to, I'll be right here."

>>>

Callie took Keeshan to church with her Sunday morning, though by the time she'd helped him bathe and dress and eat, she wanted to go back to bed herself. In all her years as an aunt, she'd never noticed how slowly children moved. Keeshan seemed to function in some kind of time warp—like a bad science fiction movie. Nothing she said hurried him. He had one irritatingly slow pace, and it threatened to drive her mad.

They were late getting into the car, later still arriving at the church parking lot, and by the time she wrote Keeshan's name on the classroom visitor's sheet, the other four-year-olds had already assembled in a semicircle around the teacher's chair. Singing came from the closed class-room door as Callie took Keeshan's coat.

"I don't want to go," Keeshan said, his fists clutching the end of his sleeves. He drew back, pulling loose.

"It'll be fun," Callie said. "You might even have friends here."

"No!" He began to cry, tears streaming down his cheeks with the sur-prising intensity of a faucet. Backing away, he slipped his thumb in his mouth. "I don't want to."

The assistant teacher, a younger woman, shot Callie a condescending smile. "I'm just taking care of him," Callie said, embarrassed. Keeshan chose that moment to run, his little legs motoring down the hall toward the stairs.

With long strides, Callie caught up, snatching him around the waist and lifting him from behind. Her back objected strenuously to this action. She hadn't had any practice lugging around forty-pound children. Undaunted, she continued her pitch. "You'll love class here. They have great toys and lots of other kids." She sounded like an encyclopedia salesman.

"I don't want to," he said, this time with more volume. To his tears he added a woeful wailing. "No class," he cried, shaking his head and kicking his feet. As people walked by, they turned to stare at the boy struggling to free himself from Callie's arms. "Shh-shh," she whispered, her stress mounting. She felt the beginning of yet another headache.

She turned him to face her. By this time, his nose had developed a significant leak, and the fluid dripping from there had drained onto his forearms and shirt. He wiped his nose with his palm, but the tears con-tinued to flow. His dark eyes begged for understanding.

Callie caved. "Okay, Keeshan. No class today. But you'll have to sit in the main service with me."

Hope lit his face. She put him down and fished through her purse for a tissue. She had business cards, a single bicycle glove, a package of breath mints, but no tissue. Why did she even bother to carry a purse? She never had what she needed. "Let's go to the bathroom and you can blow your nose. Okay?"

He nodded.

From the far end of the hall, Callie turned to the assistant teacher. "I guess we'll try again next week," she said. The teacher's expression had changed from welcoming smile to disapproving glare. *Even the teacher knows I'm clueless.*

Taking Keeshan's slimy hand in her own, she waved. "You have a great morning," she said, a fake smile plastered over her irritation. Then, with all the self-respect she could muster, Callie led Keeshan out the door and up the stairs.

By the time they entered the sanctuary, they'd missed most of the worship service. She found a place near the back and slid into a pew. Placing Keeshan on the bench, Callie tried to join the singing. But Keeshan wiggled. He picked his nose and wiped the contents onto the bench. He took off his shoes. He stood on the pew and tugged on her skirt.

She leaned down and he whispered into her cheek, spit spraying across her skin. "I'm hungry," he said in a stage whisper. She heard twitters from the row behind them. Sighing, Callie wiped spittle from her skin.

She didn't have enough courage to see who might have noticed. "You just ate breakfast."

"But I'm so hungry," he repeated with emphasis.

She opened her purse and handed him the tin of breath mints. "Have one of these," she said. He took the purse with one hand, the container with the other. Once again, Callie thanked God that she would only have him for a few days. She hadn't been cut from mother-cloth. She could never handle this kind of pressure full-time.

By the time the congregation sat for announcements, Keeshan had eaten all of the mints and spread every item in her purse across the bench. With what she hoped was an intimidating frown and severe shake of her head, she began picking up after him.

Before she could finish, he snatched a pen from the pew and began drawing on the cover of the bulletin. *At last,* Callie thought, *an innocent activity.* Grateful, she relaxed.

The pastor stood up to speak after the announcements. Once again, Keeshan pulled at Callie's blouse. She leaned over, almost certain of what was coming next. He did not surprise her.

"I need to go potty," he said into her hair.

"Can't you wait?" Callie pointed at the pastor. "The sermon just started."

"I really need to go bad," he answered, grabbing the zipper of his jeans for emphasis. "I can't wait."

Sighing, Callie picked him up and stood to leave. Carefully stepping over the people at the end of the row, she had almost made the aisle when the wayward strap of a misplaced purse caught her shoe. She lunged forward, narrowly avoiding a fall by grabbing the shoulder of a fellow parishioner. Keeshan lunged forward, clutching her neck.

"Excuse us," she whispered. "I'm so sorry." She felt her face grow warm. Somehow she managed to untangle her foot from the purse strap and continue to the aisle. At the sanctuary exit, an usher held the door for her, nodding as she passed by. There had been nothing subtle about their exit.

Callie made it to the bathroom and helped Keeshan into a stall, offering to help him with his belt. "I can do it myself," he said. She waited as his little fingers struggled with the hardware. He pulled. He tugged. He fought. But the boy was trying to open the belt without first pulling the end out of the loop. She bent to offer a hand. He backed away. "No!"

Frustrated, Callie bit her upper lip and stepped out of the stall. Leaning against the door, she brushed away a stray tear. "How ya doin'?" she asked.

There was no answer. Instead, she heard the first evidence of his need for a bathroom. After what seemed like an eternity, Keeshan emerged from the stall. "I can't get the zipper," he said, his face etched with concern.

Callie bent down to retrieve the zipper pull from the depths of his denim. Carefully, she worked it up until his fingers could reach it. "There you are. You can finish yourself."

As far as church was concerned, Callie was finished as well.

Thirteen

By the end of his first week at the mission, Marcus realized that his previous building experience had little application in an all-volunteer operation. He'd already let go of his expectations, especially those concerning efficiency, quality, and time. Clearly, the addition to the medical clinic would not follow the well-organized path of commercial construction. In fact at this pace, he reasoned, they would be lucky to finish building the small addition by the following Christmas.

In this light, Sean's desperation for skilled help made sense.

The promised crew arrived in the form of a single helper named Socorro. Introducing himself as Soco, Marcus quickly discovered that he understood very little English. He spoke even less, and this was so heavily accented as to be nearly indiscernible.

Because Marcus spoke no Spanish, the two were reduced to communication via hand signals, pictures drawn on the back of floor plans, and an occasional, almost laughable, pantomime. Occasionally desperate, they went in to the clinic waiting room, where an already overworked receptionist translated their conversations.

Soco was friendly enough, quick to smile, with glossy black hair that hung low over his dark eyes. A heavy mustache covered his upper lip.

Though he sweated profusely, he drank almost no water, a man completely unencumbered by the heat that drilled them during the workday. Marcus, on the other hand, could hardly wait to get a roof up so that he could hide from the spring sunshine.

As nearly as Marcus could tell, Soco had never before held a hammer. He had no idea how to use the claw end. Of course, he knew almost nothing about the building trade. With every new assignment, he required a thorough explanation. He would not begin a task until he understood how to complete it and how it fit in to the project as a whole.

This slowed their already leisurely progress to the pace of a seasick snail.

At the end of five days, Soco had removed most of the siding on the end of the medical clinic. He'd drilled holes in the existing foundation, only after he understood that they would serve to tie in the new addition.

While Soco worked at these tasks, Marcus used a rented backhoe to level the ground where the new addition would eventually stand. This allowed his injured ribs another week of relative rest. For this he was grateful, even though his chest continued to complain when he climbed in and out of the backhoe's cab. By Wednesday, he finished trenches for the footings.

Together, they set the forms for the concrete footings and foundation, and dug trenches for plumbing and electrical conduits. Soco's thick frame gave him nearly supernatural strength, and he dug two feet for every one Marcus managed.

Soco took great pride in outperforming his boss.

Late Friday afternoon Marcus headed over to Sean's office, stopping first at Marianna's desk. "Is he in?" he asked.

She smiled. "He's in, but it isn't pretty."

Marcus nodded. "Thanks for the warning." He knocked lightly on Sean's door.

Seated across from Sean, Marcus couldn't miss the concern etched in his boss's expression. "I came to let you know we're ready for concrete."

Sean's eyebrows rose. "So soon?"

"If I'd had the crew you promised, we'd have poured on Tuesday, Wednesday at the latest. I've done the best I can with what I've got."

"Soco is a good man."

"I'm not complaining about Soco." Marcus shifted in his seat. "I'm just saying I could use some more help."

"Everyone here could use more help."

"I know that. I don't mean to diminish that. But about the concrete, can you order a Monday delivery? And can you come up with a crew?"

"I wish I could," Sean answered, shaking his head.

"You promised me a full crew."

"I did. I just don't know if I can deliver."

"What happened?"

"The immigration people came through yesterday afternoon. They took ten men from our shelter and deported them."

>>>>

Church had been a bad idea from the very beginning; Callie decided to head home. Maybe Keeshan would do better on another Sunday. As she stepped outside the church's front doors, a hand caught her elbow, swinging her around. "Callie, how about lunch?"

Surprised, Callie turned to greet a familiar face. "Angie, hello," she said, accepting her embrace. "You alone today? Where are Don and the boys?"

"The boys have a tournament in Olympia. Don is chauffeuring."

"I thought you never miss a match."

Angie shrugged and hitched her purse up over her shoulder. "It was my week to prepare communion. So, you hungry?" Her glossy dark hair, cut short, shone in the morning light. In her black raincoat and dark tights, she looked like a French runway model.

Though she and Callie had worked together on a project for a food bank, they weren't, strictly speaking, the best of friends. Both women juggled demanding careers. Today though, with the added responsibility of Keeshan and the worry over Celia, the idea of lunch out seemed like divine leading. Callie considered her friend's eager face. "I'm starved," she said, smiling. "Oh, by the way, this is Keeshan. He's with me." She held up his hand. "Keeshan, this is Angie."

Angie bent down to offer her hand to Keeshan. "Hello, young man. You don't know me, but I know your mother." He backed away, unwilling to accept her handshake. Undaunted, she continued, "My name is Angie. May I call you Keeshan?" Still cautious, he nodded.

Once again, the Prospect grapevine had preceded Callie. "I didn't know you knew Celia," she said as they walked through the parking lot.

Angie smiled and nodded. "She and my sister work at the same school, though I've only met her a couple of times. What happened?"

Callie glanced down to find Keeshan looking up at her, his tiny features twisted in a concerned frown. She smiled at him. "Hey, how would you like to eat at McDonald's?"

His smile broke out like sunshine on a cloudy day. Grabbing her hand with both of his own, he pulled her forward. Winking at Angie, Callie said, "I guess that answers that. Lunch it is, then. You can ride with us."

While Keeshan crawled through a sea of plastic balls like a swimmer against a strong tide, Callie explained the accident to Angie. At the end of the play space, oblivious to the other children, Keeshan stood, spread his arms, and fell blindly backward. Giggling as the balls caught him, he repeated the maneuver.

"He's a happy boy," Angie said. "She must take great care of him."

"I think so. He's got a mind of his own, though. I wouldn't want to deal with it forever. But then, what do I know?" With her plastic fork, Callie stabbed a piece of chicken and dipped it in fat-free salad dressing. "Besides, I'm the most unqualified woman in history to care for a child. Anyone could tell you that."

"Nonsense," Angie pushed at Callie's shoulder with her palm. "I'm sure you're doing fine. Mothering isn't exactly rocket science."

"I think you're overestimating my potential."

Angie frowned. "What does the doctor say about Celia?"

Callie watched Keeshan climb the ladder leading to a tunnel and disappear inside. The contraption reminded her of something a pet store would sell for hamsters, and she wondered how long it would take him to come out the other end. "We went to the hospital yesterday. I didn't speak to the doctor, but the nurse was pretty honest about it. She said they expect Celia to begin waking up any moment, but so far there hasn't been any real response. Not to voices or pain. She doesn't even open her eyes."

"Only two days after the accident?"

"I guess the longer she stays like this, the worse it is. Waking up doesn't always happen all at once. Sometimes the eyes open, but the patient doesn't follow directions. It can come a little at a time."

"I can't imagine anyone having to go through something like that. It must be horribly frightening for you."

Callie shook her head, refusing to go down that road. Fear was like an addiction. Once you gave in, even a little bit, it took control. She couldn't afford to let fear take over now. Keeshan needed her. "They have a monitor in Celia's brain to watch for swelling. So far, the nurse says her brain is still getting bigger. They're using medication to keep the blood moving through it."

"It's amazing what they can do these days."

"That's not her only problem. She has a broken leg—you know, the big bone above the knee. And they can't even set that—at least, not while she's in such fragile condition. So they have her leg propped up in the air. There's a pin going right through the skin. I can hardly stand to look at it."

Angie shivered. "Just hearing about it makes me goosey."

Callie rested her elbows on the table, watching as Keeshan popped out of the end of the tube. He returned to climb the ladder again. "She looks bad. I hope they find her family soon. If Celia were my daughter, I'd want to be with her. I'd want to care for my grandson."

"You were such close friends."

"We *are* close friends."

Angie nodded. "Caring for Keeshan is a way of helping her. She must appreciate it."

Callie blinked away fresh tears. Who knew what Celia appreciated? Callie hadn't seen any sign of her friend lying in that lonely ICU bed. The possibility of losing Celia loomed larger than ever. "The hospital asked me to go over to the house and go through her things. I found her address book, a diploma, a birth certificate, and a few pictures. I took all that, along with her telephone records, to the hospital, but the social worker wasn't there. I suppose they'll start looking for family again tomorrow."

"It shouldn't take long to track them down."

"I don't know. Celia often spoke to Keeshan in Spanish. What if her family was from Mexico? Her family could be in some remote village and the hospital would never find them. I can't take care of him forever."

"They aren't asking you to."

Unbidden, old thoughts, terrifying thoughts, selfish thoughts circled through Callie's mind; around and around they flew, determined to nest and raise their young. Callie shook her head, but the thoughts would not abate. *After all, you'll never marry. Why not keep Keeshan? You could care for him as well as anyone. He could become the family you've always wanted.* Callie felt her face turn crimson with guilt.

"I scare him to death," Callie said. "You should see it. Half the time he looks at me with a face that says, 'Have you ever taken care of a child before?' Honestly, I think he knows."

"Children don't know anything but kindness and love. If you're generous with those, the rest will fall into place."

"What about discipline? He takes me right to the very edge. What do I do?"

"You'll know what to do when you get there. Besides, with all the things happening to him, you should probably cut him some slack. He misses his mom. He's little, but he still has feelings."

In spite of her encouragement, none of Angie's platitudes gave Callie confidence. "You know, maybe you should have him. At least you're a real mother. You know how to do it."

Angie laughed. "I saw that coming a mile away. No thanks, friend. Besides, he doesn't need any more trauma than he's already suffered. He doesn't even know me."

"But you're a real mother."

"With three boys of my own," she shook her head. " No, Callie, living with us would be hazardous to his health. This job belongs to you."

DETOURS 121

By three in the afternoon, Callie and Keeshan were headed back to the house. Watching in the rearview mirror, Callie noticed his little brown eyelids drift sleepily as his thumb slid out of his mouth and dropped onto his lap.

How long did little boys take an afternoon nap? Perhaps, if she were very careful, she could sneak him onto his bed without disturbing him. Leaving him in the car, she unlocked the back door. Then, from the passenger side, she leaned into the car and grasped him around the waist, tugging. Keeshan didn't come out of his car seat.

She'd forgotten to unbuckle his safety belt.

The boy moaned. Gently, she slid her hand over his belly and unlocked the latch. With both hands she pulled him out and draped him over her shoulder. Tiptoeing into the house, she managed to shut the door behind her, pass through the kitchen, and make it to the front hall just as the telephone began ringing.

Keeshan's head shifted on her shoulder and he found his mouth with his thumb. "Stupid phone," Callie muttered. "Only rings when you can't answer."

>>>

On Monday, after Marcus ate pancakes in the school cafeteria, he headed around the fenced schoolyard and across the church parking lot to the medical clinic. By the time he arrived, the back of his neck stung from the intense morning sun. He used the front of his T-shirt to wipe perspiration from his face.

Last night's forecast called for clear skies and high temperatures. Normal weather for spring in Tucson, but the heat would not help Marcus's plans for the clinic addition. He'd scheduled today to pour the concrete footings.

Though Sean had promised to round up men to help with the foundation, Marcus had no idea what kind of help to expect. *It won't be easy to work concrete in this temperature,* Marcus thought, *even for a well-trained crew. Who knows what kind of men Sean will show up with this time?*

Even though he'd been on the campus for some time, Marcus had very little contact with those who used the services. Though he saw them, he never spoke with them. For the most part, the clients, as the volunteers referred to them, spoke Spanish, a language Marcus had not studied. Beyond this, Marcus worked long days and then spent his evenings studying plans and specifications.

In the midst of his new life, Marcus never forgot that he needed to stay hidden and unrecognized. He avoided church services, stayed away from crowds, and rarely introduced himself to other volunteers. In this new place, isolated by his past, among those who spoke a language he did not understand, Marcus felt deeply alone.

He told himself that isolation was better for everyone.

He checked his watch. Where were the men Sean had promised? He glanced back at the driveway. Though cars came and went, not a single man approached the addition. Maybe this time Sean couldn't come through. *No,* Marcus thought. *This place is different.*

Back home, in the projects, there was always some short-lived effort to better conditions for the poor. Most of those came and went in less than a year—unless they were government funded. These lasted until the funding went dry—whether they helped anyone or not.

Churches in the projects tried to help their own people, but resources were slim and enthusiasm was hard to come by. The people *in* the churches often needed as much help as the people *around* them.

The church of his childhood had managed a thrift store for the poorer people in the neighborhood. Kept in a tidy space in the church basement, the store opened for patronage only on Sunday afternoons. Along with this, the ladies served a free meal of beef stew and biscuits for those who shopped there.

Marcus could still remember the smell of biscuits baking in the church kitchen. But as much as he begged his mother to let him go for the afternoon meal, she refused. Neither would she consider shopping at the store, though Marcus had certainly suggested they try it.

"Don't you ask me again, Marcus," she'd said, her tone biting. "I don't care how nice them things is. We ain't gonna show up at church wearing no throwaways that came from some guild member."

"But, Ma," he'd argued. "Danny Whitman found a Colt's Jersey at the guild store."

"I gave you my answer, son" she said, turning away to polish the kitchen counter. And that was the end of it. When Ma put her foot down, no one in the Jefferson family tried to change her mind. Marcus least of all.

Not in all his years had Marcus ever seen anything to match the energy and scope of the Oasis Mission. Somehow Sean would come through. Marcus picked up a shovel. Backfilling the outer footing, he reinforced a long stretch of two-by-tens. He kicked at the footing and checked his watch again.

With the concrete truck due in fifteen minutes, Marcus felt an edge of desperation creep into his gut. Without help, he couldn't possibly get the footings poured and all the screeding done before the stuff began to set. If someone didn't show, he would have to reschedule the concrete truck, and the ministry would pay for the error.

The muscles in his jaw tightened. Deliberately, he opened his mouth and stretched to ease the tension. He refused to bungle his first job. Not when Sean had been so kind. Not when he needed this job so badly. A long honk caught his attention, and he turned in time to see Soco pull his pickup into the parking area behind the clinic. He waved his stocky arm at Marcus and pulled on a baseball cap. "You ready?" he called as he slipped out of the cab.

"You're late," Marcus answered, taking a deep breath as he tried to relax his shoulders. "Sean hasn't shown up with a crew."

"Then I'm not late. They're coming. Over behind the church building," he said, pointing.

"You saw them?"

"Jes," Soco said. "They are coming right away."

Marcus heard the rumble of a diesel engine, and spotted the concrete truck waiting at the corner light. "I don't think they could cut it any closer."

"They're here," Soco said, shrugging. "No worries, man."

No matter how sweet the deal or how much he needed the work, Marcus wasn't sure he would survive the stress.

Fourteen

Hurrying, Callie carried Keeshan into the bedroom and put him down on his back. As the phone continued to ring, she dragged a coverlet from the chair and placed it over his legs and chest. Then, as quietly as she could, she pulled the bedroom door closed.

By the time she reached the kitchen, the phone had stopped ringing. "Ah well," she said. "I'll catch the message." She'd no more than turned away when it began to ring again. She looked at the caller identification screen. Harborview Hospital.

Callie's fingers trembled as she reached for the telephone. With her heart pounding, she said, "Callie O'Brian."

A deep voice spoke. "Ms. O'Brian. This is Dr. Jacobson. I'm covering the ICU at Harborview today. I'm so sorry to have to tell you this, but your friend, Ms. Hernandez, passed away about thirty minutes ago."

>>>

Over the next few weeks, Marcus began to heal. The swelling around his eye disappeared and he began to see normally again. Every day, his ribs moved more comfortably. Eventually, he removed the tape around his chest. He felt stronger, more at peace with himself and his new existence. In spite of his injuries, Marcus finished the foundation of the new addition.

As promised, Sean always managed to find Marcus a construction crew—though calling them a crew was like calling a hammer a nail gun.

Every morning Marcus arrived at the job wondering who would show up to help. Every day he started over with a completely different group of men. Unfortunately, most of these had little construction experience. Day after day, before the real work began, each new worker had to be instructed in safety techniques and the use of power tools.

Marcus never knew what to expect. Some of these men came from the campus recovery programs. Others came from the feeding program. Some studied English at the language institute. Sometimes, when he was desperate, Sean showed up with an associate pastor or even a cook. Once, one of the preschool teachers added her feminine hands to the crew.

It wasn't easy, starting over day after day.

Soco became quite the expert at heading off mistakes, mostly because the new men were so predictable. Day after day, the new crew made exactly the same mistakes as the new men who helped the day before.

For the most part, the men were anxious to please. They laughed easily and chided one another over their errors. With time, Soco taught Marcus to use Spanish phrases in managing the men, though sometimes Marcus thought Soco taught him Spanish solely for his own amusement. No matter how hard he tried, Marcus could not roll the Spanish consonants. The results were brittle and forced, leaving the men doubled over with laughter.

Though the language did not come easily to him, eventually, in halting Spanish, Marcus learned to remind them to drink water and told them when to take a break. He learned specific phrases as well. "Good job," he said, whenever he could. Or, "No, not like that."

With every new phrase, the men invariably broke up laughing. Marcus refused to take their mirth personally. They were not all that different, after all, he and the men who worked on his crew. They were both poor, with darker skin than the wealthy and powerful around them.

Both knew the misfortune of being born in the wrong place at the wrong time. All of them, Marcus included, depended on the kindness of Oasis Mission. All knew the pain of being taken from the family and cultures they loved. Each lived a kind of haunting loneliness, even in the presence of other people.

Marcus continued to call his contact as often as he dared, though always from a different phone booth in a different part of town. To his unending frustration, nothing about the trial had changed. The missing witness had not yet been found, and Marcus could not help but wonder how much effort the sheriff was actually putting into finding him.

Though part of Marcus longed to return to real life, something inside him felt peace in Tucson, in spite of these disturbing phone calls. He couldn't quite explain this feeling. It wasn't that he felt especially safe or that the work was especially satisfying. Though he couldn't quite put his finger on the source of his tranquility, he drew strength from it, allowing the quiet of the place to bring a new peace to his soul.

More than anything he wanted to finish what he'd begun. He wanted to give back some of what Sean had given him. He would not forget his hunger, his near brush with jail, or the very real possibility of being found by those who wanted revenge. Sean had saved him from those things, and Marcus felt a measure of gratitude he could never repay.

Gradually, the walls of the clinic rose over the sill plates. Sheeting covered the trusses and before long, Marcus had a group of volunteers hanging plywood over the outside walls. Soco measured and called the numbers as Marcus cut the lengths. Then, with a compressor and nail gun, they hung the wood.

Even though they made no great haste, the addition progressed nicely. Unfortunately, the details from his past life didn't follow such a predictable path. On a cloudy Thursday morning, Marcus stopped at a pay phone to call his contact.

"It's me," he said into the telephone.

His contact swore softly. "About time you called. The prosecutor was making noises about putting me on the stand."

"They're only pressuring you to get to me. What's happening?"

"The prosecution decided to bail. I guess they knew they didn't have enough evidence."

"Bail?"

"Bad choice of words. The prosecution dismissed charges."

"Against Ortega? They can't do that!"

"They can and they did. They let him go."

"Why? Why let him go?"

"Look, it was the only way. They can't make him stand trial twice. They had to make it stick or they had to let him go. If Presario gets caught, they'll charge Ortega again."

"That's a big if. They can't charge Ortega if they can't find him. Besides, with Ortega loose, I don't think Presario will ever turn up—at least not alive. Ortega will find him before the police do."

"I'm sorry, Marcus. It looks like it's over."

"It's over in more ways than one."

"What do you mean?"

Marcus hung up without speaking.

>>>

Feeling weak, Callie pulled out a chair. Though she did not cry, her trembling grew to shaking and she felt cold—so cold that she could hardly feel her fingers. Her teeth began to chatter. She reached for the phone book and looked up Angie's number. Who else could she call? Who else did she have in the midst of this nightmarish web?

"The hospital just called, Angie" she said, holding her head with one hand, focusing on the words, willing herself to stay calm. "Celia passed away half an hour ago."

Angie, apparently stunned, made no response.

"Are you there? Did you hear me?"

"I don't understand," she said, sounding confused. "You said they expected her to recover."

"They have to do an autopsy. She went very suddenly, I guess. The doctor thinks it may have been a clot from the leg fracture. That somehow it got into her blood stream and went to her heart." Callie closed her eyes, and the image of Celia climbing into the Ford Explorer flashed through her memory. A wave of guilt passed over her and the trembling increased. She clutched the phone. "I never should have loaned her my car. She wasn't experienced in the snow. What was I thinking? A car isn't safe unless you know how to drive it."

Angie's advice turned practical. "Come on, Callie. You have to let go. The accident wasn't your fault. It wasn't anybody's fault. These things happen," she said, her voice catching. "Who knows why? You can't blame yourself."

"If I hadn't offered her the car, she'd have stayed home. She was afraid, you know? Afraid of driving in that stuff."

Angie blew her nose. "I can't believe she's gone. I didn't expect this. It has to be a mistake. You said—oh, it doesn't matter what you said. I'm so sorry. So sorry."

Though her grief had been walled up inside, Callie gave in to her weeping. Embarrassed by the display, she tried to gain control. She sniffed, wheezed, and wiped her face with her sleeve. "I know. I mean, you answer the phone, and this strange doctor announces that she's gone. He didn't even sound sad. She was my friend. What on earth do I do now? What about the boy?"

"What do you mean, what do you do?"

Callie resented Angie's question. "I mean, what do I do?" Callie rubbed her forehead, trying to regain control. "Listen to me; I can hardly talk. How do I tell Keeshan about this? I can't do it. I'll make a mess of it. I'll ruin him for life."

"Okay, first take a deep breath." Angie blew a long sigh into the telephone. "Okay. Now relax. First of all, Keeshan isn't yours forever. You aren't the only person who loved Celia. Somewhere she has a family. The hospital will find them. No one is going to saddle this child with you—unless you want to keep him."

A shiver passed through Callie.

There it was again. Hope. Callie recognized it and pushed it away, ashamed of her own selfishness. What kind of woman entertained these kinds of thoughts? What kind of egocentric person would hope for a child only moments after her friend died?

Callie shook her head. "Don't even say it."

"What? Want him? Don't be silly; no one expects you to raise Celia's child. In the meantime, you have some time to think through your approach. When he wakes up, you tell him what happened to his mother. But I warn you, I don't think he'll understand. Death isn't real to a child his age."

The headache, which began at church, settled in between Callie's eyebrows, now a raging forest fire. She rubbed her forehead. "What do you mean?"

"I mean that he hasn't experienced death. He doesn't understand that it's permanent. You're going to have to tell him over and over and over."

"As if once isn't going to kill me." Callie brushed hair out of her face and turned to lean against the counter. "I can't do it over and over."

"Yes, you can." Angie said with exaggerated patience. "He's going to need help understanding. You start by explaining it as simply as possible. Don't make a bunch of excuses. Just tell him."

"But if he won't understand, why am I doing it?"

"Because eventually, he will. It takes time."

"I can't do this. Maybe you can come over and talk to him?"

"I can if you insist. But I think quieter is better."

"What if I mess it up?"

"Now you're the one who sounds like a child."

At this Callie let her tears flow freely. She choked back a sob. "I am a child. I can't even run my own life, let alone help a four-year-old through this kind of thing. I miss Celia myself. How can I possibly help a boy who's lost his mother?

"With prayer."

Her answer sounded like one of those greeting cards from the sympathy section of a Hallmark store. Callie could hardly contain her frustration. "Oh, please. I'm serious."

"Remember that old poster, 'Life is tough, handle with prayer'?"

She'd like to forget pat, oversimplified answers. "I remember."

"This is the kind of situation it was referring to."

Thanks for nothing. "I guess so."

"I'm not kidding." Angie said, her voice deadly serious. "The only way any of us can get through life is with prayer."

"I know. It's true. But at the same time, it seems so—so oversimplified." Callie felt a measure of desperation she'd never experienced before. Not when her mother died. Not even when she found out about Scott's marriage. She could hardly contain the urge to run screaming through the house. It all felt so unfair. So arbitrary. Why would God take Celia now? She was so young. Keshan needed her.

"Are you there?"

"I'm here," she answered, barely recognizing her own defeated voice. "I'm here," she repeated. Callie looked up to find Keeshan ambling down the hall, his face sleepy, his hands struggling again with the zipper of his jeans. "You're right," she said, putting on a cheerful tone as she brushed the tears from her cheeks. "Keeshan's up from his nap. I've gotta go."

>>>>

On the day the spring rains began in Tucson, Marcus walked through the building with an electrician, a volunteer who'd offered to help supervise and certify the electrical installation. They'd just marked the new location of a hallway electrical box when Marcus heard his name called from outside.

He rose from his haunches. "In here." He tucked a square pencil into his tool belt and spotted the administrative assistant stepping over a wall brace.

"Marcus," she said, smiling. "I'm glad I found you. Sean wants you in his office."

"Now?"

"As soon as you can make it."

Marcus exchanged a glance with the electrician. "All right, tell him I'll be in as soon as I finish here."

"Thanks," she said. "I'll tell him." She turned to leave, but hesitated. "By the way, this is coming along nicely. Good job, Marcus."

He smiled to himself, taking satisfaction in her words. Not everyone appreciated a work in progress. Turning back to the electrician, he said, "Let's finish marking all the boxes. Your time is money. I don't want to keep you."

An hour later, Marcus knocked on Sean's door.

"Come on in."

Inside, Marcus found Sean in jeans and a University of Arizona polo shirt, bending over blueprints for the new school building. He and Sean had spent long hours discussing the plans and making changes where necessary. Marcus smiled. "Back again?"

"Yeah. Come look at this, will you?" Sean pointed to the curb view of the exterior facade. "What do you think?" He held the roll open with his palm. "They just came in this morning."

"I like it," Marcus said. "The change in the roofline suits the exterior. It won't cost much to frame that way. The drive-through will keep children from dashing through traffic. Might even save a life."

"It was your idea. I never would've thought of it." Sean turned to face Marcus, leaning one hip against the table. "You never told me about your past," he said. "You've had more training than you let on."

Crossing his arms across his chest, Marcus faced Sean, poker-faced. Neither man blinked.

Sean continued. "My guess is that you're an architect, maybe an engineer. You know too much about building to masquerade as a framer. You should try harder to act dumb—though I doubt you'd get away with it."

Unbidden, the picture of Marcus's graduation party passed through his mind. His wife had been so pleased, so proud of his accomplishment. "We agreed not to talk about my past."

"I'm afraid we have to," Sean said, his face clouding. "I wish I could ignore it, but I can't, not any longer."

Marcus felt his heart rate accelerate. Though he trusted Sean, he couldn't tell him about his past. It was too big a risk. "I told you, I can't tell you anything."

"You don't have to. Yesterday, while you and Soco were out picking up siding, someone came looking for you. A man. Marianna was the only one at her desk. He asked questions, lots of them. She told me he was pretty ugly about it—must've hoped to frighten her into talking. She was smart enough to call me. Marianna doesn't scare easily."

Marcus felt his throat tighten. Deliberately, he swallowed. "You spoke with him?"

"He told me he was an old friend. But he didn't seem too friendly, and he didn't stay long once I showed up."

"But he knows I'm here?"

"He thinks he knows. He had a picture."

Marcus nodded. This was bad news, worse than he imagined. "What'd he look like?"

"He wasn't a big man," Sean slipped his hands in his jeans pockets. "About 5'8" and maybe 170 pounds. Dark hair and eyes. He had a scar along one cheek," Sean fingered his face as he demonstrated the scar. "But there was something funny about his face—his mouth actually."

"One side sort of slides downhill?"

"That's it exactly."

"Presario."

"Who?"

"Doesn't matter. He's found me."

"Marcus, I know you're struggling with some demon from your past. I don't know what's going on. But I'd like to help. Maybe if you told me the whole story—I have friends in the Tucson police department. They can put a stop to this."

Marcus searched Sean's eyes, wondering how much he already knew. Had he already checked his background? He might have figured out the whole sordid mess. "I've gone to the police. That's what started the whole thing in the first place." Marcus shook his head. "No. I hoped the police would take care of it, but they didn't. They can't, really. Now I've got to take action." He put his hands on his hips. "No. No human can help me with this."

"Marcus, you've got to trust someone. You can't keep running forever."

He shook his head. "This isn't about trust. The guy is crazy. He's not afraid of the police. If I don't leave, I'm putting all of you in jeopardy."

"We can handle it."

"Out of the question."

"I hate to let you go," Sean said, walking around the desk. "Will you leave right away?"

Marcus nodded. In his mind, he'd already moved on. Part of him had already closed down, shut himself off from the friends he knew here. He couldn't afford to care for anyone, not even this gentle, furry giant. Until this was over, Marcus could have no relationships, not without risk. "I've stayed too long."

"I can't talk you out of it?"

"I'm afraid not."

"Where will you go?"

"Back to Florida, where the whole thing started."

"Well, then," Sean stepped forward, offering his hand. "God go with you."

Marcus took Sean's hand only to be pulled into a fierce embrace. Marcus found his eyes filling with tears. This man had trusted him when he didn't deserve it, and now, when the time came for departure, Marcus could hardly bear to let go. He felt Sean pat his shoulder.

Marcus knew what he had to do. Though Presario was a wanted man, it seemed that for him, revenge was a stronger motivation than freedom. Marcus would have to take a stand, to take his chances against Presario and finish this thing.

Sean stepped back. "Is there anything I can do for you? Anyway I can help?"

"You can pray. I know it sounds trite, but I need it. I need it bad."

"I've already started."

Fifteen

The hard truth about Celia didn't hit Callie until she placed the telephone into its cradle. Her friend was gone. Not recuperating. Not recovering. She was gone, and grief struck Callie with the force of a karate kick to the gut.

She could hardly breathe for the pain of it. Ignoring Keeshan, she turned to the window and bent over the sink, supporting herself on her elbows. How could it be true?

Callie jumped as Keeshan spoke. "I'm thirsty," he said. "Can I have some pop?"

She wiped tears from her face with the back of her hand and took a deep breath. "Not now. I have some orange juice, though." She went to the fridge and pulled out a pitcher. Pouring it into a half-sized tumbler, she fought with the tears that threatened once again to cascade over her cheeks. What she wanted more than anything was to have a good long cry. But that luxury would have to wait. For now, she needed to think about the boy.

Later, after she fixed a macaroni and cheese dinner, they sat down to a nearly silent meal. Still sleepy from his nap, Keeshan had trouble eating. Callie couldn't get her mind off Celia. When they finished cleaning up, she knew the time had come. She let Keeshan play with Eddy as she built a fire in the old fireplace. Then, putting a string quartet on the CD player, Callie invited Keeshan to sit with her in the rocking chair.

"Can Eddy sit with us too?" he asked.

"Maybe later."

His face collapsed in a pout as he climbed onto her lap. "Eddy likes to sit with us," he said. Eddy purred as he rubbed against her ankles. He did indeed seem to know it was time for what Celia used to call "a cuddle."

"Does Eddy lie on your lap when you sit with your mom?"

Keeshan nodded, his face solemn.

"Then I guess Eddy should join us."

"Come on, Eddy," Keeshan coaxed, slapping his thighs as he leaned over to speak to the kitty. The cat stopped his rubbing long enough to look up. With the grace of a ballet dancer, he jumped onto Keeshan's lap and began kneading with his paws.

With a twitch of his tail, he curled up, purring again as Keeshan pet his dark, silken fur. Callie put one arm around Keeshan's shoulder and began rocking. "I heard from the doctor today," she said, her voice low. "He called to tell me about your mama."

Keeshan turned to look at her, his face bright with expectation. What he saw must have startled him, for he reached up to touch her cheek. "You're sad," he said simply.

"I have some bad news, Keeshan," Callie said, her voice shaking. She cleared her throat and prayed. *Father, help me. Help me to say this right.* He glanced up at her again, his face etched with confusion. How could she tell this sweet little boy that his mother would never again read a bedtime story? Never tuck him in? She took a deep breath and plunged in. "Your mama was very sick, even sicker than the doctors thought after the accident. When the doctor called from the hospital, he told me your mama died."

The crease between his eyebrows deepened, and he put his thumb in his mouth. "When will she come home?"

"Keeshan, your mama won't be coming home, honey. Not ever."

The boy said nothing. Instead, he turned back to the fireplace and continued petting the cat. Through tears Callie watched the flames, feeling as burned out as the ashes on the hearth. She longed to say more, to reassure the boy, to see how much he understood of what had been said. But she didn't know where to begin. And Callie was afraid—both of her own emotions and of the boy's grief. Would his sorrow add to her own? If the two pains became one, would she be able to survive the weight of it?

For a long while, in the dimly lit room, Callie heard only the sound of Keeshan's mouth working on his thumb, the purring of the cat, and the occasional sputter of the fire. Feeling helpless, wishing she knew how to help the boy, she continued rocking in silence, and as she did, she let her own tears roll.

>>>>

Marcus made a show of leaving Tucson. Saying goodbye to those he had worked with, including suppliers and volunteers, he made sure that everyone knew he had tickets for Florida. Certain that Presario was somewhere nearby, probably watching his every move, Marcus wanted to be absolutely positive that Presario knew where Marcus was headed. More than anything, Marcus wanted Presario to follow him.

Though he didn't know exactly how, once Marcus landed in Florida, he planned to draw Presario out in the open where Florida authorities could nab him. Somewhere along the way, Marcus would figure out the details and finish this chase once and for all. He couldn't live this way. If the police couldn't nab Presario, Marcus would have to lead Presario to the police.

At the airport, Marcus thanked Soco for the ride. As they shook hands, Marcus felt a keen sense of loss. They had worked well together, the two of them, and Marcus hated to leave his new friend. He stood on the sidewalk and watched as the old truck rumbled out of sight.

A strange feeling overcame Marcus as he entered the terminal. Something was wrong, though he had no idea what. Ignoring the twist in his gut, he checked in, picked up his boarding pass, and made his way to the security checkpoint, where he stood in line behind a group of girls in track warm-ups. His uneasiness grew until he could no longer ignore it. He turned away from the flow of travelers, circled around the concourse, and then went upstairs where he watched from a balcony, unobserved. He saw nothing suspicious below him, nothing more than travelers, airport security, and airline crewmembers.

Still unnerved, he made his way to a pay phone and made another call to Dade County. "Something's wrong," he said without preliminaries. "I know it."

"I'm glad you called," the contact answered. "I hate not knowing how to reach you."

"What's happened?"

"Who told you?"

"No one," he said. "It's a feeling. Just tell me what happened."

"I had a request from my lieutenant. He asked for the file on Peter. Apparently, a hospital in Washington State is looking for him. Wants to know where he's serving his sentence."

"My brother? Why?"

"I don't know. Could be they've connected something in Washington to the drug ring we busted. Maybe they want to talk to him about our case. But I'm out of the line of information here. Dixon didn't tell me anything. If I ask about the request, I'll draw his suspicion. He'll wonder why I care. And remember, I'm not supposed to know anything about where you are."

"I understand. But how can I find out?"

The voice hesitated, cleared his throat. "Where's Peter's wife?"

"I honestly don't know. I told Celia to wait until Peter was arrested and then clear out. Once I got out of jail, I helped her load her stuff into a U-haul. The last I saw, she pulled out of the driveway and headed for the interstate." Marcus tried to remember if he knew anything, had heard any hint about where Celia had gone. He assumed she'd gone to be with her family. "Do you think something has happened to Celia?"

"Could be. She had a child too, didn't she?"

"Keeshan."

"The authorities would want to contact your brother in either case."

Marcus had sensed something wrong. And now, more confused and discouraged than ever, he hung up the phone. Had something horrible happened to Celia? Had the child been injured? There was no way to know from the airport. No way for Marcus to find out why a hospital was looking for his brother.

And then a more horrible thought crossed his mind. If Presario found Marcus in Tucson, had he also found Celia? Had Presario done something to Celia in retaliation for his arrest?

An involuntary shudder rumbled through his shoulders. Marcus could not answer these questions on his own. Though he hated the thought, he had no choice. He would have to go to the source. He would have to go to the penitentiary and ask his brother.

>>>

Though Callie tried to stifle her own emotion for the boy's sake, her tears fell in a nearly endless stream. No matter what she was doing, or where in the house she was, they returned as soon as she wiped them away.

She managed to put Keeshan to bed, though their routine felt sodden—like a wool blanket left out in a heavy rain. She tried to read a bedtime story, but her voice trembled like an old woman's, and she could not finish. She tried to pray for him, but the words would not come.

"God, help us," Callie whispered. It was all she could manage.

Keeshan seemed sensitive to her sorrow, unwilling or unable to express his own. More than once he stroked her face, wiping tears from her cheeks. His tenderness nearly undid her, and it was a great relief to turn out the light and shut the door to his bedroom.

Callie hadn't heard anything new about the search for Celia's family. She would have to call in the morning and check with the social worker. In fact, there were dozens of calls she needed to make. She began to wonder about a memorial service. Celia deserved a celebration service in honor of her life.

And more than anything, the people who loved her deserved to say goodbye.

With a pen and paper, Callie sat down at the kitchen table, making a list as the thoughts came to her. She needed to call the pastor, the pianist, a soloist. She needed to choose a funeral home and a place to bury her friend's body. What about an obituary? Who would write a tribute for Celia?

Even as she made notes, Callie wondered. Was this her place? Shouldn't her family be the one to make this final offering? But what if the social worker had not yet found the family? How long could such planning wait? She had no idea.

Neither did she know what had become of Celia's body. Had the hospital sent it off? The doctor mentioned an autopsy. Who would take care of that?

There were so many pieces to the puzzle that Callie wondered where to start. It felt as if someone had handed her a tangled ball of yarn. She couldn't begin to unravel the yarn until she found the loose end.

The thought of planning a service for Celia drove the whole disaster home again, like yet another stab to an already fatally wounded heart. Celia was gone. Now who would be her friend, her confidant? Keeshan had lost his mother, and Callie had lost her only real friend.

Sitting at the kitchen table, Callie laid her head on her hands and wept.

At bedtime she washed the tears from her face and brushed her teeth. She slid between the sheets and tried to find comfort in the Bible. Much as she loved the Word, on the night of Celia's death it read like a foreign language newspaper. She turned to the Psalms and began reading out loud. At least David knew sorrow.

After three tries at going to sleep, Callie gave up and took an herbal sleep aid. Still, her heart raced, and in the darkness of her bedroom she dripped silent tears into her pillow. She could not erase the picture she had of the three of them, eating popcorn at the guesthouse and watching a Disney movie. The image of her friend, wonderfully alive, haunted Callie. Hours later, she watched the numbers of her alarm clock change. Again she tried to read. She got a drink of water. And still she lay awake.

Later, Callie was not surprised by the sound of her door opening and of little footsteps crossing the carpet. The bed creaked as Keeshan climbed up and crawled under the covers with her. Lifting the blankets she made room for him; he scooted backward, as close to her as he could get and curled up front of her chest.

"Can't sleep, eh, Keeshan?"

She heard only the sound of his mouth working, chewing, slurping on his thumb. Putting an arm around his waist, she pulled him closer. He squirmed and settled in. When at last he stopped moving, her hand fell upon something unusual. Something satiny and soft.

Keeshan had brought Celia's nightgown into bed with him.

>>>

One day after arriving in Florida, Marcus endured the procedures for entering the Dade Correctional Institution in Florida City. Leaving all his personal belongings in a locker near the lobby, he signed in at the front desk, providing two forms of identification—identification he'd left in a safety deposit box when he fled Florida three years earlier. He passed through a metal detector and took off his shoes for inspection. He gave the guard his jacket and watched as the officer pawed through the lining and pockets for contraband. Moments later, a drug-sniffing dog gave him a few sniffs about the knees.

All through the procedure, Marcus silently thanked God that his father had not lived to make this same trip.

It would have killed William Ovid Jefferson to know that his younger son lived in this prison. William always wanted more for his boys. Every day of his life, Marcus heard his father preach about his aspirations for his sons. Never had Marcus heard his father acknowledge racial prejudice as an excuse for any disadvantage. Education, he'd thundered, that was the key to everything. Every evening, every Sunday afternoon, his father's mantra was the same. "All men got to get an education," William had said. "Don't matter if they black or white or red or purple. All men got to get one. And if they don't, they ain't goin' nowhere."

William Ovid Jefferson dreamed enough for both his boys.

His hope served as inspiration to Marcus. It had encouraged him to earn a scholarship to the University of Evansville. It had challenged him to play football, to work thirty hours a week while getting his degree.

However to Peter, the younger son, those same dreams felt like a ball and chain. When he'd grown old enough, Peter had finally cut the chain. Cut it, heck, he'd axed the thing. And his freedom had landed him in a twelve-year sentence in a maximum-security prison.

Though Marcus hated everything about this place, about all the memories it conjured up, he gritted his teeth, determined to tolerate almost anything if it would lead him closer to the answers he sought. He couldn't shake the feeling that Celia needed him. If somehow, by being here, he could help her, it would be worth it. After what she'd been through, she deserved his help.

Having passed through the initial security screening, Marcus waited, trapped in a twelve-foot zone while the outer gate crawled closed behind him. Unable to move in or out, he felt his shoulders tense.

He glanced up to the concertina wire crowning the twelve-foot cyclone fence. Couldn't they secure the area without the extra wire? It looked gruesome there, waiting to tear the flesh off anyone daring to escape. Marcus sighed and watched the guard tower as the sentry sent the electronic signal to open the inner gate.

It took all of his composure to keep from dashing through the opening. In all, Marcus passed through five sets of double gates before reaching the visiting area for his brother's cell block. There, Marcus waited another forty minutes while other visitors were called in.

He didn't know what to expect, exactly. He hadn't spoken with, or written to, his brother since his trial. And considering his brother's track record, there would be no way to predict his current mental status. Marcus steeled himself for the inevitable confrontation.

Sixteen

Callie woke on Monday morning feeling sluggish and heavy, her eyes swollen from crying. Even with so much evidence of her grief, she could not bring herself to believe that Celia was gone.

She left Keeshan in bed and headed for her beloved bicycle. Sweat always made her feel alive. In the few years she'd lived in Prospect she almost never missed a morning on her bicycle. On this morning she hoped it would revive her again. Callie left open the back door to the shop and climbed on the bike.

She put on her earphones, turned on her music, and pedaled hard, waiting for the endorphins to kick in. But today even her bicycle could not bring her joy. She dropped the earphones around her shoulders and began praying, first for Keeshan and then for Celia's family. Before long, visions of the time they'd spent together played again through her mind.

She remembered how gentle Celia had been with the boy. She thought of the joy Celia and Keeshan shared, their secret jokes, their inner world. Their laughter—so innocent, so pure. She wondered what it would be like to share everything with a child like that. To be so unconditionally loved, so absolutely certain that someone was there for you, all the time, in every circumstance.

You're envious. You want this child for yourself.

Instantly guilty, Callie rebuked herself. "Lord, you know where they are. Let the social worker find Celia's family," she prayed.

Twenty-five minutes into her exercise, a ringing telephone caught her attention. She considered letting the answering machine take a message. Instead, she climbed off the bike and picked up the workshop extension.

"Hello, Ms. O'Brian, this is Wendy Newton calling from Harborview. I have a note saying that Dr. Jacobson called you yesterday?"

Callie wiped her face with her sleeve. Still panting, she said, "He did."

"I've caught you in the middle of something."

She took a deep breath and tried to quiet her breathing. "Just exercise. I was on the bike. Don't worry about it."

"I wanted to tell you how sorry I am about Ms. Hernandez's death. It must be hard."

Though she tried to stay detached, once again tears pooled in Callie's eyes. "Thank you," she said, turning to lean against the wall. "Actually, I was going to call you this morning. I have some questions."

"I'd be glad to help if I can."

"I was wondering where Celia's body is now."

"The doctor asked for an autopsy. He's sent it to the medical examiner."

"How long will that take?"

"Depends on how backed up they are. Not long, though. I can have them call you."

"Please."

"There is one other thing you should know. Because Ms. Hernandez did not survive the accident, I won't continue looking for next of kin."

"Why not?" Callie felt her alarm rise. How could she handle being assigned to yet another staff person? "Who will notify the family? I mean, in the space of four days, the job of finding Celia's family has passed through so many different hands—three if you count the police at the scene of the accident. Somebody's got to take responsibility here."

"That falls to the medical examiner's office now. But you must understand. Finding family isn't easy. If the family came into the country illegally, they may have already relocated in Mexico. That would make them almost impossible to find. If they're still in the States, and they don't want to be found—well, then it's anyone's guess where they've gone."

"What about Celia? Who will bury her?"

"You have a couple of days to think about that. If the medical examiner doesn't find her family by the time the autopsy is finished, I'd suggest you take care of it yourself. Perhaps your church family or her coworkers can help."

"She deserves that. Keeshan deserves that."

"And about the boy. How is he doing?"

"I think he's fine. He seems amazingly unaffected."

"I wouldn't be fooled by his behavior," the woman said. "Things could change quite dramatically now that his mother has expired."

The woman made Celia sound like an outdated coupon.

>>>

"Peter Jefferson," a woman's voice announced.

Marcus moved through the double doors into the prison visiting area. A female guard met him at the door and escorted him to a seat at an empty desk. "He'll be out in a minute," she said.

The room itself was lined with identical desks, each covered in fake wood, each facing away from the center of the room. A thick plastic panel divided every table, thus separating visitor from the inmate. At the base of each divider, a two-way speaker amplified both voices. The room looked very much like something from prime-time drama. Marcus felt himself begin to sweat.

Feeling self-conscious, he wiped his palms on his jeans. Nausea rose in his gut as he watched the doorway, waiting for his brother to appear. Marcus began to wish he'd skipped lunch.

Eventually the door opened and Peter appeared. Slimmer than he had been, his hair longer and more unkempt, he shuffled toward the desk. It wasn't until he saw Marcus that his expression changed from impassive to an almost animal hatred.

Marcus saw it in the narrowing of his eyes, the tightening of his lips, the almost imperceptible raising of his chin. Peter defied his brother, dared him to speak by the set of his eyes and shoulders.

He sat down and leaned back in the chair. "What're you doing here?"

"I came to see you."

"I'll bet. After three years."

"I've been out of state."

"Right." Peter placed his cuffed wrists on the table and leaned forward.

Marcus hesitated, wishing somehow he could make it right. "How are you?" He cleared his throat, aware that his voice sounded higher, thinner.

"I live in prison," his brother answered. "How do you think I am?"

"What can I get you?"

"You put me in jail and now you want to know what you can bring me?" A low mocking laugh escaped his brother as he shook his head. He swore. "You're somethin'."

Marcus leaned forward. "I know it's hard. I didn't want you to end up in jail, but it had to stop."

"You have no idea what I've been through."

"And you'll never know what I've saved you from."

"Oh, please. Don't go heroic. You're starting to sound like dad."

"It could be a worse." Though Marcus expected his brother's reaction, it still struck him with deep sadness. How could two boys raised in the same home come out so differently?

Peter scoffed. "Never."

"Maybe someday you'll change your mind."

"Don't waste the sentiment. What'd you really come for?"

"I'm looking for Celia."

Peter raised suspicious eyes. "Why?"

"I heard a hospital was looking for you. I think she may be in trouble."

"Why would you care? We're divorced, you know. Unless, of course, you want her too."

Marcus almost choked. "How can you say that? I only want to help her. She was the best thing that ever happened to you. If she's in trouble, she deserves some help. She has a child. What about the child?"

"My rights were terminated in the divorce."

"So you don't know anything?"

"I didn't say that."

Marcus fought with an urge to pull out his own hair. How many times had he gone around like this with his brother? "What have I done to make you hate me?"

"You mean other than be the good brother? The son who always did everything right?"

Marcus shook his head. "You made your own choices. Don't blame me."

"I could never measure up. Dad only had one son."

Marcus felt his temper rise. At times like this, he wanted to strangle his little brother. "I can't fix that for you. Somewhere inside you know it isn't true. Dad loved you every bit as much as he loved me. You just couldn't accept it, somehow." Marcus put his hands on the desk, laced his fingers, and tried to relax. If he didn't stay calm, he'd never get anything out of Peter. "Do you know anything about Celia?"

His brother leaned back against the chair, putting his cuffed hands behind his head. "Yeah. I know something."

Just say it, Marcus wanted to scream. "Tell me. What do you know?"

"She's dead. In a car accident. Somebody contacted me through the prison chaplain. They were looking for family."

"What did you tell them?"

"I told them the truth. I told 'em Celia had nobody."

"What about me? Why didn't you tell them about me?"

"You were gone. Disappeared to save your own skin. Like I said, Celia had nobody."

I'm too late to help her. Marcus struggled to understand what might have happened. Had Presario already taken care of her? Had he done it knowing that this would hurt Marcus more than his own death? Suddenly he lost touch with the room around him. Unaware of the voices and people, he could think only of the loss. And then it occurred to him. "What about the child? What about Keeshan?"

"What about him?"

"Where is he?"

His brother smiled, a bitter, cold smile. "You want to swoop in like a hero, don't you?"

Marcus bit his lip, controlling a rage so deep that it seemed to come from the center of his being. "Not a hero. Like family. Someone needs to help the boy."

Peter's lips curled in an evil smile. "I don't know where he is."

"Who contacted the prison? Where was she killed?"

"I'll tell you. It won't help, but I'll tell you." Peter leaned back and his expression took on a malicious smirk. "She died in King County, Washington. Biggest county in the state. So there," he said, standing up. He shuffled to the exit. "Go find her, big brother. Be the hero." Without looking back, Peter nodded to the guard and the door opened. In a moment, he was gone.

>>>

On the Monday after Celia died, Callie hired an old employee to work her shift. It was only for one day, after all. Today of all days, Callie could not face customers. Could not mix steamed milk and make small talk. Could not wipe counters and clean equipment as if nothing had happened.

But neither could she stay home. She needed to get out, to go somewhere, to talk with someone. But whom? Since she'd moved to Prospect, Callie had never taken the time to make friends. Quite intentionally she had kept herself isolated, alone. She never expected to lose the one woman who had managed, in spite of her defenses, to crawl into her heart.

Callie decided to drive into town and visit her dad. Though they weren't as close as she would have liked, he was family. Maybe he would have some words of wisdom. Some encouragement.

Callie put Keeshan in the car and drove the twenty miles into Puyallup.

"Where are we going?" Keeshan asked.

"To visit my dad," Callie answered. "He lives in a very special place. You'll like it. They have lots of grandmas and grandpas living there. And they have ice cream and a big toy and swings. It's a fun place for little boys to visit."

Callie turned into the retirement community, parked in front of her dad's duplex, and helped Keeshan from the car. Stepping onto the front porch, she rang the bell. They waited for long moments with no response.

"No one's home," he said, disappointed.

"He's home," Callie answered, squeezing Keeshan's hand. "You just have to wait a long time for him. He's pretty slow."

As if to prove her point, they heard a commotion inside. As the door swung open, Callie saw her father's wheelchair spinning away from the door. "Hi, dad," she said, waiting for him to get out of the way. "I brought someone I'd like you to meet."

"Calliandra! Come in!"

"Calliandra?" Keeshan looked up at her.

"It's my name, squirt," she said.

He shrugged and slipped his thumb into his mouth.

She led Keeshan into the small slate entry and paused before her dad. "This is Keeshan, Dad, the boy I told you about. Keeshan, this is my dad. You can call him Jack."

Callie's father held out his hand. "Hey, Keeshan," he said.

Unable to move, Keeshan stared at the stump hanging below Jack's left knee. "Where's your foot?" he asked, pointing.

Callie felt her face heat up. "Keeshan!"

"I lost my foot a few years ago," Jack said, turning away from the boy and starting into the living room.

"Where did you lose it?"

He turned back to face the boy, his hands folded across his lap. Jack's smile seemed thin. "I mean that the doctor had to cut off my foot. It was infected."

Whether or not he understood, Keeshan gave a solemn nod. Still staring at the stump, he slipped his thumb into his mouth. Callie crossed to give her dad a hug. "Good to see you, Dad."

"Good to see you too. You'd never know we live in the same state."

"I've been busy," she said, slipping off her coat. "Busier than usual."

"I can see that," her father said, nodding at the boy. "Keeshan, come with me." His spun the chair by the wheels. "I have a jar over here that I can't quite reach. Could you open it for me?" Jack pointed to a cookie jar at the back of the counter separating the living area from the kitchen.

Keeshan hurried to catch up, stopping beside the wheelchair to look up at the cookie jar.

"I think there is something in that jar you would like. But you'll have to crawl up and get it yourself, if you're brave enough."

Keeshan dragged a chair from the dining table. Climbing onto the counter he lifted the lid from the jar. "Oreos!" he yelled, filling both fists.

"Just two," Callie corrected.

"You sound like a mother," Jack said, turning to look at Callie, a curious expression on his face. It was as if some new thought had just occurred him. Whatever it was, it hadn't made him happy. Keeshan climbed back down to the floor. Stuffing a full cookie into his mouth, he said, spewing crumbs, "Thank you, Jack."

"Shall we go over to the big toy?" Callie asked, aware of the sudden freeze that had come over their little interaction. "It's a nice day. We can talk while Keeshan plays."

One eyebrow rose on Jack's stiff face. "Sure," he agreed, without enthusiasm. "Let's go visit the big toy."

Seventeen

Leaving the penitentiary, Marcus took the freeway north toward Miami. He drove mindlessly, only vaguely aware of the scenery he passed. He could not shake the feeling he'd waited too long. He should have left Tucson sooner. Should have had his contact try to find Celia, to check on her. No, he shook his head. He should have done it himself.

Celia was dead because he'd chosen himself over her.

As the sun sank on his left, Marcus thought back over the events that had driven him from his family. It seemed, at the time, that there was no other way. Was he wrong? Should he have done something more?

He remembered the day he recognized his brother's game plan. And once again, though it had been almost four years, Marcus felt his stomach lurch with revulsion.

It had been hot, so hot that Marcus left work early, anxious to escape the irritable temper of the office staff. He'd taken off his jacket and tie even before getting into the car. The air conditioner had not been working, so he rolled down all the windows as he pulled out of the parking lot and headed to the body shop where Peter worked as a painter. Marcus stopped only at a drive-through for a cold drink.

An hour later he parked in front of the body shop, went into the office, and asked for his brother. "He should be in the paint shed," the shop owner told him. "He's finishing a job."

"I don't want to disturb him," Marcus answered. "I'm a little early."

"No problem. You can head around back," he said, pointing. "Door should be open."

Marcus stepped out of the office and walked along the side of the aluminum building, careful to stay out of the sun. The sound of compressors, grinders, and torches overpowered the noisy traffic of the old highway. Just as Marcus came to the corner of the building, he heard voices. Though he could not explain his decision, he stopped moving, afraid to interrupt the conversation. Recognizing one of the voices, he leaned forward, trying to catch the words.

Peter spoke. "How much?"

"About one kilo apiece."

"Pure?"

"The best."

"When?"

"Depends on you."

"On me?"

"We need a decoy."

"Keeshan? No way." Peter seemed adamant.

"It's too late for other kids. The shipment is ready. We have to move quickly or it will go somewhere else."

"Celia would never let him go."

"Tell her you're taking him to visit relatives."

"She'd see right through it."

"Then lie. Send her to visit her parents. Tell her you'll take care of the baby."

"Why not someone else's kid?"

"Because we need yours. Now!"

"Look. I manage the stuff once you get it into the country. It isn't my job to get it here. Go find someone else to do your dirty work."

"It's only Panama. We'll have him back in three days."

"I can't."

"You can. I can make you. You know it."

As Marcus listened, his anger grew. It didn't take a detective to understand the conversation. Peter was back in the drug business. After all the lectures, all the jail time, all his promises to change, Peter had returned to his old way of life.

Disgusted and sick, Marcus turned and crept through the shadow to the front of the building. Careful not to be seen, he got into his car and drove away. About four miles south of the shop, he'd stopped at a tavern and hidden in a dark booth while he considered his options.

The sound of a horn dragged Marcus back to the present.

He was sweating, though not from the heat. A car passed him on the right, and he ignored the crass gesture of the other driver. Marcus signaled and moved into the slow lane.

Though years had gone by, Marcus could still smell the smoke that hung in the tavern on that day. He'd sat for more than an hour wondering what to do. He'd prayed. He'd worried. He'd let himself feel anger and betrayal. He'd considered strangling his brother with his own bare hands. And then he decided.

In the end, he'd done what he had to do. From the telephone booth on the corner, he'd canceled his dinner with Peter. Then he'd called a friend in the police department and turned Peter in.

Marcus didn't know enough to be a witness. He hadn't seen a drug deal. He'd only overheard a conversation. But he knew enough to help the police complete their own investigation. He'd given them names and addresses, suspicions and past history. They'd put the case together on their own.

Marcus didn't convict Peter; he'd only set the wheels of justice in motion. By the time his brother was arrested, the police had uncovered one of the largest and most successful drug rings in Florida history. Once Peter was in custody, Marcus helped Celia pack up her belongings and leave. It had been the hardest day of his life, helping to destroy his brother's family. He'd told himself he was keeping her safe. Keeping the infant safe. That it was necessary.

It cost Marcus. Presario had threatened him. Once, on his way to church, he'd spotted someone following him. Later, someone broke into his apartment. He felt vulnerable, violated.

He decided to run, to disappear until all of the trials were over.

Even now as he drove down the highway, he wondered. Had he made the right choice? Maybe he should have gone with Celia. Maybe he should have protected her.

Instead, he ran, though he continued to watch both the investigation and the prosecuting attorney from a distance. Marcus became an expert at keeping up via television and Internet sources. When he could, he called his contact.

One by one, the police took the drug ring apart, charging and convicting its members, using them one against the other until at last, nearly three years later, only two men awaited trial. Presario disappeared. Walked right out of the courthouse.

Ortega went free.

And now Celia was dead. He shook his head, still unwilling to think of her that way. As Marcus drove north, he made his decision. No longer would he cower in fear. No longer would Presario's threats control him. No. He would face Presario if he had to. And he would find his nephew. Marcus Jefferson would find and raise the boy.

>>>

As Keeshan crawled up the slide of the big toy, Callie sat down on a nearby bench. Her father parked his chair beside her and locked the brakes. "Why do you have the child?"

"His mother was killed, Dad. Someone needed to take him."

"They have foster care for cases like that."

Keeshan crept across a plank bridge toward a set of monkey bars. She smiled, remembering Officer Moriarty as he begged her to take the boy. "I know. The police officer investigating the accident said the system was overcrowded. They would've sent him across the state."

"And that's your fault?" Her father glanced at her, his face tight.

Callie took a deep breath. "No. Not my fault. I wanted to take him. It's the least I can do for Celia. At least until they find her family."

"He's a half-breed."

Callie turned to stare at her father, too stunned for a moment to speak. Even his voice had changed, had become low and hateful. She barely recognized him. "How can you even say that? What does that have to do with anything?"

"I'm just making an observation."

Callie's father had always held firm beliefs about racial segregation. He'd never wanted her to date anyone of another race. But this observation, even from him, seemed surprising. "So what are you saying? I shouldn't care for him because his skin isn't the same color as mine?"

"I'm not trying to be hateful here. I'm a pragmatist. He would be better off with his own people."

"That's ridiculous. He lived next door. Celia was my friend. I know him. He knows me."

Her father spun his chair to face her, his features hardened by anger. "You want to keep the boy."

Callie sputtered. "I didn't say that...the authorities are looking for her family..."

"It's been days since the accident. She's dead, and they haven't found anyone yet."

"True, but it's still early."

"You want to keep him," he repeated.

Though she hadn't yet allowed herself to think these thoughts out loud, she realized that her father was right. As usual, he'd brought out the truth, a truth so fearful she could hardly bear to face it. Could it be? Might it be possible for her to keep Keeshan? To raise him herself? "It's too early, Dad."

"Callie, you aren't getting any younger. What would a man think, seeing you with that boy? I'll tell you. He'd think the boy belongs to you. That you were part of an interracial marriage. A mixed relationship. "

Callie could hardly believe her father. This conversation seemed to get weirder by the minute. "If having Keeshan makes a difference to a man, I wouldn't want him. I don't want to be with a man who's concerned with color."

"That's easy to say now. But wait. Wait until you're old and alone, and all you have is a child who's grown up and forgotten you." Her father turned his chair to face Keeshan, now sliding down a pole like a firefighter. "Then you'll wish you'd thought about it," he said. "You'll wish you'd never thought of keeping him."

Though they parted amicably, Callie was deeply disturbed by her father's warning. As she ran errands, she tried to attribute his irrational prejudice to bitterness. After all, his own life had taken a painful and unalterable turn. He'd recently been widowed. He'd lost a foot, and with it, his ability to walk, his independence, his hobbies. Though he'd chosen to leave his dream home and move into a retirement community, it couldn't have been an easy adjustment. He had yet to make friends. He'd lost ties to the people in his old church. Perhaps he was depressed and so enveloped in his own pain that he could not spare any sympathy for the heartbreak of others.

The more she thought about Keeshan, the more defensive Callie became. What if this accident, horrible as it was, was something more than bad luck or a twist of fate? Until this morning, Callie thought of Keeshan as nothing more than a detour in the path of her life. An obligation—temporary as it might be—that she could discharge before moving on. But what if this accident, and the boy himself, were not a detour? What if this was the path God meant for her? Could God use this horrible accident to bring the boy into her life? Might this detour actually lead her down her own divine path?

Keeshan seemed blissfully unaware of Jack's hateful attitude. For this Callie was grateful. As he napped in the car, Callie considered her father's words. What did it matter to him if she hoped to keep the boy? Would it be so horrible?

After all, Callie would never marry. Though she'd come close, too close, the betrayal she'd experienced at the hands of Scott Friel had cauterized her heart forever. She would never allow herself to be that vulnerable again. In the years since she'd moved to Prospect, she had learned to accept this pain. This chosen loneliness.

She had a church family, a business life, a home. She didn't need to be married. Why couldn't other people see that? Though Callie O'Brian could live without marriage, she did not think she could survive if she let this opportunity pass by. Her father was right. If it were possible, she would keep Keeshan forever.

>>>

Callie took the phone call from the medical examiner's office on Tuesday afternoon. "Ms. O'Brian, this is Bob Wright from the King County Medical Examiner's office."

She glanced at Keeshan, who sat coloring by himself, oblivious to her conversation. "Thank you so much for returning my call."

"You left a message asking about the next of kin for Ms. Celia Hernandez?"

"Right. I was wondering what you'd found."

"Actually, I worked on it most of yesterday. The information you provided the hospital was very helpful. We were able to trace the baby's father to a prison in Florida, where he's serving a twelve-year sentence. The name on the birth certificate is incorrect. She was married at the time of the birth to a man named Peter Jefferson. According to vital records, Ms. Hernandez divorced her husband two years ago. His parental rights were terminated in that action."

"So he doesn't count."

"Essentially, that's correct. However, we did arrange to have him notified about her death. Obviously, he won't be claiming the body."

"What about her family? Have you found anyone?"

"No. In fact, I suspect they may be illegal aliens who've returned to Mexico."

"How did you come up with that?"

"I talked with the counselor at the high school where Celia graduated. He remembered Ms. Hernandez because he helped find a college scholarship for her. Apparently, your friend was a remarkable student."

"That doesn't surprise me. She was very bright."

"The family had several children in school at the time. Several years after Ms. Hernandez graduated, the others were pulled out of school. The family disappeared entirely."

"So how do we find them?"

"We don't. If they returned to Mexico, it would be virtually impossible. As for me, I'm out of it. The law only requires that I make a reasonable effort to locate the family. I've done that. Now I'll just put the body on rotation."

"Rotation?"

"We keep a list of local funeral homes. When we have indigent remains, we simply call the next business on the list and ask if they'll take the body. The morticians take turns caring for unclaimed remains at their own expense."

"What about friends? Can friends claim the body?"

"Of course. The law allows friends to claim the deceased when there is no relative."

"Then we want Celia."

"I'll make a note of that. Just call our office after you make arrangements."

After Callie hung up, she put her head in her hands and cried. Just five days ago, her friend was happy and healthy. Now, everything had changed. Callie had only begun to comprehend the loss. Every reminder opened the wound, and once again Callie bled fresh grief.

When her crying eased, she realized she had promised to arrange for the body. What was she thinking? She didn't know anything about burial services, funerals, or even memorials, for that matter.

Callie called the pastor of her church. "I just talked to the medical examiner's office. They can't locate Celia's family. I agreed to claim her body, but I don't have the money to pay for a burial. What should I do now?"

Pastor Roger chuckled. "First take a deep breath and calm down," he said. "I'm sorry about your friend. You did the right thing. We'll take care of it. We can have the memorial here at the church, and I can call someone from our Kiwanis group to make the arrangements for burial.

Why don't you and Angie see if you can plan a light dinner after the memorial? Her friends will want time to visit after the service."

Four days later, Callie took Keeshan to the service for his mother. Wearing a miniature suit and tie and brand-new shoes, he looked like a model in a children's catalogue. He seemed blissfully unaware of his surroundings—that is, until he spotted the life-sized picture of his mother on the platform. Keeshan pointed to the picture and began to cry.

In the course of the afternoon, he got all the attention of a rock star. People patted his curls, picked him up and hugged him, and squatted to ask him questions. Keeshan remained reserved, often backing up to hide behind Callie's skirt. His thumb never left his mouth.

Though Callie worried that the event would overwhelm him, she felt it essential that he attend. In spite of his age, she hoped that some part of the day, some moment would remain with him. At the very least, Callie hoped that Keeshan would remember the number of people who loved and respected his mother.

Callie and Angie arranged to videotape the open mike section of the memorial. Someday, Keeshan might want it to remember his mother.

When the day was over, Callie felt more alone than she ever had in her life.

Eighteen

Callie first began to understand the social worker's warning on the morning after the funeral when she went to get Keeshan out of bed. "Hey, squirt," she said, "time to wake up. You need to get some breakfast."

She wiggled his shoulder gently. "Keeshan, are you awake?"

He stirred and stretched. She sat beside him, leaning on her hand. "Oh, yuck," she said, lifting her hand from the wet spot she discovered spreading out from under the boy. Keeshan, who had been potty trained for years, had wet his bed. The strong smell of urine made Callie's stomach lurch. "Keeshan, get up and head to the bathroom. I'll run some water in the tub, and after your bath we can make breakfast."

"I don't want a bath."

"Sorry, buddy. You've wet the bed. You have to clean up."

He looked down at the sheets as though to confirm her story. With one thumb in his mouth, he wiped the sheets with his other hand. Tears formed in his eyes, and he looked up at her, emotion squeezing his features. Was he embarrassed? Frustrated? Or had he just remembered that his mother was gone? There was no way for Callie to know what the boy was thinking.

"Don't worry about the bed, honey. I can change the sheets."

He nodded, blinked, and crawled out of bed. With one hand he slid off his pajama pants, stomping them with his feet as he pulled them off his legs. Without another objection, he headed for the bathroom.

Callie followed and started water in the tub. She stripped the sheets and threw them in the hallway. The mattress pad was soaked, and urine had found its way to the surface of the mattress. Callie grimaced.

With many tears, both hers and Keeshan's, Callie managed to bathe and dress the boy. She boiled eggs for herself while he ate Dynobuddies. As she finished getting ready, she turned on the television and let Keeshan watch Sesame Street. From the kitchen telephone, she called the coffee shop. "It's not going well this morning" she told Jan. "We're running a little late. I'll be there as soon as I can."

Then she called the day care. "I'm going to bring Keeshan in this morning just like normal," she said. "But I think he's having a hard time of it; he doesn't seem to respond when we talk. It's like part of him understands, but the feelings are so deep he can't get to them."

"That's the way it is with kids," Peggy Mortensen said. "Thanks for letting me know."

"Keeshan, time for school. Go get your coat." He did not move. Instead, he stared straight ahead, his thumb in his mouth, his eyes focused on the television screen. "Keeshan, your coat is in the laundry room," Callie said.

When she turned off the television and helped him off the floor, she discovered he had been sitting on his mother's nightgown, the satin fabric pulled up between his legs. His fingers moved constantly, rubbing the blue fabric. The sight of him, comforting himself with his mother's gown, nearly broke Callie's heart. Stifling her own tears, Callie headed to the laundry room for the coat.

After putting him in the car, she set out for the day care. Try as she might, she could not engage him in conversation. "Do you remember what we talked about last night, Keeshan?" she asked.

He did not answer.

"We talked about your mama. Now do you remember?"

Again he did not respond. She adjusted the rearview mirror so that she could see his little face. His lids were held tightly closed, the eyeballs moving wildly beneath his silken skin. Unable to shut out her words, Keeshan had chosen to shut out the world.

She gave up.

At the day care, she parked the car and helped him from his seat. Keeshan pushed against her and held firmly onto the sides of the seat. "No," he said, tears filling his eyes. "No Peggy."

"It will be fun. Come on Keeshan."

"NO."

"Your friends are waiting for you."

"NO."

"If you go, I'll buy you some ice cream on the way home this afternoon."

"NO." His lower jaw jutted forward, and he closed his eyes in fierce determination. "I want to go home!"

Callie, being older and stronger and every bit as determined as the boy, leaned over the seat. Sliding her forearm in under his behind, she pried him loose. "Keeshan. You're going to day care. You'll be fine. You like Mrs. Mortenson and you like the other kids." She backed out of the rear passenger door. "Now," she said, throwing his body over her shoulder, "let's go."

>>>

The pilot's voice woke Marcus from a shadowy, dream-filled sleep, urging him to look out the left side of the airplane. Marcus obliged, fascinated by the ragged appearance of an enormous mountain poking its head through heavy clouds. The mid-morning sun reflected off its snow-covered peak. Moments later, as his plane floated low over the Seattle metro area, he spotted lakes and forests and Puget Sound with green-and-white ferries crossing the water, their wake extended over a wide V behind them. Marcus had never been anyplace so beautiful.

Carrying only a duffle bag, he boarded a metro bus, and inside of forty minutes had arrived in downtown Seattle. His driver, a wiry black man, pointed down a broad avenue. "You can't miss it, son. It's three blocks that way," he said, as Marcus climbed down the steps. "That library is somethin' you just don't miss."

Marcus waved as the driver pulled away from the curb. *How many times did Dad help strangers that same way?* William Ovid Jefferson had served the city of Indianapolis for more than twenty-three years as a bus driver. Today, in this strange city, his father's life seemed a worthy investment.

Slinging his duffel over one shoulder, Marcus crossed the street and headed south on Fourth Avenue. Though he knew he could get the information he needed at the King County Coroner's office, Marcus did not feel strong enough to handle the questions of bureaucrats. He knew he could not tell them where he had been or why they could not locate Celia's family. He did not want their questions to keep him from the child. No. He wouldn't go to the authorities unless he had to.

Nothing could have prepared Marcus for this library. Shaped like an elaborate hat, it was a honeycomb of steel and glass, filled with wide-open spaces and expansive ceilings. Strikingly decorated, with bright colors and natural light, it was the kind of structure that thrilled Marcus and reminded him of his first calling.

Pushing away his memories, he started up a bright yellow escalator and went immediately to the reference desk. "I'd like to find out about a death," he said without elaboration.

>>>

Callie was more than an hour late to work. Parking behind the shop, she shut off the engine and turned in her seat. "Keeshan, you wanted to come with me and here you are. Now I expect you to behave. No more temper tantrums."

His hand was stuck in his mouth, his lips pulling his thumb in and out. His eyes still shone from the tears he'd shed at the day care. Callie tried to shake the memory of his outburst from her mind. She didn't know how long she could stand his unruly conduct. Part of her wanted to spank him. Another part wanted to comfort him. And somewhere very near the surface, Callie still wished she'd never spoken to Michael Moriarty.

Keeshan got out of the car willingly and Callie led him across the street and through the back door of the coffee shop. Inside she took off his coat and hung it on the hook under her own. She put his hat and mittens on the upper shelf, and ran her fingers through her disheveled hair. Grabbing her baseball hat off the shelf, she pulled a fistful of hair through the opening in the back. Then she slid on her apron.

"I want a hat," Keeshan said, holding up his hands.

"Fine," she said, handing him hers. "Be my guest."

Callie heard the sound of the cash register. Jan called out, "You're late."

"I know. I'm sorry." Callie led Keeshan into the dining room and plunked him on a chair.

"Have a great day, Mollie," Jan said, closing the till. The shop door had hardly closed before Jan came around the counter. "What on earth is this?" she said, raising her eyebrows as she pointed at Keeshan. "I thought he was going to day care."

"I thought so too." Callie said, bending over Keeshan. "You can color while I work. But you have to stay here and be very good, all right?" She placed coloring books and crayons in front of him and knelt down. "I'll be right over there in the kitchen, okay?"

He nodded. "I could help you."

"Thanks," she stood up. "But you can help me most if you'll just stay here and color." She reached out and rubbed the top of his head. Looking at Jan, she tipped her head, indicating they should move out of Keeshan's hearing. She led the way to the storage room doorway.

"What happened?" Jan whispered.

"Wish I knew."

"You took him to day care, didn't you?"

"He wouldn't even get out of the car. I dragged him in and he pitched a fit in the lady's living room. He was screaming and crying, kicking and rolling. I couldn't leave him there with her. It didn't seem fair to either of them." Callie twisted her shoulder length hair into a rubber band. "I didn't know what else to do. The lady suggested I take some toys and see how he does with me at the store."

"But he's been going to that day care for years, hasn't he?"

"Ever since Celia moved to town, as far as I know." Callie washed her hands at the big sink, drying them on a bar towel.

"I wonder what happened?"

"Come on, Jan, his mother died. We just had the funeral."

"But you told me on the phone this morning that you didn't think he even knew."

"Who knows what he knows? He hardly ever talks. I've been thinking about my niece and nephew lately. At this age they said more in five minutes than he's said in three days. And then, when you least expect it, he swings from this charming, quiet little boy into a raging monster."

"Almost like a teenager."

"Very funny."

"It's not funny if you actually have a teenager. What're you going to do?"

"I don't know. I'm going to try to get through today. I can't plan any further than that."

"Listen, this is serious. You could be saddled with this kid forever."

Once again hope fluttered through her mind like a feather in the wind. She shook her head, determined to keep her secret. "Don't be silly. It wouldn't happen. In the first place, I'm not qualified. Besides that, no sane person would ever leave a child with me permanently. I'm single. I'm broke. I can hardly take care of myself, let alone a child."

"You know, I've been thinking."

Callie frowned and lifted a sack of coffee beans from under the shelf. With a pair of kitchen shears, she opened the top of the bag and poured the beans into the grinder.

"Don't you even want to know what I've been thinking?"

The smell of coffee beans permeated the air. Callie stuck her nose above the empty bag and took a whiff. "Doesn't matter what I want. You'll tell me anyway."

"I'm thinking that somewhere, this little boy has a father. Certainly he would come for him if he knew what had happened to Celia. Then you'll be back to opening the store in the mornings."

"One week and you're already tired of it?"

"Me? Four in the morning? How can you think that?"

"I hate to break it to you, sweetie, but Keeshan's dad is out of the picture. He's in jail."

>>>>

The small-boned librarian in heavy glasses listened carefully as Marcus explained his request. "Yes, sir," she said, nodding, her tiny mouth puckered as if she'd just finished a glass of lemon juice. "We have several ways to obtain that kind of information. I can start by checking with the Social Security Administration. We're paid subscribers to that site."

Marcus waited, leaning against the counter, while the reference librarian checked her computer. She sat facing him, the reflection of the screen completely obscuring her eyes. She typed and waited, and typed and waited. Marcus stifled his impatience. At last she rose and moved toward him, a sort of Goth in dark stockings and a shapeless black dress. "Her name is not listed, but the listing is about two months behind. My guess is that your sister-in-law died some time within the last sixty days."

"How can I find out where it happened?"

"Well, one way would be to check the obituaries published in local papers. You're certain the death happened in Washington?"

Marcus nodded. "I think so. Which ones?"

"We have a registered service. I'd be able to look up your relative in a matter of minutes. It's much more current than the SSA."

"Sounds like it might work."

"Only if the obituary appeared in a paper covered by our service. Otherwise, you might have to do an individual search, paper by paper. If there was a news story about her death—even if you don't know where it happened—you might find that the article mentions a hometown or even a neighborhood. That would give you another clue."

While the librarian checked the obituary files, Marcus sat down at the library's Internet connection. He began with a broad search for articles in Washington State. As he worked Marcus prayed that whatever had happened had found its way into a local newspaper. He had to find something, some hint of where his sister-in-law had gone.

Newspaper by newspaper, he entered Celia's name. Nothing. *This will never work. I might as well go out on the street and call her name.* Sliding off the stool, he stood and stretched. Discouragement pressed down on him until he felt bone weary. Hungry and frustrated, he considered giving up. There had to be another way. An easier way. He leaned against the counter and prayed for inspiration.

Try again. Use her maiden name.

Hernandez. He had searched for Celia using his family name— Jefferson. It hadn't returned any matching hits. This time, using Hernandez, Marcus struck gold. Within minutes, he had the full text of the accident story, published in the *Tacoma News Tribune*. A follow-up article reported that Celia had died on March 4 in a Seattle hospital. Her hometown was listed as Prospect, Washington.

Marcus leaned over the keyboard. Covering his eyes with his hands, he gave way to his grief. Surprised by his own tears, Marcus realized that even as he searched, he'd hoped to come up empty-handed. Hoped that Celia was alive. That his brother was lying. That it was a mistake. But it wasn't.

Celia was dead, and wherever he was, the boy needed him.

"Excuse me, sir," the librarian bent over his desk, whispering. "We didn't find the obituary you requested. Perhaps we don't have the correct name?"

Wiping away tears, Marcus spoke, his voice broken. "I found a news story that led to the obituary." He pointed to the computer screen. "Thanks for helping me look."

Even the Goth had feelings. She touched his shoulder in sympathy. "I'm sorry, sir," she said. "Would you like a copy for your records?"

"That would help," he said. "Thank you."

With the paper tucked in his wallet, Marcus walked out of the library. He didn't have much time. He needed to find his nephew.

>>>

At three in the afternoon, Callie began her cleanup routine. Though she hadn't closed the shop in months, the procedures came back to her without a problem. She emptied the trash in the dining room and wiped down all the tables. She filled the straw and napkin holders and brought coffee stirrers from the pantry and refilled the dispenser by the cash register.

After moving all of the fresh pastries in the bakery cabinet onto the top shelf, she removed the display trays and carried them to the kitchen sink. She filled a pail with hot soapy water and began wiping down the lower two shelves. Kneeling on the rubber floor pad, with her head caught between the lower two shelves, she scrubbed. After pulling a paper towel from the roll, she crawled back inside to dry the plastic. With a toothbrush, she brushed the crumbs hiding in the tracks for the sliding doors. She felt a tap on her shoulder.

"Callie, I have a stomachache."

She backed out of the cabinet and turned, still kneeling. Her head slammed into the upper shelf of the display unit.

"It hurts." He rubbed his protruding belly.

I'll bet. Callie rubbed the back of her head. "Where?"

"Here," he pointed. His eyes filled with tears and he said again, "It hurts in my tummy."

Callie stood up, put an arm around his shoulders and led him back to the table where he'd left his toys. She put him in the chair and bent down before him. Concerned, she felt his forehead. His skin felt cool and dry. "Do you hurt anywhere else?"

He shook his head.

"What about your throat?"

Again he answered no.

"Your head?"

"Just my tummy." As his whine began to grow, Callie feared it would stretch itself into a wail. "It hurts so much."

"How about some milk? Maybe that would settle your tummy?"

He shook his head.

"What about pop? I have some ginger ale in the frig."

He nodded, his eyes brightening. "I could drink some pop. I like root beer."

"Let's try the ginger ale. That's best for a sore tummy," she said. On her way to the kitchen, she closed the sliding doors to the pastry cabinet and picked up her bucket. Half-filling a paper cup with soda, she brought it to Keeshan, carefully transferring it into his small hands. "Here drink this," she said. "Be careful not to spill."

Filling his cheeks with pop, he swallowed one enormous gulp.

"Slow down, kiddo. I'm going to finish cleaning while you drink that, okay?"

He nodded, and she moved to the corner of the dining room, where she began stacking chairs upside down on the tables. When she finished, she brought out the broom and swept the red tile floor. Callie took care to clean the grout lines and corners. Even so many days after the last snowstorm, all of her customers' shoes carried sand into the shop. The grating of sand on tile gave her goosebumps, like fingernails on a blackboard.

She brought out the bucket again, and began mopping the floors. Keeping an eye on Keeshan, she worked her way across the floor from counter to front door. He watched her as she worked, slowly drinking the pop. After every sip, he replaced the cup on the table, sliding it toward the center of the table and leaning back in the chair. Between sips, he held his stomach, always in the same place, rubbing it with one hand as followed her progress.

She'd just reached the center of the dining room when he began to cry again. She frowned and continued cleaning. The cry escalated and Callie turned her back to him, determined to finish the floor without further distraction.

Finally, Callie turned around to find the boy rolling on the floor, his hands holding his stomach, his body folded around the pain in his gut. This new position frightened her, and she went to him at once.

"Keeshan," she said, picking him up. "Come here, baby." She sat in a chair and held him on her lap, rocking as she spoke. "I'm sorry, honey," she said, rubbing his stomach as she rocked. "I'm so sorry."

He quieted again, and she offered him more ginger ale. Carrying him to the telephone, she called the only parenting advisor she knew. "Angie, this is Callie," she began, without wasting time. "Something's wrong with Keeshan. He's got a terrible stomachache." The boy held the cup out to her, and she took it. "I don't know what to do. Do I take him to a doctor? I don't know whether or not it's serious."

Angie asked about Keeshan's symptoms.

"What do you think?"

"I think it might be a good idea to call someone," Angie said.

"Who? I don't know who his doctor is. How many pediatricians are there in the valley?"

"You're in luck," Angie said. "I happen to know that Celia uses my doctor because she uses my sister's doctor, and I use my sister's doctor."

"I think it's easier if you don't try to explain it."

"I'll get the number."

Callie hung up quickly and dialed the pediatrician's office. In a matter of minutes, she realized that her entire evening had just been shot.

Nineteen

Callie had to explain her relationship with Keeshan to the receptionist at the pediatrician's office. Once again, having to tell someone about Celia's death opened Callie's pain like an envelope. Her voice trembled as she spoke.

"No problem," the woman responded. "All our parents sign a permission form allowing us to treat the child no matter who brings him into the office. How soon can you come?"

Callie drove to the office in record time, beside herself with worry. Keeshan continued to complain about his stomach through the entire trip. After signing in at the front desk, she took a seat in the waiting area. Keeshan began the wait on her lap, his thumb in its usual location. For the first time, he leaned up against her, sliding one arm around her chest as he rested his head on her shoulder. He was quiet, still.

More than once she felt his head for a temperature.

The waiting room was full at this late afternoon hour. In the chairs beside Callie, moms and dads with babies and school-aged children waited to see the doctor. All the paraphernalia of the parenting life— the car seats, the diaper bags, the baby blankets—covered the floor around the chairs. In one corner sat a play area full of wooden bins of blocks and cars and puzzles.

As the toys beckoned, Keeshan eventually slid off her lap. He crossed the room, careful to keep an eye on the other children as he moved to the bin containing the building blocks. Before long, he had built a castle of oversized yellow blocks.

Callie picked up a magazine and tried to concentrate. She hadn't heard a single complaint from the boy since he'd gone to play. In fact, he seemed perfectly happy. He didn't hold his tummy. He no longer rolled along the floor.

By the time the nurse called Keeshan's name, Callie felt completely duped. The little monster was faking it, she decided. He'd developed an imaginary illness, and now she was undoubtedly going to pay to see a doctor unnecessarily.

"Keeshan," she said, moving across the waiting room. "Time to go in and see the doctor." He did not look up. "Come on. Let's go." Ignoring her, he focused on his building project. "Keeshan. Now!"

Callie felt the steam begin to roll out of her ears. She glanced at the nurse, who watched with an amused expression. Callie bent down over Keeshan. "Get up now," she said through gritted teeth, hoping she sounded as threatening as a member of the Mafia.

He ignored her. Desperate, Callie took him by the wrist. "Come now, Keeshan. We have to see the doctor." The boy went limp, and Callie found herself dragging him across the waiting room by one arm.

"I want to play with the toys."

"You can play after we've seen Dr. Fisher."

He began to cry. "I want to play now."

"Later."

"You're hurting me."

"Then walk."

Over his loud objections, Callie heard the office staff laugh. The eyes of everyone in the waiting room followed her progress to the exam room. She'd never been so grateful to close a door behind her. Embarrassed and frustrated, Callie collapsed in another chair and waited for the doctor.

Younger than she expected, Dr. Fisher had intense blue eyes that drew Callie like a magnet. When he spoke, a large dimple flashed on the right side of his mouth. "So tell me about Keeshan," he began.

Callie explained about the boy's stomachache, carefully avoiding the accident or Celia's death. Keeshan stood with his tummy against a chair, paging through a children's book.

Dr. Fisher walked across the room and squatted behind the boy. "Hey, Keeshan, that's a nice book you have there."

Keeshan glanced at the doctor.

"Can you find Waldo?"

Keeshan stuck one pudgy finger on the page.

"Right on! You have a good eye there. Hey, your friend Callie tells me you've been having a tummy ache. Is that true?"

Keeshan nodded.

"Why don't you jump up here on my table," the doctor began. He pulled out the footstool below the exam table and let Keeshan climb up by himself. Callie took a deep breath and relaxed. *At last,* she thought, *someone who knows how to handle children.*

As the doctor made requests, Keeshan responded. The boy coughed, turned, breathed, and held still on cue. The more obedient Keeshan appeared to be, the more Callie began to question her desire to keep him. Whatever she asked, Keeshan did the opposite.

Either this doctor was a magician or she was a failure.

When he was finished, Dr. Fisher took off his stethoscope and dropped it into his jacket pocket. "Well, Keeshan, you are one healthy specimen," he said, offering the boy his palm. Knowing what was expected, Keeshan slapped the hand with his own. "I'm thinking you'd like a lollipop. How's that sound?" He stepped over to the door and opened it. "Ms. O'Brian, why don't you come with us?"

Following blindly, Callie watched as the doctor settled Keeshan and his prize in the play area. "He'll be fine here," the doctor said. "Lydia, would you keep an eye on Keeshan for us? I'd like to visit with Ms. O'Brian in my office."

Moments later, Callie faced the doctor across a coffee table. "What is it? What's wrong with Keeshan?"

"Nothing, physically," he said, crossing one foot over his knee. "But the boy has been through a lot. He's grieving."

"Grieving?"

"Children grieve differently than adults. He can't tell you what he's feeling. But let me assure you, he's feeling it just as keenly as you might feel if you lost your husband."

"So you're saying the stomachache is psychological?"

"Not exactly. His pain is as real as if he had an ulcer. His stomach genuinely hurts."

"I don't understand then."

"Has he had any sleeping problems?"

"He's been wetting the bed. He never used to do that."

"What about behavior? Is he upset easily?"

"He wouldn't go to day care today."

"You see, these are the kinds of things preschool children do when they grieve. They don't process death the way we do. They don't know how to talk about their loss. They don't understand the permanence of death. We know mommy is gone forever, and they wonder why won't mommy come back? They think they did something to cause the death. Why aren't things the way they ought to be?

"They notice the adults around them acting differently—crying, whispering, coming around in droves. When normal life stops, children notice—even if they don't understand.

"So the children, who can't process what they see, are confused. They act out. They regress. They may not be able to concentrate. They may become destructive. Obedient children have temper tantrums. An independent child may become clingy one moment and push you away the next."

It seemed to Callie that the doctor had been living at her house. She pictured Keeshan clutching his mother's nightgown and remembered the temper tantrum at the babysitter's. "I think he's experienced a lot of those things."

"Then he's perfectly normal."

"Easy for you to say. He's not the same boy I knew when his mother was alive."

"The real Keeshan will be back."

"But what do I do in the meantime?"

"Let's try an antacid for the stomach pain." Dr. Fisher took a prescription pad out of a drawer and began writing. "If we treat his discomfort, eventually the other stuff will work its way out. I have a booklet on grief and preschool children." He walked to a four-drawer file. "I think this will help you help Keeshan. In the meantime, call me if you have questions. We'll treat the physical symptoms as they occur. Your job is to concentrate on the emotional symptoms."

Callie confessed, "I have no idea how to do that."

He handed her the brochure. "Some of it is in there. The rest will come to you. Start by assuring him that you won't leave him. Give him what he needs—lots of reassurance. Hold him. Hug him. Listen to him. Let him regress. It won't last forever."

"I don't know if I can do this. I've never had children."

"Well, you have one now," he said, offering his hand. "Just remember four words: routine, love, honesty, and security. I'll help whenever I can. But really, I think you can do it. No matter how he behaves, he needs all the security you can give him."

>>>

As the days passed, and Keeshan continued to grieve, Callie came to understand the patterns of his pain. Shortly after his visit to the doctor, Keeshan began carrying his mother's nightgown with him everywhere. Callie made no effort to keep him from dragging the dirty satin garment along. Even his bed-wetting took on a pattern. It happened regularly after days that included visits to the guesthouse.

For several days after one of these trips, Keeshan insisted in drinking milk from a baby bottle. His behavior did not surprise Callie; she now knew enough to expect it. The little brochure from the doctor had suggested this might happen. Callie chose not to discourage him. Fortunately, after only two weeks, he gave up the bottle by himself.

Keeshan had moments of progress as well. Gradually he returned to his day care, at first spending only twenty minutes there with Callie playing alongside of him. Together, they drove trucks across the green rug in Peggy Mortenson's playroom. Three days later, they ate lunch at Peggy's, Callie and Keeshan at the same table with the other children.

On the first day that Callie left Keeshan alone, he cried as though his heart would break. And driving away, Callie shed tears of her own. When the lunch rush at the coffee shop ended, Callie called Peggy and asked about Keeshan.

"It was tough after you left," she admitted.

"What did you do?"

"I rocked him. He settled down eventually," she said. "He told me you wouldn't come back."

"How could he think that?"

"Well, the last time he stayed with me, his mother never came back. Kids make connections, you know."

Over the weeks Keeshan's quiet demeanor gradually gave way to a curious, effervescent talkativeness that alternately endeared him to Callie or frustrated her to death.

"Where does God live?"

"Why do deer live at our house and not in town?"

"Why do you plant flowers?"

"Can I help you plant vegetable seeds?"

"Can you make a truck?"

Occasionally, he punctuated his questions with absolute statements. "I can do it myself," referring to all areas of dressing. "I hate that," referring to any type of cheese product. "Look at me," referring to his frightening love for climbing furniture, fixtures, and trees.

Keeshan clearly expected Callie to listen when he talked, and any sign of inattentiveness was rewarded by an outburst of temper that challenged Callie's objections to corporeal punishment. In the end she actually did spank the boy, though not for an outburst of temper.

One morning before work, Callie came into her room to discover Keeshan on top of her dresser. He had left the drawers open, stacked like stairs leading to the top, where Callie kept her mother's favorite crystal bowl.

When he saw her Keeshan frowned, holding the bowl's lid in one hand, strands of necklaces in the other.

"Keeshan, what are you doing on my dresser? I've told you not to play with that bowl. Please get down."

"Can I have the pretty?" Keeshan held the jewelry toward her.

"No."

"Can I play with it?"

"No, Keeshan. I've told you. You may not play with my mother's bowl."

"I won't break it."

Callie moved over to the dresser and took away the crystal top. She picked him up, setting him on the ground with firm hands. "Don't you ever let me catch you playing with that again." One by one, she shut the drawers.

He stuck out his lip and turned abruptly, stomping from the room. Callie dressed hurriedly, pulling a sweater over her head just as the telephone rang. She jogged to the kitchen to answer it.

It was Jan. "Callie, can you come in early today?"

"How early?"

"Half an hour?"

"I can try. What's up?"

"My dentist's office just called with a cancellation. I can take it if I leave here fifteen minutes early, but thirty would really help."

"Go ahead..." a crash came from the back of the house. "Take it. Gotta go, Jan." Callie hung up and ran for the back bedroom.

Once again, she found Keeshan kneeling on top of her dresser, his face screwed up in horror. She stepped toward him, unwilling to believe that he might have done exactly what she told him not to do. As she came near the dresser, she recognized pieces of the crystal bowl scattered over the carpet. She glanced into the open drawers. Splinters of glass covered her underwear and below that, shards stuck up from her wool sweaters. "Keeshan, what are you doing?"

He began to cry.

"What did I tell you?"

Leaning back on his heels, he closed his eyes, his fingers spread. Callie leaned over the broken glass and snatched him from the dresser. This time she did not put him down. Instead, she shook him, watching as splinters of glass fell onto the carpet from his corduroy pants. "How can you disobey me like this? I told you to stay off the dresser." Callie could think only of the danger that might have come with so many shards of glass.

Keeshan sobbed.

She carried him into his own bathroom, anxious to move as far away as possible from the glass. "Keeshan, you've been a bad boy," she said, brushing off his clothes as she prepared to remove his pants. "You might have been cut or fallen off the dresser." The more she thought about the danger, and about her mother's crystal bowl, the angrier she felt. Then, before she could even think, Callie turned his little body around and gave him one enthusiastic swat on the behind.

His cry turned to anguished wails.

Then Callie began to cry with him. She sat down on the floor beside him, covering her face with her hands. How had she gotten herself into this? Would nothing ever be the same in her life? The more Keeshan wailed, the sorrier Callie felt for herself, and the more she cried. She pulled her sweater up over her face and sobbed. For her mother. For herself. For her life.

Then a miracle happened.

Callie felt small arms wrap themselves around her neck and squeeze. "Don't worry, Callie," Keeshan said. "I love you."

And for the first time, Callie knew she loved him too. And at that moment, with absolute clarity, she realized that she had to make their arrangement permanent.

》》》

The news of Celia's death hurt Marcus with a fresh pain he didn't expect. He couldn't think of her that way. He stumbled out of the library and out into the biting wind blowing off the Seattle harbor. Even as he walked, memories haunted him.

When Marcus last saw Keeshan, he'd been weeks old. A newborn, with all the personality of a dishtowel. From the first time Marcus saw mother and child together, he'd admired Celia's fierce, protective love.

Marcus remembered laughing when Peter told him the baby's name. "What made you choose Keeshan?" he'd asked, bewildered.

"You should talk," Peter had answered. "A man who was named after a doctor on a television show."

Marcus shook away the memory, and spotting a metro bus stop, he crossed the street. The bus company would know how to get to this tiny town where Celia had hidden.

By now, Keeshan would be—Marcus counted back the years—four years old. Walking and talking. A real human being. He could hardly imagine the boy. His nephew, almost a kindergartener.

Marcus was the only family Keeshan had left. The boy, who'd survived such a brutal beginning, deserved a father as faithful and hardworking as the one who'd raised Marcus. A father like the one Peter missed. Maybe, if Marcus could father Keeshan, he could prevent the loss of another generation. Keeshan deserved that much.

Marcus jogged toward the stop, unable to shake the anticipation that drove him forward. At last, everything was so clear. The questions were answered. Though he didn't know how, he would somehow manage to find and raise the boy.

As he ran, he prayed. Without divine help, there would be no way to find Keeshan.

In less than an hour, Marcus bought a Washington State map and made his way to the metro bus kiosk. "I need to get to Prospect," he told a white-haired customer service advisor named Carolyn.

Her eyebrows rose. "Prospect?" She shook her head, confused. "Where is Prospect?"

Marcus smiled and opened his map. "Right there," he said, pointing to the tiny letters printed nearly one hundred miles south and east of Seattle. "How do I get there?"

"Can I borrow this?"

Marcus nodded, and Carolyn carried the map over to another agent. After some discussion, they chose several pamphlets from a rack below the counter.

"Well, you have a few choices," she said, taking a highlighter from behind her ear. "Nothing will get you all the way to Prospect, but you can get close." She laid the pamphlets out on the counter. "And at this hour, we don't have many routes running out of town. You could take a bus, but you'd have to make several connections." She opened one of the schedules and traced the route with a yellow highlighter.

"In a couple of hours, there will be several routes running south again." She handed Marcus the pamphlet, shrugging, "Or you can head down to Union Station, and take the train all the way into Puyallup. That's much faster; there's no freeway traffic. From there, you can take a bus south to Graham. Of course, you'll have to take a taxi from there," she said, again pointing to the map. "Or I suppose the easiest thing would be to just rent a car."

With detailed instructions written on the outside of a bus schedule, Marcus made his way down Third Avenue. Though he had a three-hour wait, he would take the train to Puyallup. From there, he would take a bus as far south as he could. He would get to Prospect even if he had to walk the last 20 miles.

Twenty

As Callie entered the attorney's inner office, she couldn't escape the heat she felt building under her jacket. Perspiration dampened her sweater. It was one thing to care for the boy and quite another to make the whole thing legal.

This must be what a bride feels like on her wedding day.

Keeshan had needs, after all—for security, for permanence, for health insurance—and Callie told herself again that she was doing this for him. For his benefit. She had only come to ask questions. To gather information so that she could make an informed decision.

As Callie followed the secretary into the office, she took comfort from the calming hues of taupe and champagne. The attorney was already seated, waiting for her. She stood and came around her desk, her hand out in greeting. "Welcome, Ms. O'Brian. I'm Dorothy Powell. Please have a seat," she said, gesturing to a softly printed couch. Her smile seemed genuine, her hand warm and soft.

Dorothy Powell's hair was what some called salt-and-pepper, perfectly complemented by her olive complexion and deep brown eyes. The tiniest laugh lines betrayed her age, which Callie guessed to be nearly sixty. The woman wore charcoal pants with a blazer in steel blue tweed. The turtleneck underneath might have been cashmere. Callie liked the look of her. Somehow, the combination of class and beauty gave Callie confidence. She wondered if Mrs. Powell had the same effect on members of the court.

"Would you like some coffee?"

Callie detected the slightest Southern drawl. "No, thank you."

Mrs. Powell dismissed her secretary and retrieved a yellow tablet. "If you don't mind, I'd like to take notes while we talk." She sat down in a wing chair. "I understand you've come to talk to me about a custody issue?"

"That's correct."

"Tell me about the situation."

"Well, it's a long story," Callie said.

"I like long stories," she answered, and the laugh lines appeared again.

Beginning with renting the guesthouse to Celia and moving through the car accident, Callie explained how Keeshan had come to live with her. "The medical examiner's office tried to find Celia's family, but they seem to have completely vanished. The boy's father is in jail—serving a sentence for drug dealing. He won't be paroled for years."

"What about other family members—brothers, sisters, cousins—that kind of thing? Has the medical examiner looked for those?"

"They've looked everywhere. But so far they haven't found anyone."

"How can I help?"

"Well, I've talked to the intake counselor with Child Protective Services and with my insurance provider. Both suggested that I file for temporary custody."

"Why do you think you need temporary custody?"

"For a couple of reasons." Callie paused to order her thoughts. "First, Keeshan was covered by his mother's health insurance. Now that she has passed away, he has no coverage. My insurance will include him, but only if I have legal custody."

"That's a legitimate concern."

"There is one other thing," Callie stopped to clear her throat. No matter how she said it, her next concern would come out sounding like a gold digger. She took a deep breath and plunged forward. "I'm not a wealthy woman. I bought my home from my father, and I still owe a great deal of money on that contract. I used most of my savings as a down payment. Then, about four years ago, I started my own business. Two businesses, actually. Anyway, I hate how this sounds," Callie paused and brushed perspiration from the top of her lip. "The truth is, I've never had to budget for a child. Keeshan needs dental care and health care and day care. These are all expenses I didn't plan on."

"You don't need to apologize." Dorothy Powell put her pen and pad down on the table in front of her. "You're single, is that correct?"

Callie nodded.

"And your age?"

"Thirty-four."

"Single people rarely anticipate these kinds of expenses. That's the reason temporary custody exists—so that you can have access to resources to help you through this crisis."

"Thank you. This has all been very awkward."

"You do know that social security provides assistance for dependant children?"

"I had heard that. I've taken Keeshan to the pediatrician already, and I know how suddenly things can go wrong. I can't possibly provide medical care without insurance."

"All right, Ms. O'Brian," Dorothy said, picking up her notepad. "If you decide to take this next step, I think I can help you. However, we will have to document the medical examiner's attempts to locate the family."

"How?"

"I'm quite certain the ME's office can provide documentation when we request it." She jotted a note to herself. "There is one other thing. In this case, the court will want us to document that we've made an attempt to locate the family as well."

"What will that entail?"

"A thorough search of public records. Perhaps some personal ads in papers near the family's last home. Once I was required to hire a private detective to trace family. However, there was a substantial estate involved in that case."

"Will you do the search?"

"I can help you, but it will look better if we can document your own involvement." She stood and walked to the door, where she called the secretary. "Melody?"

"Yes, Mrs. Powell?"

"I'd like to begin a file for Ms. O'Brian. I'll need you to take notes, please. We're going to file for temporary custody for a Keeshan Hernandez."

>>>>

Two nights after visiting the attorney, Callie decided it was time to empty the guesthouse and advertise for a new renter. No matter what happened with Keeshan, she needed the rental income in order to pay her property taxes. She would have to take some money out of her savings in order to make the April 30 payment. But the second installment, due on October 31, would depend on renting the house.

Together, she and Keeshan went through the rooms, making a list of things to do before she could place an advertisement. She had walls to paint, carpet to clean, a light fixture that needed replacing, and a doorknob to fix.

The biggest chore—and by far the most painful—would be to empty the house of Celia's belongings. Callie had little hope of finding Celia's family. Still, she planned to store Celia's things in her garage. If someone ever showed up, Callie wanted to return all of Celia's possessions.

On Saturday of the next weekend, Callie did nothing more than box up Celia's household goods. With her favorite worship CD on the stereo, Callie began in the kitchen. She emptied cupboards, wrapping items as she stowed them. As she worked, she made a neatly printed list of the contents, taping the paper on the top of each box as she sealed it.

With Callie in the kitchen, Keeshan played in the living room, driving Matchbox cars through stacks of blocks set up on the carpet, apparently unconcerned about emptying his former home. She had worried that it would upset him to see his mother's things put away.

It took all morning to empty both the kitchen and the hall linen closet. After lunch Callie went into Celia's room and began working on her closet. Lovingly, Callie folded clothes, unable to drive away the memories that surfaced with each article of clothing. Try as she might, she could not forget how Celia looked in her dark wine dress. She could not drive away the image of Celia in her ski jacket or her flared jeans. One after another, memories flashed into Callie's mind, forcing her to grieve. As she worked, she fought with tears, praying as she folded and boxed.

She thanked God for the opportunity to know Celia. She remembered the nights they'd spent laughing over an old movie, the girl talk they'd shared on long walks through the woods. But the gratitude did not last long. When she let her thoughts come to rest, her gratitude was replaced by the deepest sense of loneliness she had ever felt. In those moments, Callie asked God how she would ever survive alone.

Callie made no effort to hide herself from God. She prayed for peace to replace her grief. She prayed for trust to replace her dismay over the horrible events that had happened in Prospect.

Callie emptied the hangers and moved on to the shelves. Here, her work progressed more steadily as photo albums stacked neatly into boxes. Callie could not open the albums. She could not allow herself to look at the memories Celia had so obviously treasured.

After a short break for dinner, Callie returned to finish Celia's room. She folded all of the things in Celia's dresser, making up a memory game to keep her mind occupied, her grief at bay. It nearly worked.

When Callie moved to the small table beside Celia's bed, she thought she'd made it. Then, in the open space under the nightstand, Callie found several novels, one written in Spanish, a cookbook, a book on child-rearing, and Celia's leather-bound Bible. Leaving the Bible on the bed, she stacked the rest in a box, indexing the titles on one of the flaps.

Callie could not resist the Bible. Celia's faith, though expressed in a different denomination, had been strong. She had often challenged Callie about passages of Scripture and things she'd read in books. Since her death, Callie realized that Celia's faith must have been forged in pain. It was the kind of faith that anchored her in the worst of storms.

Callie could use that kind of faith. She opened the Bible.

Inside, she found underlined passages, hand-printed margin notes, and full outlines of sermons written in the blank pages between books. Most of her notes were dated, and Callie skimmed the pages, wondering how long Celia had used this Bible. The oldest note was written just three and a half years ago.

Callie set the Bible aside. This was a treasure, far too precious to box up and leave in her garage. Though she didn't know what she would do with it, Callie would not leave it to mildew. Someday, Keeshan would come to know his mother through these notes.

Exhausted, she sat down on the couch behind the boy. "Well, that's it for today. You ready to go home?"

Pausing in his play, he flopped over on his bottom, and looked up at her. "This is my house," he said. "My mama lives here."

She patted the cushion next to her. "Come sit by me."

He scrambled up beside her, still clutching the ambulance he had been driving. She threw an arm around his shoulders. With the music still playing and the feel of his soft baby shoulders under her fingers, Callie began to cry.

She couldn't shake the resentment she felt about the accident. It seemed so unfair of God to leave him alone like this. He was only a child. Every child deserved to be raised by his mother. She grieved for herself as well. She deserved to have Celia too. Now without her, she felt desolate, lost.

Then, quite suddenly, Keeshan turned over and knelt on the couch next to her. "Don't cry, Callie," he said, putting his arms around her neck. "I will take care of you."

>>>>

On Sunday Callie arranged for friends to help her empty the furniture from the guesthouse. After church Angie and Don brought their two boys, and Jerry, Callie's friend from the bike club, brought his oldest son. Keeshan nominated himself supervisor.

They began by breaking down the beds and piling the parts in Callie's garage.

"You know," Don said to Callie, as he backed under the garage door with one end of the headboard, "you probably aren't obligated to keep this stuff."

Callie followed him, carrying the other end. "I know. I talked to the attorney. I could have auctioned it."

"So why didn't you?"

"I just want to have it in case the family ever shows up."

Jerry and his son came in with the box spring. "This mattress set ought to be thrown away," he said. "It's a piece of junk. I don't know why you're keeping it."

Callie laughed. "Tell me what you really think, Jerry." She pointed to the place they'd cleared for the mattresses. "Actually, I wish you guys were attorneys. It'd be great to get this much advice for free—especially if it were worth something."

"Don't criticize the help," Don said.

Angie came into the garage with two cushions from Celia's couch. Keeshan carried a single throw pillow. "Where do you want the boys to put the couch?"

"Lets leave the cushions there for a minute," Callie answered, pointing. "And then, if we could slide these boxes over here, we'll put the couch against the wall. We can stack boxes on top as soon as we get it in place."

They tugged and shoved and grunted until five large boxes had been moved out of the way. "That'll work fine," Callie said, wiping her hands on her jeans.

"I noticed the couch has a hide-a-bed," Angie said.

Callie nodded. "I checked the brand. It's a good one."

"Really? The fabric is terrible. Completely threadbare."

"Happens with the best brands."

"The frame is good?"

"Absolutely. All hardwood."

"Could you recover it?"

"Sure. It'd take a lot of fabric, though."

"Hey, Don, can we buy that couch?" She turned to her husband. "I'd like to put it in the den. We need extra space for guests."

"Right, so when your parents come to town, we get to sleep on the hide-a-bed."

"My mom needs to be near the bathroom."

"Time out, you two." Jerry said, holding his hands like a referee. "We're moving furniture here. No arguing until after we empty the house."

"We aren't arguing," Angie said. "We're discussing." She turned to Don. "Callie could re-cover the couch. We'd save a bunch of money in the long run."

"What happens when Celia's family shows up?" Jerry asked.

Angie frowned. "I'd pay them for the couch."

"That wouldn't save us any money," Don said.

"Are you kidding? In this condition, the couch isn't worth fifty bucks, is it Callie?"

Callie held her hands in mock surrender. "Don't pull me into this."

Angie looked up at Don, excitement in her eyes. "Can we do it?"

"I give up," he said. "Just promise me I don't have to sleep there when your parents come to visit."

Callie laughed. "Well, you guys can probably afford to put in one of those really good mattresses."

"Thanks, Callie," Don said. "I needed that."

The crew of friends emptied the little house in a little less than two hours. Though Callie wouldn't be able to park her SUV in her garage again, it felt gratifying to save Celia's things. When they'd finished, Angie and Don made one last trip back to Callie's workshop. With the hide-a-bed tucked in place, Callie gave Angie and Don sample fabric books to take home.

"It's up to you, but I'd stick with nylon or olefin," Callie said. "Try to stay away from rayon or cotton. With boys, you need it to wear, and your den gets too much natural light for cotton."

"How long will it take to cover?" Angie asked.

"What's the hurry?" Don asked. "Until this morning, we didn't even own it."

"I know. But now that we do, I'd like to get it over to the house. I'm excited."

"You should be. It'll be beautiful." Callie said. "If you like, we can change some of the details—like throw cushions instead of attached cushions—or a more modern arm shape. Once we order fabric, I can cover it in a couple of weeks."

"Great. That gives me time to paint and hang wallpaper."

Don rolled his eyes. "Oh, heavens. We start with a couch and now we have a complete makeover of the den? What about my favorite chair?"

"I'll let you keep that." Angie caught Callie in a swift hug. "I can hardly wait. Do you think you could help me pick paper?"

Callie laughed. "Of course."

Don picked up two fabric books and handed them to Angie. "Here, let's get out of here before you redo the whole house." He put one arm around his wife's shoulders. "Come on, dear," he said. "This morning has cost us too much already."

Callie and Keeshan walked Angie and Don to their car. Then, waving as they backed out of the driveway, Callie wondered how she would ever find time for this additional job.

Just what she needed, one more thing to accomplish.

>>>

One week after visiting the attorney, Callie worked the lunch rush at the coffee shop. Busier than normal, she kept her hands moving, forcing herself from sandwich to sandwich, from order to order, without thinking. When the bell over the shop announced a late afternoon customer, she did not look up from the beef-and-provolone sandwich she was making. Instead, she sliced it in half, wiped off the knife and returned it to the magnetic holder above the butcher block. Wrapping the sandwich in waxed tissue, she dropped it into a paper bag.

"Thomas," she called, reading the first name from the receipt in her hand.

She handed him the bag and his coffee. "Come again," she said, through a false smile. She faced her newest customer. "Can I help you?"

"Yes, please," answered an exceptionally tall, well-shaped African-American standing before the pastry counter. Few men were taller than Callie, but this man had at least five inches on her. He had the rough, hardened look of someone whose work demanded physical strength.

Thick brows hung across the darkest eyes she had ever seen, and Callie found that she could hardly look away from them. In her college years, she might have termed the eyes as sexy—though she was far too old now to consider such a phrase. A well-trimmed goatee surrounded lips that were not full, but rather—she tried to think of a word—shapely.

He was, perhaps, somewhere in his thirties, though the expression on his face seemed that of a man who'd seen the harsher side of life. Above one brow a scar—more of an indentation, really—slashed diagonally across his forehead, ending just above his nose. She found herself wondering what had happened, and too late she realized she was staring. She felt heat rise into her neck. "I'm sorry. What can I get for you?"

"I'd like a sandwich," he said. "What kind of bread do you have?" His voice was a pleasant tenor, not the deep bass she'd expected from his height.

She answered in her most professional voice, "Sourdough, whole wheat, nine-grain, and farmer's white."

"I'll take ham on nine-grain."

"Whole or half?"

"Whole."

"What kind of cheese?"

As he smiled, a glint came into his dark eyes. He was laughing at her. "What kind do you have?"

Without warning, Callie felt like a sophomore serving lunch to the captain of the football team. She didn't like the effect his smile had on her. It made her heart beat a little too fast, and somehow she felt horribly self-conscious. Irritated, she pointed to the menu board with her thumb. "Cheddar, Swiss, provolone."

"Cheddar," he answered.

"Mayo, mustard, lettuce, and tomato?"

"No tomato. Do you have juice?"

"Strawberry-kiwi, orange, and grapefruit."

"No apple?" Again the amused smile.

Callie bristled. "Did I say apple?" *This guy thinks he can charm me.*

The eyebrows rose, and though he did not move, he seemed to take a step back. "Right," he said. "I'll take coffee."

"What kind?"

"What kind?"

"Do you want a latte? Something over ice? Granita? I can make almost anything."

"Just coffee," he said. "I don't do fancy drinks. Just black coffee."

"You got it," she said. "For here or to go?"

"For here," he said.

Callie felt her emotions sink. The funny feeling this guy gave her made her uncomfortable. She'd have liked to get him out of the shop. Inwardly sighing, Callie rang up the sale, took his money, and poured his coffee into a tall paper cup. "I'll have your sandwich in a moment," she said. As he turned to look for a table, she sliced fresh bread. As she spread the mayo and layered on the cheese, questions scattered through her mind like shot from a hunting rifle. Who was this man? What brought him to Prospect?

Twenty-One

Marcus chose a table by the front window and sat down with his back to the corner. Though he'd been in Prospect less than twenty-four hours, he couldn't ignore the haunting sense of Celia's nearness. She had been here, walking these sidewalks, shopping at the grocery store across the street, buying gas at the self-serve. According to the text of the newspaper article about her accident, this was her town, and Marcus could feel it.

She had hidden here, in this small community at the foot of Mt. Rainier.

Somewhere very near, Marcus knew he would find the child. He took out the notepad and pen he'd purchased at the grocery store and made notes. Schools. Church. Library. Social Security Administration. Hospitals. Police. Someone on this list knew Celia. Someone had her address. Someone knew who had the child. It would take a little time and patience, but Marcus would find him. Nothing would keep him from the boy.

Nothing.

The clunk of a plate hitting the table brought Marcus out of his reverie. He looked up to see the woman who ran the coffee shop staring at him, her lovely eyes intense. "I'm sorry," he said. "Did you say something?"

She smiled. "I asked if there was anything else you need."

Her mirth seemed genuine enough, though Marcus wondered if she were laughing at him. "I'm sorry. I was thinking about someone. I guess I didn't hear you."

"No problem." She wiped her hands on her apron, and Marcus noted that she wore no wedding ring. "If you do need anything, let me know." She pointed behind the counter. "I'll be over there."

The sandwich looked delicious, a thick pile of ham on homemade bread. Though his mouth watered, Marcus paused to give thanks. As he ate, he watched the woman work. She was striking, the kind of woman any man would notice. Still, she was not beautiful, at least not in a classical way. Her jaw was too wide, leaving her with an almost square face. The whole effect was made more pronounced by her broad though admittedly charming smile.

She was tall and slim—and strong—in an athletic yet feminine way. She wore a baseball cap, her long, dark ponytail hanging loose from the space in the back. Her hair caught on her shoulders as she moved, and Marcus noted that it was so glossy that it shone—even from across the room.

Her eyes were green, he decided, a warm, muddy color that reminded him of saltwater marshes. She had pale, clear skin with a hint of pink high on her cheekbones.

She worked quickly, efficiently. Washing counters, putting away dishes, filling containers with condiments. Something about her manner conveyed confidence and responsibility, and Marcus guessed that she owned the place.

He watched as she took care of other customers, addressing them by name, asking about their lives, recalling their favorite drinks. She was older, nearly as old as he was, and he couldn't help but wonder what story was hidden behind her charismatic presence.

She glanced his way and caught him staring at her. He looked down at his plate, avoiding her eyes. *The one good thing about being black*, he thought as he chose a potato chip, *is that no one can see you blush.*

He hadn't stared at a woman this long since his college days. *I've been alone too long. I need to get back into the real world. White women don't tolerate being stared at by black men.*

Gazing out the window, he focused his attention on the street, where a long line of cars were passing through the town's single traffic light. The number of cars surprised him, perhaps because Prospect was so far from a major city. Marcus wondered why people would choose to live so far from their work.

When her business seemed to die down, he stood and went to the counter. "Excuse me," he said to the woman. She turned from the coffee machine, where she was wiping milk from a frothing nozzle. "I wonder if you have a telephone book I could use."

"Sure," she said. "County or local?"

"Both."

She smiled again, and Marcus noticed that her head tipped as she did. Her congenial, open approach appealed to him. "I keep it in the office." She pointed over her shoulder. "Just a minute, and I'll bring it out to your table—unless you need to use a telephone?"

"Not yet," he said. "I'm just making a list."

"All right," she said. "I'll be right there."

When she came toward his table, he tried not to notice how she moved. Tried not to notice the long legs in flared, dark jeans or the fitted T-shirt with the coffee shop logo on the breast pocket. She leaned down to put the books on the table. He tried not to notice the scent of her perfume. "There you are. I hope these help."

"Thanks."

She reached for his plate. "You finished with this?"

He nodded. "It was really good. Do you make your own bread?"

"Glad you liked it. We buy it from a cottage business here in town. More coffee?"

"That would be great. And how about one of those big cookies in the display."

"Chocolate chip, peanut butter, or lemon bar?"

"Peanut butter."

"I'll be right back."

Marcus began with listings of schools and day cares. Using the yellow pages, he noted all of these numbers in the local book. Then he looked up all of the hospitals in the larger book and wrote down their numbers as well. As he turned to the listing of churches, he remembered the map he'd bought when he rented the car. With a map, he might be able to include both Prospect churches and others near enough that Celia might have attended.

He stood and moved to the front door. "I left something in the car," he said as he stepped out of the door. "I'll be right back."

Moments later he had a state map spread across the small table. On one side of the map, he had the telephone book and his list. He'd just written down the third church number when the coffee woman brought him a cookie on a small paper plate. "Wow, that looks like a project," she said. "What're you up to?"

"You wouldn't believe me if I told you."

"Try me. Nothing much surprises me lately."

This attractive coffee shop owner seemed genuinely interested. She stood with one hand on the back of a chair, the other on her hip. Her eyes held nothing more than curiosity. Maybe she could help. "I'm Marcus Jefferson." He held out his hand.

"Callie O'Brian," she said, taking his hand. "So, Marcus, what are you doing here?"

"It's crazy, really. I'm trying to find someone who might have lived here, or at least near here at one point."

"That doesn't seem so crazy to me. How long ago are you talking about? Are we talking an ancestor or something?" Again the disarming smile.

"Not that long ago. She would have lived here recently. But I don't really know where. I don't have an address. I can't find her name in the phone book. I'm just trying to make a list of people who might have known her—you know, churches, schools, that kind of thing."

"Sounds sensible."

"But will it get me anywhere?"

She shrugged, smiling. "Who knows? What do you have so far?" She leaned forward, tipping her head as she read through the list. "Wow, that's most of the churches around here. But you're missing a new one. Mountain Meadows started two years ago."

"It isn't in the book."

She reached out and turned to the front cover of the smaller telephone book. "Sorry. This book is two years old. I didn't know I was lending it to a detective."

He added Mountain Meadows to the list. "Do you know where I could find the phone number?"

She laughed, a lighthearted, jovial laugh. "Sure. I go there."

"Then maybe you can save me a telephone call." He put down his pen. "Could I ask a question?"

She nodded.

"I wonder if you know my relative. Her name was Celia Jefferson."

>>>

Too late, Callie realized that her mouth had dropped open; she couldn't hide anything now. She closed her mouth and forced a tight smile. "I *knew* a Celia Hernandez," she said. "But she never used the name Jefferson." Did this stranger mean *her* Celia?

He blinked hard and pinched his nose as he turned his face away. "My brother married a woman in Florida about four years ago. Her maiden name was Hernandez. She was killed recently. The newspaper said she lived here in Prospect." He caught a stray tear with his thumb just as it escaped his eyelashes. "Sorry. I'm not quite used to the whole thing yet."

"Maybe there's a mistake," Callie suggested. "Do you have a picture?"

"I do." He reached back into his back pocket and pulled out a folding wallet. Opening the bill area, he removed the copy of the picture that had accompanied Celia's obituary. He paused, staring at the image in his hand. Callie noticed that his fingers trembled. He looked up as he handed Callie the clipping.

There was no mistaking the woman in the image. It was the photo Callie had chosen for the newspaper. Smiling up from the paper was a younger, happier Celia. The new mother. The happy wife. The image brought back the unfairness of her death. A shudder ran through Callie.

"I knew her as Celia Hernandez. She rented the guesthouse at my place." The shock of meeting this man weakened Callie's knees, and she pulled out the chair to sit down. "We're talking about the same woman."

Her words seemed to take him by surprise, and he shook his head, smiling. "I can't believe this. I didn't have any idea where to start looking, and here I just walked into you."

Callie didn't feel like rejoicing. Instead, her heart began to pound. If this man were who he claimed to be, he would be Keeshan's uncle. A relative. She felt as if the air had been knocked from her lungs. She took a deep breath and forced another weak smile. "Seems to be your lucky day."

"I guess so. I wonder..."

The bell over the shop door rang, and Callie took that as divine intervention. "Excuse me," she said. "I have a customer."

She hurried off to take an order for a couple on their way home from work. As she ground the coffee, she prayed. As she steamed the milk, she worried. Why now? Why couldn't anyone find this man when they had needed him most?

She thought of Keeshan, already so troubled by the loss of his mother. What would become of the boy if a veritable stranger walked into his life? Would it send him over the deep end? Callie begged God to intervene. *Make this guy disappear, Lord.*

But after the couple left and the cash register drawer closed, Marcus Jefferson—the stranger claiming to be Keeshan's uncle—still sat by the front window, drinking coffee and reading today's copy of the *News Tribune.*

She wiped down the latte machine and discarded the old coffee grinds. As she turned around to wipe the counter, he stood in front of her. She caught her breath.

"I wonder, since you knew Celia so well, if you could tell me what happened to the boy."

Callie played stupid. Averting his eyes, she wiped the counter. "The boy?"

"Her son."

"Oh. Well, yes. I know about him." She wiped faster, pausing to scratch a dried drop of milk with her fingernail.

Marcus Jefferson smiled, and Callie noticed that his whole face seemed relieved. "I've been so worried about him. I haven't been able to sleep since I heard that Celia was gone."

Callie had a headache. Her shoulders felt tight all the way to her earlobes. She tipped her head from side to side, desperate to ease the discomfort. "His name is Keeshan. He's four."

"Keeshan." Marcus shook his head. "I never understood why they named him that."

"It suits him." Callie crossed her arms.

"Where is he now?"

"I think he's in day care."

"Day care?"

Callie heard resentment in his voice—as if the child should not be in day care. With difficulty, she resisted the urge to pounce on this man's foolishness. "Celia had a wonderful lady caring for him while she worked. After all, when your husband is in *jail*, you don't have the luxury of staying home with the children."

"I didn't mean it the way it sounded. I'm sorry."

Callie suddenly didn't like this man. She didn't like his nerve. How could he just waltz in here like this and ask about the boy? She shrugged, unwilling to let him off the hook so easily.

"Can you tell me who's been caring for Keeshan since Celia's death?"

Callie nodded. "I could."

He shook his head as a sly smile spread across his lips. "Boy, you don't make anything easy, do you?" Reaching out to lean against the pastry counter, he said, "I don't know what I've done to offend you, but I'm sorry. I just want to know about the boy. I've flown all the way across the country to find my nephew. I didn't come here to play games. I didn't mean to insult you. If you'll tell me what I came to find out, I'll leave you alone."

"Look, I don't know who you are. You walk in here—a perfect stranger—and you expect me to believe every word you say. You ask about personal, painful things, and you expect me to drop what I'm doing and tell you everything. Well, I'm not that gullible." Callie threw her rag on the counter. "How do I know who you really are?"

He seemed genuinely surprised. "What do I have to do to prove it?"

"I don't know," Callie confessed. "If you really are the long lost brother, where were you when the authorities were looking for Celia's family?"

He looked away. "I've been out of touch."

"In jail—like Keeshan's dad?" Callie couldn't believe she'd said something so cruel—so unfounded. Gasping, she slapped one hand over her mouth.

He winced. "I wasn't in jail," he answered, his voice even, the tone hard.

"That was out of line." It was the closest Callie could come to an apology. Even when things were going well, apologies didn't come easy for her.

"I can't explain it all now. But as it was, the authorities couldn't reach me. If I'd known, I would have been here. In an instant." Even as he said it, Marcus wondered if it were true. He'd been a coward. He knew that now. At least he'd come to rectify his mistakes.

Callie rolled her eyes. "Right. You would have come running."

He checked his watch. "We seem to have gotten off on the wrong foot. I don't exactly understand what's wrong, but I'm not going to worry about it. Now that I know Celia lived here, it shouldn't be too hard to find the boy. If you won't tell me, someone will. In a town this size, probably everyone knows."

Callie realized that he was right. Nearly everyone in town knew she had Keeshan. If she didn't tell the truth, someone would. Perhaps she could stall. Maybe she should call her attorney. Certainly Dorothy Powell would know what to do. "I don't know what to say," Callie confessed. "You have to understand my position. I can't just give this kind of information to a stranger. As I said, how do I know who you are? Even if you provide identification, I'm not sure you're really related to Keeshan's father. His name wasn't Jefferson."

"How do you know?"

Callie chose her words carefully. "I saw the birth certificate."

This news seemed to startle him. "Who was listed as the father?"

"Andre," Callie admitted. "Andre Williams."

"William was our father's first name," Marcus said. He crossed his arms over his chest, and eyed her intently. "I have a proposition to make. If I can prove that my brother is Keeshan's father, will you talk?"

She thought about it, wishing there were some neat way to avoid this conversation. After all, there were gossips all over town willing to give away the information she kept hidden. "I suppose that would work. How will you do that?"

"Give me a couple of days. When do you get off work?"

"I own the place. We close at five."

"Could you have dinner with me?"

Callie hesitated. How could she have dinner with Keeshan's uncle? She would have to ask someone to take Keeshan for the evening. She hated to be away from the boy for that long.

"I can come and get you."

"I'll meet you."

"Where?"

"Camp Eighteen. It's a restaurant about three miles east of town."

"When?"

"Friday night."

"That's five days away. What about Wednesday?"

"I can't. Friday is my final offer."

He seemed to scowl as he considered the opportunity. "I guess it doesn't matter. I've come to see the boy. I'll stay as long as I have to. Friday it is."

>>>>

Callie called Dorothy Powell's office as soon as Marcus left the coffee shop. The attorney was on another line, according to her secretary, and would return Callie's call as soon as possible. Callie could hardly concentrate as she waited for the call. When the telephone rang, she left a customer in the middle of an order to run into her private office.

"I don't know what to do," she said, after telling Dorothy about Marcus Jefferson's afternoon appearance. "He wants to meet me for dinner. I don't even know who he really is."

"You'll know who he is if he shows up with proof."

"He promised to bring it on Friday."

"And you're meeting him in a public location, correct?"

"Yes—a restaurant near the park entrance."

"If you feel comfortable with him in public, go ahead and listen to what he has to say. The only other option is to meet him here at my office. I could offer to negotiate for you if you'd feel better."

Callie thought about Marcus, about his dark eyes and earnest expression. "No. I don't think that's necessary."

"Meeting him here might seem adversarial. Whatever you decide, the truth is, he can find out who has the boy without any trouble. Everyone in town knows. Your whole church knows. The temporary custody order is public information."

"He wants the boy."

"You don't know that. You told me he's just asking about Keeshan."

"Why would he have come this far?"

"He could want to reconnect or to recover Celia's possessions. He might want to pay his respects. Don't make assumptions. Besides, Callie, all this time you've been telling me you wanted to find Keeshan's relatives. That's what we told the commissioner in court. Now a relative shows up. You should be happy."

"I know." Callie wished it were true. She wished that she didn't want to keep Keeshan. But she did. With all her heart she wanted to keep him as her own. She did not offer an explanation to the attorney; instead, she changed the subject. "What if he's no good for the boy?"

"Take it one step at a time. You've been granted temporary custody. He can't just walk off with Keeshan. You have the stronger legal position. See what he has to say. Check him out. Maybe he's not who he says he is."

"I wish things could be simpler."

"Life rarely is."

After Callie hung up, she went back to the cash register and took the interrupted order from a resentful customer. As soon as he left the shop, Callie unplugged the window sign and drew the shades. After rushing through her closing routine, Callie drove to the Mortensons' to pick up Keeshan. As she headed down the highway, she checked her rearview mirror to make sure she wasn't being followed.

Marcus Jefferson's appearance in Prospect had definitely thrown her. Whoever he was, whatever he wanted, she wasn't going to let him take her by surprise again. From now on, Callie was going to be on the offense.

Twenty-Two

In the weeks after Celia's death, Callie's life had spun out of control. Now, with Marcus in town, Callie felt as though a hurricane had blown through, leaving her world in shambles. As much as she tried to ignore her upcoming appointment—"date" would be a completely inappropriate term—with Keeshan's uncle, she could not erase the dark shadow it cast over her world.

Changing her work schedule, combined with the pressure of instant motherhood, seemed to steal time from her day. Her fledgling upholstery business had already suffered.

In an effort to keep projects moving in and out of the workroom, Callie purchased a nursery monitor and began rising two hours earlier to spend time in the shop by herself. Though not enough to get ahead, these hours helped her to clear out the projects she'd neglected after the accident.

It didn't take Keeshan long to realize that Callie began her day in the workshop. He often appeared at the back door, thumb in mouth, Celia's nightgown in hand. Every morning without fail, his first word remained the same.

"Dynobuddies?"

When he appeared, Callie stopped working. He had no patience for upholstery projects. Keeshan had no patience for anything that didn't focus on him.

With this schedule, she'd managed to finish a wing chair she'd promised to a teacher in the local elementary school and make seven throw pillows to decorate the new family room belonging to a friend of a friend. Soon, Callie was ready to begin recovering Celia's couch for Angie and Don.

Angie found fabric at a local mill-end store. However, because the material was slightly imperfect, Callie had to candle the yardage and mark each flaw. She began by rolling it out, yard-by-yard, scanning for tiny blemishes in the weave. After marking these, she re-rolled the fabric and stored it in a closet.

The couch itself gave off an unusual smell; Callie suspected it had been wet at some point in its life. It didn't matter. Eventually she would replace all of the stuffing with fresh material. She only hoped that the frame had not suffered the same fate. She did not want to replace the wood.

Callie began by removing the existing fabric and marking it for use as a pattern. Between the moisture and the age of the couch, the staples Callie uncovered were rusted and brittle. Often, as she pried them loose, they fractured, forcing her to remove the broken pieces with tiny snub-nosed pliers.

Callie teased the staples from the wood, gently pulling the cloth to loosen them. As she stretched the worn fabric, it disintegrated in her hands, leaving her nothing but dust and broken thread. The staples stayed behind, and her pattern grew more and more distorted.

Every staple, every brad, every nail had to be plucked out by hand.

Callie very nearly swore at her friend's old couch. She eventually removed the bed frame, and uncovered the outside back and both arms. To her delight, the frame of the couch was every bit as well constructed as she had guessed with no evidence of mildew in the wood. It was a great piece of furniture, well worth the effort and expense of recovering.

On Friday of that week, her appointment with Marcus hanging over her head, Callie had only the lower front and the inside back fabric to remove. She rose at 5:00 A.M., made herself a pot of coffee, and ate a bowl of homemade granola. After her devotions, she reported to her workshop determined to finish stripping the couch. She turned on the fluorescent lights and switched the radio to smooth jazz.

She knelt in front of the couch with her tool tray beside her. "Okay," she said aloud to the half-finished frame. "Be good to me this morning. We're going to strip you today or die trying."

Callie tipped the couch onto its back, humming along with the radio as she worked. Carefully, she eased the inside back from the wood frame and marked the back with a permanent felt-tipped pen. She drew arrows showing the top and bottom, as well as lines marking the straight of grain and the center of the frame. Then she carefully removed the fabric.

Underneath, the polyester batting was black with mildew. Callie marked it with the pen and pulled it away, trying not to breathe as she did so. She carried it out the back door and left it on the sidewalk, where it would not smell up the workshop.

Underneath, she discovered large pads of horsehair stuffing held in place by burlap sewn through the padding. Before removing these, Callie took a clean sheet of paper and made notes.

Below the pads, Callie found several sheets of cardboard that served as a base for the stuffing. These pieces had been cut and molded around the frame, serving as support for the padding that went above them. It didn't surprise Callie that the cardboard was broken in several places. Just something else to replace.

So, once again, Callie marked every sheet of cardboard and removed the staples holding them to the frame. She had taken off three pieces when the sound of falling objects caught her attention.

Normally, Callie found all kinds of things in couches—pens, knitting needles, toys, hairbrushes, money, even television remotes. But in hide-a-beds, personal things fall completely through to the floor under the couch. She had never found anything in a hide-a-bed—let alone something like this.

Callie walked around the couch and bent down to get a closer look. Four identical zip top bags made of clear plastic lay on her cement floor. The material inside looked like baking soda or perhaps powdered sugar. Callie picked up one of the bags and held it to the light. White powder clung to the sides of the bag.

She shook it slightly and squished the sides between her fingers. Small, unevenly shaped crystals—the size of granulated sugar—were evenly spread throughout the powder. All four bags appeared to hold the same material.

As she held the bags, Callie's hands began to tremble. Though she had never seen it before, she was certain this was some kind of illegal substance. Callie had never used drugs. Never even seen drugs up close and personal—not in all her years in the city, not in her bachelor's or master's degree programs. This kind of find was way out of her league.

Where had this stuff come from?

She was certain Celia had never used drugs. Ever the careful mother, she would never have allowed these things in her home. Though she wasn't careful about food, Celia was vigilant about safety issues. She covered her plugs with childproof covers; she kept cleaning solvents in overhead cabinets. Celia even locked her medicine cabinet.

Then it occurred to Callie; Celia must not have known the drugs were in the couch. Someone else had hidden them inside. But why? And who?

"Dynobuddies!"

She looked up to see Spider-Man pajamas standing in the doorway. She stood up quickly, leaning against the couch to block Keeshan's view of the packages. She had not heard him leave his room through the monitor. "Morning, Spider-Man," she said. "How'd you sleep?"

"Okay. Can I have Dynobuddies?"

"Sure," Callie smiled. "Have you been to the bathroom and washed your hands yet?"

He shook his head, shifted Celia's nightgown to the other hand, and brought his thumb to his mouth. "I want breakfast," he said, sending the words around his thumb.

"Tell you what. You go back in the house and use the bathroom. By the time you wash your hands, I'll be in to make you breakfast. I promise."

He looked at her, clearly surprised by her unwillingness to cooperate. "Go wash your hands," she repeated.

He pulled his hand out of his mouth, showing her his thumb. "It's clean. I just woke up."

"Wash, Keeshan," Callie said with as much authority as she could muster.

He shrugged and turned to go. She leaned against the couch until she heard him open the screen door to the big house. Then, with one hand over her chest, she thanked God that he had not seen the packages.

What should she do? Call the police? Report the find? What would that do to her? Would it endanger her chance of keeping the boy? She couldn't think straight, and she had only moments before he returned. Bending over again, she picked up the packages. Then, desperate, she looked around the workroom for a place to hide the stuff. Keeshan must never find them. Where would they be safe?

Suddenly, she spotted the freezer standing near the back door. She went over to the doorway and opened it. Moving ground beef with one hand, she slid the packages down behind the meat in the very back of the second shelf. Shutting the door, she leaned against the freezer.

Tonight, after Keeshan goes to bed, I flush the stuff, Callie decided.

>>>

Late Friday afternoon, Callie dressed carefully, choosing black slacks and a purple silk top. She wore her hair down in back, the bangs clipped into a loose twist at the top of her head. Whatever happened at the restaurant, she wanted to appear serious, reasonable. Keeshan was her responsibility now, and she had no intention of letting this stranger misinterpret her relationship with the boy. Callie O'Brian would not be taken for a fool.

She arrived at the restaurant early, parking near the front door. As she walked in, she remembered how dark the interior of Camp Eighteen was; she wished she'd chosen a place with more natural light. Here, wood paneling combined with widely spaced windows to cast a deep shadow over the dining room. On every table, small hurricane lanterns, decorated with fresh spring flowers, held broad white candles.

Some women might have called the soft candlelight romantic. Callie wished for bright fluorescent tubes.

"You're early," Marcus said, stepping toward her. In a ruby red sweater over dark jeans, he looked casual, confident. In one hand he held a large manila envelope. "I've asked for a quiet table so we can talk," he said, and then he added, "I hope you don't mind."

She nodded her agreement, tucking her purse under her arm. The hostess came toward them carrying two menus. "Are you ready?"

She thinks we're a couple, Callie thought, feeling the heat rise in her neck. She followed the waitress to a corner table, where the window overlooked the meadow behind the restaurant. In the background, Mt. Rainier basked in the late afternoon sunshine. Marcus pulled out a chair for her, and Callie sat down. How long had it been since someone did anything so simple, so thoughtful? She thought again of Scott, of the way he'd always anticipated her needs, rushing ahead to meet them. He'd always held her chair for her. Callie shuddered.

Scott was part of her distant past. It was her job to keep him there.

"Are you cold?" Marcus asked.

"Nothing like that," Callie answered, reaching for the water glass. Determined not to let Marcus into her thoughts, she turned her attention to the view.

He put his menu down, folding his hands over the cover. "Thank you for coming tonight," he said. "I know that I'm a complete stranger to you. It was risky to agree to dinner. I appreciate it."

She nodded and looked away. Why did he do that? Why did he disarm her just as she was thinking the worst? It wasn't easy to see him as an enemy, here with the mountain view, surrounded by flowers and candles. The guy looked normal, even friendly. All right, he looked breathtakingly handsome. Callie unfolded her napkin and spread it across her lap, wiping nervous fingers on the linen.

"I've brought the documentation you asked for. I hope it will prove that I am who I say that I am." He picked up the menu. "But let's order dinner first. We can talk while we wait for our food."

"Sounds good to me. I'm starved," she said. *Overenthusiastic,* she chided herself. *You sound like a high school student.*

"Me too. What do you recommend?"

"The beef here is excellent; the steak is especially good."

"Sounds great. I'll have that."

When they had given the waitress their orders, they fell into an uneasy silence. Callie played with her water glass, turning the stem in steady quarter turns to the right.

"Tell me about Celia," Marcus said. "How did you know her?"

Callie eyed him. Did he really want to know? Or was he simply making conversation? She decided to give him the benefit of the doubt. "I met her when she moved to Prospect about three years ago. She answered a newspaper ad I placed for the guesthouse on my property. I rent the house to make ends meet. Keeshan was only a baby at the time."

"You were friends?"

"Not for a while."

"But you were when she died."

This guy should work for a newspaper. "I came to Prospect rather unexpectedly. My mother had cancer, and I was out of state, working on a project. Mom died only days after I came home." Callie took a drink of ice water. "I was still grieving when I placed that ad. I wasn't ready to be a friend to anyone." It wasn't the whole truth, but it was close enough for strangers.

"What about your father?"

She looked at him, wondering if he knew how personal these questions were. "Dad lives in a retirement community about forty minutes from here."

"He didn't want to stay in the house?"

Marcus Jefferson looked interested, leaning forward, his eyes focused on hers. His expression on his face seemed genuine. Callie answered the question. "I think Dad was glad to move. With almost forty acres, the place was too much for him to manage." She thought about it a minute, and decided not to mention her father's health problems. Instead she added, more quietly, "Actually, I think he'd have hated to stay without Mom."

"So you became friends with Celia."

"Eventually."

"How much did you know about her life?"

Callie found herself thinking about the packages in her freezer as she wondered about Celia, about her past. *I hardly knew anything,* Callie thought bitterly. *I wasn't much of a friend.*

The waitress, a tall woman with blond hair and heavy makeup, placed their salads on chargers. "Ground pepper?" she asked. Marcus nodded, and they fell silent as she sprinkled his salad with pepper. "And you?" Callie shook her head.

When they were alone, he began again. "You were telling me about Celia."

"Actually, you were asking too many questions."

"I'm sorry. You keep answering."

"Maybe I shouldn't."

They ate in silence for a while, watching the sunlight fade and the snow on the mountain turn a deep shade of apricot.

>>>>

Marcus watched Callie as she picked at her salad. She was disturbed by his presence, he sensed that much. Her short, terse answers landed somewhere just short of polite. He wondered why she was so protective, almost secretive.

What did she have to hide?

As they finished their salads, the silence grew monstrously uncomfortable, and Marcus chided himself for even trying to charm her into talking. What was he thinking? He had all the charm of a rattlesnake.

After the waitress removed their salad plates, he tried again. "Obviously, you don't want to talk about Celia. So why don't you forget about that? Tell me about yourself."

She looked up and rolled her muddy green eyes. Taking her napkin, she dabbed at her lips. "Don't you think maybe we should establish just exactly who you are?"

"I suppose you're right."

"In this day and age, with serial killers all over the place, a woman would be nuts to carry on this kind of conversation with someone she doesn't even know."

"Are you? Nuts, I mean?"

His question caught her off guard, and a sly smile escaped before she had time to stamp it out. "I might be."

He reached over to the empty chair and lifted the manila envelope. "I pulled these off the Internet. It wasn't easy. I had to hitchhike into Puyallup to the library. I think you'll find them interesting." He handed the envelope to her.

Clearly he'd won her curiosity. She reached for the envelope, her features clothed in anticipation as she opened the clasp and pulled out a stack of papers. She glanced up at him, her eyebrows asking the question before she spoke. "What is this?"

He pulled his wallet from his back pocket. "Go ahead. Read. It will take you a while."

He watched as she started at the top of the stack. The envelope contained newspaper articles he'd found and copied at the Pierce County library. The first had the most recent dateline, describing the release of Armando Ortega. She skimmed it, pausing with her finger on the text. "Why am I reading this? I don't know any of these people."

"That's correct," Marcus said. "Did you notice the scam?"

"They're using babies to sneak drugs in and out of the country."

"Right. Drug-addicted women from the poorest parts of the city carry babies out of the country on trips to Central and South America. When they return, they have both the baby and sealed cans of baby formula. Problem is, the formula wasn't formula. It was cocaine."

"I don't understand…" she began, and then she stopped speaking.

Marcus saw something in her expression change. It was as if a light went on. *She does understand,* he thought. *She knows something.*

Twenty-Three

Marcus couldn't shake the suspicion he felt. Though she was attractive, bright, and opinionated, he would not be deterred. Callie O'Brian knew something. He had to figure it out. He pointed at the papers. "Keep reading."

She went on to the next page and the next. "This is all very interesting, Mr. Jefferson, but I have no idea what this problem has to do with you and me."

"I'll spare you several pages," he said. "But you might want to read them later." He gestured to the stack of papers. "You can keep that. Bedtime reading. Besides, you'll no doubt want to check this with your own sources." He reached for the papers. "May I?"

She handed him the stack.

He shuffled down to the bottom, pulled out a sheet of paper and handed it to her. "This one should start to make some sense." He watched as she read, her eyes skimming over the words as she used one delicately pointed nail to keep track. The nail moved to the middle of the page, stopped and began again, this time moving down more slowly. She leaned forward, holding the paper in the light of the lantern, her face a lovely question mark.

She looked up, confusion covering her features.

"Did you see who was arrested?"

"Yes. It was Peter Jefferson."

"And you noticed the alias?"

She nodded. "Andre Williams. The name on the birth certificate."

Grateful that he had kept his personal belongings in a Florida safe deposit box, Marcus opened his wallet and removed his driver's license, tossing it lightly onto the top page of papers. "As you can see, I'm Marcus Jefferson," he said. "My brother's name was Peter. He's four years younger than I am. Right now he's sitting in the Dade Correctional Institution, in Florida City, Florida. He won't be out for another nine years. We grew up in Indianapolis, Indiana, the only children of William and Alma Jefferson."

Her mouth dropped open, and she made no effort to cover her surprise. It bothered Marcus, more than a little bit, that this woman, who could be so suspicious, so mistrusting, could be quite so lovely wearing a stupidly blank expression.

"I've startled you."

"You *are* his brother."

"I think I said that. Of course, you'll want to check it out yourself. The records are public. I can help you with dates and addresses."

"I didn't think anyone would ever come forward."

"Well, I'm here."

She closed her mouth and shook her head. With her elbows on the table and both hands in the air, she asked the question. "Where *were* you?" She sounded perturbed. Irritated. "We looked everywhere for Celia's relatives. The whole family just disappeared. Vanished. Gone. Why couldn't we find you?"

"I told you. I was out of touch at the time," he hedged. Marcus knew he hadn't quite told the whole truth. But at this point, he wanted to be in charge of who knew what, and when. It wasn't her business, knowing where he'd been. "Maybe you didn't know where to look."

"Obviously." She rolled her eyes. "When Celia had the accident, the whole world was looking. The hospital. The medical examiner…" she stopped herself. "Everyone wanted to find Celia's family. They were entitled to know what happened. She died alone, you know."

"I'm truly sorry about that," Marcus said. "She didn't deserve that." It was true. Celia had been the best thing that had happened to the Jefferson family. He hated to think of her alone in a hospital room, broken and battered from an accident that never should have happened.

If he hadn't been so busy taking care of himself, she might not have died.

Their dinner came, and Marcus was thankful for the interruption, hoping the food would give both of them time to cool off. While he cut his meat, Marcus pictured Celia—petite, young, beautiful. Her energy and optimism had been contagious. When Marcus met her, he believed she would be the one to turn Peter from his past. If anyone might have done it, it would have been Celia.

For a while she was magic for Peter. Celia believed in him, encouraged him to complete trade school. They married after discovering she was pregnant. What Celia didn't know was that Peter often worked after hours in a chop shop for stolen cars—where his skill with metal was more seriously rewarded. He hadn't told her until the baby was born, when he used an alias for the birth certificate. That was when Celia lost faith in him.

Marcus had lost faith long before that.

He spoke up. "Just so you know, Peter didn't start out bad. It happened after our dad had a stroke. I was in college, and Peter was in high school. Mom had to work two jobs to make ends meet, and Dad couldn't do much of anything. Left to himself, Peter fell into the wrong crowd. It's the same old story."

She pointed at the papers with her fork, sarcasm dripping from her voice. "And this drug thing was his only mistake. He was a virtual angel, really."

Marcus didn't miss the implication. "I didn't say that." He thought about the years of anguish Peter caused his parents, the drugs at school, shoplifting, stints in juvenile detention. It had been torture. This woman would never understand any of that. Marcus resented her self-satisfied smirk. "You don't know anything about my brother, or our family, for that matter."

"And you don't know anything about me."

"I tried. You wouldn't tell me."

She put down her fork. "Let's be honest here. You aren't really interested in me. You want information."

"You are a very suspicious woman."

"I'm a very wise woman. I'm being wined and dined and questioned. I'd be stupid not to realize what's happening here tonight. You only want to know where the boy is." As she spoke, her raised voice drew the attention of other diners.

Marcus signaled her to quiet down.

"Don't tell me what to do," she hissed.

"We don't have to let everyone in the room share our misery. I'm trying to be civil here. Trying to reassure you about my motives."

"Right. Your brother is a felon in a federal penitentiary, and you want me to believe that you have pure motives."

"The boy is my nephew."

"And he's living with me," Callie said, scooting her chair back from the table. "As if you didn't already know. And, frankly, I think he should stay with me." She stood up. "I'm suddenly not very hungry. I think I'll be leaving now," she said, grabbing her sweater from the back of the chair.

Both mesmerized and frustrated, Marcus watched her leave.

>>>

Callie tried to carry on as though she had never met Marcus Jefferson. They had not made any further contact, and she refused to go looking for trouble. By early April, spring had come to Prospect. The rhododendrons bloomed. The grass had started growing again. The trees uncurled their first leaves. As always, Callie began to itch for the garden. Though the rain still came too frequently, she laid plans for the fenced plot she considered nearly sacred.

Her tomato seeds arrived from the East Coast on the Monday before Easter. Coming home from work with Keeshan, she drove into the driveway and discovered the package waiting for her on the front porch. Delighted, she took the box into the kitchen and sliced open the tape as Keeshan sat on top of the table watching.

Callie opened the tray of prepackaged starter containers and showed Keeshan the seed pack. "We'll put these seeds in the dirt and watch them sprout. They'll grow into tomato plants," she explained. "We'll have fresh tomatoes all summer long. Have you ever had fresh tomatoes, Keeshan?"

"No," he said, shaking his head. "Our tomatoes come from Pac 'n' Save."

Callie laughed. "Those are fresh too. But not as fresh as the ones we take right off the vine. Would you like to help me plant the tomato seeds?"

He leaned over the box and peered inside, nodding with great seriousness.

"Good. As soon as we have dinner, we'll plant the seeds and water them, and then we'll put them in the window where we can watch them grow. How does that sound?"

"Can I put the seeds in the dirt?"

"Later," she said. Callie slid the tray onto the center of the dining table. "Why don't you go check on Eddy's water dish? Then would you please wash your hands and set the table while I cook the spaghetti?"

"Okay," he said. Keeshan climbed off the table and started off down the hall, turning on lights as he went. "Don't burn the hang-ge-bur."

Watching him go, Callie shook her head. Keeshan had begun to show such confidence lately. These days he seemed as comfortable in her home as if he'd lived there all his life. Though he still didn't like the dark, he managed the lights on his own.

He was now sleeping in the big bed by himself. He even looked forward to his time at day care. Still, every night, when Callie went in to check on the boy, she found him clutching Celia's nightgown. Keeshan slept with the satin wrapped around his neck.

In the kitchen she pulled ground beef from the fridge, put a pot of water on the stove, and chopped an onion to brown with the beef. As worked, she felt the cat circle her ankles, rubbing against her calves. Callie shooed it away with one foot, but it returned. She glanced down and frowned. Eddy seemed to be gaining weight.

Keeshan came into the kitchen and went directly to the dish cupboard.

"Does Eddy have water?"

"Yep."

"Did you wash your hands?"

"I forgot."

"Why don't you use the stool and wash in the kitchen sink?"

Dragging a stool across the floor, he backed up to the sink, unfolded it, and climbed up. In moments, Keeshan had splashed water all over the counter and window. Callie took a deep breath and ignored it. "I need a towel," he said, shaking his hands.

"Here you go," she said, offering him a clean towel.

He climbed off the stool and catching sight of Eddy, pursued the cat into the living room. "Keeshan. The dishes. You were going to set the table."

"Oh, yeah," he said, returning to the kitchen. Taking a single dinner plate from the cupboard, he headed for the kitchen table. He came back for the second as Callie added the onion to the hamburger. "Good job, Keeshan," she said. "Put them right on top of the place mats."

With a little stamp of his foot he spoke. "I can do it."

Moments later he returned for silverware. He pulled the stool over to the drawer and climbed up. With small hands, he pulled out utensils, closed the drawer, and climbed down from the stool. Callie heard the silverware bang as he put it in place. "Can I plant the seeds now?"

"No, Keeshan. Not until we finish dinner."

He did not answer.

Assuming he'd gone after the cat, Callie switched on the television hanging over the kitchen counter, hoping to catch the national news. Pulling spaghetti from the cupboard, she snapped the long pasta into bite-sized pieces and added it to the boiling water.

She'd just opened the refrigerator door when an all too familiar crash came from the dining nook. "What now?" Rolling her eyes, she shut the

door. As soon as she stepped into the dining nook, she realized what
had happened.

Keeshan stood on a kitchen chair, his face turned toward the floor.
Below him, the tray of starter containers lay upside down. Dirt was everywhere, on the floor, the chair, the kitchen table. In one hand, Keeshan
held a torn envelope, tiny seeds spread across the table, some clinging
to his hand and his clothes. Callie stifled an urge to strangle the little
critter. "Oh, Keeshan, why can't you just do as you're told?"

"I didn't mean to. It just fell."

"But we were going to plant the seeds after dinner."

"I wanted to help."

Callie felt her anger burn, ignited by both exhaustion and hunger.
"If you want to help, you have to start by obeying me." She moved toward
him. "Now, the seeds are all lost. I'll never be able to find them all. The
dirt is everywhere. We won't be able to have tomatoes after all. You've
ruined everything."

She had no more than sent the words out into the air when they hit
their intended target with the accuracy of an intercontinental ballistic
missile. Keeshan's face crumbled and he started to cry. "I didn't…" he
gasped and choked. "I didn't mean to…"

"I know you didn't mean to," she said, taking the sobbing boy into
her arms. "I know," she repeated. "I didn't mean to, either."

Hours later, when the spaghetti was eaten, the floor was clean, and
the little seeds had been safely placed in sandwich bags, Callie put on
her bathrobe and helped Keeshan into his Spider-Man pajamas.

Together they sat in the little rocker by the fireplace and read
Goodnight Moon as if nothing had ever happened between them.

>>>

In the days after Marcus had dinner with Callie, he could think of
little else. Though he managed to rent a room in Prospect and scoured
the newspapers for a job, his resentment grew. The more he thought
about how she had treated him, the angrier he felt.

It didn't take a detective to figure out that she had temporary custody of the boy. Marcus heard the same story at the grocery store, the drugstore, and the hardware store. By the time he bought an old Honda with the last of his cash from the Tucson project, he could hardly stand the thought of her. What right did she—a perfect stranger—have to treat him this way? After all, Marcus was the boy's only real family. Blood.

Certainly blood was worth something.

He would have to take action. Do something drastic. But the action he had in mind required money, lots of money. And he was running short on that valuable commodity.

Though he had experience, he could not land a job with a construction crew. It seemed that those who started in construction in Prospect came by their positions via connections—connections that Marcus had not yet made. Desperate, he took a job at a supply store a mile west of town. For minimum wage he wrote up orders, ran the cash register, and helped customers load lumber. It wasn't great money, but the work was consistent. By keeping his expenses low, he would eventually save up enough to pay for an attorney. Only an attorney could take Keeshan from that woman.

After his first week at work, Marcus could stand it no longer. He ached to see Keeshan, to hold him. To see his brother in the boy's face. Even if he wasn't ready to launch a legal battle, Marcus had to know the child was all right. That the woman was taking good care of him.

On the first Wednesday in June, Marcus asked his boss for a late lunch. Driving his broken-down Honda into Prospect, Marcus parked in front of the coffee shop.

The shop was empty when he first entered, the woman nowhere to be seen. For a moment he wondered if she had disappeared. A shadow of fear floated over his consciousness. What if she had taken the boy and run?

He stepped to the counter and called out, "Anyone here?"

Callie O'Brian came around the corner, wiping her palms on the back of her jeans. As before, she wore a baseball cap, black T-shirt, and jeans. Her apron was somehow different today, and it took Marcus a moment to recognize that the bright red color had made her skin come alive. Her broad shoulders and fresh face gave her an almost boyish appeal. *Refreshing*, he thought.

"Are you busy?" he asked.

She frowned. "Of course I'm busy. I'm working."

"I mean do you have a minute to talk?"

She glanced toward the kitchen. "I was making cookie batter."

"Can it wait?"

She folded her arms across her chest. "You really are a piece of work. Every time you show up, you expect me to drop everything and take care of you. What is it with you?"

Clearly, she'd been thinking of him as well. The only problem was that she was still angry. This surprised Marcus. After all, she was the one who had stomped out of the restaurant. "It isn't anything with me," he said. "I was just wondering if we could talk. Without all the barbs."

She put her hands on her hips, still hesitating. "All right. Would you like some coffee? I could use some myself."

He nodded, and she took two mugs from the stack beside the coffeemaker and filled them. "The table in the corner is clean," she said, coming around the counter.

She put the cups down and sat facing him. For a long moment, neither of them spoke. She put her elbows on the table, fingering her coffee mug. "I suppose I should apologize," she began. "I've been a little rude."

This lady was a never-ending source of surprise. After all, she'd been more than a little rude. She'd been downright nasty. "It must have been quite a shock," he conceded, "having me show up after so long."

She nodded, putting her chin in her hand. "I wasn't expecting anyone."

"I got that impression."

"So now what do you want?"

This woman moved from apology to brusqueness at light speed. "I think you know what I want," he said. He leaned forward, trying to catch her eyes. "The boy is my nephew. I want to see him. It doesn't seem like a big request."

"I don't know," she hedged.

"What could it hurt?"

"He's been through so much. I don't want to lose the progress he's made."

"What progress?"

"You don't know much about children, do you?"

"I didn't say that. I'm just asking you to explain what you mean."

"He's lost his mother. It's been traumatic. He's just beginning to settle down."

This was news to Marcus. Of course a child would respond to his mother's death. But what had happened to his nephew? Was this woman holding something back? "Settle down?"

"He's just started to sleep through the night. He isn't wetting his bed anymore. He's going to day care again. I don't want to undo the progress he's made."

"I won't upset anything. I just want to see him."

She looked at him, mistrust in her eyes. "I don't think that's possible."

Marcus couldn't believe his ears. After all, he'd come to the coffee shop with his hat in his hands, desperate to strike a peace treaty with this overbearing woman. "Why not?"

"I have temporary custody. It's my job to care for him. To make certain he's okay."

"And to see me would change that?"

"It might."

"I think you're afraid."

She sat up straight, setting her mug on the table with a thud. "How dare you! Have you ever stayed up all night with a crying child? Have you calmed nightmares? Have you changed sheets two and three times a week? Have you taken a child to work with you day after day because he couldn't stand to be left alone?" She stood up, her eyes sparking anger. "I don't think so. I don't think you have any clue about what we've been through."

"Just calm down. We can talk about this…"

"Don't you tell me to calm down. I didn't waltz into town thinking I could save the boy." She stopped speaking suddenly and lowered her voice. "It's my job to decide what's best."

"I promise I won't hurt him."

"I know you won't hurt him. You won't because I won't let you," she said, adding even more quietly, "I think you should be going now."

Twenty-Four

Callie waited for the door to close behind Marcus. What was it about the man that got under her skin? Though she'd only seen him twice, she'd managed to lose her temper both times. The nerve, to think he could insist on busting in to Keeshan's life.

Callie went to the door and threw the lock. Unplugging the neon sign, she went into the office and called Dorothy Powell. The attorney happened to be sitting at her desk. "He just came by the shop."

"The brother?"

"Yes. The nerve of that guy."

"I'd expect it," she said, patience coating Callie's anger like frosting. "Take a deep breath and tell me what he said."

"He wants to see Keeshan."

"What did you say?"

"I told him I didn't think it was a good idea."

"How did he leave it?"

"I threw him out."

Dorothy Powell chuckled, a deep-throated, genuinely amused chuckle. "It's a good thing you aren't an attorney. You'd never make it in court."

Callie swallowed an urge to defend herself. "I can't help it. The man makes me crazy. He thinks that just because he's an uncle he can waltz in here and change things around. I don't like it. I don't like him. He shows up just when I'm getting things under control."

"Callie, I don't want to discourage you, but I don't think things are as under control as you suspect."

"What do you mean?"

"In the first place, you hired me so that the child could receive the benefits for which he is entitled. In those days, you couldn't wait to find the boy's actual family. Something has changed here."

"What are you saying?"

"You tell me. It looks to me like you want to keep the boy. Otherwise you'd be happy to see Keeshan's uncle show up."

Callie began to regret that she had not yet told her attorney the truth. She paused, thinking through her words carefully. "I haven't said anything to you yet because I wasn't sure about it. But I've changed my mind. I do want Keeshan. I think he deserves a home near everything familiar to him. He deserves more than to be jerked around by some guy who shows up at the last minute pretending to be concerned."

"I wondered if things had come to that. I understand."

Dorothy Powell did not understand. She hadn't lost her closest friend. "Keeshan has been through so much. He deserves some stability."

"Like the stability you provide."

Callie leaned over and put her forehead down on the desk. No wonder she had trouble explaining. She didn't even really understand her own motives. She sat up, gesturing with her free hand—as if the attorney could see. "All right. Yes. Like the stability a woman provides. A home. Day care. Routine. Every child deserves as much."

"Callie, I'm going to recommend something that may frighten you."

Now what? What could be more frightening than the things she'd already been through? "I'm listening."

"I think you should start a motion for third-party custody."

"Didn't we do that?"

"No, we've asked for and been granted temporary custody. The court was receptive because the family had not yet been found."

"So why this step?"

"Because I think this will be the uncle's next move—what was his name?"

"Marcus. Marcus Jefferson."

"Right. If I were Mr. Jefferson, and I had come clear across the country to find that my nephew was living with a third party, I'd file for custody. I think he will. We should file first—that is, if you really want to keep the child. It will mean adopting Keeshan."

Callie felt her heart pound. This was a big step. A huge step. Though she wanted Keeshan, fear squeezed her throat. "It's such a big decision."

"I wouldn't wait too long. It might be important."

Though she didn't want to say it, Callie worried about the funds necessary for this kind of legal action. She barely made ends meet as it was. Between the cost of her mortgage, her business expenses, and now the care for the boy, Callie didn't have the funds to keep throwing money at the legal system. "Can I call you back?"

"Of course, Callie."

"How long can you give me?"

"As long as you need. This isn't something you should start until you feel absolutely certain that it's the right course. Remember though, the whole process takes time. The wheels of family court roll very slowly. Besides that, the boy deserves to live with someone who loves him, who wants him. Someone willing to fight to keep him."

As quickly as it had come, the fear disappeared. Emboldened, Callie spoke. "You're right," she said. "Let's do it. Go ahead and file."

>>>>

Marcus left the shop discouraged and frustrated. As he drove back to work, he worried. *What is it about this woman that makes her so determined to keep me from seeing Keeshan? After all, she isn't blood. She can't provide for the boy the way real family can.*

Marcus had gone out of his way to avoid offending her. He'd cooperated when she demanded evidence of his relationship with Keeshan's father. He'd been polite, honest, forthright. Though she didn't know anything about him, she'd already decided to hate him.

Marcus had experienced ordinary prejudice before, but he'd never had anyone react quite so intensely. Her response baffled him.

Unless... Maybe she was struggling with a different kind of prejudice. Perhaps Keeshan doesn't look black. Perhaps the woman had not expected a black man to show up claiming to be the boy's uncle. Could race underlie her seething fits of anger?

It seemed the only explanation. Marcus shook his head. Up in the north, where white people claim to be color-blind, he'd found prejudice as thick as homemade molasses bread. *Just like the south,* he thought, *although much more carefully hidden.*

As Marcus worked the cash register and loaded plywood, his frustration bloomed and went to seed. After all, he was kin. She had no right to keep him from the boy. None at all. Marcus thought of his father and of his father's deep commitment to his family. William Ovid Jefferson would never let a woman keep him from his grandchild. And with that thought, Marcus made up his mind.

He would see the child no matter what Callie decided.

But how? There had to be some way. Marcus stewed as he went back to marking the price on PVC pipe. The answer actually came to him with the arrival of the next customer.

"Pastor Roger," his boss said, his enthusiasm catching Marcus's attention. He looked up to see a tall, gray-haired man standing at the service counter. "You ready for that cement mixer?"

"I guess so, Bill," the man answered. "We have a crew coming in tomorrow morning at eight. My job is to pick up the supplies."

"Better than shoveling concrete," Bill said, laughing. "I have it all clean and ready to go. If you'll sign this form, I can have you out of here in a second."

Marcus watched as the pastor signed the rental agreement and provided a credit card for his deposit. His boss handed the receipt across the counter while gesturing with his other hand. "Back your truck up through the south gate, and I'll have Marcus here hook you up."

"Thanks." The pastor waved and went back out the front door. Marcus watched him walk to a white pickup truck near the door. The truck reminded Marcus of Sean Boyer, and he felt a stab of loneliness.

"Marcus, could you hook that trailer onto Pastor's truck for me?"

"Sure, no problem." Marcus went out through the back and opened the gate. He signaled as the pastor backed into position. Then he lifted the trailer onto the hitch. After he had connected the safety chain, he stood up. "That should do it."

"When do we have to return the mixer?"

"Before closing tomorrow. It needs to be rinsed out."

"Shouldn't be a problem. The youth picnic is Sunday afternoon. We have to have the barbecue set by then anyway. Sure isn't easy building a new church," he said, removing a work glove to run his hand through his thinning hair. "I used to think that a pastor's job was pastoring—you know, preaching and praying. Sure never thought I'd be building a barbecue pit."

Marcus laughed. And then something the pastor said caught his attention. A new church. Building a new church. "Excuse me, sir," he said. "I'm new around here. Which church are you talking about?"

"I thought you looked new to me. I've been shopping here since I moved to Prospect in '87. I should have introduced myself." He stuck out a thick hand. "I'm Roger Weir, the pastor at Mountain Meadows."

"Mountain Meadows?" Though he couldn't place it, the name seemed familiar.

"Two years old. We built our building out northeast of town. By the new elementary school. You're welcome to join us," he smiled. "We aren't too big, but we love Jesus, and we preach the Bible. We have good programs for kids. Bring your wife and join us."

Marcus smiled, remembering that this was the church that Callie admitted attending on his first visit to the coffee shop. "That's a nice invitation. I need a good church. Maybe I'll visit. When's the service?"

"We start at 10:00," Roger said. "No Sunday school yet. That'll have to come later. But the service is good. You'll see."

"I'll be there," Marcus said with genuine enthusiasm.

Roger gave him a jolly wave of his baseball cap. "Then I'll be waiting for you," he said as he climbed into the truck.

>>>

On Sunday morning Callie drank raspberry tea and read the Sunday *Tribune* in the great room, enjoying the quiet. Keeshan came in and climbed up into the chair beside her. He dropped Celia's nightgown in Callie's lap and rubbed his eyes with both fists. "Good morning, Spider-Man," she said, giving him a little squeeze.

He pointed at the paper. "Cartoons?"

"You got 'em." She peeled back the sections of the paper until she reached the funny papers and handed them to him.

He held the paper with one hand, the other thumb in his mouth. She watched his gaze skim over the colorful drawings. "Now, read them?" he asked, shoving the paper at her face.

"I will," she said, "if you ask nicely."

"Please?"

"Much better." She took the paper and held it down where he could see it as she read. Then, with her finger pointing to the words, she began with Peanuts, and moved to Fox Trot. At the end of the first page, she asked, "Do you think we should stop and have breakfast? We have church today, you know."

"Really?" Keehsan's eyes sparkled as his face broke into a wide grin. "Austin will be there." Though she'd watched the change unfold, Keeshan's growth over the last few weeks still pleased her. He scooted forward on the chair, turned onto his tummy and slid off. Pulling her hand, he dropped the nightgown on the floor and grabbed the funny paper. "We can read while we eat."

"We?" Callie laughed at this statement, though she knew that Keeshan considered looking at the pictures exactly the same as reading. "Okay, we'll read while we eat," she agreed, following the boy into the kitchen.

Ninety minutes later, showered and dressed, Callie and Keeshan arrived at Mountain Meadows Community Church. Callie took Keeshan directly to his classroom, where he joined the boys in coloring on the whiteboard. After a moment visiting with Jerry, Callie took the front steps into the lobby.

She had just stepped through the double doors when she spotted Pastor Roger pumping the hand of someone coming in from the parking lot. From his enthusiastic greeting, Callie guessed that her pastor welcomed someone he knew. Callie smiled at Roger's enthusiasm, and tucked her purse over her shoulder, hurrying to find a seat in the sanctuary.

She'd nearly crossed the lobby when Marcus Jefferson stepped through the church's front doors. Dumbfounded, Callie stumbled over her own feet.

>>>>

Though Marcus had every intention of seeing the child, he had not planned on running into Callie before he even reached the sanctuary. And yet he had. He'd hardly had time to adjust to the light inside the building before he saw her.

She wore a dress of midnight blue, fitted and draped at the waist by gathers that showed off her slim figure. Her hair hung over her shoulders, and he realized he had not seen it this way before. In the light of the high stained-glass windows, its shine rivaled that of a model on a shampoo commercial.

She had no more than spotted him when her face opened up in surprise and then withered in fury. For a moment Marcus wished he did not have to be the source of such intense misery. He moved toward her, holding out his hand. "Good morning, Callie," he said, as though he came to church every Sunday. "It's good to see you again."

"I wish I could say the same," she answered, ignoring his hand. "You just don't seem to get it, do you? I thought I made myself quite clear the last time we spoke."

"I'm sorry," he answered, folding his hands. "I thought this was a church. You know the concept. A place where everyone is welcome?"

"Don't even pretend that you're here to attend church."

"What? I'm too much of a monster?"

"I didn't say that. Why do you make me out like some kind of witch?" She hugged her purse as she spoke, and the way that she did it betrayed fear and mistrust.

Her strong words were a front, Marcus decided. She was not as confident as she wanted to appear.

"Look," she said, "you can go to church anywhere you want. It's of no consequence to me. Now, excuse me. I was just on my way to find a seat."

For the second time since he'd arrived in Prospect, Marcus watched her walk away. It was beginning to feel like a bad habit.

Only after Callie disappeared behind the sanctuary door did it occur to Marcus that the boy had not been with her. Where was he? Marcus chided himself for not asking.

He followed her to the sanctuary and chose a seat in the back, determined not to call any more attention to himself than he already had. It felt strange to him, sitting in a congregation again. How long had it been since he'd allowed himself the simple pleasure of a church service? Marcus felt the sting of tears and pinched his nose.

He'd been hiding for so long. Even in Tucson he'd avoided the church service. He didn't want to chance being seen, being recognized. He had too much to lose.

For three years Marcus had hidden from the vendetta Presario had promised. From the day of Peter's arrest, Marcus lived in constant fear—the fear of being recognized, of being located, of being killed for nothing more than cold-blooded retaliation.

Presario killed for pleasure; Marcus had seen the bodies to prove it.

He wanted to live. He'd traded three years of his life for the pleasure of living to old age. Fear had been his unrelenting companion. It had driven Marcus from the very things most precious to him. Family. Church. Work. Even things as simple as worship with the ones he loved.

And on this morning, as he experienced it again, the swell of voices, the emotion of music, the genuine humility that comes with recognizing the greatness of God, Marcus could hardly control the feelings that

swelled within him. It didn't matter if the whole underworld knew who
had turned them in. Marcus would never run again.

As he recognized the strength of his decision, he immediately
regretted that he had not come to this conclusion before Celia's accident.

Marcus reveled in the song service. Though the music was new, he
entered in with as much gusto as he dared; he had no singing voice. And
there was no way to hide a tall black man, his voice the bellow of a moose,
in the middle of a milky white congregation. Still, he put his whole heart
into worship.

Afterward he greeted the family sitting next to him and enjoyed
meeting the elderly couple in front of him. As his hands touched the
skin of his brothers and sisters, Marcus felt truly alive.

While a small blond woman sang a solo, he found himself watching
Callie—not that he could avoid it. She sat several rows in front of him,
on the other side of the center aisle. Beside her sat another woman, nearly
the same age, who appeared to be married to the man on her other side.
Marcus watched as Callie whispered in her friend's ear, and they shared
a giggle.

During the greeting time, Callie freely gave and received the hugs
of those around her. She shook hands and exchanged pleasantries,
looking for all the world like a high school cheerleader campaigning for
prom queen. Only different.

She seemed genuine.

She had the kind of healthy aura Marcus expected from a soccer star
or a professional golfer. She never seemed to wear makeup—at least not
like other women. There was nothing artificial about her. No garish
colors. No long bright nails. Her skin glowed with the faint pink of fre-
quent exercise, and her bright eyes were surrounded by thick brown
lashes.

She had a natural grace, a confidence that both intrigued him and
made him crazy.

He concluded that it was her confidence that made her despise him.
The same confidence that made her absolutely certain that she was the
best one—no, the only one—capable of caring for a grieving boy. It was

that same confidence that made her assume that he'd come to church to see Keeshan. And in that she was absolutely right.

A squirming two-year-old in the row ahead of Marcus caught his attention. His mother tried to busy him with a stuffed bear, but he would have none of it. His squirming grew to include a whine. As he struggled with his mother, the boy hit his head on the shelf holding the hymnals. The sound of a tiny skull hitting hard wood made Marcus cringe.

The child's loud cries rang through the sanctuary, and his mother lifted him into her arms and stood to leave. Marcus watched her edge her way to the aisle, deeply aware of her desire to escape before eroding the attention of the entire audience.

Recognizing that her hands were full, he slid out of his seat to open the door for her. He'd no more than done so when it hit him. The boy. Keeshan had to be in a class for children! He hadn't seen him because he was already in class.

As the woman passed in front of him, she smiled her appreciation. Marcus stepped outside and closed the door quietly. Falling into step behind her, he said, "Excuse me. Could you tell me where I might find the four-year-old classroom?"

"Of course," she answered, pointing to the exit of the lobby. "At the bottom of the stairs on your left."

Marcus hurried down the stairs, his heart beating more from excitement than from exercise. No doubt the teacher would not let a stranger speak to the children. Perhaps Callie had even warned them of Marcus's presence in Prospect. Still, he could look, couldn't he? No one could stop him from looking.

The stairs ended in the middle of a long hallway filled with fluorescent light. Marcus turned left as the woman instructed, and read the signs beside every door. At the third door on the left, Marcus read "Threes and Fours."

He stopped, suddenly aware that Keeshan was in the room beyond the door. He crossed the hall, and peered through the narrow window above the door handle. Boys and girls ran around the room, searching behind the furniture, under the chairs, along the whiteboard—apparently in a game of hide-and-seek. The action reminded Marcus of the

Easter egg hunts he'd experienced as a child—only different. He watched as the children found small squares of colored paper and brought them to the teacher. One by one she lined them up on the tray below the whiteboard. A single word was printed on each one.

With each word recovered, children skipped and jumped and hopped with glee. It didn't take long for Marcus to recognize the lesson. They were collecting the fruits of the Spirit. Unfortunately for Marcus, the children danced by the window with too much speed for him to inspect their features. He had not yet recognized Keeshan.

He watched until all nine papers had been collected, and the children gathered around the teacher for what appeared to be story time. They sat facing away from him, their backs to the window. One by one Marcus examined the children. First he eliminated the girls. Then he discarded boys with fair skin and blond hair. What would Keeshan look like now? Would he have his mother's almond eyes? His father's ebony skin?

Though he could not be certain, he spotted a child near the outer edge of the front row. His dark hair curled about his head in ringlets. From behind Marcus could not identify the color of his skin, though his hands seemed dark. As his heart picked up speed, Marcus knew with certainty that the child had to be Keeshan.

He felt his hands grow damp in anticipation. He'd waited so long, wanted so badly to see the child who needed him now.

The teacher dismissed the children, and they skipped and hopped their way to the table where their snacks waited on napkins. The last child to stand was the dark-haired boy in the front row.

Marcus watched as the teacher went to him and bent down, touching his soft curls as she spoke. When she stood, she took the child's hand, and they turned to face the door. Instantly, Marcus recognized Celia's eyes, the curly hair of the infant he'd last seen in Florida, and the smile of his brother.

He'd found him; Marcus had found Keeshan!

Twenty-Five

As the weather warmed, Callie's daily routine expanded. Continuing to care for the boy, she spent the first hours of her day in the workshop, where she struggled to finish Angie's couch. After taking Keeshan to day care, she took the second shift at the coffee shop. Then, as was her habit in the spring, Callie added another project.

She re-created her mother's garden.

With her father's rototiller, Callie turned the soil in the vegetable garden. Then, adding fertilizer, she turned the soil again. Together she and Keeshan cleared the rocks and staked perfectly spaced rows with string. She allowed him to plant zucchini, beans, carrots, and corn along the top of the mounds. She helped him transplant tiny tomatoes plants into the row nearest the back of the greenhouse, where they would benefit from reflected heat.

It was an adventure Keeshan relished. His excitement was contagious, and every evening, when the last of the dishes had been put away, they put on their work clothes and headed for the garden. She taught him to pull weeds and water from a watering can.

His was a random approach to weeding, and it often included plucking healthy vegetable plants. Finding an offending plant, he would yank it from the ground and run across the garden, bringing it to Callie with the enthusiasm of lost treasure. He often presented other favorite discoveries—caterpillars, beetles, and earthworms. Keeshan seemed to flourish as the garden grew.

One morning nearly two weeks after running into Marcus at church, Keeshan came early into her workshop. Callie, in the middle of covering the back of Angie's sofa, had just finished nailing brads through a cardboard strip at the top of the back, turning the fabric to expose a neatly finished edge. When Keeshan arrived, she was in the midst of hammering an aluminum tack strip into place. "I'm hungry," he said.

"I know, honey. Can you sit down and wait for me a minute?"

"I want Dynobuddies. I can make it myself."

She envisioned the floor of her kitchen covered with cold cereal and opted for a practical consideration. "You can't pour the milk."

"I can too."

"In just a moment, I'll be finished. Please be patient."

"But I'm hungry."

Callie could not stop. She'd battled the left edge of the back for too long to give in now. The strip wanted to pop out, and she had to lean into the frame as she hammered. "I promise. Just a minute." Bent upside down, with her head very near the floor, Callie gave one final swing of the hammer.

Keeshan began to cry. It was not the frustrated cry of a hungry boy, but the agonized cry of the injured. Straightening, she spotted him behind her, sitting on the floor, one foot crossed over his knee. Tears rolled down his cheeks as his cry turned into a near scream. She went to him, bending down over his foot.

"What happened?"

He cried all the louder.

Frightened, Callie sat beside him, taking his foot in her hand. "Turn over," she instructed, and Keeshan lay on his tummy. His cry continued unabated. She examined the small, bare foot carefully. There was no blood. No obvious injury. "What is it?"

"My toe," he howled.

Callie shifted her attention to his toe, squeezing the bulb of flesh on the sole of his foot. Blood trickled from a tiny wound at the base of his great toe. "Keeshan, what did you step on?"

"A nail," he said, crying louder. He twisted to the side and handed Callie a blue upholstery tack. "I stepped on a nail."

"I'm so sorry," Callie said, scooping him into her arms. "I didn't mean for you to step on a brad. It must hurt very much."

He settled into her lap, slipping his thumb into his mouth. "It hurts."

She brushed the tears from his cheeks. "I think maybe you need some pancakes to recover from that wound," she said.

"Yes, that would help a lot."

"Okay. Let's go make pancakes. You can stir the batter."

>>>

Marcus could not get over seeing the child. Somehow, wherever he went, whatever he did, he carried Keeshan's image with him. It consumed him, the presence of his brother's child, so near and yet so unavailable. Marcus no longer wanted just to see him; he wanted to spend time with him. To know him. To be known by him.

This was his brother's boy. His father's only grandson. The boy needed a man in his life. He needed the firm guidance, the male influence, that only another man could give. He needed the good things that Marcus had been given. Encouragement, education, challenge, character, a relationship with the living God. The boy needed Marcus.

Marcus needed the boy.

Seeing Keeshan changed everything for Marcus. What began as curiosity had grown to protectiveness, and somehow in the days that passed after the church service, his concern crossed the line into obsession. Marcus had to have the boy.

He began to look for a better job. Every morning as he loaded the materials on his customer's trucks, he reminded the crews that he was a framer. Experienced. Fast. Professional. Reliable.

He began to pray about the child. To pray for him. For his care. For Callie. In the process, he began to understand her protectiveness. He felt the same way. As the days passed, Marcus knew that somehow he must gain custody of his only brother's child.

But the fight for custody required money. And money was the one commodity that Marcus did not have. One day after work, Marcus went home to his rented room in Violet Werner's old house. His little nine by eleven space had never felt so empty.

He turned on the television, skipped over several channels, and found nothing to interest him. He picked up a novel, flipped to the opening chapter, and could not focus on the words. He wandered downstairs, hoping to find Mrs. Werner at work in the kitchen.

With the cutting board fully extended, she gently rolled pastry into a perfect circle. Beside her a glass pie plate waited.

"You look lost, Marcus," she said as he came in. "Would you like some iced tea? I just made fresh."

"Sounds good," he answered, smiling. What allowed women to read men this way? He might as well write his feelings on his forehead.

She wiped her hands on her apron and poured deep amber liquid into a glass. After adding lemon slices, she handed it to him, saying, "Might as well tell me about it. I'm all you've got. What's bothering you?"

"The boy," Marcus answered.

"Your nephew? The one at Mountain Meadows?"

"I didn't tell you that."

"You don't have to. It's a small town."

Marcus laughed, a hollow, sad laugh. "I grew up in Indianapolis."

She nodded. "What bothers you about the boy?"

He leaned against the counter, his arms across his chest. "Keeshan needs me. I want custody. I owe it to my brother. But that takes an attorney, and I can't afford that. I've been asking around for more work, but no one's ready to hire."

"The economy is off." She folded her pastry in half and lifted it into the pie plate, tucking it in and pinching the lip without a single break in the dough. Though her hands flew around the pie, Violet kept her eyes on Marcus. "So you want work? What kind?"

"I can do just about anything. I've been in the construction business all my adult life. You name it, I've done it."

"What about renovation?"

"I've done it all."

"Would you consider doing some work for me? I could give you a large advance."

"Would I?" Marcus echoed. "Are you kidding?"

>>>

On the morning after the incident with the tack, Keeshan woke tired and grumpy, demanding rather than asking for breakfast.

Resigned to caring for the child—and his emotional ups and downs—Callie followed him from the shop into the kitchen. Walking behind him, Callie noticed that he limped. *He must have hurt his foot more than I realized,* she thought. *I'll have to keep an eye on that.*

While they got ready for the day, Keeshan had no patience with Callie; she was too slow with his breakfast, too demanding with his table manners, too helpful with his dressing.

She very nearly ran out of patience with him.

Shortly after one in the afternoon, she received a phone call from Peggy Mortenson. "I'm sorry to bother you at work, Callie," she began, sounding worn out. Knowing how much energy one child demanded, Callie couldn't begin to imagine a grandmother caring for a whole house full of children.

Peggy continued, "I think you may need to take Keeshan to the doctor. I'd have waited until you came to pick him up, but I think you might want to do it today."

"Doctor?"

"It's his foot. He'll hardly walk on it. When I took off his shoe, I noticed a bandage on his toe. I tried to unwrap it for a better look, but he wouldn't let me touch it. His toe is swollen and red. I think it might be infected."

"It can't be," Callie objected. How could a tack cause an infection so quickly? "Does he have a fever?"

"I haven't taken his temperature. If I were you, I'd make an appointment."

"Thanks for calling, Peggy. I appreciate it. I'll get right back to you."

Callie managed to get a four o'clock appointment with the pediatrician. She called Jan, who, though she'd already worked a full seven hours, agreed to come in and close the shop.

By the time she arrived at Peggy's, Keeshan refused to walk no matter how much she coaxed and bribed. His face felt warm, and Callie struggled with guilt for having let this little injury get so far out of control. She carried him to the car and buckled him into his seat.

At the doctor's office they waited for more than two hours as sick children with prearranged appointments came and went. It seemed to be the season for spring colds, and Callie had never seen more runny noses in one place. Sneezing, wiping, touching, Callie could almost feel her next cold creeping into her lungs as the minutes passed.

Keeshan cuddled in her lap, unwilling to venture over to the toys or the television. Uninterested in the toddlers who came near to inspect him, he waited, his eyes drifting closed.

It wasn't bad, holding a sleeping child.

When her turn came, she carried him to the exam room. With the child on her lap, the nurse practitioner managed to unwrap the toe, confirming Callie's worst suspicions—the beginning of a nasty infection. Even though she'd looked at the toe in the morning, Callie was surprised by the changes that had occurred since breakfast.

Reading from her computer screen, the nurse practitioner said, "We don't have a record of his immunization schedule during his first few months, so I'd like to start with a tetanus booster." She paused to adjust her glasses and continued, "And, of course, we'll start a course of antibiotics. This infection is aggressive. I'd like to hit him with an antibiotic smart bomb, so to speak."

"Anything you suggest," Callie agreed.

The nurse stroked the keyboard and the printer underneath chugged to life, spewing out a prescription, which she signed with a flourish. "I have a sample of this medicine here in the office. I'll give you the first dose now. Then you head straight to the pharmacy. Make sure that he takes every single dose. Try to space the doses as evenly as you can. Don't skip a single dose. Don't stop taking the prescription before you use all the medicine."

"I understand," Callie said.

"Be sure to call me if he hasn't improved within twenty-four hours. When you are finished with the prescription, he should be symptom free. If he isn't absolutely better, I want him back in the office."

"What does that mean?"

"We won't worry about that now. If this doesn't work, we have other approaches." She smiled. "Call us if you have any questions."

Callie thanked the nurse and carried Keeshan to the front desk, where she wrote a check for the co-payment. She chose a sugar-free lollipop for Keeshan, and offered to unwrap it. Keeshan shook his head, leaned into her chest, and closed his eyes.

>>>

With a touch of anxiety, Marcus turned into the paved driveway. The woman at the coffee shop told him Callie lived here, deep in forty acres of untouched woods. He'd followed her instructions exactly, but nothing she said prepared him for the unabashed beauty of the place. Did all this belong to Callie?

Covered by a thick carpet of needles, the private road was lined on both sides by tall firs, some with diameters as great as a grown man's outstretched arms. Heavy underbrush covered the forest floor. Some of these plants Marcus recognized—huckleberry, Oregon grape, ferns. But most were completely unfamiliar to a man who had grown up in the poorer sections of Indianapolis. His understanding of botany ended with the Indiana State parks.

The driveway seemed to go on forever. Just when Marcus had begun to give up on finding her house, the drive made a sharp left turn, and the trees gave way to a vista of sunlit green. Before him the house stood alone in what appeared to be a natural meadow, where Marcus caught a glimpse of the mountain.

He slammed on the brakes and put the car in reverse.

Mt. Rainier, a sleeping volcano of more than fourteen thousand feet, dominated the skyline around Prospect. Locals lived in the ever-present shadow of the mountain. As a man raised in the Midwest, Marcus would never get used to seeing the mountain like this, close enough to touch. He nearly stopped breathing whenever it emerged suddenly from a cloudy sky. He shook his head.

It seemed to have been painted on a canvas of blue, so close that it took up the greatest part of the sky. Marcus let the car idle as he took a few moments to gaze at the vista.

Dragging himself away, he paused before the big house. There was no car parked here, and Marcus wondered if perhaps Callie wasn't home. He turned into the carport beside what appeared to be a guesthouse and parked. In the sunlight the lawn and tree leaves sparkled with leftover drops of an early afternoon rain. The yard was perfectly neat, cut and well trimmed with not a single weed in sight. He got out and walked toward the big house.

Rather than the usual grass plot surrounded by a small border of shrubs, Callie's yard invited the observer inside. Flagstone pathways traveled through the garden. Huge rocks, stacked against the hill, provided a visual anchor for terraced displays of exotic plants. A small waterfall trickled over the rocks. Unable to resist a closer examination, he stepped onto the walkway.

The plants here bore little resemblance to the standard fare surrounding most Prospect homes. In one corner, though it held no blooms, he recognized the spiky leaves of a tropical flower. In another, Marcus spotted a diminutive species of palm. In spite of their bizarre origins, the landscape had the thoughtful feel of a luxurious refuge.

He had never seen anything quite like it.

Determined to accomplish his mission, he went to the door and rang the bell. Trying to appear calm, he deliberately relaxed his shoulders and folded his hands. No one answered.

The empty house puzzled him. The woman at the coffee shop had directed him here, implying that Callie and the child were at home. Marcus stepped sideways into the planting area below the front window. The soil was damp from the rain, and he sank into the mud, leaving deep footprints. Cupping his hands on the window, he looked inside.

The window opened over a narrow corridor separating what he guessed to be the two main living areas of the house. On the far side a low wall of warm-colored stones separated the great room from the main hallway. The room had a cathedral ceiling, and even from outside he could see a wall of windows opening the room to the view east of the house.

A huge fireplace of identical stones anchored one end of the room. The beams in the ceiling were stained dark, and the ceiling itself had been sprayed with popcorn, a texture rarely seen anymore. Marcus guessed the house was perhaps fifteen years old.

He noticed that the house was clean, almost meticulously so. The window had no fingerprints. The great room had no toys, clothes, magazines, or even collectibles. For that matter, Marcus could not identify a single sign that a living person actually used the room. It looked as clean as a model home.

Strange, he thought, shaking his head as he stepped back onto the sidewalk. His curiosity aroused, Marcus wondered what other hints the property might hold about the mysterious and ill-tempered woman who lived there. *As long as she's not home, I might as well take a look around.*

Across the driveway and up several stone steps, tall posts supported chicken wire strung around what appeared to be a garden. A solid cedar gate, painted a soft fern green, hung between posts. On this, a tiny hand-printed sign hung. Curious, Marcus walked across the drive.

Garden tours—ten cents. Vegetables—all you can eat.

Glancing up the drive, Marcus wondered how long it would be before Callie actually showed up. Did he dare give himself an unescorted tour?

The latch to the gate was on the inside; Marcus pulled a thick cord to enter. The gate swung away easily. Inside he found the largest vegetable garden he had ever seen. Growing in neat rows, plants flourished in the sunshine. Marcus knew his vegetables; his mother had always kept a small garden. But the vast assortment of plants in this space astounded him. What on earth was she going to do with all this?

Marcus walked down one row and continued up the hill. Behind the garden he discovered a small grove of fruit trees containing at least six carefully pruned dwarf varieties, all heavily laden with fruit.

Beside the orchard stood a small, hand-built greenhouse. On the end facing the sun, Callie had planted more than a dozen tomato plants. Though not yet bearing fruit, blossoms already covered the plants.

He'd never expected this—an almost gentleman farmer—from the woman who cared for the boy. She seemed too cultured, too social to live in this way. Still, whoever cultivated this space had invested her heart and soul into the plants she grew.

Confused, Marcus left the garden, carefully closing the gate behind him. From above the driveway, he caught site of the smaller house. Celia had undoubtedly lived here.

He wanted to see inside. He wanted to know, even though it was too late, that she had been comfortable here, that she'd made a good transition, that she'd moved on to a happy life.

Marcus went around to the back of Celia's house, where, on the mountain side, he found a covered porch completely bathed in shadow. Two pieces of white wicker furniture, each with a worn chintz cushion, lined the porch. The guesthouse, like the big house next door, also had windows on the view side, though Celia's were covered by pleated shades.

Back at the driveway, Marcus watched an SUV pull into the carport of the big house. His heart rate accelerated. It wasn't going to be easy, doing what he'd come to do. But he had no choice. Marcus had to finish what he'd started. Or better perhaps, to start what he had decided to finish. He wasn't sure which statement accurately described his position.

He waited patiently beside the carport while Callie got out of the car. She ignored him as she opened the rear passenger door and leaned inside. After throwing something over her shoulder, she pulled the boy out of the car.

It was Keeshan. The same boy Marcus had spotted in the church classroom. His head, covered in soft dark curls, rested against the woman's shoulder. *He seems tired,* Marcus thought. Sleepy perhaps. He did not lift his head as she started around to the back of the car.

Without speaking, Marcus stepped out of her way.

"This isn't a good time," she said, unlocking the cargo door with a remote.

"It's never a good time."

"You're not funny. We just came from the doctor."

"Sick?" Suddenly Marcus reinterpreted the child's posture. "What's wrong?"

"He stepped on a tack," she said. Opening the rear door of the vehicle with one hand, she pulled out a plastic grocery bag. "He's got a bad toe."

Marcus stepped forward, concerned. "What did the doctor say?"

"They said Keeshan has an infection." She turned away and walked toward the house. "I can't stand here visiting with you. He weighs a ton."

Marcus leaned down, and picked up several grocery bags, and shut the door. "Here, I'll help you bring these inside."

She turned, eyeing him suspiciously before nodding. "I guess I could use the help."

Marcus set the bags on the kitchen counter while Callie settled the boy on the couch. He put the milk in the refrigerator and began to take the groceries out of the bags. He might not know where things went, but he could at least empty the bags for her. She came into the kitchen and grabbed a bottle of water from the refrigerator. Before closing the door, she asked, "Want one?"

"No, thanks," he said. Marcus ran his thumb across his mustache, wondering how he should proceed. He certainly hadn't planned all of this, to find her with a sick boy on her hands. "I suppose I ought to be going."

"Wait," she said. "You haven't told me why you're here."

Her tone betrayed suspicion. Wishing he did not have to confirm her strong opinions, he confessed, "Actually, I came to give you these." He opened his jacket, retrieved a bundle of papers, and held them out to her.

Though she accepted the papers, which had been folded lengthwise, she did not open them. "What are they?"

Marcus looked away.

"You might as well tell me."

Her eyes narrowed, and even clothed in mistrust, he thought they must be the most striking eyes he'd ever seen. He hated to tell her the truth. Hated to have her despise him even more. "They're legal papers. I've filed for third-party custody."

Twenty-Six

Before Marcus had pulled out onto the highway, Callie dialed her attorney at home. "He's filed for custody," she blurted as soon as Dorothy Powell picked up.

"It'll work itself out," Dorothy assured her. "We have a court date in late August."

Callie could hardly contain her disappointment. "Can't we do something sooner?"

"The court calendar is jammed. We fast-tracked the first order, but I can't do anything about this. Until then, temporary custody remains in place." She paused to clear her throat. "Callie, you're paying me for advice, and I need to tell you something. I want you to listen, and listen carefully." She paused, and Callie leaned forward, wishing her to go on. "If you want to keep this child, you must not infuriate the uncle."

"I can't be responsible for his emotions!"

"I'm not kidding here. If you're not careful, you may create a monster."

"He's already a monster."

"Look, I've had custody disputes go on for years. Years, I'm telling you. In some cases I'm convinced that as long as either party has any money left, they'll use it to battle over the children. Custody battles become a kind of cancer—always coming back—especially when one party begins to see it as retribution. It could happen here. And it will, unless you figure out how to pacify this man."

"Pacify? Are you saying that we won't win?"

"No. I'm saying that even if you do win, it may not be over anytime soon."

"How do I pacify him?"

"Let him see the child. Don't be so heavy-handed. Show the court you're willing to cooperate so that the child has the best of both worlds. After all, Marcus Jefferson is his uncle."

"What if he isn't good for Keeshan?"

"You'll have to document that. If it's true, I might be able to speed things up. But first we'll have to appear before a commissioner. You can't just make an assumption and react. Besides, it's possible that if he has access to the child, he will lose interest in custody."

"What if it backfires? What if by spending time with Keeshan he becomes obsessed?"

"Then we'll have to see what the court decides."

"I can't do that."

"You don't have any choice. I'm guessing the court will appoint a guardian ad litem. He'll interview both you and Marcus and spend some time with the boy. He'll make a recommendation based on what he observes. The court will likely follow his suggestion."

Callie could feel herself start to tremble. "It sounds risky."

"It's very risky. Of course, we'll try to color things our way so that the commissioner will decide you'll make the best custodial parent. In the meantime, try to stay busy. Take care of the child. Don't let this battle consume you."

>>>>

Callie tried to follow her attorney's suggestions, though it was far easier to suggest that Callie think of other things than it was for Callie to accomplish. Still, the beautiful weather helped her to find ways to stay busy.

She and Keeshan developed some summertime routines of their own. After work, on nights that they did not spend in the garden, she and Keeshan shared an early dinner. Then, after piling him into his car seat, she strapped her bike on the back of her car and drove to the park by the river. There, in the late afternoon sunshine, she put Keeshan in the buggy she'd borrowed from Jerry and rode the flat paved trail alongside Prospect Creek. Though these outings were different from her usual rides, Callie grew to enjoy them.

On hot days the glacier-fed river gave off a cooling spray. The cover of trees protected them from the intense heat of the late afternoon sun. Though not as long as the bike trips she had taken when she lived alone, Callie rejoiced in her ability to ride at all. Her legs grew stronger as she pulled the heavy trailer day after day; her heart and lungs stopped complaining at the workload. She settled into the rhythm of pulling Keeshan along the trail behind her.

Callie enjoyed greeting the same people every afternoon. Older couples out for their after-dinner walks. Women wearing Lycra and earphones, desperate to exercise after a long day at work. Kids riding with training wheels. Grandpas walking their hunting dogs. In a surprising way they all became familiar to Callie, a pleasure she never expected.

Keeshan loved riding in the trailer. He pointed out the horses, called out to the dogs, and waved at all his new friends. One afternoon they stopped to watch a cow give birth. On another, they saw an eagle catch a salmon in the river. As the summer progressed, they watched the corn grow high along the trail.

They enjoyed other activities as well, though some were not nearly as pleasant. Callie continued to visit her father with Keeshan. Though Jack did not approve of her keeping the boy, he grew to enjoy their visits. And Keeshan, unaware of the tension, grew to love Jack.

Angie picked up her new hide-a-bed and other projects found their way into the workshop. Her upholstery business grew, bit by bit, and Callie benefited from the additional income. It paid her attorney bills.

Though she understood Dorothy Powell's suggestion to include Marcus in Keeshan's life, she found it very difficult to do. She didn't trust him, and she would not consider allowing the boy to spend time with his uncle alone.

Fortunately for Callie, Marcus continued to attend Mountain Meadows. This gave her at least some way of maintaining civil contact. At a church party for high school graduates, they shared a table in the fellowship hall. He sat by her during a children's program celebrating Independence Day. Keeshan greeted Marcus every Sunday with enthusiasm worthy of an uncle.

Marcus behaved himself during these brief interactions, though he always seemed too eager to please, too friendly, too…well, it was almost as if he didn't think his bid for full custody would hurt her. Callie resented that. Why didn't he understand how desperately she wanted to keep Keeshan?

Still, he was kind to the boy, and he had a good sense of humor. He was gentle. Encouraging. He knew how boys liked to play, and he met Keeshan at Keeshan's level. Though she was aware of these attributes, and of his handsome good looks, Callie resisted the urge to soften toward him. It bothered her that Marcus Jefferson had little to disqualify him from parenting Keeshan.

>>>

As spring turned to summer, Marcus kept his job at Contractor's Supply and was promoted to lumber supply manager. Now in charge of all the ordering and delivery of lumber and trusses, the job didn't provide much of a challenge, but it came with a raise, and Marcus managed to put some money away toward his legal expenses.

In his spare time, he worked for Mrs. Werner. "My brother died last fall and left me his estate," she'd told him as they discussed proposed changes. "He never married, so I'm his only surviving relative. I think he'd like me to fix up the old place. That's where you come in," she said, smiling. "I want a new kitchen, with one of those big breakfast nooks. I want new cabinets too—with the trays in the cupboards that pull out. I don't want to crawl in after my pressure cooker anymore.

"And I want a brick patio, big enough for comfortable lawn furniture, so I can sit outside and read a good book. And I want it surrounded by flower boxes. Can you do that?"

"Everything but the furniture," Marcus said, laughing.

After drawing plans he framed a small addition to the back of Mrs. Werner's fifty-year-old home. He enclosed the space, opened the kitchen to the addition and spent the very first week of summer tearing out Mrs. Werner's kitchen cabinets.

It frustrated Marcus that he could only work for Violet part-time. "You could get someone else to do this faster. Your kitchen will be out of commission for a long time."

"I don't want anyone else."

"You won't be able to cook." Looking at the disappointment in her face, Marcus realized that she had not thought that far ahead.

"I promised you room and board," she said.

"Well, do you have any camping gear?"

"I think my husband may have kept some in the garage—up in the rafters."

"I'll take a look. Maybe we can set up a kitchen in the garage."

With the old oven and a two-burner propane stove, Marcus soon had Mrs. Werner back in business. She continued to cook, though she always waited for Marcus to come home and start the stove. Lighting the burners frightened Violet.

Every evening, Marcus ate with her in the backyard. When it rained, they pulled the picnic table into the garage. When it was cold, they wore sweaters. Mrs. Werner let Marcus have his pick of the sweaters she'd knit for the late Mr. Werner.

Marcus wore them with pride.

Somehow he knew that he would win the custody battle. He had every confidence that the state would prefer a blood relative over Callie. His confidence gave him peace, and he didn't feel the need to push Callie to let him spend time with Keeshan. He ran into the two of them occasionally, once in town and several times at Mountain Meadows, where Marcus continued to attend.

The boy was growing even as he watched from a distance.

He hadn't realized how confident he'd become until one day he found himself behind Callie in the line at the church picnic. She was scooping food onto two paper plates balanced in her left hand. She seemed to sense him there, and she glanced up to acknowledge him with a nod.

"Hello, Callie."

"Hello, Marcus." She had her hair in the same old pony tale, hanging out the hole in the back of a baseball cap. She wore cargo pants, cut short, so that some of her lovely legs tempted him. Her shirt, a white sleeveless model, was tied around the middle with a sash of the same material. She smelled of plumeria.

Marcus tried to ignore the scent. "Hello, Keeshan." Marcus bent around Callie to offer his palm for the traditional slap. Keeshan obliged. "Hey, how's your summer going?"

"It's good. I'm learning to ride a bike."

Marcus looked at Callie for an explanation. "It has training wheels," she said. "He's doing pretty well so far."

"Do you like the bike?"

"I can ride anywhere I want," Keeshan said. "I can go fast. Faster than the cat."

"I'll bet you can," Marcus agreed. "Do you wear a helmet?"

"She makes me," he pointed to Callie.

"And how is Eddy these days?"

"Fine," Keeshan said. "Eddy had kittens."

Marcus couldn't suppress the laugh that rumbled up out of his throat. "He did, did he?"

Keeshan nodded. "And I get to sell them."

"Sounds like a plan." Marcus leaned over the table to accept the hamburger offered by the host. "Thanks, Nick," he said. "You like hamburgers, Keeshan? Or are you having a hot dog?"

"I'm having a hang-ge-bur. See?" Keeshan pointed to his plate.

"Hang-ge-bur, eh?" He pronounced the *g* with a hard sound as the boy had. "You sure are. Looks good too."

At the end of the line, Callie turned to face him. "Well, since we're all here together, how about if you sit with us?"

Marcus nodded, trying to cover his surprise. "I'd like that very much."

She pointed to an empty blanket with her juice bottle. "Over there. We're all set up."

He followed them to the blanket, folding his big frame into a sitting position while still holding his drink and utensils. He landed with a thump.

"No cookie, Keeshan," Callie said, "until after you eat your hamburger."

Marcus looked up in time to see Keeshan drop an Oreo cookie back onto his paper plate. The boy looked as though he'd just missed catching a fly ball to center field. Marcus felt his heart soften. "He can't help it," he said, gesturing with a plastic fork. "He comes by it genetically. His dad loved Oreo cookies." Marcus put down his plate and snapped open his pop.

He looked up to see Callie staring. The boy seemed surprised. "My dad?"

Marcus looked at Callie.

With the slightest shake of her head, she warned him. *Don't say anything.*

He couldn't believe her nerve.

Keeshan doesn't know who I am. She hasn't told him the truth. What could be so upsetting about having an uncle? In an instant, he decided. "Yeah. Your dad was my little brother. Just like Angie and Don have three boys, our parents had two boys. Peter and Marcus. We grew up together, brothers." Marcus took a swig of pop. "That makes me your uncle."

His information clearly confused Keeshan. "My uncle?" He looked at Callie. "What's an uncle?"

Marcus hadn't planned on this. Didn't every child know what an uncle was?

"It's a relative. Like a grandpa or a grandma. Like a mom or a dad. It's a relative. A member of the family. You're a member of my family," Marcus explained.

"I don't think it's quite that easy," Callie interrupted with a determined air. "Families are more than just relatives. There are relatives that aren't family at all. And there are families that aren't even related."

Marcus knew by the bright red in her cheeks that he'd made her angry. Very angry. "Well, that makes it about as clear as mud, doesn't it?" Marcus asked.

"Keeshan," she said, "would you like to go play while your hamburger cools off? I think it's too hot to eat right now."

Boy, that's for sure.

"Can I take a cookie?"

She nodded. "Stay over by the swings, where I can watch you." The boy grabbed an Oreo and ran toward the other children. She turned on Marcus like a starving lioness. "How dare you make that kind of announcement here—now, of all times?"

"I thought he knew."

"Why would he know?"

"You should have told him."

"Why? What does it matter? He's only a child. He doesn't understand shirttail relatives."

"Shirttail?" Marcus couldn't believe it. "An uncle isn't shirttail! It's about time you start thinking ahead."

Her eyes narrowed. "What do you mean?"

"I mean that you'll have some real explaining to do when I take full custody of the boy won't you? Don't you think it would be easier if you told the truth now, rather than waiting until you deliver him to me?"

"I don't intend to deliver him to anyone."

"Your intentions are very clear. But when you lose the case, you won't have any choice, will you?" Marcus, having had just about enough of this woman, took his dinner and his Coke can and stood up. "When you run out of choices, you might just wish you'd been a little more thoughtful." With that, he strode away.

〉〉〉

Callie sputtered her way through several days, trying to get over her anger with Marcus. How dare he take an occasion as simple as a picnic and use it as an opportunity to endear himself to Keeshan! What made him take such liberty?

It wasn't until Dorothy Powell spoke to her about it that Callie realized she'd made a mistake. No matter how she felt about his behavior, she shouldn't have angered him like that. Anger wouldn't help her campaign to keep the boy. Her attorney had warned her, but Callie had plunged on in spite of good advice.

"You should try to mend your bridges," Dorothy told her. "It won't help to have him mad at you. Besides, he is the boy's uncle. Keeshan has a right to understand some of what is going on. You don't want Keeshan to be blindsided. Marcus might win custody."

"He won't. He can't. What judge would do that to a little boy?"

"It happens, Callie."

No matter how much she hated the idea, Dorothy's advice made sense. So, when the first of her cherry tomatoes ripened, she and Keeshan headed out to the garden with a white plastic bowl and picked them. Harvesting the fruit thrilled Keeshan, and it was all Callie could do to keep him from plucking every single tomato, including the green ones, hanging from her plants.

"Just the red ones, Keeshan," Callie told him. "Like this. See?" She held up a tiny marble-sized tomato. "It's red all over, even at the stem."

"Here's one," he said, crushing a tiny ripe orb between his thumb and fingers. He laughed and plopped the fruit in his mouth, squishing it with his teeth and showed her the results.

Callie shook her head. "What would I do without you?"

With the tomatoes picked, they put the sprinkler over the vegetables and turned on the water. Then, they got into the car and drove the ten miles into town.

Callie could only hope that Marcus was in the mood to let her grovel.

Twenty-Seven

Violet Werner's house stood three blocks off Main, her backyard facing the parking lot of Alfred's Hotel. Sol Werner, the founder of Werner's Department Store, built the house on a piece of property he bought in the 1950s, back when Prospect was nothing more than a filling station on the way to the national park. He'd managed to subdivide and sell the land just before he died, leaving Vi with the only vintage house among a large grouping of tiny ramblers.

Vi kept the two-story clapboard looking like a dollhouse. Fresh yellow paint covered the siding and white trim surrounded the narrow old-fashioned windows. Wisteria grew along the covered porch, and full pots of lush marigolds stood on both sides of the front door. Huge bushes of blooming dahlias grew along the gravel driveway. Every week, Vi mowed her own lawn with a reel mower and trimmed the garden with hand shears.

Even Callie, who loved her garden, stood in awe of Violet Werner.

Taking Keeshan by the hand, Callie approached the front door and knocked. After a long pause, Violet opened the door wearing a pale pink housedress, her shoulders draped with a white cardigan. A silver clasp and chain held the sweater in place.

Though she did not open the screen door, she stepped forward. "Yes?"

"Hi, Mrs. Werner, I'm Callie O'Brian. Remember me?"

She pushed thick glasses higher on her nose as she peered out. When she smiled, her entire face lifted several inches. "Oh, yes, Callie. Come in. Come in." With a screech of old hinges, she opened the screen door. "I expect you're here to see my Marcus."

My Marcus? Callie stepped inside. "Actually, I just brought a little something from my garden." She offered the bag of tomatoes. "We've had so many I can't possibly eat them all."

Vi accepted the brown bag without looking inside. "And who is this?" she said, turning her attention to the boy.

"This is Keeshan." Callie dropped his hand. "Keeshan, this is Mrs. Werner."

"I picked them," he offered. "Do you have a cat?"

Smiling, Vi bent down to have a better look at the boy. "Well, no, young man. I don't have a cat."

"Eddy has kittens," Keeshan said. Suddenly shy, he backed away. At last, bumping into her couch, he stopped. His thumb disappeared into his mouth.

"Isn't that nice, dear," she said, turning back to Callie. "Marcus is out back. Perhaps you'd like to give these to him yourself. Come along." Violet Werner set off toward the back of the house at a trot.

Callie hurried to catch up with the white bun as it disappeared through the dining room into the kitchen. "Oh, no, that won't be necessary," she objected. But Vi had already vanished. As Callie stepped into the kitchen, she found Marcus looking down at her from the top of an aluminum ladder. He took two nails from between his lips.

"Well, hello," he said, his right hand in the air, his hammer caught in what appeared to be mid-swing. "I wasn't expecting you."

Callie couldn't believe the changes in the room. Since the last time she'd been in Violet's home, someone had managed to create a bump out, a kind of octagonal space sticking out behind the house and into the yard. At the far side of this space, new French doors opened onto an enormous area outside. From the framework, it looked as though

Vi planned to add a patio. "Wow, this is great," she said, honestly impressed. "Who did all of this?"

"Why, Marcus, of course," Vi said. She handed him the bag as she trotted across the kitchen. "Look what Callie brought us. Won't they be just lovely with dinner?"

"I didn't know you did this kind of work," Callie said.

"I guess we haven't had much time to talk about what I can do." He stepped down from the ladder, pausing to drop his hammer into his tool belt.

"Oh, no, I'd almost forgotten," Vi said. "The dryer is finished. I've got laundry to fold. You'll excuse me." With that, she disappeared.

Suddenly Callie felt shy. "I didn't mean to interrupt. I, uh, we…" Callie stuttered like a seventh grader. She looked at Keeshan, who shrugged. "We just finished picking tomatoes from our garden. We have more than we could ever eat, so we brought some to you."

"A peace offering, eh?"

She felt her blood pressure rise and her cheeks grow warm. "Not really," she lied. *I'd like to chew and swallow my own crow, Mr. Marcus Jefferson. I don't need you to stuff it down my throat.* "Like I said, we thought you could use the fresh vegetables."

He smiled and leaned one elbow against the ladder, opening the bag to look inside. "Well, then, thank you very much. I do like fresh tomatoes."

Callie nodded, crossing her arms in front of her chest. "This really is amazing."

"You've been here before?"

"It's been a while. I dropped by with my dad."

"The whole idea was Violet's. She wanted more light and space. Kind of an eat-in kitchen. Most of all, she wanted to be able to go outside without having to tackle those steep stairs to the back door," he gestured to the door. "We left them there, but with this big deck and French doors, she can really enjoy her backyard."

"What about cabinets?"

"In the kitchen? We ordered them. I don't have time to make them myself."

"You could?"

He shrugged. "If I had to. My dad taught me."

Again Callie nodded. "New appliances?"

"That space is for a washer and dryer," he pointed. "When we're done, she can do laundry right here in the kitchen." He covered his mouth with a single finger. "But the whole thing is top secret. She's sure the people in town would think it's foolish to have everything redone."

"Why? It's her house."

Marcus smiled. "It's her age. That and the fact that she's blowing the inheritance from her brother's estate. She's doing everything. New appliances, new floors, new cabinets. It'll be beautiful when she's finished."

"She'll never keep a secret in this town," Callie said, shaking her head. "But it won't come from me. Cross my heart." She took one last look around the space. When Marcus finished, it would be a wonderful kitchen. Whether she wanted to or not, Callie had a whole new appreciation of him. He knew what he was doing with his tools. The kitchen would be much lighter and more useful than it had been when it was built. She shook herself from her thoughts. "Well, I think we should be getting home. We haven't had dinner. Come, Keeshan."

Keeshan, sitting in a corner filled with sawdust and scraps of wood, had already begun building his own house. He did not even look up.

"Keeshan, we need to be going."

"Why don't you stay and eat dinner with us?" Marcus said, his dark eyes sparkling. "Vi would be thrilled to have company."

>>>>

Marcus watched Callie consider the offer. She looked doubtful, like a teenager being asked to a prom by the pimply-faced boy in her physics class. "It's just a simple dinner," he added. "I promise not to start any arguments—my best behavior, honest. Vi will be here to send us to our separate corners if we misbehave."

"Well, I suppose dinner would be okay. I can't stay long. Keeshan goes to bed early."

"Good. I'll tell Vi. Be right back," he said. Marcus headed out to the garage, where he found Vi bent over a basket of clean sheets and towels. "Hey, Mrs. Werner. Would you mind if Callie and Keeshan stayed for dinner?"

"I was hoping you'd ask," she answered. "I already took out some extra meat. It's in that bag there. Take it inside and pop it in the microwave, will you?"

When Marcus came back inside, Callie was squatting beside Keeshan in the sawdust, playing as if she'd always been a mother. He couldn't help but smile. "Vi is thrilled. I think I must bore her to death. I'll stick this in the microwave to thaw." He held up his package.

"Can I help?"

"I don't know if you want to."

"Why not?"

"We do all the cooking in the garage these days. The refrigerator is out there, and we cook on a camp stove and a barbecue grill. I set up a Ping-Pong table for a counter."

"I can handle adverse circumstances," she said.

"Good. Then I'll put you in charge of the salad."

An hour later, the four of them sat down to dinner at the picnic table on the lawn.

Marcus made a conscious effort to be courteous, thoughtful, and attentive. But it worried him, this best behavior stuff. He hadn't had a meal with a real family in so long that he wasn't sure he could manage it all. As it happened, he shouldn't have worried.

"Callie, how is your dad these days?" Vi asked as she passed the salad. "Does he like the Gardens?"

"He's doing fine, I think. He likes his duplex—everything is geared for the wheelchair. He can take care of himself, cooking and cleaning. And he takes care of all kinds of ladies—you know, fixing drains, rewiring lamps, that kind of thing."

"Just like my Marcus," Vi answered. "I suppose Jack's the belle of the ball. He was always such a handsome man."

Callie laughed. "I don't know about that. I think it's a simple matter of statistics—more women than men in those kinds of places. Dad loves to be needed."

Marcus asked, "What kind of place is it?"

"A retirement community," Callie answered. "He moved there about four years ago, right after my mom died."

Once again, Marcus realized that he'd managed to bring up a painful subject. "I'm sorry."

"Laura O'Brian was the best gardener in the county," Violet said. "She could make anything grow anywhere, no matter what the Western Garden Book said. She was always over here giving me cuttings and bulbs. I don't think I've bought anything at a commercial nursery in ten years. She was a good friend."

Callie smiled. "She was a good mother. I still miss her."

"I grew these," Keeshan put in, holding up a cherry tomato.

"And they're the best I've ever had," Vi answered.

"We planted them and watered them every day," he added. "And I picked them."

Callie reached over and tussled his hair, using her thumb to brush off a bit of barbecue sauce. "Keeshan is a great helper. I couldn't grow vegetables without him."

Her tenderness struck Marcus. How many times had his own mother touched him just that way?

"Callie, it seems to me your mother told me you were engaged."

Marcus glanced up in time to see Callie suddenly invest all of her attention on her salad. A splotch of red started at her neckline and rose to her cheeks. "No. Never engaged." As she took a sip from her water glass, their eyes met.

"Hmm. Must've gotten my story wrong," Vi said. "I was sure your mother was excited about some man in your life. But," she said, sighing, "now that I have hearing aids, I either hear too much noise or not enough talk. There doesn't seem to be anything in between. So, is there someone special in your life?"

"Violet Werner! I can't believe you're asking me these things."

"Oh, come now, dear. At my age I can't afford to be discreet. Who knows how long I have to gather important information?"

"I hope you have many years left to live, Vi," Marcus said. "But you don't have to interrogate Ms. O'Brian. I think you've made her uncomfortable.

"You don't have to defend me," Callie said. "I'm single. I'm not seeing anyone right now. It's fine with me. I'm very happy with my life." She turned to look directly at Marcus. "And what about you, Mr. Jefferson. Are you single?"

"I live here by myself, don't I?"

Her eyes narrowed, and Marcus thought he saw a flash of pain. "These days, you can't assume anything by that, now can you?"

"I'm divorced."

Her eyebrows rose.

He'd caught her by surprise. "My wife left me for another man about five years after we were married. They're happily married—as far as I know—and they have children now. She lives in Indiana."

"I'm sorry," Callie said. "I was being flippant…"

"It's all right. It was my fault, actually. I worked too much. I said I was doing it for her, but she didn't buy it. She was young and very disappointed."

"So she blamed you and found someone else." Callie's surprise had turned to sympathy. "I'm sorry."

"That's a hard lesson to learn," Violet added.

"It was a long time ago," Marcus said, shaking his head. "I'm still learning lessons about people. I can't quite seem to get it right."

"Aren't we all?" Vi said.

"I learned how to make a K," Keeshan said. "Can I have some more milk?"

"Now that's impressive," Marcus said, standing up. "I'll bet you'll be able to write your whole name soon." He looked at Callie. "Can he have more milk?"

She nodded.

"I'll get it for you, then," Marcus said. As he crossed the lawn to the garage, he replayed the conversation he'd just heard. So there had been someone. Callie had nearly married. But something had gone wrong. Something had driven her from her life in the city.

What was it? And why did he suddenly care so much about her past?

>>>

Through the rest of the summer, Callie continued her usual activities. She and Keeshan spent the warm days outside, enjoying the sunshine and activity. The child seemed to grow more and more confident as time passed. He stopped sucking his thumb, and eventually he stopped carrying Celia's nightgown with him everywhere. He helped to take care of Eddy's six kittens. He began asking about his mother with a kind of detached curiosity that made Callie wonder if he didn't quite remember her.

Worried that he might forget Celia, Callie took several of her own photos and added them to the picture from the guesthouse, putting them in a collage, which she hung on the kitchen wall. As often as possible, Callie talked to Keeshan about his mother, relaying funny stories they'd shared over the years. He laughed along as though they talked of someone he'd never met.

There was no doubt in her mind; Keeshan's broken heart was healing.

She and Keeshan saw Marcus more frequently, sitting with him occasionally at church, visiting with him when he came into the coffee shop, saying hello on the street. Callie came to expect these encounters. After all, when living in a town that covered all of six blocks, it would take a miracle to avoid Marcus.

The people of Mountain Meadows accepted him as though he'd been raised there. One morning out of the clear blue sky, Callie went to church and discovered Marcus serving as an usher. He seemed to like the new role. Entirely too often, his was the face that greeted her at the door to the sanctuary.

As handsome as his face might be, it still unsettled her.

Throughout the long summer, one worry hung over every moment and danced constantly at the edges of her thoughts. Even as she spent treasured time with Keeshan, she could not escape her uneasy wait for the custody hearing. She didn't know what to expect. She hoped that the whole process would be over quickly, put to rest in a single visit to the courthouse.

She couldn't have been more wrong.

The day of the hearing dawned cloudy but bright, and Callie awoke confident that the day would end with sunshine and success. Rising early, she dressed carefully, choosing a sage green pantsuit for her first appearance in court. Checking herself in the mirror, she opted for a different top under the jacket. Then looking again, she restyled her hair. Aware of how her appearance might affect the judge, Callie wanted desperately to appear finished, professional, reliable.

By the time she came out for breakfast, her confidence had given way to anxiety. Her stomach twisted upon itself, and she couldn't face even a single piece of toast.

Without letting Keeshan in on her fear, Callie prayed all the way to Peggy's. *Lord, let me keep him. He needs me. Please, Lord.* She sighed. *I need him.* Effective or not, it was the only prayer she could manage in her current emotional tumult.

Parking in front of the day care, Callie pasted on a bright smile and took Keeshan inside. Peggy greeted her with a hug. "Today's the big day, isn't it?"

Callie took another deep breath, letting it out slowly as she smoothed the front of her jacket. "I think so."

"You look great. Any judge worth his salt would see how much you love him."

Callie smiled a flickering, halfhearted smile and bent down to hug Keeshan. "Hey, Keesh, you have a good day, you hear?"

Putting both arms around her neck, he hugged her tight. "It'll be all right, Callie," he said.

Callie held him a moment longer. This kid amazed her; she had not told him about the preliminary hearing. Somehow, he'd picked up the vibes on his own.

After another hour in the car, Callie turned off of Sprague toward the courthouse and began the relentless pursuit of free curbside parking.

The sun had burned off the cloud cover, and even with air conditioning the temperature inside the car rose. Her linen pants, so crisp and sharp when she left the house, melted into a limp, wrinkled mess. Her hair, neatly up on top of her head, now drooped with perspiration, and when Callie caught sight of it in the rearview mirror, all her confidence turned unexpectedly to terror.

What if she couldn't keep the boy? What if blood were more important than stability?

Callie felt her hands begin to tremble. *This will not do. Fear will not change the outcome. I have to face this thing.* Suddenly anxious to get the hearing over with, Callie decided to pay for parking and pulled into an expensive lot across the street from the courthouse. After dropping a ten-dollar bill into the payment opening, she threw her purse over her shoulder and strode to the courthouse.

But her fear had not left by the time she passed through security. Her stomach had not calmed by the time she found her name on the monitor in the lobby. In fact, by the time she put her hand on the door to the courtroom, Callie thought she might actually be sick. Her stomach ached, and severe nausea threatened to send her running for a restroom.

Dizzy, she let go of the door and turned back to the hallway. Spotting a wooden bench against the wall, she reached for it, gently easing herself down into the seat. She'd waited all summer for this very event. How could fear incapacitate her now?

Twenty-Eight

Gritting her teeth, she hugged herself, rocking back and forth on the courthouse bench as she waited for the nausea to pass. Right now she wanted a glass of water, cold clear water. That might do the trick. She wondered if she had passed a fountain nearby.

"You're here already." She glanced up to find Marcus standing at the door of the courtroom. "I got caught in traffic; thought I'd never get here," he said, smiling. Then, as though seeing her for the first time, he said, "You look pale. I mean, even for a white woman. Are you feeling all right?"

She couldn't help the smile he provoked. "Actually, no. I'm a little under the weather."

"Can I get you something? Water?"

"Water would be heaven."

"I'll be right back."

Callie leaned back, resting her head against the wall and closed her eyes. Even in this position, she felt the room spin.

"Here."

Still dizzy, she felt Marcus sit down beside her.

He offered her a large cone-shaped paper cup. "This should help."

She took the cup from him, and because the paper was fragile and the shape of cup was awkward, his fingers touched hers. Why did he have to be so darned nice? Didn't he know they were at war? By the end of today, one of them would win and the other would lose. There was no other way. Here, in this matter of critical importance, they were enemies.

How could he blur the edges by being so thoughtful?

She sipped the cold liquid slowly, unwilling to provoke her stomach by large swallows. After several long moments, she finished the last of the water and crushed the cup. "Thanks. I feel better."

He took the trash. "No problem. Will you be all right?"

"Absolutely. We don't want to postpone this, do we?"

He shook his head, and though he didn't say anything, Callie wondered if she saw regret in his dark eyes.

》》》

He waited with her until she felt like moving into the courtroom, aware even now of how his appraisal of her had changed. When he first met Callie, he thought of her as a handsome, athletic woman. But today, even when she was feeling badly, she seemed to him one of the most strikingly beautiful women he'd ever known. In a summer-weight pantsuit, with her hair up on her head, she looked almost regal. Somehow, the color—some shade of dark green—made her eyes come alive. He thought about the Hawaiian print shirt he'd worn over khaki pants and felt a little sorry for himself. They hadn't even started the hearing, and already Marcus felt like the underdog.

He should have at least bought a sports jacket for the occasion. Vi had tried to loan him one of her husband's coats, but it had been three sizes too small. He'd come out of his room looking like a linebacker in a leprechaun suit. Instead, he'd gone for understated. And now he was so understated he resembled someone from a homeless shelter.

"I really am feeling much better," she said, standing. "We should probably go in." Her skin was still deathly pale, and she held onto the bench as she stood; Marcus shook his head. *She's one determined woman.*

He opened the courtroom door and she stepped inside, swaying slightly as she walked. Marcus gestured to a bench near the back of the room and Callie slid into a seat. She looked grateful to collapse. Only a few people sat waiting on the audience benches at the back of the room. Most were alone, neither reading nor talking. He was about to sit beside Callie when he spotted his attorney sitting up front at a table. He walked forward to greet Philip Westover.

The size of the room surprised Marcus, who'd expected something larger, more stately, more like the television courtrooms he'd seen over the years. Up front, a large two-level desk took up nearly half of the room. The top level held a wire frame with a collection of manila files all standing on edge. Beside this a sign said: Robert Bolognesi, Commissioner Pro Tem.

A woman occupied the lower desk, working before a flat-screen computer monitor. Below her, a half wall separated the audience from the courtroom participants. Marcus moved through the gate, his hand extended.

"Good morning, Marcus," Philip said, patting Marcus on the back. "Are you ready?"

"I think so."

"The docket has us listed as fifth in line. By the time they get to us, I hope opposing counsel will be here. When they call our name, I'll go stand at that table there." He pointed to a counter just below the woman. "I'll use the microphone on the right. You'll stand on my right as I make our argument."

"The other attorney isn't here?"

"Don't worry. She'll come. As I was saying, you won't say anything unless the commissioner asks you a direct question. Then you may answer."

"All right," Marcus said, feeling a little overwhelmed by the whole event. It reminded him of the times his brother had gone to court and of his parents' disappointment, associations that made his mouth go dry. "I don't think I could manage to talk anyway."

As Marcus spoke, a voice called out, "All rise. Pierce County Superior Court, Commissioner Pro Tem, Robert Bolognesi presiding, now in session." Both Marcus and Philip stood as the commissioner, a thick, gray-haired man with black wire glasses, came in from an adjoining office and took his seat.

"You may be seated," the commissioner said.

Marcus felt his heart speed up as he watched the black-robed man converse in low tones with the woman in front of him. The moments passed. Then, picking up a file, the commissioner called out, "Nichols vs. Nichols."

A heavy woman in a poorly fitted navy suit responded, "I'm here your honor. Opposing counsel is not yet present."

Nodding, he picked up another file. "Roberts vs. Norton."

Again the same thing happened. As the tension of waiting mounted, Marcus felt his blood pound in his ears.

"Jefferson vs. O'Brian," the commissioner called. At that moment, a stately woman stepped through the gate and sat down at the other table.

Philip stood. "Both attorneys present, your honor." Philip tipped his head, and Marcus followed him to the microphone. The woman beside them strode forward to the other microphone. Marcus watched as Callie slid out of her seat and walked toward the front.

She looked even more ill than she had in the hallway, and her eyes had a tight edge to them. Marcus felt very sorry that it had come to this. Callie had let her anxiety build until she'd made herself sick.

It didn't have to be this way. She should have just given him custody of the child. After all, he was family. The child was his nephew. Who had more right to raise Keeshan?

Marcus couldn't understand why she wanted to keep the child. She had a happy life. She had friends. A community. Family. At some point, she would settle down and have children of her own. Then how would she feel about this boy she had taken out of pity and guilt?

Phillip began speaking, and Marcus forced himself to listen. "Your honor, we have presented documents to the court."

"I have them here."

"As the father has relinquished his parental rights, and the child's mother is deceased, the only living member of the family is Mr. Marcus Jefferson, whom we have proved to be the father's brother. Marcus is the uncle to the orphaned child, known to the state as Keeshan Marcus Hernandez.

"Currently Mr. Jefferson is gainfully employed and living in the same location as the boy. We have submitted affidavits as to his employment and current address. We have also included affidavits of character from his employer, his landlord, and his pastor. We have also submitted a criminal background check.

"Mr. Jefferson is willing to maintain the same day care, church, and relationships the boy has already established so as to keep continuity in the child's environment. Mr. Jefferson has spent some time with the boy this summer and feels that the boy both knows and trusts him.

"Mr. Jefferson requests that the court terminate the temporary custody of the child with Ms. Calliandra O'Brian and establish permanent third-party custody with Mr. Jefferson."

It sounded simple to Marcus. A simple case of returning the boy to his rightful family. What more could anyone expect? He folded his hands and rested them on the bench, certain that he would prevail.

"Counsel for Ms. O'Brian?"

Marcus glanced sideways, wondering about the woman representing Callie. Her hair was cut short. She was tall, though not as tall as Callie, slim, and almost as regal as her client. She wore a silver-gray suit that complemented her pale blue eyes and translucent skin. "Your honor. I'm Dorothy Powell, representing Ms. Calliandra O'Brian." She spoke with a slow southern drawl, every word drawn out, Marcus believed, to pull listeners in.

"You may proceed."

"For the past three years, Ms. O'Brian shared her home with the child's mother, Ms. Celia Hernandez. The two women were best friends, spending a great deal of time together. The child, being in the care of Celia Hernandez at the time, became a part of this friendship.

"The child has known Ms. O'Brian since his infancy. When Ms. Hernandez was hospitalized following her car accident, Ms. O'Brian stepped in to care for the child until other family members could be notified. She obtained temporary custody in order to provide health insurance for the child.

"As you can see, your honor, none of the social workers assigned to this case—in fact, not even the medical examiner's office—was able to locate a single relative of the deceased. According to the medical examiner's report, which I've supplied to you, officials suspect that Ms. Hernandez's family may have been illegal immigrants who have since returned to Mexico. No attempt has been made to locate her family outside the United States. Such a family would be unsuitable for a child who has spent his entire life in the U.S.

"However, I would ask the court to consider this: If Mr. Jefferson were indeed so committed to the care of this child, why exactly was he unavailable, indeed completely untraceable, when the authorities were looking for him?"

Dorothy Powell adjusted her reading glasses and continued. "No one knew Mr. Jefferson's whereabouts. Ms. Hernandez had no record of him in her belongings. And I would contend that if this uncle were as genuinely concerned about his nephew as he would lead us to believe, he would perhaps have kept in touch with the child's mother. Mr. Jefferson did nothing of the kind. Instead, at this late hour, Mr. Jefferson shows up in Prospect, Washington demanding custody of a child he has never seen, never cared for, never spent time with."

As Dorothy Powell took off her glasses, making wide gestures with both hands, Marcus began to sweat. The whole effect of silver hair, tailored suit, and eloquent speech gave the impression of an expert witness speaking before a senate hearing. The judge leaned forward, shuffling his papers as she referred to them, hanging on to every word. For the first time, Marcus realized that this hearing might not be the slam dunk he had so confidently imagined.

The judge turned to Marcus's attorney. "Mr. Westover?"

"Your honor, I would contend that Ms. Powell is misleading the court. In truth, Ms. Hernandez lived in a guesthouse, not under the same roof with Ms. O'Brian. In fact, both of the women worked full time, and Ms. O'Brian actually has two full-time positions, which I shall address in a moment. As you can see, because of time constraints, neither woman had extensive contact with the other. Thus, Ms. O'Brian has not been a continuous presence in the child's life.

"Furthermore, we would contend that since Ms. O'Brian continues to own and operate two separate businesses, the Mountain High Coffee Company and also O'Brian Upholstery, Ms. O'Brian has very little time to dedicate to the care of a small child.

"We can support this by an incident which occurred on," he shuffled between the notes on his yellow pad. "On the twentieth of June. On this day Keeshan Hernandez managed to step on an upholstery tack, even though supervised by Ms. O'Brian. The injury was serious enough to cause a severe infection, which might have jeopardized the life of the child. Now I ask the court, is this responsible care?

"I might add, if the court allows, that neither of these businesses is more than three years old. We would contend that Ms. O'Brian's financial situation is highly fluid, leading to precarious stability at best.

"We contend that full custody should be immediately and finally awarded to Mr. Jefferson."

"One last comment, Ms. Powell?"

"I would take issue with Mr. Westover's picture of Ms. O'Brian. Mr. Jefferson is himself working two jobs at this moment—one as counter help at Contractor's Supply, and the other, a renovation in a private home. I hardly think Mr. Westover should be throwing stones concerning work issues. Related to this, the court should know that Mr. Jefferson is working for nearly minimum wage at his full-time job. The job does not include insurance benefits, and presently, Mr. Jefferson has no medical insurance for himself. He is renting a single room from an elderly woman in Prospect, hardly a suitable environment for raising a child.

"Though Mr. Jefferson can prove relationship to the child, he cannot prove financial stability, emotional stability, or physical stability—all important aspects of responsibility in the eyes of the court.

"My client, Ms. O'Brian can prove financial, emotional, and physical stability. She should be awarded permanent custody of Keeshan Hernandez."

"Thank you, Ms. Powell." The commissioner closed the file and said, "The court will appoint a guardian ad litem for the child Keeshan Hernandez and delay a permanent custody decision until the guardian has made his report to the court."

"Nichols vs. Nichols?"

>>>>

Callie blinked. She couldn't believe it. She sensed Dorothy Powell moving beside her, and she felt her attorney's gentle touch guiding her away from the bench. Callie vaguely perceived the movement of other attorneys, of other clients moving to the front of the room. She allowed Dorothy to lead her to the very last bench, where she collapsed into a seat.

In only a matter of minutes the hearing was concluded. Callie's thoughts collided with her emotions. No one had bothered to ask the most important question of all. It hadn't even occurred to the commissioner to consider the issue. How could they overlook the most critical of facts?

I love Keeshan, the voice inside her screamed. *What else matters?*

Callie sat stupefied, unaware of the voices now arguing at the front of the courtroom. She was not angry. She did not replay the expositions offered by the opposing attorneys. Instead, baffled by the impersonal, inconsequential items that concerned the court, Callie wondered how they could decide the fate of a child based on such things.

Still in shock, she could hardly think. She glanced up to see Marcus move out of the room, his arm held by Philip Westover's firm hand. Marcus looked at her as he went by, his eyes clouded with hurt, his face an expression of intense disappointment.

Dorothy whispered, "Let's go outside."

Blindly, Callie followed her into the hallway, where they sat on exactly the same bench she had occupied before the hearing. "Well, it didn't go as well as I'd hoped," Dorothy drawled. "But it isn't over, either."

Callie fought through her numbness, trying to give her attorney the attention she deserved. "What is a guardian ad litem?"

"It's a representative of the court, appointed to investigate opposing parties in custody disputes," Dorothy said. "Most often, it's an attorney. Occasionally, it's a social worker. They volunteer for the position. They have some training, but really, it's potluck. Who knows what we'll get?"

"Please. I can't take any more bad news."

"Don't worry. It wasn't as bad as it seemed."

"How can that be?"

"We have a clear idea of what their tactics are. We know what they consider to be our weaknesses. We'll have to shore up our story, prepare a clear offense, and do our best with the guardian. I think I'm going to do some investigating on this uncle. I want to know where he's been all this time."

"How long will it take? To finish this, I mean."

"Another four to six months, minimum."

"Why so long?"

"The court calendar is filled with civil cases. Mostly parenting agreements. Custody fights. Some divorce settlements over property issues. We live in a litigious society. You're lucky Keeshan is so young. Some children grow up before the whole issue is resolved."

After thanking Dorothy, Callie drove home. Instead of going back to work, she went to the day care and ate lunch with Keeshan. If she were going to lose him, she would spend every possible moment in his presence.

Twenty-Nine

Marcus had taken the entire day off from work. So when the hearing finished before noon, he drove back Prospect to have lunch with Violet. Today of all days he could use her comfort, her devotion, and yes, her wisdom. He found her on the front porch watering her beloved flowerpots. In a broad-brimmed straw hat, baggie blue capris, and white tennis shoes, she was the picture of the old lady gardener. Wisps of white hair peeked out from under her hat, and as she heard the car in the drive, she turned and waved.

Marcus took the front steps slowly. "Whew! What is that smell?"

"Fish fertilizer," she said, stopping to catch a stray hair and stuffing it back under the hat.

"Why would you use something that smells so bad?"

"Because it works. I use it once a week."

"I'm glad you do it when I'm not home." Marcus sank into the glider that hung at the end of the porch. Absently, he pushed himself with his foot, swinging in the warm afternoon sunshine. Vi put down her watering can and came to sit beside him, her gloved hands in her lap. Her small shoes didn't quite touch the porch.

"Things didn't go as well as you hoped?"

"That's putting it mildly. You know, I was so sure. I just thought that after all that prayer, it couldn't go any other way. I was sure we'd win custody."

"What happened?"

"The commissioner didn't think either of us had a good enough case to decide. He appointed a guardian ad litem—whatever that is. Some court representative, I guess. Anyway, after he interviews both of us, Callie and me, and probably Keeshan too, he'll decide what's best for the boy and make a recommendation."

"I'm glad that isn't my job."

"Thanks a lot. I thought you'd be pulling for me."

"Don't you forget that Callie's folks have been my friends from the day they moved to Prospect. They're good people. Callie is good people."

"I've never argued that."

"And you're good people, Marcus."

Marcus patted Violet on her knee. "Thanks, Vi."

"The whole thing reminds me of those women who took the baby to King Solomon."

"Are you suggesting we cut Keeshan in half?"

"Hardly." Vi seemed to consider her words as she sat, her tiny feet swinging back and forth from the swing. Carefully, she pulled off her gloves and placed them neatly in her lap. "I think there's a simpler answer, and it doesn't take Solomon's wisdom to come up with it."

Marcus really didn't want to hear the old woman's idea, but he could hardly ignore her now. Putting aside his disappointment, he asked, "Wisdom?"

"Men. They're as dense as concrete sometimes." She shook her head and then pointed one bony finger at Marcus, her brown eyes intense. "You seem so sharp and yet here you sit. Think about it. Callie is single. She's smart. She's beautiful. She's a great mother. Of course you can't divide the child in half, but you can make the two into one." She folded her hands in her lap and shook her head. "You'd be a fool not to pursue her."

Marcus could hardly believe she'd said it. This was the last thing he expected from Violet Werner. He opened his mouth to respond, but no words came. He felt certain that he looked like a fish in a small aquarium.

She laughed, waving him off with one hand. "See? I told you. You aren't even smart enough to think of it yourself. It's a wonder the world can survive with men in charge."

"What are you saying? Me? Date her?" He shook his head. "She hates me."

"Don't be silly. She hates what you represent."

"Because I'm black?"

Vi threw both hands in the air, her face turned up to the sky. "Honestly, I don't think I can help you, dear." She slid her hips forward and dropped off the seat. "How did you graduate from college?"

"Wait. I want to hear what you think."

She turned to face him. "She's afraid you'll take that little boy from her. She loves him. It's as simple as that. She isn't taking care of him until family comes. She wants to keep him because she loves him. It's her only chance to have the family she always wanted. She doesn't hate you, Marcus. She's terrified that you will leave and take the boy."

"You think she might feel differently about me—as a person?"

"Not as a person, silly. As a man."

"Really?"

"At my age, I don't have enough time left to repeat myself, young man." Violet slipped her garden gloves back on and walked over to her watering can. Humming a light tune, she pinched blossoms with one hand as she watered with the other.

She completely ignored Marcus, who couldn't speak for his surprise.

>>>>

After the hearing Callie managed to resume her normal life, though nothing about it felt normal. One snowstorm in late spring had changed everything, and now, in late summer, Callie prayed that things would not change again.

She spent her days waiting for a phone call from the guardian. At night, she prayed for God's favor with the court system. She and Keeshan continued to garden and to bike. Bits and pieces of the trial came back to her, and she remembered the testimony of Marcus's attorney. She fought a growing bitterness about the battle.

On a Wednesday one week after the hearing, Callie realized that her pear trees had begun to drop ripe fruit. On the following afternoon, she and Keeshan came home, ate quickly, and spent the entire evening picking and dragging buckets of pears into the laundry room, where they would have to remain until she found time to preserve them.

She retrieved her mother's dehydrator from the garage and brought it into the kitchen. Then, with music on the stereo, she sliced pears and Keeshan placed the slices on the dryer shelves. He loved the ripe fruit, and while she sliced, he slipped piece after piece into his mouth. Before long his tiny fingers were covered in pear mush, and sweet juice dripped from his chin. Though she warned him about the consequences, he continued eating fruit.

Around 8:30, he began complaining of a stomachache. She filled the bathtub with warm water and gave him a long relaxing bath. He had to use the toilet twice during the bath. As she put him in his pajamas, he held his aching stomach with both hands. "I'm never gonna eat another pear again," he promised. "Not ever, ever, ever."

After he went to bed, Callie canned fourteen quarts of pears. That left five full buckets and two huge piles of pears left to preserve. Since she'd moved into her parents' home, Callie had never had this kind of harvest before. While her mother was ill, the trees had gone untended, the orchard unwatered. It had taken three years to coax the trees into production again.

And now, it seemed, they had made up for lost time.

Just after midnight, Callie began cleaning up the kitchen. The counters were covered with juice, the stovetop sticky with spilled syrup. Fruit flies seemed to be everywhere. Her shoes stuck to the floor. *It would be easier to clean the kitchen with a garden hose.*

As she cleaned she considered how much fruit she had left. She would have to can every night and most of Saturday if she were going to keep those pears from spoiling. Hoping to avoid a long confinement in the kitchen, Callie decided to give away as much fruit as she could. While she washed the floor, she made a mental list of recipients. Nearly an hour later, the floor clean and the counters wiped, Callie headed down the hall to bed.

She checked in on Keeshan, who snored in delicate breaths from the depth of four-year-old dreams. Then, hot and sticky, she took a long shower and got ready for bed. She spent some time in prayer and turned out the light.

Later, from the depths of her own sleep, Callie heard a strong persistent sound, but she could not identify it. She tried to roll over, to turn away. She put a pillow over her head, but the sound continued. Waking from a dream where she had been boxing Marcus, she turned on the bedside lamp and strained to focus on the clock radio. Three o'clock? Who would call at three in the morning? Why hadn't the machine picked up? She reached for the ringing telephone. "Hello?"

"Callie? Is this Callie O'Brian?"

"Yes. Yes, it is." Callie rubbed her eyes with her free hand, wishing she hadn't stayed up so late. She could hardly think.

"This is Andrew Bird. I'm calling from downtown."

She struggled to stay with the conversation. Did she know anyone named Andrew? And then the thought came to her. Andrew from the fire department. "What? What's happened?"

"Your building is on fire. We have two trucks and the whole crew. I think you should get down here."

Callie hung up without speaking. Ripping off her nightgown, she threw on a sweatshirt before she reached the bedroom door. She pulled on her jeans as she stumbled down the hall. Pausing at the bathroom door to grab a rubber band, she threw her hair into a ponytail. By the time she opened Keeshan's door, Callie was wide-awake and praying with all her might.

Lord, save the building. Help them save my business.

Grabbing Keeshan, she wrapped him in the quilt that covered his bed and ran to the carport. The boy groaned only slightly when she belted him not into the car seat, but into the shoulder harness in the front seat.

Just five minutes after answering her phone, Callie hit the highway. By the time she reached the far end of Main Street, she could see the sky above the town glow red. The street was blocked off, and a large group of cars were parked just outside the barricade. Callie wondered where she could park and still be close enough to watch the car from her building. She did not need to have Keeshan loose around the fire. She turned into an alley and parked in the grocery store lot across from the coffee shop.

Locking the car, she ran down across Main, skirted the barricades, and passed the fire engine parked in the middle of the street. Pushing her way through the crowd of onlookers, she came to the side of the coffee shop. The view made her knees tremble, and tears filled her eyes and coursed down her cheeks.

Already flames had broken through the roof at the back of the building and were leaping into the dark sky. Despite streams of water, the fire refused to back down. Instead, growing, licking, eating the timber of the old building with a speed that seemed impossible, it continued to grow. She wouldn't have believed it without witnessing it herself.

It surprised her that even in the darkness she could see the color of the smoke billowing out above the flames, a black cloud illuminated by the ghastly red glow. The heat burned her face, and a strong wind tossed her hair—a wind she realized was created by the power of the flames themselves. Through the side window, Callie saw a wall of red roaring through what had been her kitchen.

Firemen in sooty yellow jackets and heavy boots swarmed the parking lot like bees over a summer picnic. But no effort of the men seemed to deter the fire. Instead it grew, until at last the crowd was driven back by the explosion of the windows in the dining room. Callie watched as flames began to consume the front of the building.

"Oh, Callie." She recognized Jan's voice and looked up to see Jan push her way through the crowd. The two women leaned against one another, both giving in to the grief they felt. Jan, having worked for the shop since its grand opening, seemed lost in shock. Silent. Tearful.

Callie felt hands patting her shoulders, business owners offering condolences. Someone wrapped her shoulders in a wool blanket. Another brought her a bottle of water. But Callie could not think, could not look, could not respond.

She could not see anything but the flames that consumed her dreams.

>>>

"Callie, I'm so sorry." Marcus stood beside her, his face staring at the now receding light of the flames.

She nodded, unable to turn away from the cadaver of her business. "Thanks."

"What happened?"

"I don't know. They called me; I came. I haven't talked to anyone yet."

"Where's Keeshan?"

Callie pointed. "Asleep in my car. I have him wrapped in a blanket with the seat down."

"Where?"

"The parking lot at the grocery store."

"Give me your keys. I'll go stay with him."

Callie dug down into the kangaroo pocket of her sweatshirt and pulled out her key ring. Unbidden, the tears began again. She handed Marcus the keys, and buried her face in her hands. "It's gone. Everything is gone," she said, letting go in one tidal wave of grief. And as she cried she thought of her former life. Of her former love. Of her mother. Of Celia.

Would the losses never end?

Still weeping, she felt Marcus pull her into his arms. He held her, patting her shoulder gently as she cried. And through her grief, something about his being there, something about his comfort, something about his arms felt exactly right.

>>>

Marcus held Callie until her violent shaking gave way an occasional shudder. Then, lifting her head with his two hands, he wiped her tears away with the pad of his thumbs. "It'll be all right," he promised, kissing her forehead. "We'll get through this." He rewrapped the wool blanket, tightening it around her shoulders.

Something about her vulnerability, her pain, made him ache. He hated to see her like this, lost, hurting. He knew he would stay with her until she was herself again.

"I'm going to go take care of Keeshan," he said, bending to speak into her ear. "Don't worry," he said. "I'll take him over to Vi's house. He can sleep there tonight. She'll stay with him. I'll be right back."

"I don't want to bother Violet," Callie said, her agitation returning. "And Keeshan shouldn't wake up in a strange place."

"She's already awake. Everyone in town is awake. Vi will sit with him, don't you worry." Marcus gave her shoulder a squeeze. "You're needed here. I promise he'll be fine."

Certain that she was okay for the moment, he hurried across the street to her car. Inside, Keeshan slept on, completely unaware of the crowd and activity. Marcus unlocked the car and slid behind the steering wheel.

At Vi's house he carried Keeshan upstairs. Still dreaming, Keeshan slipped his thumb back into his mouth as Marcus rolled him into bed and pulled the covers up around his neck.

"What a lamb," Violet said, leaning against the doorway. Her long white hair hung around her shoulders, and in the light from the street, it reminded him of angel hair—like the stuff his mother put under the nativity when he was a boy.

"That he is," Marcus agreed, standing. "The coffee shop is a total loss. Callie's down there watching it burn. I told her you would stay with Keeshan."

"Of course," Vi said, nodding. "I'll sit with him."

Marcus noticed the old woman's bare feet below her housecoat, aged and bony. He had never seen her feet before. Like her hands, even Violet's feet were ready to serve whenever needed. "Callie would appreciate that. I'd appreciate it." He stepped around her. "I'll bring you a rocker from downstairs."

"That isn't necessary," she said, catching his arm.

"I know." In the living room, Marcus turned Vi's favorite swivel rocker upside down, his head holding the seat cushion in place as he hefted it up the stairs. Turning it sideways, he brought it through the door jamb and placed it beside the bed. Vi stood at the window, her silhouette outlined by the glow of lights and fire. "Here, sit down, Violet. You need your rest."

Holding one hand over trembling lips, she did not answer. Marcus went over to stand beside her in the dark, and together they watched the embers of Mountain High Coffee Shop die.

Thirty

It was nearly five in the morning when Callie returned home. Her clothes and hair smelled like smoke, and soot clung to her face. Her fingers stuck together, whether from dirt or soot she did not know. The fire had blurred her memory. She had tried to help the firemen as they pulled furniture from the burning building. Callie and Jan, along with a host of Prospect citizens, had dragged it as far away from the fire as they could.

She needed to shower again.

But she had neither the energy, nor the desire. Marcus had taken Keeshan for the night. The coffee shop was gone. What did it matter if she washed before she collapsed? Nothing mattered anymore. Callie felt a growing fear, a terrifying emptiness that sat just under the surface of her thoughts. Unwilling to give in, she stuffed it back, moving automatically through the house as she turned out lights and locked her doors. Callie even remembered to check on Eddy and the kittens before washing her face and hands in the laundry room sink.

As she scrubbed her hands with the scratchy side of a kitchen sponge, she thought about Marcus. He had come back, just as he promised. He had taken Keeshan to Violet Werner's house and returned to help them save whatever furniture they could. He'd stayed as long as she, talking to the firemen, helping them return their equipment to the trucks.

He'd been there when she needed him, she remembered, drying her face on a towel. He'd held her while she cried. He'd touched her face with his hands. He'd kissed her forehead. He'd promised to help her through this.

His actions didn't fit the picture she'd made of Marcus Jefferson. She couldn't understand this sudden kindness. Couldn't see behind his concern for her welfare. Was his the kind of thoughtfulness that only surfaced in tragedy?

But even that was too much to think about now. She decided to put his lovely eyes and gentle touch completely out of her mind. She needed rest, and nothing sounded more comforting than the thought of her own bed.

In her room, she sat down and untied her tennis shoes. Then using the toe of one foot, she kicked off the other shoe. She pulled her filthy sweatshirt over her head and unzipped her pants. Then, sliding between the sheets, she pulled the covers up around her neck. Staring out through the gloom of predawn, Callie heard her bedside clock click as the numbers rolled over to 5:00 A.M. It occurred to her then, as she stared at the clock, that she had no reason to get up, no job, no obligations at all. Callie rolled away from the clock and pulled a pillow into her embrace. Only then did she allow her pain to come forth.

As the dam broke, Callie cried herself to sleep.

>>>>

Sunlight streaming in through her bedroom window beat down on her face, warming her eyelids even before she opened her eyes. The memory of the fire was with her instantly, though she did not feel the stab of pain that she expected. She lay quietly, her face in the sun, thinking about what the mess might look like in the broad light of day.

A thump startled her, and she opened her eyes to find Eddy rubbing against her knees, pushing at the covers as he prepared to claim his spot on Callie's bed. *Her spot*, Callie corrected herself. The six kittens now sleeping in the laundry room had erased any questions they might have had about Eddy's gender.

Both Callie and Keeshan still enjoyed the joke Eddy had played on them.

We should probably rename the cat.

She rolled over and slid out from under the covers, surprised to notice that she had slept till almost ten o'clock. Grabbing a robe, she headed for the spare bathroom, where she started her bath water. She went into the kitchen and made herself a pot of strong coffee. As the coffee dripped, Callie selected the largest ripe pear on the counter and returned to her bedroom. Munching on the pear, she stripped the bed, rolled her clothes into the sheets and carried the whole mess to the laundry room. She dumped the collection straight into the washer and added twice the normal amount of detergent.

She could only hope that the smell would wash out. If not, she'd have to trash the whole mess. She couldn't stand to live with the stench forever reminding her of the fire.

She poured herself a huge cup of coffee and padded back to the bathroom, where she found her tub threatening to overflow. She added bath salts and stepped into the water just as the phone began to ring. Tempted to ignore the world, she stood there for two or three more rings considering it. Then, grabbing her robe, she returned to the kitchen, her feet dripping, to catch the telephone.

"You're awake," a voice said without introduction. She recognized Marcus, sounding upbeat, rested. The man had to be made of steel.

"Lucky for you."

"I figured you might not sleep too well."

"I slept like a dead man."

"Yeah, it was quite a night."

Tears sprang to her eyes. "Thanks for taking care of Keeshan."

"Don't worry about it. He's fine."

"Where is he now?"

"He's here, with me."

"Don't you have to work?"

"I called and told them I wouldn't be in." He paused long enough that she began to wonder if they'd been cut off. "How are you this morning? I mean, how are you really?"

She understood what he meant. For the first time, she did not try to think of something smart or clever to say. "I think I'm a little numb. It doesn't seem real to me. Like a dream."

"It wasn't a dream. It was a nightmare."

"You're right. I haven't even begun to think about what's next. I'd like to rebuild. It was a good business. We were just getting off the ground, you know?"

"I've been thinking about that too. Were you insured?"

"The bank required it for the equipment loan. I don't know if I have enough to re-create the whole thing. Equipment is expensive—and rebuilding—well, I haven't even talked to anyone about that. It's a little early, don't you think?"

"How'd you like to meet me there—at the shop? I could bring Keeshan."

"I was just getting into the tub."

"I'll give you an hour."

She carried the phone back to the bathroom, took a sip of her coffee and frowned. She'd let it get cool. "All right. I'll meet you in an hour."

"Sounds good," he said, and then added, "hey, Callie, bring some tools, will you? A couple shovels, any rakes you have. A broom? We can start cleaning up."

This guy was full of surprises. "Sure," she agreed. "But you know you don't have to help."

"I know. I want to."

She smiled. "One more thing," she added. "Do you like pears?"

》》》

Marcus made blueberry pancakes on the camp stove in the garage and served them to Keeshan on the picnic table. Violet had not yet gotten out of bed, and Marcus intended to let her sleep as long as she needed. After breakfast, Marcus took Keeshan to Werner's Department Store. In the boys department, Marcus helped Keeshan try on a few items, which they took to the front register, where Marcus paid with cash. Then Marcus led Keeshan back to the changing area, where he put on his new clothes.

"There," he said when the boy emerged. "That looks like a real carpenter—someone about to build a building."

Keeshan stood in front of a mirror admiring himself. "Can I have a tool belt just like yours?"

"Absolutely, my boy," Marcus said, clapping Keeshan on the shoulders as he led him to the car. "I'm going to need your help. Are you ready for that?"

Marcus and Keeshan parked on the street behind the charred remains of the shop. In the sunlight, the damage surprised Marcus. There were no walls still standing. Yellow tape surrounded the carnage. Twisted and scorched timbers lay like pickup sticks over a thick pile of ash. Two men sifted through the remains.

Marcus got out of the car and helped Keeshan from his seat belt. "If you're going to travel with me, buddy, we're going to have to get you a car seat," he said. "Don't let me forget that." He held Keeshan's hand as they walked to the shop.

"What happened?" Keeshan asked, his eyes wide.

"There was a fire last night, and Callie's shop burned down."

"Why?"

"That's a great question, kid," Marcus said.

As they approached the remains, one of the men stepped over the yellow tape surrounding the site and walked toward them. "Morning," he said. "I'm Tim Schmidt from Pierce County Fire Marshall's office, Arson Division. And you are?"

"Marcus Jefferson, friend of the owner." The two shook hands. "Do you suspect arson?"

"We haven't made an official determination, but whenever there's a fire in a volunteer district we have to file a report." He put his hands on his hips and turned to stare at the building. "Right now, it looks like it started in the electrical panel. A total loss, though. Too bad."

"It was quite a fire."

"That's what I heard. Can I ask why you're here?"

"Sure. I'm meeting the owner. We're going to make plans to clean up this mess."

"Well, we should be finished soon. You'll want to take photographs. Have you called the insurance carrier?"

"That's on the schedule."

"Don't delay. The sooner the better."

"Thanks for the advice," Marcus said, smiling. "Do you mind if we take some outside measurements?"

"No problem." He reached into his shirt pocket and pulled out a business card. "Call us if you have any questions."

"When will you have a determination?"

"Probably by tomorrow afternoon. You can call the office. We'll give you a case number and you can track it yourselves."

"I appreciate it." Marcus watched as the man reentered the bowels of the old business and caught up with his partner.

Marcus opened his toolbox—filled with tools Violet had contributed—and selected a measuring tape. Together he and Keeshan measured the cement pad under the old coffee shop. They had just stretched the tape across the front entry when Callie pulled up to the curb. Marcus felt his heart accelerate. He had concocted a two-part plan, a carefully selected, precisely premeditated scheme. But if the plan were to succeed, the first part had to fall into place now. It all depended on her. Marcus threw up a prayer. *I think I know her, Lord. But only you can give me success. Help me to find favor in her eyes.*

She had a long-sleeved T-shirt over dark jeans and was wearing old-fashioned canvas tennis shoes. Her hair was caught up in a twist. As she came closer, Marcus noticed that her eyes were swollen.

She bent low and offered her arms to Keeshan. It was all the encouragement he needed. The child ran into her embrace and the two held one another for a long moment.

She stood up, holding him at arm's length. "What have you got on?"

"My work clothes," he answered, a measure of pride in his voice.

"Work clothes?" She looked at Marcus. "Where did he get a pair of overalls, and what is he talking about?"

"We've decided to help you rebuild."

She looked confused. "You?"

"Why not?"

"I don't know if I want to rebuild. I haven't even talked to my insurance company."

He laughed. "I know it's been a short night, but there's no time like the present."

She rubbed her forehead. "You're obviously several steps ahead of me here. Give me some time to catch up."

Marcus smiled. "I'd be glad to bring you up to date. First, let me get you something." He turned back to the toolbox and lifted a large paper cup, handing it to her. "Here, drink this."

She recognized the logo on the cup. "You bought coffee from my competitor?"

"And so will everyone else in town, starting this morning, unless you rebuild and do it quickly. Every morning you let them buy from the competitor, you are less likely to win them back. You need to act and act fast."

Her green eyes clouded and Marcus recognized her pain. "I've learned that much."

"So, here's the plan," He reached into his back pocket and removed a folded piece of white copy paper. "I drew this over breakfast," he said, handing it to her. "It isn't much, but it's a start. I can do real plans if you approve these. It won't take me more than a couple of days. We can pool our resources, and if you'll get the whole thing through the planning department, I'll start on the building end. I can have the whole building framed in less than a week. It's a simple structure this time—not a renovation of an existing building. We can give it the same country, herbal garden flare you had before—if that's what you still want—and save a lot of money starting from scratch."

"Wait a minute. You're going a little fast for me."

"Sorry," he reached up to smooth his goatee. "I get excited when I talk about buildings."

"Just like a man," she said. "You seem to have forgotten. You have a job. And for that matter, you have two jobs."

"Actually, I only have one job."

"One? You haven't finished the work on Violet's house."

"No. There's a lot left to do there." He smiled. "This morning I called my boss at Contractor's Supply and quit."

"Quit? Marcus, that's crazy. You need that money."

"No. Well, yes, actually I do. But you need to rebuild this business even more. You have insurance. If you use the insurance money to build, you can pay me as your general contractor. You know you can trust me. You've seen my work. I'm available to start today."

"If I didn't know better, I'd think you burned it down so you could get the job."

"That's a low blow," he answered.

"I know," she said, shaking her head. "I didn't mean it." Carefully, she unfolded the paper. Holding the drawing in one hand, she examined Marcus's ideas. "This is good. Really good." She looked up at him, staring intently into his eyes. "Marcus Jefferson, you haven't told me everything. Who are you and why would you do this for me?"

"We can talk about that later. First, have you called your insurance company?"

Thirty-One

In the days after the fire, Callie's emotions felt like a car chase in a San Francisco action movie.

It comforted her to have Marcus work on the building. No matter how irritating he had been, he was a man of his word, a hardworking man who arrived at the shop every morning long before she did. He was single-minded, stubbornly overcoming every obstacle that threatened to deter their progress. Having spent so many hours with him, Callie decided that he was both a skilled builder and a man of character.

But she experienced moments of sorrow as well. Only days after the fire, Jan announced that she'd taken a job at a local diner, putting an end to her employment at Mountain High. Since their relationship had revolved primarily around the business, Callie grieved the loss and worried that their friendship might suffer as well. Her sadness was compounded by the loss of Jan's creativity. Jan had advice about everything—from decorating to marketing.

At the same time, Callie was forced to withdraw Keeshan from day care. Of course, Peggy Mortenson understood. With the loss of income from the coffee shop and the added expense of rebuilding, Callie had no money left for his tuition. Since she no longer worked during the day, Callie could watch Keeshan herself. Though she hated for Keeshan to face any more changes, it seemed the only solution.

Gradually Callie, Keeshan, and Marcus fell into a daily routine. While they waited for insurance inspectors to approve benefit checks, they cleaned up the old building, filling a dumpster with chunks of burned debris and buckets of ash. Marcus found endless ways to let Keeshan participate, and the boy flourished under his constant attention.

For one whole morning, as Marcus swept, Keeshan dutifully held his dustpan. Though he would have saved hours working alone, Marcus chose to include the boy. On another morning, while Callie cut back the charred plants in the patio garden, Marcus taught Keeshan to pick up her cuttings. Together, they filled bucket after bucket with branches, which Marcus emptied into the dumpster.

Most afternoons, Keeshan stayed with Violet Werner. Sometimes, exhausted from his "work" at the coffee shop, Keeshan napped. Often, he helped Vi with her chores. Keeshan charmed Violet as though she were his own grandmother. The old lady didn't have a chance.

At the same time, as they worked together, Callie struggled with a tinge of jealousy. Though Keeshan continued to live with her, he talked endlessly about Marcus. Every morning he insisted on wearing the brown overalls Marcus had purchased, buckling his plastic tool belt around his hips. Keeshan began walking exactly as Marcus did. Every time they got into the car, Keeshan asked, "Are we going to see Marcus?"

When they went to church, Keeshan asked, "Can we have lunch with Marcus?"

Callie understood that Keeshan had never had any male attention. Of course he delighted in Marcus. Still, as Keeshan grew to love Marcus, Callie felt him move away from her. Though she knew Marcus was good for the boy, she longed for the closeness they had once shared. At the same time, she worried about his growing attachment to the stranger who had invaded her world. What would happen when Keeshan talked with the court-appointed guardian? Would the boy prefer to live with Marcus?

Rather than worry, she decided to confront the issue head on. "I can't tell you how grateful I am for your help in all of this," she said one day, as she drove her car toward Prospect. "If it hadn't been for you, I might have curled up and quit."

"You don't have to thank me. I've gotten everything I asked for."

Callie glanced over at him. A tiny smile played at the edges of his lips. "I know you're getting paid," she said. "Still, you don't have to be so kind. You've included Keeshan in everything." She slowed as a car pulled into the highway in front of them. "I wonder if you've noticed how attached Keeshan has become?"

He shrugged. "I like him too."

"Do you think it's wise?"

"What do you mean, wise?" He turned in his seat to face her. "It isn't like I have plans to steal his affection from you. Is that what you think?"

Callie felt her defenses rise. "You didn't plan that he would fall in love with you? You weren't thinking that Keeshan would choose to live with you instead of me?" Out loud, she had to admit, the idea sounded a little paranoid. Still, Keeshan had clearly given Marcus his heart. She had to protect him. Someone had to protect him. He was too young to protect himself.

"Tell me, Callie, who hurt you?"

She gave him a fierce look. "Don't avoid the question."

"I'm not. Who was it?"

"What makes you think that I've been hurt?"

"Oh, come on. You constantly assume the worst of me. You think I planned to have Keeshan choose me. You see the world through suspicious eyes. Someone has hurt you Callie, or you wouldn't be so busy trying to protect yourself."

Callie blinked hard, trying to avoid the tears that threatened to spill over her cheeks. Was he right? In spite of all she'd done since moving to Prospect, did her past still dominate her present? She never meant to become jaded.

"Well?"

"I try to give you the benefit of the doubt." She looked at him again, gauging his response. "I'm just afraid for him. He can't afford to lose someone else."

"Afraid for him? Or afraid for you?" His dark eyes appealed to her, and something in his expression challenged her to be honest with herself—perhaps for the first time since she'd moved back home. At that moment, somewhere between the lumber store and Prospect, Callie realized that Marcus Jefferson had managed to crawl into her soul as well. He'd become a friend, more than a friend, a good friend. *Still,* she wondered, *can I trust him? Can I tell him the truth without having it come back to bite me?*

He settled back against the door, as if for a long story. "So tell me."

Callie looked down the highway, and saw instead the face that had started it all. "Before I came back to Prospect, I loved a man. He was older, gentle, thoughtful—a kind of Renaissance man wrapped up in urban cowboy." Self-conscious, she laughed. "I know it sounds crazy. He told me he was a believer. We worked for the same corporation, so we often ended up in the same city, far from where either of us lived."

"You got burned."

"I guess that's the short version," Callie agreed, her cheeks flaming. "He was married."

"You didn't know?"

"Do I strike you as the kind of woman who would pursue a married man?" She shook her head. "I'm not evil, just stupid. Dim-witted enough to believe what he told me. If we'd lived in the same town, or worked out of the same office, I would have known better."

"What happened?"

Callie sighed; she'd already gone too far. There was nothing left but to finish it. "Even after I found out, I couldn't believe how it hurt. I'd already let him into my heart, you know? Fortunately, that's when my dad called and asked me to come home. My mom was dying."

"How did you find out he was married?"

"Scott never told me, that's for sure. One of the men in our company let the cat out of the bag. He assumed I knew. He thought I'd gone into the relationship with my eyes wide open." Callie stretched her sweaty fingers, peeling them off the steering wheel. "Here I'd been so open about my faith around the office, and this guy thought I'd deliberately fallen in love with a married man. I was humiliated. Completely blown away—both my own stupidity, and by Scott's deception. He was good, you know? An Oscar-winning performance."

"He didn't know you very well."

"It had to be the dumbest thing I'd ever done."

>>>>

Marcus let the miles pass, unwilling to break the spell of trust that had grown between them. Finally he spoke. "You shouldn't be so hard on yourself, Callie. I know what it feels like to be duped—not necessarily in my love life—but by someone you trust. It was that way with my brother."

"Your brother?"

Marcus nodded. "I found out Peter was involved in a drug ring, a huge syndicate, operating out of different ports all over the country. Peter was only a small cog in a very big wheel. I would have let it go—you know, let the authorities take care of it. But then I found out he was planning to use his own son."

"Keeshan? How did you know?"

"A conversation. I'd gone to pick up Peter at work, and by chance I overheard him making plans. It didn't take a rocket scientist to put the pieces together."

"How?"

"They gave newborns to female drug addicts and had them take the babies out of the country. The infants served as decoys. When the women came back in the country, they sailed right through customs without any problems. The importers hid cocaine in sealed cans of baby formula. I guess they got away with it for almost three years."

"So what did you do?"

"I turned him in." Marcus blinked hard and turned away. The truth still hurt him, even after all this time. "It was the hardest thing I've ever done."

Still, letting Callie know felt good. It relieved him to finally explain everything. She listened without judgment, waiting patiently for him to explain as much or as little as he needed. Marcus knew how hard it must be to hear these things, and yet she did not pepper him with questions or accuse him of missteps. He went on. "Our dad had a stroke just after Peter got into high school. Without Dad's income, we nearly went under. Mom took a second job to make ends meet. Bad timing for my brother. Without any supervision, he got into trouble—just little things at first. But before long, he was stealing cars, using drugs, and working in a chop shop."

"He didn't get caught?"

"Oh, he got caught all right, but it didn't stop him. I was in college at the time. I had my own agenda, you know. I tried to talk to Peter about it, but he wouldn't listen. My parents were too self-involved to do any thing more. It wasn't that they didn't care. They just were too busy trying to survive. Peter missed Dad, and he was angry about being poor and alone and, of course, like lots of kids, he blamed it all on being black."

"How did he meet Celia?"

"I couldn't tell you. By the time they got together, I'd been married a few years and was working for a company that encouraged long, hard hours. After a few promotions, I was pretty impressed with myself. I set my sights on making money and didn't have time to care about what was going on with Pete. I didn't even make it home to my dad's funeral."

"We all have something we wish we could change," she said.

"I'm ashamed of that," Marcus admitted. "After all my dad did for us, I was too busy and too important to come home for his service." He sighed and shifted in his seat. "Peter moved to Florida, and the next thing I knew, he had this girlfriend. That was about the same time I developed problems of my own.

"My wife began to feel neglected and decided she'd had enough of me working all the time. We argued. I tried to convince her I was doing it for the family. I think I may have believed it myself. She didn't.

"She was beautiful and funny, and she loved people. She couldn't stand being cooped up at home in the evening waiting for me. Before long she found the attention she was lacking. I couldn't believe she'd had an affair." The pain of her betrayal stabbed Marcus again, as fresh and sharp as ever. He winced. "I promised her I'd change. I tried to convince her to stay. But it was too late."

Callie looked at him, tears clouding her eyes. "I'm sorry, Marcus."

He cleared his throat. "I learned my lesson; too bad it was too late. She married the guy, and I moved to Florida. I felt like such a failure. I knew Peter was up to his old tricks, and I was determined to save him from making the same mistakes I had. I felt that I could make it up to Dad by helping Peter straighten out."

"Ever the elder brother."

A mirthless chuckle escaped from Marcus. "When Peter married Celia, I thought responsibility would force him to settle down. It didn't work that way. By the time I got there, Celia was pregnant."

"And you found out about the drugs?"

"Not right away. By the time I moved to Dade County, nothing would straighten Peter out. He was back in the stolen car business. Then, when I found out he was associated with that bunch of thugs, I panicked. It's one thing to ruin your own life; it's something else to risk an innocent child."

"What did you do?"

"I had a friend who worked for the sheriff's office. I called in a tip. I didn't have enough information to convict Peter, not even enough to be a valid witness, but I had enough to let the police figure out the details. They worked hard to take out the whole ring."

Marcus wondered what effect this story would have on Callie. Would she change her mind about him? Would she resent him for turning in his own brother?

"That must have been a hard call to make."

"I struggled with it. In the end I realized there was more at stake than my brother. I couldn't let them risk those kids. Especially Keeshan. I didn't know how soon the police could act. So, once Peter was arrested, I told Celia to take the boy and run. I thought she'd let me know where she went. But before she could, I ran myself."

"Why?"

Marcus shook his head. "I was afraid. The police broke the whole ring too soon, and in the process, one of the defendants figured out where the tip had come from. He said he was going to kill me. I believed him. These guys played for keeps. Wherever they went, people died. I decided that Celia and Keeshan would both be safer if I disappeared." He brought his hand to his face, working the goatee with his fingers. "If I'd stayed around to protect her, she might be alive today."

In the silence that followed, Marcus worried about what Callie thought. Had her opinions changed? Did she know that Celia might have survived if he'd had the courage to protect her? They were almost back to the coffee shop, and still he had not told her about Presario. Should he tell Callie that Presario had nearly caught up with him in Tucson? Wouldn't that frighten her unnecessarily? After all, Presario didn't want Callie. He wanted Marcus.

No. He could not tell her that part of the story, not now. Besides, it had been several months since Marcus had last heard anything about Presario. Talking about him might invite trouble. Marcus could not invite that kind of disaster to Prospect, not now, not with so much riding on his success.

"So, say something," Marcus said. "You think I'm a scumbag. Just say it."

"Marcus, Celia died in a car accident. It wasn't your fault."

"You don't know these people. They might have found her. They might have connected her with the arrests. They might have murdered her to get back at me."

"It was my car. The police looked it over after the accident. There wasn't anything wrong. It was just an accident, nothing more than an overcrowded, snow-covered highway. You can't take the blame for that."

She rolled down the window of her car, and took a deep breath, reveling in the fresh mountain air filled with the smell of cedar and firs. "You've got to let it go. You did the best you could, Marcus. That's all anyone can do. Truthfully, no one knows what might have happened if you hadn't acted. Today Keeshan is alive and well. Maybe you should give yourself credit for that."

》》》

Two days later, Callie woke to a ringing telephone. She rolled over and glanced at the clock, surprised to see that she'd overslept. Marcus was probably waiting for her at the coffee shop. She picked up the receiver. "I'm on the way," she said, her voice gravelly with sleep.

"Excuse me?"

The male voice was not Marcus. Embarrassed, she sat up and tried again. "I'm sorry. I was expecting a call." She turned on the bedside lamp. "I guess I should start over. May I help you?"

"I understand you have a house for rent?"

"I do. A guesthouse. Nine hundred square feet. Are you interested?"

"Yes. But I'd like to look at it first. Would you be willing to show the place today?"

"I could arrange that."

"Is it furnished?"

"No, but it has appliances. Washer, dryer, refrigerator, stove, and wall oven."

"Oh, I was under the impression it was furnished." He paused. "Well, I guess unfurnished would be acceptable. When could you show it? Would this afternoon be too soon?"

Callie tried to think through her plans for the day. She'd promised to help Marcus pull electrical wire. "Not at all. When would you like to meet?"

"How about two o'clock?"

"Sounds fine. The house is difficult to find, though. Why don't you meet me in Prospect at Black Ink Tattoos? Are you familiar with the highway that leads out to Prospect?"

"I've been there once."

"Once you come into town, the highway swerves to the left. You'll want to take the right-hand fork. The last business on the right is the tattoo parlor."

"I drive a pale blue Escort."

"I drive a red SUV. And your name?"

She heard the slightest pause. "Paul. Paul Lund."

"Well, Paul, I'll see you at two."

Thirty-Two

By 3:00, Callie was back at the coffee shop, her hands clutching a dowel that ran through the center of a wire spool Marcus had given her. As they talked, he pulled wire through the studs, running strands to every switch and plug and appliance in the shop. Callie kept the reel rolling smoothly as she fed wire into the wall. "He was a nice guy, Marcus. I don't know what you're so upset about."

"How smart is it to rent the house next door to some strange man?"

"He's a stranger, not strange. Don't overreact." She'd never seen this side of him before, and it galled her to think that he felt that he needed to protect her. After all, she'd made it almost thirty-five years by herself. "He seems like a serious, hardworking guy. He's no stranger than you or I am—a little funny looking—you know, lopsided somehow. But other than that a normal guy."

"Lopsided? What kind of description is that? When is he moving in?"

She shrugged. "Saturday morning, I think."

"He didn't waste any time, did he?"

"I haven't had a renter since Celia. Believe me, I've tried. Not more than two or three calls at the most. I need the money, Marcus. Don't be so protective. It's not like he's a serial killer."

"How do you know?"

She laughed. "All serial killers are required to wear ID bracelets."

"What's he do for a living?"

"He works from home. Some kind of consultant thing."

"So you don't even have a reference from his employer?"

"No. But he paid the first and last month's rent in cash."

"Cash. How often does that happen?"

"Not as often as I'd like." Callie frowned. "Can we please talk about something else?"

They finished pulling the wire for the kitchen by the end of the afternoon and then went over to Violet's house, where they found Vi and Keeshan at the picnic table outside, coloring in two separate coloring books. "See what I did today?" Keeshan asked, showing Callie his picture. He'd colored a picture of a single cat sleeping in her basket. Underneath, Keeshan had drawn four more blobs of color. "I added kittens."

"You did," Marcus said, with obvious pride. "How many kittens?"

Keeshan counted as he pointed.

"Is that enough?" Marcus asked the boy.

Keeshan shook his head. "I ran out of room." He shrugged, dismissing the problem by turning the page. "Now I want to color a truck."

Callie had worried that Marcus would not finish Vi's house if he did the construction on the shop. He'd compromised by agreeing to let her help with Vi's house every evening. Together, the three adults had fallen into a pattern. They cooked together, and then after dinner, began work on Violet's kitchen. On the night after she rented the guesthouse, they celebrated with steak and corn on the cob.

"So what's on the schedule this evening?" Vi asked, looking up at Marcus from her corn.

"I think I'm ready to put in your kitchen sink."

"Really?" Vi put down the corn and wiped her fingers with her napkin. "I didn't think you'd be ready for that for another week. I'll be able to do dishes inside!"

Callie thought Vi looked like a woman who'd just won a Mercedes Benz.

"Starting tomorrow, I think," Marcus said. "I picked up all the parts when we went out today. Actually, I just needed new plumbing connections."

"It's gone so fast," Violet said. "I'm delighted with the new kitchen, but I don't know what I'll do without you two over here every night."

"You're a saint," Callie said, marveling. "I'd have gone crazy by now, cooking in the garage and eating outside."

"It's been an adventure," Vi said. "And I've had Keeshan here nearly every day. I couldn't be happier."

While Marcus crawled under the kitchen cabinets, Callie and Vi heated water for the dishes. "I do love that Marcus," Vi said, scraping the debris from Keeshan's plate. "He's hardworking, reliable. I don't think I've ever met a man so good with children. You'd think he had a dozen of his own."

Callie tried to ignore the turn her conversation had taken. "Shall we save this corn?" she asked. "Maybe you could cut it off the cob and freeze it?"

"What do you think of Marcus?"

Callie rolled her eyes. No matter how kind Violet had been, she was about to get nosey. "He's been good to me."

"Why do you suppose he's still single?"

"I couldn't begin to guess," Callie answered. "Did I tell you that Keeshan can write his own name now?"

"Don't try to distract me, dear. I'm asking what you think of Marcus."

"I know exactly what you're doing, Violet," Callie carried the salad dressing to the refrigerator. "You're meddling."

"I'm supposed to do that. Every old lady meddles in other people's business. It's part of the job description."

"Well, then, you deserve a promotion. You're very good at it."

"He's single, Callie. He's handsome. He's crazy about you."

He's black, Callie thought. The idea had no more than passed through her brain than she felt a wash of guilt. What had made her think that? That was the kind of observation her father might make. *Of course he's black. I'm white. I have green eyes. His are brown. I'm not prejudiced!* She tried another tact. "I don't think he's crazy about me."

"Then you aren't using your eyeballs, honey. Anyone can see it by the way he looks at you. By the way he talks to you. It's as plain as the hair on your head."

"Mostly he'd like to strangle me."

"Love has many faces, dear."

"I think you need another occupation," Callie said, bending to wipe the dinner crumbs from the oilcloth table cover. "You're in over your head on this one, Vi. You may be the world's best meddler, but you're no matchmaker."

"I think you love him too."

"Don't be silly. He's talented. He's kind. He's generous. But that doesn't add up to love." Callie checked on the water and saw that it had begun to bubble. Using potholders, she emptied it into the galvanized washbasin. "It takes more than good character to make a husband, Vi."

"Not really. When all the zing and fireworks are over, character is the only thing left." She carried dishes over to the washbasin. "Is it because he's black?"

"Heavens no," Callie answered, much too quickly.

"Good, because I was wondering. You know, in my day we wouldn't have considered it."

"My day isn't so different. When I was growing up, my dad made sure I understood I wasn't ever to date anyone from another race."

"But you've gotten over that?"

"Of course."

"And you could marry anyone you loved, no matter what color he is?"

"Could you hand me the dish soap?"

When they finished putting things away, Vi took Keeshan into the living room, and Callie held an electric light for Marcus while he plumbed the sink. She handed him tools and watched as his skilled hands put the sink back together. "Where did you learn this stuff?" she asked, leaning over the base of the cabinet.

"My dad. He drove buses for Indianapolis Transit. It was regular work, so he was home every day at exactly the same time. He had enough time to work around the house. I think he liked it. Taught me everything he knew." Marcus rolled slightly and pointed to a can. "Could you hand me that, please?"

"This?"

He nodded.

Dipping his index finger into the can he continued. "My family has a long history of doing things for ourselves. My granddad was a sharecropper. If he couldn't do it himself, it didn't get done. Gramps taught Dad. And Dad taught me. He fixed anything. Plumbing, wiring, carpentry. Once he took my mother's mixer apart and rebuilt the engine."

"He'd be proud of what you can do."

Marcus, lying on his back under the sink, raised his head to look at her. "Thank you. I'd like to think so."

At 8:30 Marcus called Vi in from the living room. She watched with delight as he turned on the water for the very first time. "Ta da!" He'd announced triumphantly. "Today the sink; tomorrow, the dishwasher."

Callie laughed. "And so says Marcus the conqueror."

"My hero," Violet added, clapping. Then she reached up to Marcus with both hands, and pulled his face down for a kiss.

>>>

It was after nine by the time Callie put Keeshan in his car seat and headed for the house. He fell asleep before she pulled out of Violet's driveway, and the ten-mile drive gave her time to think about what Vi had said. It bothered her, the conversation they'd shared over the dinner dishes.

But Callie couldn't quite understand why.

Was Vi right? Was it Marcus's skin color that kept her from seeing him as a man? Never once, in all the months she'd known him, had she even considered him as a potential mate. Of course, they'd begun their relationship as adversaries. But things had changed, hadn't they?

Now they were friends, or so Callie believed. And in other experiences with men, Callie had found that friendships often grew into something more. It had been that way with the last man she'd loved.

*Oh, boy, am I glad Vi doesn't know about Scott. She's absolutely right.
If you don't start with character, you end up with nothing.* After Scott,
she'd been left with nothing. But why hadn't she even considered Marcus?

The implication of Violet's accusation wounded Callie. As a child
she'd been keenly aware of her father's prejudice. In an era of acceptance and tolerance, she'd grown up with a bigoted man. He made fre-
quent racial jokes. His assumptions about people of other cultures and
races embarrassed Callie. His attitude had angered her, and in some ways,
it had kept her from fully respecting her father.

Only later, after she'd finished her master's degree, did Callie come
to understand him. A product of his own upbringing, integration came
slowly to him. She couldn't hate him for that, anymore than she could
hate herself for the faith her parents had passed on to her.

Even the best parents sometimes pass on negative attitudes and
behavior. She simply chose to believe differently than her father.

Didn't she?

She remembered the night she first saw the depth of her father's prejudice. She could still hear the tone of his voice, the intensity in his expression as he'd explained the way things would be in their home. "I'm telling
you, Calliandra," he'd said, using the dreaded long form of her name.
"If you ever date a black man, you'll come home to find everything you
own on the front porch. Don't bother to ring the doorbell because you
won't be welcome in our house."

Though she had observed signs of such an attitude, this frank expression of it startled her. She had never seen him so intense, so determined.
Because she loved him, it was a rule she chose never to challenge. But
that was long ago.

And then she remembered her father's first response to Keeshan. It
was the boy's race that worried Jack. He'd always showered love on her
sister's children, but he'd needed time to warm up to Keeshan.

Callie didn't like the looks of it. Maybe Violet Werner was right. How
much of her attitude was left over from her father's influence? She loved
Keeshan, after all. Didn't that prove she had no biases? Callie arrived
home even more confused than when she'd started the car.

She pulled into her usual space in the carport, eased Keeshan from his car seat, and took him inside. She went straight to his bedroom and put him down for the night. It was too late for toothbrushes and pajamas. His teeth could wait till morning. Tonight he needed sleep.

As she stood beside his bed, looking at him in the lamplight, Callie recognized her feelings for the boy. She loved him. Violet was wrong about her. Callie was not prejudiced. This proved it. She turned out the light and closed the door.

She'd no sooner started down the hall, than a terrible thought struck her. Did she allow herself to love Keeshan because he was only a child—dependant on her care?

Did she avoid Marcus because loving him made him her equal?

With her head spinning, she went into the kitchen and stopped to check her messages. She had six. Opening the top drawer, she picked up a pen and notepad. *Funny,* she thought, lifting paper onto the counter, *I thought I left the paper on the left side of this drawer.*

〉〉〉

On the following Tuesday afternoon, after Keeshan finished his nap, Callie picked him up at Violet's house. She and Marcus had decided to take him to the coffee shop for a few hours, giving Vi some peace before they all descended on her house for dinner.

Keeshan picked up a small bucket and reported to Marcus. "Can I pick up wire with you?"

"Sure," Marcus agreed. "Just be careful. The floor is rough. I don't want you to get splinters in your fingers."

Keeshan skipped along from room to room, swinging his bucket in his hands. With the abandonment of the very young, he picked up small pieces of wire wherever he found them. "I like to help build the coffee shop," he sang.

The last system for Marcus to install included the simple security system he'd insisted on adding at the last minute. Unfortunately, soon after they started pulling wires, they ran out of staples. "Contactor's

Supply has already closed." Marcus said, glancing at his watch. "We could have worked a couple more hours if we had a staple gun."

"No problem. I can go back to my place," Callie suggested. "You keep pulling wire, and I'll bring out my upholstery gun. The staples are smaller, but they should still work. We can go to the store tomorrow."

"Are you sure you don't mind?"

"Not at all. I'll take Keeshan. It'll give him a break."

"Okay. Hurry, though. I don't want to get too far ahead of you."

Callie drove back to the house. As she pulled into the driveway, it occurred to her that Marcus might want a snack. She got out of the car and set Keeshan free.

"I want to go see the kittens," he said.

"All right," she agreed. "I'm going to bring Marcus some of those cookies we made this weekend."

"Can I have one?" Keeshan asked.

"Of course." Callie laughed. "Would you make sure Eddy has water? It's hot today. She needs water so that she can feed her kittens."

"Okay. I'll give her water."

Callie watched as Keeshan skipped toward the back door. They'd decided to keep the new family of cats in the laundry room, and Keeshan often took responsibility for their food and water. Though they were nearly eight weeks old, his excitement over the kittens had not diminished in the slightest.

Callie went through the front door to the kitchen, where she filled a plastic container with old-fashioned freezer cookies—a recipe her mother had given her.

Then she took a large pitcher and filled it with ice. She added powdered lemonade and water and stirred. After putting on the lid, she pulled out a stack of paper cups and carried everything out to the car. Putting an empty box behind the back seat, she set the food inside. Feeling as if she'd forgotten something, Callie hesitated to shut the cargo door. She stood there, her hands on her hips thinking for several moments before she remembered the staples. *I'd forget my head if it weren't attached.*

She went through the laundry room door calling for Keeshan. The kitten box was exactly as she'd left it, in front of the dryer. Eddy, lying against the box, looked up from nursing her six bundles of fur. Beside the cat box, her bowl was full of fresh water. *Well, he made it that far.* She reached for a paper towel and wiped up the floor near the water bowl.

"Keeshan," she called again. Maybe he'd gone to the bathroom. She tossed the towel into the trash. "I'm going out to the workshop for the staple gun," she called. She turned to the back door and noticed that it stood wide open. "Now that's funny..." she said.

Callie went out the back door and across the lawn toward the workshop. Somewhere, in the middle of the lawn, she broke into a run. Through the closed shop door she recognized the sound of Keeshan crying.

>>>>

As Callie turned onto Main Street, Marcus waved. He looked down to check his watch; if she hurried, they might have two more hours of work before stopping for dinner. He walked around the back of the shop to the enormous water cask Violet had loaned them.

Filling his water bottle with water, Marcus sat down on a box, took off his hat, and wiped sweat from his face with his T-shirt. Then he drank the bottle dry.

Every bone in his body complained. He wondered how much longer he could keep up the pace. For months he'd been working two jobs. Though his job at Contractor's Supply hadn't required much physical energy, he'd gotten behind on his sleep. Now the physical demands of construction, both at the shop and Violet's house, had so deprived Marcus of rest that he fell asleep anytime he stopped moving. *I'm not getting any younger*, he thought.

Leaning back against the newly framed wall, he enjoyed the warm fall sunshine beating down on his face. Knowing that he shouldn't, Marcus closed his eyes.

In a heartbeat, he fell asleep, the water bottle still in his hands.

Thirty-Three

Callie burst through the door, expecting to see blood running down Keeshan's face from a severe head wound. What she saw instead made her freeze, whether from terror or surprise she did not know. Standing in the far corner of the workshop, Paul Lund held one arm around Keeshan's throat. In the other he held a handgun pointed directly at her.

He gestured with the gun. "Come in, Callie," he said. "I wondered how long it would take for you to look for us." Lund eyed her with the expression of a coiled snake.

She stepped inside, gently closing the door behind her. Keeshan whimpered, tears rolling down his cheeks. Her presence seemed to calm him and he brought his hands away from Lund's arms. The pounding of her heart intensified until it thundered behind her eardrums. *Stay calm. Don't let Lund know you're afraid.*

She forced herself to speak calmly. "Paul? What are you doing here? What is this?" Moving slowly, deliberately, she brought her hands to her sides, keeping them always within his view. She knew better than to startle a man with a gun.

He chuckled. "You don't think I really wanted to live out here in this wilderness with you?" His right eyebrow rose, and the lopsided smile she'd labeled charming when she met him took on a sinister, frightening appearance.

"Silly me. I thought that if you rented a house, you might actually want to live there. So what is it? What do you want?" Callie looked directly at Keeshan, forcing herself to smile, telegraphing confidence. *It'll be all right, Keeshan.*

"I'll tell you what I want." He motioned for her to step closer. "I want the coke. I know the packages were in Celia's couch. I put them there myself three years ago. A little stash no one else knew about." He dragged the boy forward. "I've been looking for Celia Jefferson ever since I got out of prison." He spoke with a voice befitting a radio drama, deep and frightening. Evil. Yes, that was it. He laughed. "That friend of yours, that Marcus Jefferson, is so stupid he doesn't even know that he's the one who led me to Celia. I'd never have found her if he hadn't shown me the way."

Lund stopped moving and pointed the gun to the floor. Callie followed the gesture to a piece of the fabric that had covered Celia's hide-a-bed. Paul must have dug through the bottom of Callie's trash barrel— a fifty-gallon cardboard container she'd snagged from the feed store. "The couch is gone," he said, "but you must know where my packages are."

Paul must have loosened his hold around Keeshan's neck, for the boy squirmed and made an effort to get away. Paul caught him, jerking his little head as he tightened the hold around Keeshan's neck. He cried out in pain.

"Shut up, kid."

Callie, emboldened by his cruelty, barked, "He's only a child. Let him go."

Lund chuckled, obviously enjoying her emotion. "You know where those drugs are."

"I re-covered the couch and sold it to a friend."

His face grew hard, and his arm tightened around Keeshan, who cried out in terror. Paul Lund had no patience to spare. He growled. "So I've heard. You found the drugs. A half-million-dollars worth. Where are they?"

"Do you actually think I'd keep that stuff around here? What if the boy happened to find it?" Callie fixed her eyes on his, unwilling to blink, lest she miss something that might cost her life. "I flushed it—right down the toilet. It's gone, Lund. You're too late."

"I don't think so," he said, watching her the way a cat watches its prey. "No one would throw that much money away. It's here somewhere, that's what I think."

"Look," she said, appealing to his logic. "If you're so sure I have the stuff, search for it. Find it. Just let the boy go. He doesn't need to be a part of this."

Lund laughed, and Callie shivered at the evil sound. "I don't think so. Keeshan is my insurance, you see. You'll do whatever I ask as long as I have the boy. So, until I change my mind, you're going to search every inch of this place for me. Keeshan stays right here, and you look for the stuff. That's the plan," he said. "We start here." He jerked the child again, delighting in the sound of his cries. "And when I'm finished with you, I'm going to take care of Jefferson, once and for all."

>>>>

Marcus might have slept forever had it not been for the sound of the water bottle bouncing on the gravel parking lot. He jerked awake, startled by the clatter. Blinking against intense sunlight, he tried to remember why he'd fallen asleep.

Where was Callie?

He listened for a moment, aware of the silence in the building behind him. Then he remembered. She'd gone to the house for her staple gun. Marcus slid forward and stood up. How long had she been gone? If he didn't have more wire pulled by the time she returned, he'd never hear the end of it. He'd better get moving.

Marcus smiled as he walked around the corner and through the back door of the coffee shop. *She's a slave driver, that woman,* he thought. As he reached up to pull the end of a wire through a hole in a door frame, his neck complained. With his other hand he kneaded the hefty muscles at the base of his neck. *I must have slept longer than I thought.*

He looked at his watch. An hour? He shook his wrist and watched the second hand move around the watch face. How could Callie be gone for an entire hour? Marcus pulled the wire through three more holes, still wondering about the time. It bothered him that she had been gone so long. But, after all, he didn't have a telephone. She couldn't let him know that she'd been delayed.

Marcus threaded two more holes. Something else bothered him too. Something Callie had said—it kept coming back, this irritating fact—like a stiff label on a piece of new clothing. It chafed him, made him want to rub the irritated skin with the palm of his hand. Something she had said about the man who rented the guesthouse. What was it?

Marcus stopped working and stood still, his hands on his hips. He replayed the conversation he'd had with Callie about the new renter. There was something there; he knew it. He felt his body come alive with the complete certainty of it. He felt jittery, as though he'd just finished one of Callie's triple-shot drinks. Something. Something.

Lopsided. That was the word. Callie had called the new renter lopsided.

Marcus bolted from the shop, heading toward the little car he'd parked on the street. As he reached the sidewalk, he pulled his keys from his pocket and leapt for the door. Lopsided, she'd said.

It was Presario. Presario had rented Callie's guesthouse right under his nose. How could he be so stupid? Why hadn't he thought of it before? Marcus started the car and gunned it, squealing tires as he pulled into the street.

Callie's house was ten miles out of town. If he were lucky, Marcus could drive fast enough to catch the attention of several state patrol officers along the way. He could use their help, after all. He had no doubt Callie was in trouble.

》》》

With Lund holding Keeshan by the throat, Callie started in the far corner of the workshop, opening the drawers of her father's built-in cabinets, and item by item, dropping the contents onto the floor. As she worked, Lund stood not more than a step behind her, watching her every move, the gun pointed directly at her, the child firmly clutched in the corner of his arm. As she moved onto the next drawer, Lund bent to examine the last, dragging the whimpering child along with him.

Callie had never been so frightened. Shallow breathing made her feel lightheaded, and her fingers trembled so much she could hardly open the drawers. But as she kept searching, she struggled to think of something she might use to overcome the man behind her. Even if she had to die, she would never let him harm Keeshan. He would not win. She would think of something. *Stay calm.*

Try as she might, neither her mind nor her body would cooperate.

Lund held the boy so tightly that he cried out every time Lund took a step. Apparently, though his eyes were wide with panic, the hold was tight enough to keep Keeshan from speaking. His little fingers held Lund's forearm, pulling downward in a fruitless effort to avoid pressure on his windpipe. Callie tried to calm Keeshan, smiling at him whenever she caught his eye, but it did not work. His eyes ran with ceaseless tears, and his expression begged her to stop Lund. The sight of Keeshan's terror made Callie so angry that for the first time in her life she knew she could kill if the chance arose.

And then she remembered. In the bank of drawers nearest the refrigerator, the third drawer down had been broken when she moved into the workshop. On a cold winter day not long after her mother died, Callie had opened the drawer with too much force, accidentally pulling the whole drawer out onto the floor and dropping it on her foot.

The drawer had been heavy enough to break her toe and send her to the emergency room.

Was she strong enough to pull it out and fling it at Lund's face in one smooth motion? Would it hit with enough force to knock him unconscious? There was no way to guess. No way to be certain. She would just have to try. Her hands began to sweat as she worked, and after she opened the next drawer, she wiped her hands on the lap of her overalls.

"What was that?" Lund said, his voice instantly angry.

"I'm hot. It's hot in here, don't you think?"

"I don't care if it's hot. Keep moving."

"Don't you think we should open a window? Between the heat and that gun of yours, I'm feeling sick to my stomach."

He squinted at her, suspicion oozing from the lopsided expression on his face. He stepped back, dragging Keeshan with him while pointing the gun at the window. "Okay, but don't try anything. I'm watching. Open the window."

Callie held her hands up as she stepped to the window nearest the house. Slowly, she reached out to pull the cord to the mini blinds.

"What are you doing?"

"I have to open the blinds to reach the window latch."

"All right. Make it quick."

Thinking about Marcus, she reached up and opened the window. If Marcus kept track of the time, he might become alarmed. Would he come to see what had happened? If he did, Lund would hear the sound of his tires on the driveway. Without surprise, Marcus would end up captive, just like Keeshan and Callie. She needed to add something to cover the sound of Marcus arriving—if he did. "There," she said. "Much better. Can I turn on the fan?"

"No!"

"The sun hits the back of the workshop in the late afternoon," she said, shrugging. "In an hour, it's going to feel like an oven in here. That's why I work in the morning."

He glanced at the back of the building as he considered her words. Callie shuddered. *Perhaps this goon has been watching us for months.* He hesitated and then took the bait. "All right. Put the fan in front of the window."

Callie lifted the box fan from the floor and set it on the counter. Turning it on high, she made a great show of taking a deep breath. "There," she said, "that's much better."

She went back to where she'd left off. In the next drawer, she had several yards of folded seat decking. She pulled it out, still folded, and showed the yardage to Lund. "Open it up. Shake it," he said, again gesturing with the gun as he spoke.

She held the fabric between both hands opening it wide before him. She heard something outside. *Was that Marcus's funny little car?* Callie glanced at Lund. *Had he heard the sound?*

Hoping against hope that Marcus had come for her, Callie turned toward the center of the room. "It's a big piece," she said. "I don't want to hit you with it," she said. She shook it wildly, deliberately stumbling over the tools she'd emptied from the previous drawer.

"Be careful, you clumsy ox," he hissed.

Desperate to cover any sound Marcus might make, she made a show of anger, shouting, "It's a little difficult you know, with you pointing a gun at me and this garbage all over the room! I'm a little nervous—who wouldn't be?—with a gun stuck in my face!" She dropped the fabric onto the floor with the rest of the mess. "Now, can I move on to the next drawer?"

Callie watched in horror as Lund dragged Keeshan over to the window and looked outside. Keeshan's crying turned into a wail. If Marcus were outside, the crying would bring him running. He'd never take the time to think. Callie began sweating from sheer terror. They didn't have a chance. *Lord*, she prayed, *help us overcome our enemies.*

Lund took one last look over the lawn and toward the house. Turning to her, he indicated the next drawer. Callie turned and reached for the handle. As she removed several spools of upholstery thread, Callie looked ahead to the broken drawer. Three more drawers. Three more. Could she time her attack with Marcus's arrival in the workroom?

Lord, give me strength to lift that drawer.

>>>

Marcus pulled in behind Callie's car and got out. Seeing the rear gate still open sent his heart pounding. His instinct was right. *Callie should have made it back by now.* He glanced over toward the guesthouse where he spotted a beaten Ford Escort. Someone else was here with her, that much he knew.

He reached inside Callie's car and touched the pitcher of lemonade. It was cool, but not cold. How long had it been in the sun?

Seeing the front door wide open, he decided to begin there. "Callie," he called, stepping into the entryway. "Callie, are you all right?" Quickly, he ran through the bedroom wing, looking into rooms, calling her name. He went into the kitchen, where he found lemonade powder on the counter, the cookie jar open and empty ice trays waiting beside the sink.

Knowing Callie as he did, the messy kitchen confirmed his suspicion. Marcus grew wild with alarm. Where could she be? Then he remembered the staple gun. Had something happened to her in the workshop? Marcus started out through the laundry room.

Then something he could not explain told him to stop.

He paused, aware only of some deep instinct, some strong voice, telling him to avoid the path across the lawn. He turned and went out the door to the carport, past Callie's car and on into the driveway.

He jogged toward the guesthouse, absolutely certain, according to his instinct, that Presario was not inside. Still, he crept around the far side of the little house and took the back porch by stealth. From the porch, he jogged across the lawn to the workshop.

With no windows on this side of the building, Marcus was certain that he would not be seen from inside the building. As he came around the corner, he stopped, pressing his ear to the siding. He heard what he clearly recognized as Callie's voice though he could not make out the words. Then a man's voice. He crept toward the door, and again pressed his ear to the wood.

"...with a gun stuck in my face!"

Desperate, Marcus looked around for something he could use as a weapon. Beside the door, a pile of mildewed stuffing waited to be taken to the trash. Marcus lifted the stuffing to find several lengths of 2x2s. He chose one, the length of a baseball bat, and returned to the shop door. Crouching there, he prayed for strength and then exploded through the door with the finesse of a black bear in a pup tent. He had barely caught his balance when he spotted the lopsided grin of Presario. Marcus did not pause to evaluate the scene inside. Instead, he threw himself across the mound of garbage on the floor, aiming the club for Presario's face.

When he heard the gun go off in his ears, Marcus felt only deafening rage.

>>>

As the door banged against the wall behind it, Callie dove for the broken drawer. Leaning back, she pulled it open with a swift jerk. Sensing the moment that the back of the drawer cleared the opening, Callie changed direction and heaved the whole drawer up toward Presario. With a wholehearted grunt, she felt the bone give way where the wood met his skull.

Then, startled by a sudden, burning pain in her right shoulder, Callie felt her body driven backward, away from Keeshan, away from Lund. It was the same strong kick she'd once felt from a horse's rear leg, and it sent her crashing against the bank of drawers below the window. Somehow on the way down, Callie lost her footing. Her last sensation was of her head slamming against the edge of the counter.

>>>

Much later Callie lay on a stretcher in her driveway, aware of lights flashing all around her. The headache banging against the inside of her skull made her so dizzy she could barely open her eyes. "I've told you everything I know," she said again.

"That's enough for now, Officer." It was Marcus's voice. Dear Marcus. "You can interview her later. After she sees a doctor."

"I'll be in touch," the second voice said. "At least he'll never hurt anyone again."

Callie willed her eyes open, and she spotted Marcus standing beside her in the waning light, Keeshan in his arms, the boy clinging to Marcus's neck.

"Marcus," Callie whispered. Breathing hurt too much to waste words. "Lund?"

"I'm here, Callie." Even through the fog of pain, she heard emotion in his voice. "This is all my fault. He was Presario. The one who was after me. I led him right to you. If I'd stayed away, this never would have happened."

"No." Though she said it, no sound came out. She tried again. "No. Not true." Callie did not try to shake her head. She pulled one hand from under the blanket. "Keeshan?"

Marcus took her hand. "He's fine. Worried about you, but fine. I've got him, I promise."

"We need to transport her to the hospital now." Marcus nodded at someone behind her.

"Will you come?" Callie whispered.

He nodded, his eyes filling with tears. "We'll follow in your car."

The stretcher started moving, and Callie winced as it hit a rock in the driveway. Her shoulder screamed and white spots clouded her vision.

"Wait!" Marcus called.

Callie opened her eyes, turning her head just enough to see Marcus jog toward her, Keeshan bouncing in his arms. He had tears on his cheeks as he bent low over the stretcher. His face came nearer, and nearer still. Finally, he spoke, his cheek touching hers, his breath against her skin, warm against her ear. "Callie," he whispered, his lips touching her ear-lobe, his voice hoarse with emotion. "I can't let you go without telling you. I love you."

"I love you too," she whispered.

He lingered just long enough to brush her cheeks with his lips.

Epilogue

Two days later, the hospital sent Callie home with a very sore shoulder and a healing bullet wound. According to the doctor, her headaches would disappear in a matter of days. In the meantime, antibiotics and pain medication kept her comfortable. She was so grateful to be alive that she refused to complain.

By the time she returned to the coffee shop, Marcus had hired a crew to hang sheet rock and mud the new building. He'd made a lot of progress in her absence. She and Marcus and Keeshan continued working on the shop as if nothing had happened.

Though Callie felt shy in his presence, especially after the kiss they'd shared in the driveway, she couldn't bring herself to mention what had transpired between them. Maybe she'd simply imagined it. Or perhaps Marcus had expressed himself out of an emotional rush, nothing more than relief that the three year ordeal was finally over. Callie could not be sure.

As if he felt the same way, Marcus said nothing. Instead, he behaved with the utmost civility—like the perfect general contractor. Only his eyes betrayed his feelings. Though she should have been patient, Callie was beside herself with frustration.

Why did men have to be so stubborn?

Either Marcus did or did not love her. Why didn't he just say some-thing? If he'd changed his mind, why keep her in the dark?

For several days Callie bit her tongue, absolutely unwilling to ask questions. In this relationship, Marcus Jefferson would just have to take the lead. After all, he'd come into her life when she least expected him, appearing as a minor irritation and growing into a major threat. Somehow he'd managed to steal her heart, or at least a huge part of it—whatever piece Keeshan had not already stolen. Though she felt as though she might grow old without knowing, Callie O'Brian would wait as long as it took for Marcus to make his move.

As the grand reopening of the coffee shop approached, their work took on a feverish pace. Marcus and Callie often found themselves on opposite ends of the little building, each finishing some last detail.

On a Thursday afternoon, four weeks after leaving the hospital, Callie knelt on the dining room floor, shoving grout between flagstone tiles. Keeshan, who had been playing outside the door with his trucks, tugged impatiently on her sweatshirt. "Can we go for a ride this afternoon?"

"I don't know," she said. "Have you asked Marcus?"

"He told me to ask you."

She sat back on her heels, pushing hair out of her face with the back of her hand. "I don't know, sweets. There's so much left to finish."

"Please? I'm tired of playing here."

Callie stood up, groaning from hours on the hard floor. "I'll check with Marcus." She went through the coffee bar to the kitchen, where he was trimming new laminate with a router. "Hey," she shouted, touching his shoulder.

He switched off the motor and raised his safety goggles. "What do you need?"

"Not me," she said. "Keeshan wants to go riding this afternoon."

Marcus looked at Keeshan and frowned. "You do?" The boy nodded. Marcus looked around the kitchen. "I don't know. I've got a lot left to do."

"Please," Keeshan whined.

"I guess we can go for a short ride." Marcus pulled off his goggles and set them on the counter.

>>>>

As summer warmth gave way to fall chill, the leaves along the river trail turned russet, and on that afternoon, fog nestled among bare limbs in pockets of misty white. Callie loved the changing faces of the river valley.

Marcus parked Callie's car in the lot nearest the city park and unloaded the bikes.

"Hurry," Keeshan begged. "We have to hurry."

"The river isn't going anywhere, squirt," Marcus said, hitching the buggy to the seat post of his used road bike. "Climb in."

Callie mounted up and started down the trail, enjoying the cool afternoon air, and the hint of pink on the horizon. With sunset only an hour away, they didn't have much time before they would have to turn around. She glanced back to see that Marcus had fallen far behind. *He's not much of a biker.*

She slowed so that he could catch up. As he came along beside her, he was breathing heavily. "You doing okay?"

"A little tired today. Do you think we could stop up here?"

"At the wetlands?"

"There's a bench were we can watch the birds."

She shrugged. "I guess." *He's more of a wimp than I thought.* "Maybe we shouldn't have come."

"I'll be okay. Come on." Marcus turned his bike onto a narrow path and disappeared into the trees. Callie followed, watching the ground carefully. She did not feel like changing a flat in the dark.

Up ahead Marcus let Keeshan out of the buggy, and Callie noticed that the boy jumped up and down beside a bench at the end of the path. She shook her head; he was so full of energy. From this spot she saw nothing but hills and trees and river, a vista so full of wild energy that she was actually grateful that Marcus needed a break. She would enjoy sitting here for a moment. "Come sit down, Callie," Keeshan called, skipping toward her.

She dismounted and took his hand. "I'm coming, you chimp."

She did not see Marcus, not until Keeshan shoved her onto the bench, and she turned to look for him. He stepped out from behind a group of vine maples, his upturned hand holding a silver platter with three crystal wine glasses and a bottle. Stunned, Callie watched him approach, dimly aware of Keeshan sitting down beside her, his little legs swinging from the bench.

"Mr. Keeshan Marcus Jefferson," Marcus said, his voice quite official. "I've come today to ask for the hand of your foster mother, Ms. Callie O'Brian, in marriage. Would you give your blessing to our union?"

Keeshan clapped, his eyes laughing, his feet swinging. "Yes!" he said. "Marcus is going to marry Callie!"

And just as the horizon turned crimson, Marcus knelt before the bench, offering her the tray. On one side stood a tall iced bottle of sparkling cider. Between the crystal glasses was a tiny velvet box. Callie's eyes filled with tears as Marcus spoke. "And you, Miss Calliandra O'Brian, would you consent to marry an old black contractor?"

Callie took the tray and placed it on the bench beside her.

"Oh, yes," she said, throwing her arms around Marcus's neck. "I most certainly would!"

More Fine Fiction from Harvest House Publishers

A SEASON OF GRACE
Bette Nordberg

Colleen is wary when her brother Stephen arrives, but she refuses to dwell on his homosexuality. After a family fight, Stephen angrily leaves. Colleen follows him, discovers he has AIDS, and invites him to live with her family. As Stephen's illness progresses, Colleen encounters fear, prejudice, and judgments from "it's a shame" to "God is punishing Stephen."

Slowly Colleen considers a new answer. Maybe AIDS isn't a condemnation. Perhaps God has granted Stephen time to evaluate his life and discover the love of the Master Healer.

THE MILLION DOLLAR MYSTERIES
A PENNY FOR YOUR THOUGHTS
Mindy Starns Clark

Callie's latest assignment—go to Philadelphia and present an old family friend of Tom's (her employer) with a check for $250,000. Wendell Smythe heads a relief organization and needs immediate funds. When Callie goes to his office, check in hand, she discovers him dead on the floor. At Tom's request, Callie moves into Smythe's home and begins a murder investigation. But it's a dangerous place to be, for the family has secrets they would rather not have uncovered.

Callie's only hope is that God will help her use her investigative skills to discover the murderer and escape the web of deceit that surrounds her.

CHAMBERS OF JUSTICE
THE RESURRECTION FILE
Craig Parshall

When a small-time preacher asks Will Chambers to defend him against accusations that might not only destroy the man's ministry, but the very foundation of Christian faith, everything in Chambers' nonbelieving heart says "run away." But the preacher's earnest plea; his lovely and successful daughter, Fiona; and the prosecutor's high-powered efforts to discredit the Gospels' historical integrity prove too heady a mix. Chambers takes the case. Quickly caught up in a conspiracy involving terrorism, top-level government intrigue, and wild legal maneuvering, Chambers is in for the ride of his life.

The Resurrection File is a legal thriller with tightly drawn characters, page-turning twists and, at its core, a compelling story of one lawyer's discovery of the truth and power of Christ's message.

HARVEST HOUSE
PUBLISHERS

About the Author

Bette Nordberg graduated from the University of Washington as a physical therapist in 1977. In 1990 she turned from rehabilitation medicine to writing and is now the author of *Serenity Bay*, *Pacific Hope*, *Thin Air*, and *A Season of Grace*, as well as *Encouraging Words for the First Hundred Days*. She and her husband, Kim, helped plant Lighthouse Christian Center, a church in the South Hill area of Puyallup, Washington. Today she writes for the drama team and teaches Christian growth classes. Along with teaching writing workshops, Bette speaks for audiences around the Northwest. Married thirty years, Bette and Kim have four children, three living at home.

Bette may be contacted through her website:
www.bettenordberg.com

GREENWOOD PUBLIC LIBRARY
P.O. BOX 839 MILL ST.
GREENWOOD, DE 19950